Silver, Lead, and Dead

D1607767

Silver, Lead, and Dead

James Garmisch

ISBN: 1500522171
ISBN 13: 9781500522179

Part 1

CHAPTER 1

A Tale of Two Kidnappings

Juárez, Mexico, February 13, 2010, 0810 Hours

Armando Gonzalez lived in Ciudad Juárez, the largest city in the Mexican state of Chihuahua. The city had grown in Armando's seventy-nine years from scrubland and farms joined by dirt roads and footpaths to a city of over a million. Juárez was now a city of factories, Walmarts, smokestacks, and old school buses packed with workers heading to the maquiladoras. The last decade had brought an entirely different transformation.

When Armando was young, gringos used to walk across the border, buy cheap booze, dance with hookers, and buy bundles of weed and heroin, or "mud," to take back home. Drug trafficking in the 1950s and '60s was more like buying produce from a local farmers' market. Buy local; know your dealer. Sure, people got killed, but, by and large, business was done with a handshake, not a "goat horn," or AK-47.

The farmers would bring down their crops from the hills of Sinaloa in old trucks or by animals. Hippies from California, soldiers on leave, and smugglers looking to make quick cash could satisfy their needs for the right price. *There was a code back then,*

Armando mused. The police and government officials turned their heads and stretched out their hands. Gringos and Mexicans traded paper for weed. The world was in balance. Armando had been a police officer for a few years in his youth before the lure of smuggling drew him into a multidecade journey of mayhem. Several events in 1975 transformed Armando into a broken and humble man. At times, he was nostalgic about those days, but he recognized them for what they were, and he praised God for deliverance.

Armando had been shot four times and survived. His brothers had not been so lucky. The decade he spent in prison was perhaps the beginning of the best thing that ever happened to him. During an oppressive day in June, Armando decided to have his large tattoo of Jesús Malverde recolored. Jesús Malverde patron saint of smugglers, held the nostalgia of Robin Hood and the allure of a noble outlaw. Armando's tattoo covered his entire back and was quite impressive, even by prison-tattoo standards. Malverde had been executed for his crimes.

"Worship dead idols and false prophets and end up like them." The words from an inmate had at first offended Armando, but gradually the warning burned fear into him. Armando's slow conversion was not pretty. One day the scales fell from his eyes, he recalled, and he surrendered his life to a higher power.

Armando never looked back. Illiterate, he learned to read so he could see and understand the Holy Bible for himself. Armando came to believe that God did indeed have a plan for him, and it was not living a life of pleasure but one of service. His friends abandoned him, and he was mocked, yet he grew stronger each year. During Armando's ninth and final year in prison, he met the sister of another convict and fell in love. Her name was Sophia, and she was indeed the answer to his prayers. Sophia's father owned a chain of grocery stores in Juárez, and upon release, Armando began working for him. Sophia and Armando were married and had four children.

Armando paused to think about his children. It seemed like yesterday when they were born. The two oldest boys had been killed in the mid-1980s by stray gunfire. The two younger daughters, twins, now lived in the States. Maria, a teacher, and her six children lived in San Antonio. His daughter Sophia had also married, had five children, and was now living in a place called Virginia.

A car backfired; Armando jumped and returned abruptly to the present. How could fifty years go so quickly?

He now owned the grocery store with one of his surviving brothers. His wife, Sophia, had died eighteen years earlier. A night did not go by that Armando didn't plead, "Please let me die tonight too and wake up in your glory and see Sophia again."

Each morning he woke up in his one-room apartment disappointed but accepting, thinking, *You must not be done with me yet.* He recalled how his daughters pleaded with him to leave Juárez. "It's not safe! You must come live with us."

"No, my little angels. I can't be comfortable in North America, oblivious to the suffering down here. I am a disciple of Christ and am doing my best to spread blessings and his word."

His daughter Sophia would sigh, just like her mother. "But you are giving the money Maria and I send you to bums and vagrants. You will make yourself a target! You are not a poor man, yet you live like a bum!"

"What is money, my child? I spread love and help those who need it. It's God's money. He has done great things in people's lives."

"Maybe he will send a bomb to destroy all the narcos! Papa! Leave that country!"

"Mexico will be judged just like every other vile place where man lives. Look at the United States. Its acts would make the people of Sodom blush. Evil will get its reward."

Armando walked down the street to the store and thought about Sophia, his angel—beautiful like her mother. Armando still felt at home in the city even though things had gone from bad to insane. The smell of death had been baked into the ground. Shell casings, broken bottles, and shreds of clothing cut from the wounded by paramedics lay in bloody clumps in the gutter. He could smell smoke from taco stands and generally saw the same people every day standing around, waiting for something to happen. Armando handed out Bibles to anyone who would take one and would pray for anyone who would listen—especially for those who would not.

"No, my work in this city is not done!" he had told Sophia.

Rust, hopelessness, rotting corpses, and poverty were laid out and left to dry in the sun like miles of mota. Juárez had more murders in one day than El Paso had in a year. Despite soldiers and police on nearly every street and a curfew, the city was out of control. Armando drank a warm Pepsi from a bottle as he left his house. His cluttered neighborhood had seen better days. Most of the houses on his block were boarded up and empty. Some one hundred thousand people had fled Juárez over the years.

Armando had worked at the same job and gone to the same church every day for decades. He swallowed the last of the Pepsi and threw the empty bottle into a Dumpster that stank like human remains. Armando paused. It was still early in the morning, and there was a slight chill in the air. He could not ride his bike anymore; he had given it to a man on the street. He walked two blocks, passing old, abandoned sheds and houses, graffiti-covered walls, and a few gutted cars.

People were fleeing north by the thousands from all over Mexico. Armando sighed; it was not an economic problem but a spiritual one. Many of his friends and neighbors who fled to the States chasing a magic new beginning were dead within a few years or just as bad off. They just dragged their problems across the border.

Armando smelled and then saw a dead dog lying among broken beer bottles and plastic syringes. He crossed the street. He spotted the grocery store and reached for his keys as he did every day. A few homeless people lay among piles of trash. They smelled like old urine. Stray cats regarded him as an invader and looked for food. He said a prayer for the homeless people and reached in his pocket for some tracts.

A loud noise caught Armando's attention. A yellow pickup with no muffler or tailgate rounded a corner and pulled right up on the sidewalk next to him. The exhaust stank, and the truck rattled as it idled.

Is this it? Are they going to kill me? he wondered.

He looked at the truck and the driver with surprise and curiosity. Two men jumped from the bed of the rusted-out truck. One was short and fat, the other tall and thin. They both wore ski masks and moved with nervous energy and clumsy, shaky hands. Armando frowned. Back in the day, he already would have killed these two amateurs. Now he faced them without fear and with a hope that soon he would see his lost love.

The taller of the men put a gun in Armando's face. He yelled, "Get in, old man!"

The kidnappers threw a bag over Armando's head and lifted him off the ground and into the bed of the truck. He did not resist as moldy-smelling blankets were piled on him.

"Go! Go!" yelled one of the men as he slammed his fist onto the cab of the truck.

The truck took off with the exhaust booming. Armando's keys and tracts lay on the sidewalk.

Mexico City, February 14, 2010, 0800 Hours

Mexico City is a large sprawl of concrete, steel, dust, and smog. Streets weave through and around it like veins and arteries pumping and receiving blood.

At seventy-three hundred feet in altitude, the city is home to twenty-one million people packed like bees in sixteen boroughs over 573 square miles.

Nineteen-year-old Manuel Rosa did what he did best: he talked. No one seemed to be listening, so he talked louder and faster.

"*So*, Roger, you looking forward to going back to Scotland? The land of rain and clouds? You know you will miss it here in Mexico City, the kidnapping capital of the world, huh? Exams are over and we could go to the beach. Warm water here; freezing water in Scotland. Great party last night—never seen my cousins drink so much! Passed all my classes. Changing majors by the way—screw business school; screw dad! I am going to be an artist and live in Spain!"

Manuel frowned when he had no response. He sat wedged in the backseat of his father's bulletproof Mercedes speeding along to Aeropuerto Internacional Benito Juárez. His bodyguards ignored him as they often did. He was in the backseat with Salvador, while Jose drove, and Roger rode shotgun.

"*Look!* A Ducati would love to get one of those, would never happen. What would I do? Drive around with my security detail on my back? Look ridiculous."

The car exited and headed toward the airport entrance. Manuel spoke faster trying to get all his words out before it was too late. He noticed that a police truck had fallen in behind them.

"Roger, so I have a question for you. Have you always done what your father has asked? I mean did you do for a living what he wanted?"

Roger grumbled and fiddled with a new Blackberry that Manuel had bought for him as a going-away present. At six four and 250 pounds, Roger seemed to fill the car. Manuel was amused at how slow anyone over the age of thirty was with technology, and he was glad now that he had bought it, if not for the sheer joy of watching Roger struggle.

"Need help with that?" Manuel asked, laughing. "Helps, Roger, if you turn it on!"

Roger cursed and grumbled and then shoved the thing in his pocket. He spoke with a heavy Scottish accent that annihilated the Spanish language whenever he chose to speak it. Roger had retired from the British SAS six years ago and attended cooking school in Paris. Now, he was in Mexico as a chef for Manuel's family. The former chef had been shot over refusing to yield a parking space. Roger's appearance had terrified his cooking instructors at first, but that all changed when they tasted his creations. With long hair, a full beard with a few braids, and pro-Scottish tattoos, he looked more like a cast member out of a remake of *Highlander*.

"Lad, you should not speak of your father that way."

"Well, Roger, did you do what your dad wanted?"

"That's different son; my dad was a drunk. He ran me off when I was about your age. I joined the service and never looked back. Answer is no."

"So there! I am going to be an artist!" Manuel said.

Salvatore looked sideways at Manuel and shook his head. Salvatore reeked of cigarettes and breath mints.

"Art? Get a job first, boy, and then you can draw all you want. Your father is a good man. But he is not a forgiving man!"

"All of you talk too much!" Manuel complained.

"Son, we all rebel. Let's talk about this when I get back. I'll be gone for three months. Hold your tongue. If you still wanna color pictures for a livin' we can talk to your dad then," Roger said flatly.

"Fine. But I hate my life."

The car edged its way toward the international departures and slowed.

"You hate your life? Son, you got a good family and a good life here."

Manuel showed his frustration but struggled to keep his voice calm. No one ever raised their voice at Roger; his temper was legendary.

"Nice? Like when your best friend from high school gets kidnapped and held for ransom by the police and then even after the parents pay—they rape her and melt her with acid? *No!* I am done with this place. I have not been outside by myself since. No walks, no bike rides. I am moving to Spain."

Roger shook his head; no one spoke.

Salvatore coughed and pulled out his cigarettes.

Jose drove slowly up the ramp to international departures. He cursed at a tow truck stopped illegally next to the curb and parked the Mercedes beside a curbside taxi off-loading a man. Laws were merely a suggestion in Mexico.

A taxi left, and a white delivery van drove up slowly next to the curb. Roger got out and put on his backpack. Jose popped the trunk and got out. Salvador rolled down his window but stayed in the car. The engine was still running. Manuel got out quickly and walked around to say good-bye to Roger, who gave him a quick handshake, closed the trunk, and shrugged.

"I'll see you in a few months, *amigo*."

"Have a good trip, Roger. I am not kidding about school."

"Do what you got to, son. I believe in you. *Adios*."

Roger walked around the delivery van, paused to look back, and then disappeared inside the terminal. A breeze picked up, and the sound of planes and the smell of jet fuel filled the air.

Manuel turned to look as the same black-and-white police truck pulled up behind them. Two cops got out.

"Guess we must move along," said Manuel, looking around for Jose. The car's driver-side door was open, but its driver was nowhere in sight. And the large delivery truck to the right of the Mercedes blocked a view of the terminal's entrance, casting a shadow over the car. The airport seemed eerily quiet.

"*No se puede estacionar aqui!*" Two cops approached. One cop spoke to Manuel while the other walked toward Salvador between the white truck and the Mercedes.

"You don't understand, sir. My driver, he was just here!" explained Manuel.

"Come with me." The policeman looked bored and annoyed.

"My driver left, sir. We dropped off my friend, I turned around, and the driver was gone!"

"Come!"

Manuel did as told. He walked to the police truck and noticed two men sitting in the back. The truck was a pickup with a four-door crew cab.

He just wants a payoff. Freakin' corrupt cops, thought Manuel.

To the cop he said, "My driver's license is suspended." He looked back at the Mercedes. Jose was still gone—or he had left. "I don't know where my driver went."

"Your friend can drive, yes?" asked the cop, nodding toward Salvador. "And I need to run your name."

"My father will kill me if I get a ticket." Manuel started to get nervous and ramble. He wished Roger were here; he would know what to do. Something was not right, but he was too anxious to do anything.

The police officer was calm and looked annoyed. "Your name?" He picked up his radio mike.

"Manuel Rosa."

The cop's face suddenly changed, and he grinned evilly. Manuel felt his pulse jump, and he gulped. Did this cop recognize his name?

Manuel glanced at Salvador, who opened the car door to speak with the second cop.

Manuel stood next to the police pickup. He felt confused and just wanted to go. His cousin was setting him up on a blind date that night with a beautiful French exchange student. His mind drifted. A honk from the white van brought him back to reality.

"What's going on? Where's my driver?" Manuel paused and turned to see if Jose had returned. "Salvador, what is going on?" he yelled.

As the driver of the white delivery truck revved the engine and honked, the cop standing beside Salvador calmly removed his gun from his holster and shot Salvador in the head.

Manuel felt his ears explode with adrenalin. He froze. "No!"

"Get in the truck, or your entire family is dead. We have them all!"

Manuel couldn't move. He wanted to scream for Roger, but his voice wouldn't work. He felt his throat dry up, and his body began to shake as if he had been dropped in the Arctic Ocean.

The cop grabbed and cuffed him while someone else put a bag over his head and shoved him facedown in the crew cab of the pickup. He knew he was dead and began praying.

"Do not resist!" snarled the cop.

Within two minutes they were all gone. The police vehicle was speeding away by the time the Mercedes was hooked up to the tow truck. The delivery van, which had successfully blocked any onlookers from the curb, brought up the rear. No one saw a thing, and even if they had, no one would talk. This was Mexico City.

Inside the terminal, Roger ordered a coffee at Starbucks and looked at his ticket. He had plenty of time. He sat down with his back to a wall and looked around. The airport was divided into two terminals, one for domestic flights and one for international. The high, modern curved ceilings; white, shiny floors; and expensive shops reminded Roger of a mall.

He had no illusions about life in Mexico.

During Roger's first year in Mexico, the son of one of his boss's neighbors was kidnapped. The family paid the ransom and still no child. Three days later, the kid was found stuffed in the trunk of an abandoned car. His heart had been pierced by a nail gun. After that, bodyguard hires skyrocketed.

Roger drank his coffee and read his Mexican cooking magazine. Some girls speaking English walked by, and he glanced up. He loved hearing that sound. He was going home. Roger watched people for a few minutes, and then something caught his eye. A man with a red baseball hat was leaning up against a pillar, staring at him.

Roger quickly looked away. *Jesus, I'm paranoid.* He pretended to read his magazine and glanced again. The man was talking on a cell phone.

I need to get outta this country, Roger thought.

Ready to check in at the gate, he grabbed his backpack and walked through small groups of people heading to destinations around the world. He ducked into the restroom. Roger could hardly wait to talk to his old friends and drink a pint or ten of Guinness. In the men's room, he looked around for a stall. He never used urinals. They were too open, and his situational awareness made him hyperalert.

Roger saw a large African man with what looked like tribal tattoos along his cheeks and neck. Part of his ear was missing. A large earring of Santa Muerte hung from the other ear. It was so rare for Roger to see anyone taller than himself that he did a double take. The man was pretending to wash his hands, with no water running.

The massive man looked Roger right in the eye.

Roger swallowed hard. His internal alarms began to sound.

The moment shattered when the man with the red baseball hat walked up behind him.

Thank God for mirrors, Roger thought and kicked backward, catching the man with the baseball hat in the knee. He went down with a curse. Roger was more worried about the huge prison-tattooed beast.

Roger charged. The African produced a gun and grinned, revealing broken, yellow teeth. Roger just kept moving. He would rather die on the offensive. "If you bastards want a fight, you can have one!"

So this was it. His life would end in a bathroom in Mexico City.

CHAPTER 2

Waking Up from Bad Dreams into Nightmares

Cartagena, Colombia, December 1, 1993

The wind and rain hit the tin walls of the warehouse sideways with increasing intensity. The building shook for a moment as if it might blow off its foundation.

A broken man lay on a large table. His hands and feet were tied, and a plastic bag with holes stuck to his grimy face. An assortment of pliers and surgical instruments lay out of his reach.

"You have fifteen minutes before we drop him where the police will find him."

A tall, thin Colombian with a cigarette in his mouth spoke quietly as he pulled off his bloody rubber gloves and shot them across the room like a rubber band. The Colombian seemed drained as if he had just had some type of sexual release.

Rain, blood, and the scurry of rats were the only movements until a man stepped out of the shadows. A group of armed men in tactical gear lined the walls. They were soaked from being outside. Puddles began to form under their boots. Some of the men were Colombian police or soldiers;

others just wore the uniform but were in fact members of a Colombian revolutionary group.

Evan emerged from the shadows like a vapor coming into focus. He tore off his black ski mask and grabbed the face of the captured cartel member.

The cartel member tried to focus. "You?" His breath hissed in and out in what sounded like gasps.

A sign had been attached to the man's chest with duct tape. It said, "Another enemy of the people" and was signed "the People Persecuted by Pablo Escobar or Los Pepes."

"Remember me?" Evan asked.

One eye dilated and widened; the other was swollen shut. "You, Snake...you're supposed to be—"

"Dead?" Evan flicked a severed ear off the table as if he were an eighth grader punting a paper football.

The drug dealer gasped. He had given up on life. His skin had begun to turn gray and felt cool when Evan touched him. He stopped breathing every few breaths, and right when Evan thought he was dead, he would gasp and speak.

"You know what I am capable of," said Evan. "Your family is in hiding with Pablo's family at the hotel. They are protected by the Colombian military and living in fear of Los Pepes. You know if there is anyone who can get to them"—Evan paused to let his words sink in—"I can."

"You betray m-m-me." The man gasped.

"That's my job." Evan took off his thin gloves and put a dip of Skoal in his mouth. The humidity was oppressive. He shook his hand in the air to rid it of the drops of sweat. "Tell me where Pablo is."

The drug dealer rallied for a moment and spoke. "I only know...neighborhood. Not house."

"Better."

"Second floor. Safe house. In city. He makes a phone call each day to his—" The man coughed and stopped breathing for a second. "His son." He gasped. "Calls him noon."

Evan knew that the drug dealer had figured out that the Colombian police as well as the Americans could pinpoint locations by listening to phone calls. Pablo had moved so frequently that he had grown tired.

Evan placed a map in front of the man's face. "Where?"

"No kill my family?"

"Where?"

"Here." The man touched his nose to the map, making a bloody smudge. Blood and froth drained from the corners of his mouth. He tried to cough. "They live?"

Evan turned to walk away and was surprised when the drug dealer called out, "Traitor. I hope you can live with yourself."

Evan stopped and listened to the rain and his own pounding heart. This man had ordered his wife killed.

Evan turned around to face the broken man. "I stopped living with myself years ago," he said, spitting on the floor.

"Andre, Andre Pena."

Evan walked back to the dying man. "Who?"

"A-A-Andre Pena. Freelance hit man, an artist. Blew up a passenger plane to kill one man. Works for guerrilla groups, sometimes government; no cares, no loyalty. Works for Pablo. Get him. Not me. He killed your woman, not me."

Evan put his mask back on. "I have to go."

The cartel leader coughed and muttered his last words on earth: "My family…please, please."

The next day, Evan's birthday, December 2, 1993, Pablo Escobar died. The Colombian police tracked him down and killed him, courtesy of electronic surveillance provided by the United States. The collaboration with US operators, including

Delta Force, CIA, and members of the US Army Intelligence Support Activity, paid off.

Rumors and accusations by opposing political parties later surfaced that perhaps the United States had aided a paramilitary group known as Los Pepes. This vigilante group was made up of rival drug gangs, right-wing guerrilla groups, and Colombian police moonlighting outside of the law to kill off or torture anyone who was associated with Pablo. Los Pepes was the only thing ever known to strike terror in Pablo and his family.

Mason Neck, Virginia, February 14, 2010, 0800 Hours

Evan Hernandez sat up in a cold sweat. The dreams had returned, and the guilt had found him once again. He cursed and started to get out of bed muttering, "I'm in a movie stuck on repeat." He walked into the bathroom. He was depressed again, and it angered him. Today was Veronica's birthday, and, once again, he was reliving the culmination of a thousand lies and bad choices.

"Eighteen years ago or yesterday—how long does this torment go on?" Evan considered his reflection in the mirror. He stood six feet one and 225 pounds. Friends teased that he looked like a retired professional wrestler. Evan had always looked rough, distant, and disconnected, even when he tried to smile. In his younger years, he could break a baseball bat with a shin kick and shatter a full bottle of Coke with his vise grip. No one cared about stupid tricks at his age.

Evan stared, feeling like critical mass was approaching. He thought of how many stories and clichés there were about gazing at one's self in the mirror. He spoke aloud to himself and to Zeus, his Great Dane, "There's mirror, mirror on the wall and there's break a mirror and have seven years bad luck. And, of course, there's that Greek dude—what's his name—Narcissus, who fell in love with his own image."

Evan shook his head and got into the shower. He was relieved when the steam frosted the mirror, hiding his reflection. "Vanity, self-centeredness, self-destruction, depression. What best describes the tornado in my head?"

Evan thought about the shrinks he had seen, the medications he had been on, and the pain in his lower back from not one but two helicopter crashes. "Zeus, let me tell you, the witch doctors with degrees have very medical-sounding terms and politically correct ways of describing what is going on. Of course, every few years they completely change the meanings; hell, they have changed them so much that now the crazy people are the normal ones and the normal ones are nuts."

Evan kept talking to Zeus. He turned off the shower and walked past the mirror, refusing to look at it. "Zeus, you lazy dog, you're not listening." He dried off and got dressed.

"I am being profane—or maybe just thinking about profanity." Evan waved a hand in the air as he pulled on his jeans and then his cowboy boots.

Zeus raised his head and watched him with curiosity.

Evan continued his monologue: "Food and outside—that's all you can think of, huh? Guess that's why you're always happy, living permanently on the dole. I am done. Done living in self-pity, self-this, self-that, drugging myself into thinking it's all OK. Screw it! We are going to sell this house, and we are packing up and moving."

Zeus barked.

Evan laughed. "Wow, I'm talking to my dog. Oh, well, I guarantee I'm not the only one!" He walked through his cluttered living room and pushed a pile of clothes and books out of the way so he could open the door and let his oversized dog lumber out into the snow.

"Maybe I should write a book." Evan frowned, looked into the gray sky, and muttered, "How long would it take me to end up on an enemy's list and have a drone strike take me out?"

He closed the door. "No, they would probably just arrange for a nice accident and then say, 'Evan Hernandez, ex- or fired or alleged former CIA employee, ran off the road today and hit a schoolteacher before killing a poor tree.'"

Evan continued his rant as he grabbed his coffee beans from the pantry. "He has a history of blah, blah, blah, and, oh, he was a marine—oooh, that really makes him a nut."

Evan went into his kitchen and began his coffee-making ritual. He had about three minutes before Zeus would start barking to come in. He weighed his beans on a digital scale, ground them coarsely by hand, and scooped the grounds gently, like an EOD tech might move gunpowder. Evan bought green coffee beans online and roasted them himself.

He stared out the window at the light snow that had covered the ground while he slept. He wondered at how he had come to this place in life. He was not sure why he didn't feel angry this morning or depressed or like going and chopping wood for hours. He had given his neighbors enough wood over the past few months to build their own additions. They weren't sure if he was an out-of-work contractor or a lumberjack. Evan was always working on his house. He was replacing a section of roof, rebuilding his screened-in porch, and starting his second renovation on his workshop.

"Sometimes I get a little OCD," he said with pride. The noise of the coffee maker and the smell of the best medication of all filled his nose and took him back to his early life or lives.

He was forty-eight and felt twenty some days and over sixty other days. He was born in South Florida to an overbearing Cuban father whose family had been very wealthy in pre-Castro Cuba. Evan's father had narrowly escaped the revolution, fleeing to the States with nothing.

Evan had spent the first fourteen years of his life terrified that the Russians were going to attack at any moment. He grew up thinking it was normal to live in a foreign country for two to three years and then move back to the States, just to repeat the cycle. Once he hit fifteen, he began to think his dad was just crazy.

He could still see his father working the grill, wearing an old silk Hawaiian shirt unbuttoned all the way, white dress shorts, expensive brown shoes, and black socks. Sometimes he would chew on an unlit cigar for hours and just grumble to himself.

"Son, you have no idea how lucky you have it in this country," he had told Evan. "These people, these Americans, they are sheep. Someday communism will come here. You laugh at me, but a smiley-face communism will take this country down from the inside. You watch!"

Evan was never clear on what his dad did until he was about twenty. He had told Evan that he worked for the State Department helping other countries as an engineer. On his dad's retirement day, he finally got the truth.

Evan smiled thinking about his old man—his love of boats, his obsessive memorization of useless dates and facts, and his scrapbooking. Evan's father loved to clip and save newspaper articles.

"Proof," he often said, "that America is incrementally being steered toward communism. Someday you will read these old articles, and you will say, 'See, he was not so crazy.' They are like frogs in a pot of water. The heat is turning up slowly, but they don't move. They are so comfortable. By the time they are boiling, it is too late!"

Evan had been great at entertaining his siblings by imitating his father. "What a paranoid, old nut!" he had said on many occasions. He hated his dad's cigars, aftershave, and the brown shoes with socks and shorts. "What's with the socks, Dad?"

Evan was the youngest. He had two sisters and one older brother. In hindsight, Evan now had completely different thoughts about his dad: *Smartest, fairest man I ever met and freaking right about most everything!*

Evan's mother was a whole different case. She was quiet and calculating and only spoke when she had something worth saying. She was mellow and sweet and watched everything. His mother had been born in Russia, and she too had been smuggled away from an oppressive country. To her, life was grand, rules could not be bent, and there was a mathematical rationale behind all she did. His mother had been a chemistry teacher.

Evan checked his coffee machine and critically checked the brew. "Guess I was destined to be a nut," he said, sighing.

His high school teacher mother and CIA agent father had provided Evan with the genetic mix of intellect, discipline, and rigidity—plus a tinge of paranoia—to make him a stellar student. He recalled the frequent moves, the readaptation, and reacclimation to stateside life and sometimes wondered if he was being programmed to be a spy. A friend of his father had given him an empty shell casing when he was a boy and said, "Collected this at the site where Che Guevara was shot."

Surrounded by spies and people who always used aliases, did his dad have some master plan in his head? He recalled his father saying one evening, while sharing a bottle of illegal Cuban rum, "You have to be able to blend in, Son, no matter where you go. Imagine fleeing your home country!"

By the time Evan had left home at age seventeen to join the marine corps, he was head and shoulders more worldly and knowledgeable than his peers. He had grown up in Europe, South America, and Japan before he left home. Evan had a knack for languages. He loved people, and he loved figuring out how they ticked. Speaking four languages seemed natural to him. "The more people I can talk to, the more fun I can have."

The coffee was done, and the dog began barking right on time. Evan poured his coffee and waited. Proper coffee had to cool before the flavor could be tasted. He reminisced about his military time: twelve years in the marines as a grunt and then as a warrant officer flying helicopters.

Evan let the dog in and looked at his photos on the wall. "Damn, I was young and stupid in those days," he muttered to Zeus. The last twenty years of his life flashed before him as a wisp of smells, tastes, and the heartache of a million mistakes.

He had left the marine corps after his first marriage began to fail. He didn't want his ex-wife, who was sleeping with half the guys in Cherry Point, to get his retirement. "What a fitting place for her!" he said, laughing. Her nickname had been Cherry.

"Twelve years in the marine corps and eighteen years with the CIA—and what to show?" Evan had spiraled out of control when he had a forced resignation two years ago. No retirement, thanks to the assholes and political hacks. Then followed bankruptcies, DUIs, OxyContin addiction related to old injuries, and finally booze. Alcoholism had always been there, like an invisible friend, lurking in the shadows.

Evan's most recent ex-girlfriend had scammed him by opening several credit cards in his name. She had seemed so needy, so innocent, and so eager to please. He had been fooled.

"Stay away from younger girls, Zeus," he cautioned. "Be careful what trees you pee on!" The dog barked, and Evan stood up to get his food ready.

"Pretty lousy spy, huh? Got scammed by a twenty-eight-year-old Brazilian babe with an expired student visa and an Obama sticker." Evan sipped his coffee and said, "But I've turned over a new leaf, Zeus. You'll see. When I was on my game, before all this pity-party nonsense, I was sharp—a motivated marine, a cunning agent. We have to get out of here!"

Evan had made his decision. "Build a damn bridge and get over it!" He knew there was no stopping him.

The phone rang. He jumped and looked suspiciously at the caller ID on his home phone. Private caller. Evan fought back the cynical fear that it might be a trick.

"What? Answer it? Zeus! Stop barking. I have to think. What if they use a code word, and I go on a shooting spree?" He laughed, halfheartedly believing his own propaganda. He knew that experiments had been done in the 1960s under the MKUltra projects to implant memories and suggestions into people's subconscious without them knowing. *The Manchurian Candidate* stuff.

"Nothing compares to the crap we can do today," he told Zeus. The phone rang ten times. Finally, Evan shook his head and ignored his overactive imagination.

"*Hola?*"

"*Hola*, Bro. Want to meet for coffee?"

Evan paused—he hadn't spoken to his brother for three months. His dad's funeral had not been a pleasant family reunion.

"*Estas bien?*"

"Can't say over the phone, Bro."

Evan's mouth went dry, and he thought about his boat, scrapbook supplies, and everything else he had to do. He hated surprises.

"Can we meet at Starbucks?"

Evan frowned and looked at his dog. "You know I don't buy anything I can make myself," he said. "Their coffee is overpriced and burnt."

He heard his brother take a deep breath and sigh. He knew what his older brother was thinking: *Evan, so freaking difficult and picky.*

"*Lo siento,*" said Evan.

I'll come over there," replied his brother. "Clear off a space so I can sit!"

"Funny. Just cleaned the place," Evan said, tilting a chair to let books and a pair of boots slide onto the floor. The line went dead. Evan looked out the window and began to feel nervous.

Mexico City, Benito Juárez Airport, Men's Room

The gun made a metallic click and misfired. The large African's eyes were wide and bloodshot as if he were on a dozen different drugs. He cursed in an unintelligible language, and Roger seized the second with a new vigor. He clamped the African's throat with one hand and his tattooed bicep with the other. With a twisting motion, like turning the wheel of a huge ship in a storm, Roger drove the African's head, arm, and shoulder downward. For a brief second, the man canted and was off-balance. Roger's leg swept out, and the African went down, his head bouncing off the tile. The man lay still, and the gun skidded across the floor. Roger felt something like a bat or a pipe hit him in the back of the head. His ears began to ring, and he knew another blow like that would take him out.

Roger kicked backward like a mule and connected with the smaller Mexican. Roger spun around and faced the other attacker. Roger focused intensely, but he felt like the bathroom was moving slightly. "Fucking cracked my skull!"

The smaller man swung the bat again. But Roger was ready. He trapped it with his arms and jerked it out of the Mexican's grasp. The man screamed as if on the verge of panic when Roger reversed the momentum of the bat and cracked him in the face and then shoved him into an open stall.

Roger knew the man would not be down for long. Roger was not sure how he managed to drop the bat, but he did when he felt the big African's arms around his legs, trying to bring him down. The African was having a hard time getting up, so he would bring Roger down to him.

The gun was gone, and the bat lay somewhere on the floor, which was slick with blood, urine, and water. Roger knew he had to finish this quickly; he was in no condition to fight two men. He leapt on the African, punching and elbowing him. He wanted to keep the big guy on the defensive so he could finish him off.

"Never back down—always move forward," his dad used to yell during Roger's wrestling matches. He used to pin people quickly just to get his dad to shut up. Now he thanked his old man.

Roger was trying to get his arms around the African's neck when he felt teeth sink into his arm. Roger dug with his fist into the man's jaw and then carotid, causing extreme pain and reduction in blood flow. The African cursed. His face and hair were bloody. The teeth let go.

"You dirty bastard!" Roger said, groaning. Out of the corner of his eye, he saw the man with the red baseball hat scrambling around looking for the gun.

Roger had the big African pinned to the floor, head and upper arm immobilized. He had his arm around the man's neck and felt him gasp. The big man was having trouble breathing and kicked wildly. He punched with his free hand and connected a few hard blows to Roger's face. The African was in full panic now, and though he was stronger than Roger, lack of oxygen was causing him to fade like an empty lighter.

"You hit like a girl!" said Roger, spitting blood and a tooth. He did not want to hold the man forever; this was not a wrestling match. He used every ounce of weight he had and broke the big African's neck. He felt the first and second cervical vertebrae pop as they separated.

The body went limp.

Roger's heart was pounding in his ears, and he knew time was running out. The guy who used to be wearing the red baseball hat had blood streaming down his face, and his clothes were torn. He favored one leg and could not breathe through a broken nose. His jaw looked fractured; bloody drool was spilling over swollen lips. His eyes were wild and darting from side to side.

Roger stood up straight, looking like a character out of Macbeth. His long brown hair was now stringy and dripping with blood. He smiled ominously and said, "Didn't turn out like you hoped, you little wanker!"

"Gringo!" said the Mexican, finding the jammed gun and raising it.

Roger grabbed his wrists firmly with two hands. Time seemed to stop. "You just can't seem to hold on to things," Roger growled.

"Kill me, an' you no see Manuel again!" His English was rough, but Roger got the message.

"This is where you lose!" said Roger as he broke the man's wrist and elbow and then flipped him in one fluid motion. The cracking bones reminded him of chicken bones being pulled apart. Roger stomped the Mexican's face until he stopped screaming and moving. "You won't be around to find out, you shit!"

Roger knew the police would be in within seconds. Loud voices and a rush of people started to storm the bathroom. He stomped the man's bloody head one more time before it was too late.

He did not resist the police or paramedics.

CHAPTER 3

Best Laid Plans of Vice and Men

Evan knew his brother had arrived when Zeus began barking. "Zeus misses you," he said, opening the door. "He's going to follow you around the whole time you're here, just be warned."

"Animals always seem to know who's allergic." Jack petted Zeus and watched the dog's waving tail knock magazines off a low table. "Why did you get such a big dog?"

Evan shrugged. "I don't know. Small-man complex?"

"You're six one! Nah, you got issues."

Evan walked into the kitchen and got the DEA coffee cup reserved for his brother. Jack was a career DEA agent and had been at headquarters in DC for the better part of ten years. Evan figured he was, if anything, the best-dressed special agent in town. Jack loved clothes.

"How many of these books have you actually read, Evan?"

"Most of them. I usually read about four at a time—too many interests, that's the problem. I got ten times that many on my Kindle."

"How's work on the house?" asked Jack.

Evan poured coffee and added cream. He glanced out the kitchen window and spotted a pair of deer. "It's going. I want to sell in the spring. Break even, pay off debt, and get out of here."

"Houses out here are selling pretty high, Bro," said Jack.

"The whole county is nuts—nine hundred thousand in this area can fetch what? A three-bedroom dump. Go someplace you can buy a freaking ranch with a pool and a staff."

"The price of living where there's lots of money and power," responded Jack.

"And that's why the country is jacked up. Idiot academics educated beyond their intelligence. Government is just massive legal organized crime! Oh, except the DEA, of course." Evan grinned.

"Don't hold back, Bro," Jack said, reaching for the mug Evan handed him.

Evan sat on the couch across from his brother, thinking that Jack had not said anything about the mess or critiqued the yard full of lumber and unfinished projects; he wondered what he Jack up to.

"I love this spot, Jack," he said. "They can't build anymore—it's a nature preserve. I can canoe in the morning, see osprey, eagles. I can fish. And if I need to go sit in traffic for a few hours, I can go do that too. Solitude, it's all here."

"Working any, Evan?" asked Jack.

"Part time. One of my retired friends has a judo and jujitsu dojo in Woodbridge. I teach there for fun, and I'm doing some contracting work, electrical stuff and so on."

"Like it?" persisted Jack.

"Love teaching the kids. They are so enthusiastic; everything is new. Should have been a builder instead of a government type, much more peaceful."

"So you got your driver's license back then?" Jack asked cautiously, not wanting to stir anything up.

"Yes. DUIs destroy your bank account. Of course, so do girls!"

"I see," Jack said and nodded.

"Anyway, soon as I get things together, I'm moving," said Evan flatly.

"Where you thinking about moving?" asked Jack.

Evan drank his coffee and looked at his brother. Something seemed wrong, very wrong. Jack sat stiffly, turning the coffee mug nervously.

Feeling edgy himself, Evan blurted, "Got a few options. Leaving the country to travel for a bit." He wasn't ready to disclose where, even though he knew. He cultivated an aloof, free-spirit facade. But that only masked meticulous plans, countercontingencies, and backups. He wanted to leave the States and soon. A nagging burn in his stomach told him he was no longer safe.

"Evan…" Jack began and trailed off.

Evan watched him carefully, remembering that he needed to be the one to break the ice.

Honesty, no games—my new motto, he thought, looking directly at his brother. "Jack, I apologize for the way I have been acting over the past year. Withdrawn, selfish, and lost. Forgive?"

Jack coughed and choked on his coffee. "Holy crap, Evan. I don't think I have ever heard you apologize for anything."

Over the next forty-five minutes, the two brothers talked about their quirky father, their rock-steady mother, sports, politics, and then back to their father's predictions of the decline and downfall of America. The topics changed and wound around until they were back where they started.

"Dad was a wise old guy," Evan said and then counted the silence.

Jack abruptly put his empty cup on the table and stood. Stepping over the sleeping dog, he walked over to collections of photos hanging on the wall. He paused in front of a picture of an old man, probably from the early 1900s. "Who is that?" he asked.

"Jigoro Kano, founder of judo. I have some of his books in Japanese if you want to borrow them."

"No thanks. But what does this say?" Jack pointed to some Japanese writing along the bottom of the photo.

"A classic Kano saying," said Evan, reciting, "'Walk a single path, becoming neither cocky with victory nor broken in defeat, without forgetting caution when all is quiet, or becoming frightened when danger threatens.'"

Jack nodded and turned to face his brother. "Evan, how do you feel about doing something dangerous and possibly illegal?"

Evan stared at his brother for a moment, and then asked him to repeat what was just said.

Mexico City, 0900

Masked police drove Roger about twenty minutes north of the airport to Hospital Juárez de Mexico. Now they waited. Roger grumbled and tried to engage the two stoic police officers in conversation. They said nothing. The men were fairly tall and athletically built. Roger regarded them with interest. They had to be members of some elite unit, but they wore no insignia or patches. Both men wore black ski masks, black body armor, and tactical gear down to black kneepads and steel-toed boots. Roger looked at their weapons and nodded.

The men silently looked back from behind their shades, as if in a staring contest.

Roger groaned at the pain in his face. He said, "I been here for two years and never had the police help me with anything—just take a couple of bribes to tear up bogus tickets. Now, I got what? The SWAT team?"

He sipped some water, winced at the sting, and looked around his private treatment room. A doctor had sewn up his head, given him some ice, and taken x-rays several hours ago. His passport and luggage had been taken, and now he waited, like a prisoner.

"Roger!" said Victor Rosa, Manuel's uncle, as he burst into the room. Victor waved at the two armed men and spoke to them. *"Fuera de aqui!"*

The two men left without a word.

"What are you doing here? Am I under arrest?" Roger asked angrily.

Victor Rosa was high up in the Mexican Federal Police— *maybe a detective*, Roger thought. And he knew Victor had pull, but not like this.

"My bags, Victor?" Roger asked.

"No worries, my friend. Taken care of. You hear that Manuel was kidnapped?"

Victor had an urgency and stress to his face that put Roger on edge. He had only seen the man on weekends, usually with a beer in his hand and a smile on his face.

"Aye, I heard," said Roger. "They are one for one. They kidnapped him but missed me."

Victor nodded and said, "Last year, two men dressed as doctors came into this very hospital and killed a top narco hit man."

"That's reassuring!" Roger grumbled.

"And a few months ago, narco hit men dressed as Federales gunned down six police officers at the airport." Victor continued as if he were talking about the weather. "You are missing some teeth, eh?" He walked close and stared sadly at Roger.

"Aye."

"Let's go. Quickly!" said Victor. He handed Roger a ski mask, a bulletproof vest, and a large blanket. "Put this on."

Roger put on the vest and stood slowly, his whole body aching.

"Roger, my friend, we must leave before the actual police get here. They are who we are trying to avoid!" Victor said with a laugh that trailed off into a cough.

Roger froze. Then he put on the black mask and gulped. His stomach tightened, and his mouth went dry. "What are you talking about?"

"No time to explain, *amigo*," said Victor. "Right now I am not with the police!" He looked at his watch. "I will explain all in the car."

"Am I avoiding the police or the kidnappers?" asked Roger.

"Both!"

Roger left the hospital treatment room. He stumbled as a group of six armed men led and half pulled him through back hallways and staff exits out into a parking garage.

"*Darse prisa!* Hurry up," urged Victor.

Mason Neck, Virginia

Evan looked at his brother for a minute and then spoke slowly. "You're serious?"

"Evan, you're the only one I know who could help me pull this off," said Jack urgently.

"You're not talking about robbing a 7-Eleven, right?"

"Sophia Gonzales, my housekeeper—" said Jack.

"I am confused. You want me to rob your housekeeper?"

"Evan, I am serious," Jack replied. "Sophia's father, Armando Gonzales, was kidnapped a few days ago in Juárez, Mexico."

"That sucks. He's dead by now, Jack. You know the stats!"

Jack nodded, and the color seemed to drain from his face. "Sophia's like family. She's been with us for ten years. She's got five kids, all in high school, and they are all a wreck. They clearly can't go to the police."

Evan stated. "No. Half the time it is the police. Proof of life confirmation?"

"Yes," Jack said. "Yesterday, a recorded message saying, 'I am old. Don't pay these animals.'"

"What else?"

"Her father was kidnapped yesterday while on his way to work. The kidnappers mistakenly think that he has a lot of money since his daughters live in the United States. They want fifty thousand dollars in three days, or he's dead. They gave instructions—what to do and where to go."

"Juárez, eh?" Evan mused.

Jack leaned forward and spoke quickly. "I clearly can't let her or any of her family go there. They are adamant about taking their life savings, selling their cars, business, whatever it takes, to go down there and get, well, ambushed. I saw this play out dozens of times in Arizona and Texas when I was stationed there. Whole families wiped out."

"He's dead, Jack—been dead."

"And if it were our father?"

"Does she do windows?" Evan asked, trying to lighten things up, but Jack didn't smile.

"I need you to be my alibi," he said. "I'm taking ten days' leave and fifty thousand dollars of my own money and going down there."

"What?" exclaimed Evan. "You're crazy!"

Jack ignored him. "Cindy doesn't know, and if the DEA finds out, I'm fired."

Evan stood up so quickly that Zeus lifted his head and growled.

"Jack! Just stop it! I know you're a cop, but listen to yourself. You'll end up in a YouTube video getting killed by some cartel members. You got a family too and a career. No. No way!"

"I feel called to do it."

Evan paused and looked at his brother as if he were nuts. "Called? Like God told you?"

"Just called," said Jack. "Like I have the resources, like I have been helping protect victims my whole freaking career...And now I know a victim who is almost family. What does it say about me, Evan, if I do nothing?"

Evan began to pace around the room. His head ached, and as he walked into the kitchen, an idea began to burn deep in his head, like a warm coal.

"I will be in and out in two days, Evan. I just need you to say that I was with you."

Evan walked back into the living room, sipping the last of the coffee.

"A couple of years ago, I had a dream about helping a stranger, an old man with a horrible scar on his back. I refused to help, and he died."

"How?" asked Evan, looking at his brother sideways.

"Can't say, but it wasn't pretty. Look, Evan, I got to go down there, and what I really wanted to do is ask you to go with me. But when I got here, I chickened out."

Evan bit his lower lip and looked at his brother.

Zeus was snoring again.

"You know I spent a lot of time in South America and Mexico," Evan began slowly. "You know I was a pilot with the agency—no secret there—but what I did, the details...Well, it's the same with your job. You can't talk about it."

"Your point, Evan?"

"You're married, Jack. You have three kids in college. You haven't been in the field in, like, fifteen years, and, well, you have rules."

"What are you saying?"

Evan looked at his coffee cup and felt like drinking some Scotch. His head throbbed. "My lies got someone I loved and my daughter killed many years ago. I thought I drank the memories away and covered the guilt—only it's back now, stronger than ever."

"You were married? When? Where?" asked Jack. His jaw dropped, and his eyes widened for a second as if he did not recognize his brother.

"In Colombia. I had a wife and daughter. The same time I had a fiancée up here. I was an ass," said Evan.

"Why the hell didn't you tell me?"

"'Cause I am an asshole, Jack, that's why. You go to Mexico and get killed, you're no better than me. You're hurting someone with lies."

"You've been living with that for how long?" demanded Jack. He sat back on the couch, breathing heavily as if he had just run a race. He looked around the room, shook his head, and said quietly, "I forgive you, and God can forgive you. You should ask."

"But the dead people, Jack—they don't forgive or forget. There's a Mexican ballad about a hit man who arrives in hell and meets his victims. That's me."

Evan walked over to a bookshelf and moved some books around till he found a small bottle with barely a swallow of tequila. "I haven't had a drink in months, Jack. I can't believe I just told you my big freaking secret!"

Jack stared at his brother, not in anger but with gentleness and a touch of pity. "Wow, Evan," he said softly.

Evan opened the bottle and poured the contents down his throat, barely tasting the warm burn. He screwed the cap back on, set the bottle down, and looked at his brother. His lips felt warm, but his head was clear. "You wouldn't last a day down there, Jack. They'd make you for a cop. You got too much to live for. Me—well, I'm a different story."

"What are you saying?"

"I might be a little more prepared than you, Jack. You have access to real-life data, DEA intelligence. You can help me with that. But on the ground? You're worthless! No, you're better sitting at a computer!"

"Screw you. I am going," protested Jack. "This is my operation."

Evan spoke quickly as if he where betraying some secret. "Come with me, Jack. I want to show you something." He led his brother back through the bedroom and into the only place in the house that was immaculate: his closet. Inside was a large walk-in safe that was securely bolted to the floor.

Evan opened the safe and stood aside for his brother. Jack eyed the assortment of handguns and custom AR-15s in Evan's war closet and said, "Jesus, Evan, you expecting an apocalypse?"

"Every day. Here, look at this." Evan's voice grew deep and impatient as he went from slight embarrassment to guilt and then to baring it all. "Green bag, Europe. Yellow bag, Asia. Red bag, South America. Look inside," urged Evan. Each duffel bag made a solid thud as it hit the carpet.

Jack whistled and then was very quiet as the impact of what he was seeing hit him.

"You got a different jump bag for each region? Holy shit, Evan! Fake passports? Money? Gold? You're breaking half a dozen laws with this crap…cell phones, plastic weapons to sneak past security? What the hell! Are the marshals after you?"

"You just proved my point, Jack. This is normal to me. I live with paranoia that at any moment they are going to come get me. What if they have second thoughts about letting me just retire?"

"They?"

Evan shook his head as if he were explaining geometry to a chimp.

"What the hell did you do, Brother?" Jack muttered.

Evan shook his head. "Can't say."

Jack pulled a wad of euros and a small plastic knife that could fit easily in the palm out of the European bag. "Only a paranoid nut job or a—"

"Terrorist or spook would have something like this?" Evan finished the sentence and then began piling his jump bags back into the safe and locked it. He felt relieved in a way, like he had just shared a burden, given someone an insight into the paranoia of his world.

"Rest my case, Jack. You're not fit to go; I am. When do I leave?"

Jack backed out of the closet, walked back into the living room, and sat down. "Not crazy or prepared enough," he said. "Too much to live for? You have a peculiar way of putting things." He shook his head slowly and tried to process what he had just learned about his own flesh and blood. "I wanted your help or an alibi at the least—not for you to take over. But maybe you're right."

"You're getting the bonus plan, Bro," quipped Evan.

"Possibly a dead brother too," Jack said and sighed. He walked to the front window and glanced out at the snow. He took several deep breaths and then turned around to face his brother. "I don't know, Evan. My motives are to bring Sophia's family some closure—to say, 'Your father is dead or missing'—or, by some miracle, to get him back. Not likely alive though."

"Nope," Evan chimed in.

"But I want to work with you. I would feel like a coward having my younger brother go while I didn't. And you really have bad luck on top of everything, Evan."

Jack's sarcastic attempt at humor was partly based on fact but also on a desire to give Evan an out. Both knew that Evan had a better chance than Jack did of pulling off such an operation.

Neither spoke for several minutes. Jack stared out at the snow-dusted trees and said, "Don't feel like you have to, Evan, and this is no time to prove anything to anyone."

Evan coughed and shook his head. He wanted to say that he was far beyond trying to prove anything to anyone, that it was a chance to help someone other than himself. Instead, he muttered, "My problems will still be here when I get back, unless I get killed—or maybe meet a beautiful Mexican soap-opera star."

"Evan, this is serious. Stop kidding!"

"You know I'm just mumbling to myself. It keeps me chilled. Staying calm is key."

"Bad habit," said Jack. "People might think you're crazy or not serious."

"Or both. Look, I'll be fine. My calendar is empty. Yeah, this is dangerous, but Mexico really is OK if you don't act like a fool—way more good people than nasty ones. I'll see what I find out and bring them some kind of an answer either way. Deal?"

"I guess," said Jack warily. "They will appreciate it. The worry of missing a loved one—"

"I know, Jack. It never goes away. I have one small favor to ask of you while I am gone."

"Name it, Bro!"

Evan looked at his dog, then at his brother and then again at the dog. Zeus perked up his ears and barked.

CHAPTER 4

Liars, Flyers, and Bloody Pliers

Juárez, Mexico, February 14, 1300 Hours

Gerard was in a horrible mood. His eyes were bloodshot, his mouth tasted like cigarettes, and despite the Red Bull and cocaine, he was starting to see double. He had flown fifteen hundred miles from Boca del Rio, where he could be spending his day at the beach. Now he was here, in hell. Gerard Blaise, hated the barren, crime-ridden border town of Juárez. The temperature would be warm during the day and dip down into the thirties at night.

"Hellhole!" he muttered, driving the white van slowly through traffic.

The men with him had their weapons ready in case someone tried to carjack them. Even criminals were afraid to drive in Juárez.

Blaise was short and wiry like an endurance athlete. He had a narrow face with a long pointy nose, sharp brown eyes, and a thin mouth that was fixed in a sarcastic smirk. He was not French by birth but had fled a dead-end gypsy life in Eastern Europe to reinvent himself. Several years in the French Foreign Legion had given him a new name and marketable skills. Now known as

Gerard, he was a for-hire weapons expert and pilot. Trouble with the law and authorities had set him on the run, and he had ended up in Mexico.

He rubbed his face, noting he had not shaved in two days. "I need more smokes," he said.

The men with him said nothing.

"Boss?" said one of the men.

"*Yes?*" Gerard asked.

They drove past a group of police standing in a circle looking down at a body. Streams of blood stained the pavement. Shell casings glittered in the sun. Children on bikes and old people moved to get a closer look. Gerard noticed the body of a cop sprawled in his car, the windshield shredded from bullet holes. He heard a helicopter and spat out of the van's window.

"Do we have to fly back today?" one of his companions asked. "I know a great bar."

"My orders are to get the girls back to the coast," said the Frenchmen. "But I'll check. I am tired, and none of you idiots can fly a plane. Besides, this place is dangerous!"

Only a few in the gang could tolerate being around Gerard.

The van moved through traffic, passing car dealerships, banks, and homeless people. They passed Los Pueblos del Mercado and turned into a back alley. "I'll get out here. You two are backup," he said, parking the van. "Be careful. Don't do anything stupid, and don't sleep!"

He got out of the van, pausing to light another cigarette. He glanced at a telephone pole with hundreds of pictures of missing women, all stapled on top of one another, torn and bleached by the sun. A handwritten sign in Spanish read, "400 girls killed and the government has done nothing."

The store was one of hundreds of small convenience stores owned by the Eastern Cartel and was used primarily for money laundering. The Scorpions protected such stores and their managers.

"Can I help you, *señor*?"

Gerard turned to face a small, round Mexican who was missing teeth and had crooked glasses. He looked like he was out of a spaghetti western. "Store Manager Juan?"

"*Si, y usted?*" Juan spoke loudly and walked with a limp.

Gerard lifted up his shirt with both hands, turning his head to the side to avoid getting cigarette ash on himself. Smoke wafted into his eyes, and he squinted. A large scorpion tattoo covered his abdomen and torso. He kept his sunglasses on. "The scorpion says who I am."

The store manager visibly gulped and took a deep breath. He had heard of this man.

"I am Gerard. *Donde esta leche?*" he snarled.

"Back here, *señor*," Juan stammered. He was terrified.

"*Abrir* the back door. My men are parked out back," said Gerard, opening the door and letting one gang member in.

Juan led them to a large walk-in beer cooler with a chain and padlock on its door. Juan fumbled with a key, and he spoke nervously. "The doctor was here this morning. He say they are in good health." He continued in a mix of broken English and Spanish, "*Las chicas es* d-d-drugged and asleep. I-I had to put extra blankets on them. *El* doctor left instructions for us to give medication."

Gerard rolled his eyes and exhaled loudly. "Will you shut up? I have a headache! This is not the first time I have done this, you fool."

The three men went into the cooler and walked to a corner.

"Shit, does beer need to stay this freaking cold?" Gerard said.

Behind some boxes and pallets of Tecate and Dos Equis, five bodies covered with blankets lay on a mattress. Chains linked the ankles of the captives.

Gerard was about to yank the covers back when he spotted an old man sitting on a stool, staring at the young women. "Who the fuck is this?" He yanked out his .45 and put it to the old man's head. The old man did not flinch or look up; he just kept staring at the girls as if he were their protector. Gerard paused. "Is he blind?"

"No, *señor*, please, no shoot him!" pleaded the store manager. "He is my helper! He cleans and makes sure the girls breathe. He keeps them warm. *El* doctor…he…he say to watch them. He no speak or hear; he no sees too good."

"As long as that is all he does," said Gerard. He and the driver laughed. "Crazy old man…Fine, he can help us."

Gerard lifted off the blankets and looked at the girls. They wore orange jumpsuits like prisoners. Their skin looked a little blue. Gerard ran his hands over their bodies—breasts and hair. He was about to unzip one of the jumpsuits to have a look and then had second thoughts. Even he would not defy Jorge Valdez, his boss.

"Nice, and they are still breathing," he said. "Payday is coming, men! They're too cold. The drugs don't allow them to regulate temperature. They die, I kill you. Get it? Now, go get the bags. We need to move. Where are the drugs and directions?"

Gerard always transported the girls in body bags. If he was stopped by the police, he would slip them some money and say that he was transporting bodies to either a medical school or morgue. He turned to the old man, who had not taken his eyes off the girls.

"You want them, old man? Are you their knight in shining armor? Eh? They are like sleeping beauties, no?"

Gerard caressed one of the girl's faces and rubbed her body soothingly. Her skin was cool, and he felt slightly aroused. "This is a lot of money here. No prince charming rescues these girls. The big bad wolf gets them. Fairy tales are not real, old man.

This is real." He pulled out his gun again and put it to the man's temple. The man didn't move.

"I am a Scorpion. Do not forget; I can find you anywhere, you old bastard!"

Two gang members returned with Juan and some body bags. One of them said, "We have a problem, boss." His voice was shaky, and he looked at the floor.

"Problem?" asked Gerard coldly.

"*Sí*, the van, the muffler…It scraped and came off when we came up the alley. It sounds like a loud motorcycle, and we have a flat tire. Ran over something in the road."

No one spoke for a long moment. Gerard looked around. He was a very cautious person and above all else was superstitious.

"We can switch trucks, boss, but this one must be towed."

"No! I have made many deliveries in this truck. We go get it fixed."

"Could take a day or two, boss."

"Well, then, Jesus, you get to party in Juárez for two days!" said Gerard. He chuckled but clearly was not amused. He took a wad of cash out of his back pocket and peeled off a hundred-dollar bill.

"Juan! You watch these girls, and call me at this number if there's any problem. Let them wake up to pee and eat, walk around a little. Then out again!" He wrote a number on the bill. "I will be back in two days max. Don't screw up!"

"Si, *señor*" stammered Juan.

"And the old man—he can't leave."

"No, sir, he stay and help," answered Juan.

Gerard considered this. "I will have the doctor come sit with them tomorrow. They are not to be moved." He was surprisingly calm as he left, followed by the two gang members.

"Boss," said one of the men, "I called us a cab. My cousin, he will get us. My other cousin, he will tow the truck."

The three men stepped out into the alley, which stank like old urine and garbage.

"You are thinking ahead. Good. What is your name again?"

"Carlos."

"Good, Carlos." Gerard handed him a hundred-dollar bill. "This club you men keep bragging about, it better be good. I want this to go smooth. Understand? I have a ritual, and if my ritual does not go right, people die—get it?"

"Boss, anything like this happen before?" asked Carlos.

Gerard lit up his last cigarette. He paused and watched a cloud of smoke float away like a pleasant dream. "Once, when I was flying back to Boca del Rio."

He paused again as if he was watching a slow movie.

"A Peruvian overdosed last year. Dumped her out at ten thousand feet," Gerard said and laughed. "We lost a lot of money, but we just snatched some American instead," he said.

In the cooler, Juan looked from the five drugged females to the man he had kidnapped, Armando Gonzales. This was Juan's first venture into kidnapping, and he was wondering if it was worth it. He and his buddies had not really considered the logistics involved in kidnapping the old man and housing him at the same time they were working their regular jobs.

And he was having second thoughts now that the Scorpions had arrived. He knew that he and his gang would be killed if they were suspected of conducting their own operation.

Juan mustered his courage and tried to gain back some of his lost nerve.

"You will be free tomorrow when your rich American family pays," Juan said in Spanish to his prisoner. "If not, you will die. Now listen, old man, you did well with that Scorpion. Forget about those bitches. They'll wish they were dead when they wake up. Very sad."

Juan felt a tinge of guilt and thought maybe he was not as hard as he pretended. "I am not evil, just poor. The Scorpions, those men, they do this for some other reason." He shook his head and looked away from the old man's eyes.

Armando Gonzalez stared at Juan, no longer faking his ailments. "You are all the same," he said. "My daughter, she is not wealthy but will pay. You must not play games with her. You need to make your peace with God before you meet him. It will not be a good meeting."

He shook his head and hoped that Sophia would not come to this satanic place. "You should kill me if you have the guts. Save everyone some trouble. Death in this world is a new life for me. I know where I am going, Juan. Do you?"

Juan shifted his weight from foot to foot and chewed on his lip. He wished his gang members were here; they would know what to say. This old man had no fear and a surreal calmness and peace, and that terrified Juan.

Armando was sad for the girls. He looked past the tormented Juan and at the motionless, covered bodies. He prayed for their safety.

CHAPTER 5

Baggage Pickup

Outside the People's Market, two men sat in a small car with tinted windows. Miguel and Francisco had been members of Mexico's elite antinarcotics unit before defecting and joining what could best be described as an underground mercenary group known as Dark Cloud. They had been gathering information on Gerard Blaise—Gerard—and other gatekeepers in the Scorpion gang. Gatekeepers were basically area managers and had direct contact with Mario, the Eastern Cartel leader.

"Well, what do you think?" asked Miguel.

"I think something has gone wrong." Francisco, the elder of the two, spoke in a quiet, unassuming manner. "He always flies in, picks up the load of girls, takes them to the airport, and leaves. Stops at the same places every time. Today, though, the van breaks down. As a creature of habit, he has it towed away, no doubt to be fixed. They have no need for situational security, for they are in a hurry. They could easily just get a new damn vehicle, but, no, not Gerard. This obsessiveness with habit, this unwillingness to remain vigilant and observe operational security, shows me that he is lazy."

"OK, so what's the plan? Should we pass information to the police and have the girls rescued?" Miguel asked, not hiding his boredom or impatience.

"No. No tactical benefit. Nathan was clear: observe Gerard, see if he meets with any other big players. No direct action."

"Unfortunately, Francisco, we have done this a few times, and we never figure out where he takes the girls. They vanish—that is our key."

"Well, that's Nathan's job. He claims that this time he can track the plane. This time we mark it, and they track it. I hear that he has someone on the inside now, someone close to Mario."

No one spoke for a second, and then Francisco looked at his cell phone. He had a text.

"We have to go to the airport. Team Two is going to relieve us."

"Oh, great. Going to watch Mr. Zipcatonal again? What's the point?" Miguel complained. "We have all this new technology, but if you ask me, it just makes things more complex. Painting the plane with a laser, tracking, watching, using computers. I say we snatch Gerard and melt his balls with a blowtorch till he talks. That's the real world! The Mexican way! Letting innocent girls get sold into slavery to rich Saudis—despicable! Screw operational security!"

"Ah, my friend, Miguel. You are so funny!"

"And another thing, Francisco. Why watch Mr. Z? Nathan is spreading us too thin!"

"We just do our job. Get it? Mr. Z has a background in intelligence. If he is clean, we will recruit him."

They watched Gerard and his henchmen walk out to the curb and get into a cab driven by a good-looking woman.

"Traffic," said Miguel, groaning, as he eased the car into a fast-moving stream of vehicles.

Mexico City, 1400 Hours

Roger walked through the rain trying to stay under trees as best he could. Traffic was heavy on the busier streets. The cars thudded through potholes, splashing him with water. It was late afternoon and a little cool. He cursed and kept walking. The rain had stopped by the time he turned down the side street. Roger paused by a predetermined signpost. He looped the duffel bag over his shoulder and adjusted his baseball cap and his wet jeans.

"I hate being wet," he grumbled out loud to the surveillance team, wherever they were. "You realize they are going to kill me and just take the money. Manuel is probably already dead." His words made him feel depressed.

He was impressed by Dark Cloud's technology. He was wearing a tiny microphone and camera concealed in his baseball cap. He had a backup microphone on his shirt collar. His watch and cloned cell phone were providing GPS data separately. Dark Cloud even knew his heart rate. The fact that they could see him, hear him, and monitor his phone calls did little to reassure him.

Following the kidnappers' directions, Roger was unarmed and had zigzagged on foot some twenty-five blocks through the garden and business districts of Mexico City. Apparently, the bad guys did not want him going into a bad section of town and getting robbed.

The cell phone in his pocket rang. "Doesn't matter if the good guys know where I am—or where the money is, for that matter," he muttered. "They can't stop a bullet." He took out the phone provided by the kidnappers. "Aye," said Roger, slowly looking all around. Both the good guys and the bad guys were listening. Both most likely knew that the others were listening. *Let the cat-and-mouse game begin*, he thought nervously.

"OK, gringo, listen."

"First of all, you little bean eater, I'm not a gringo; I'm Scottish."

"I no care. You walk up to statue. There be motorcycle cop ten minutes. You ask for light. You give bag. You wait."

"Wait for what, you wanker?"

"No questions. We give proof of life. You give money. Second drop." The Mexican's English was choppy. He had probably lived in the States at one time.

The phone went dead, and Roger took a deep breath. "I hope you bastards know what you're doing," he said under his breath as he began walking up the street.

He felt sweaty and like he needed a shower. His head was not throbbing as badly. He purposely had not taken any Percocet so he could keep his wits about him. He couldn't ever recall a time when he was ready to die, and this was no different.

The plan had three phases. First, Roger would drop off the first bag of money, which could be tracked via a microsized tracer. Second, Roger would go to a second place, where he would get proof of life. The final phase was the final money drop and exchange.

Roger figured he would be shot by this point and wasn't sure what he was going to do.

He knew that typically the gangs would kidnap or kill whoever delivered the money on the first drop. Often gangs would either demand more money or just kill the courier and the original victim or *levantado*. Generally, a kidnap victim was never seen again. Roger recalled the narco lingo and bloody stories that he had heard from Mr. Rosa's detective brother over the years. It did little to soothe Roger but did increase the fight factor over the flight urge.

If you were a body stuffed into a trunk, you were an *encajuelados*. If you were bound and blindfolded with tape, you were known as *encintados*. *Encobijado* meant that you were one rolled up in a blanket, which seemed common with the *sicarios* or hit men. Roger began to feel more edgy and alert as he recalled Rosa's brother talking about *El Pozolero*, "the Soup Maker," a hit man in the border region who dissolved his victims' bodies in acid.

Narcocorridos, narco ballads, had been written about him. Roger shook his head. Americans complained about how gangster rap influenced kids in the States, turning suburban kids into gangster wannabes. But here, the narcos actually paid to have albums made about them and their grisly exploits.

Roger looked around him at the business of the city. Despite the violence and craziness, Roger still loved the country. The food was awesome and varied and the people were colorful and, for the most part, friendly. Life in Mexico was so different from that in Scotland or Europe. And he loved the difference. Still, Roger wished that he was ignorant of the whole subculture that ran beneath the surface. He just wanted to focus on learning Spanish, cooking, and maybe even meeting a nice girl.

"Kidnapping! Who knew it was such big business," Roger grumbled out loud. "Working is so much easier than living a life of crime!"

Negotiating ransoms was a booming industry in Mexico. Some of the agencies actually hired thugs to kidnap potential clients. The agency would then act as a mediator and solicit money from the families for negotiating the victim's recovery. Thus the agency got money on both ends. Money was king in Mexico just like everywhere else.

Roger made his way uphill to a large statue. He had driven by the impressive white statue of an Aztec before but had never really looked at it.

"They won't have to shoot me," he said. "I'll just have a freaking heart attack."

He was walking along Aventia Reforma, and traffic was heavy. He felt isolated near the traffic circle and statue. Life was moving all around him, oblivious to his predicament.

"Doing OK?" a female voice crackled in his ear.

"No." Roger leaned against the low wall that framed the long-dead Aztec king. "I am thinking too much and beginning to have second thoughts about this."

"Cuauhtémoc That is his name, Roger, known as Fallen Eagle. He was a great Aztec king," said the voice.

"Easy for you to say," Roger grumbled, recognized the voice, and tried to catch his breath. The stress of the day, the beating, and fear were all creeping into his joints and torso.

Roger decided if he survived this, he was going to start working out.

He thought back briefly to the attractive woman named Mia, a Dark Cloud technical operative he had briefly met at the Rosas' house. Roger pegged Dark Cloud to be a highly paranoid and secretive organization of ex-spooks and law-enforcement types cashing in on Mexico's growing private-mercenary industry. Roger had only seen a couple of people at a time and only the face of Mia. Members usually wore masks, did not use their names, and seemed to be divided into cells or groups. Roger had been briefed that Dark Cloud was financed by wealthy businessmen and government officials. He would have never trusted nor gone along with this whole plan had he not known that Mr. Rosa had given his blessing.

"Mercenaries, connected mercenaries," he grumbled. "Less I know about you, all the better."

"Hey, you!"

Roger spun around and looked at a motorcycle cop who pulled over to the curb and stopped. He was tall for a Mexican and looked more European. He grinned, showing crooked, yellow teeth. Traffic kept moving.

Roger reluctantly spoke the code word he had been instructed to use. "You got a light?"

"Give me bag, you!" snarled the cop, who looked stoned and had his hand on a pistol.

A million thoughts went through Roger's head as he handed over the bag. He was soaked in sweat from the uphill hike and forgot for a second how annoyed he was.

The cop smiled, slung the duffel over his shoulder, and was gone. Roger watched for a full five minutes in silence as the bike merged into traffic. He watched little VW cabs, expensive cars, pedestrians, street vendors, and tourists amble about the city. Not one of them cared or even noticed him.

Roger suddenly felt like a fool. "This is all freaking pointless," he said. "Now what?"

"Wait," Mia spoke into his ear.

"Aye, time, that's all I have," he said, noting a homeless person who was watching him with glazed, sleepy eyes.

Roger turned away. "Have you people done this before?" he asked.

"*Sí*," she said.

"If I did not know you through the Rosas, I would say your group is working with the kidnappers. Happens all the time."

The feminine voice grew hostile. "Without connections we would never trust you either, Roger. No one is asking you to join. Just participate in this operation."

"*Bueno*," Roger said and coughed. "Ten thousand security companies in Mexico—how did you guys get picked? The phone book?"

Roger heard laughter this time, but something in the tone said, *You have no idea who you are screwing with.* All cuteness drained away as she said in a serious voice, "We are not a security company."

"Can we go out sometime?" Roger blurted. "Will you let me cook dinner for you?"

The phone went silent. The homeless man began peeing on a bench. "Hey, you fucking wanker! Don't you know people sit on that! I may want to since I've been standing for hours!" Roger took a step forward, and the homeless man grunted and turned to run, not even bothering to zip his pants.

CHAPTER 6

Made in Mexico

Juárez, Mexico, February 14, 2200 Hours

Located in the high desert at 3,730 feet, just south of El Paso, Texas, Juárez was founded in the mid-seventeenth century by Franciscan friars. If their vision had been that the area would one day become a center for spreading the gospel and civilizing pagan natives, they would be disappointed. Modern Juárez has an estimated population of about 1.5 million people, give or take the time of year and who is counting. Rated as one of the most violent cities in the world outside of a war zone, its reputation stands firm. There are four ports of entry into the city or out of it, depending on where you stand: the Bridge of Americas, Ysleta International Bridge, Paso del Norte, and Stanton Bridge.

Evan stopped thinking about the mess of Juárez, history, and the dismal state of man when the pilot signaled the descent into Juárez. He turned off his iPod and looked out the window at the city lights. All cities look similar from the air. It was when you could smell and hear them and see the looks on people's faces that you really knew where you were. He wished he could drown himself in entertainment and mind-numbing consumerism—be a "sheeple" instead of someone who compulsively thought about the world and where it seemed headed.

A pretty Mexican flight attendant asked him to put his tray table up, and he nodded. From here on he would only speak Spanish and make an effort to stay in character. Evan thought briefly about his time in Colombia and half a dozen other South American countries. He tried to total the number of years he had lived outside the United States and figured it was way over ten. After decades of living in and blending into foreign cultures, first growing up and then in his work, something had shifted, either in his mind or in the collective conscience of the United States, that made him feel as if he were a stranger.

Evan was far less concerned about geography than he was about being somewhere where he could belong, live off the radar screen, and not have to look over his shoulder. "Then why the hell am I in Mexico? Not the safest of choices," he muttered. He watched the city lights below and thought about Costa Rica or a remote village in the Andes, somewhere he could just be away from it all. He longed to reduce life to its essentials, the basics.

"I am turning into one of those nut jobs my dad always talked about—a hermit—in my old age. Freaking afraid and untrusting of everything," Evan whispered to his reflection in the airplane window.

The captain made an announcement in Spanish and then repeated it in English: "This is your captain. It is fifty degrees in Juárez and ten o'clock local time. We will be landing shortly. When we land, you will have to fill out a customs form if you have anything to declare. Please have your passport ready."

Evan smiled. Not many people smuggle stuff into Mexico; it's the flight out that's the problem. He thought about the border and how that line signified a personal border that he had crossed. How far was he going to go on this mission, or how far was he willing to go? He disliked operating without any backup, but here he was. The wheels made the familiar touchdown noise and bump. He smiled wryly and texted a single word to his brother Jack: *In*.

He retrieved his bag and moved away from the crowds at the baggage carousel. He was sweating in his suit and tie and would be glad to change. Scanning the exit, he spotted a man looking directly at him.

The man was sixtyish, short and stocky, with a pockmarked face and thinning hair. He wore jeans; cowboy boots; a colorful, long-sleeved shirt; and a cowboy hat too big for his head. Evan had met Mr. Z twice years earlier. He had been a valuable asset, providing safe houses and getting items for agents for years.

"*Señor* E?" asked the Mexican tentatively. "*Cómo fue tu vuelo, mi amigo?*"

"*Largo*," replied Evan shortly.

"*Bienvenida a Juárez. No ha cambiado.*"

"Where is the car?"

"Outside. Your bags?"

"I got them. I'm booked at the Quality Inn near the American consulate. On Paseo de la Victoria," replied Evan. "You lost weight, Z?"

"*Sí*, nerves. The cartels are here. They are not small players any longer."

Evan remembered him as a man of few words, which was exactly why Mr. Z was still alive. As they left the terminal, a man on a cell phone quickly snapped a photo. Airports, bus stations, hospitals, and busy street corners in most border towns were hangouts for *halcones*—hawks—for cartels. These lookouts notified bosses of police, military, or rival gang activity. But this man was not a lookout for the underworld.

Francisco took a picture of Mr. Z and Evan shaking hands and e-mailed it to his boss. It only took moments for Francisco to figure out where the plane had departed from: nonstop from Baltimore. He e-mailed Nathan again and then called Miguel, who was circling the parking lot. "Team One said they believed Mr. Z was picking up his aunt from Peru," Francisco said.

"*Sí*, that's what they claimed," confirmed Miguel. "They intercepted calls between Z and his wife."

Francisco followed Evan and Mr. Z from the terminal, continuing his phone conversation. "Well, he lied to his wife. He met a big, ugly American who flew in from Baltimore, near Washington, DC."

"So maybe he is cheating on his wife?" Miguel laughed.

Francisco ignored the comment and paused to put gum in his mouth. "He is an American, no doubt about it. An agent most likely."

"CIA, DEA, FBI?" asked Miguel.

"Who knows? Pick one. Meet me out front. We'll follow them."

Mr. Z and Evan drove the five miles to the hotel in silence. Evan hated to admit that he was excited, but he was. He missed working but had to caution himself. This was going to be smooth. The sights and sounds of the border-town city were apparent. He noticed the busy streets packed with older small cars, half of which probably had been stolen from El Paso or elsewhere in Texas. There were military Hummers and police cars. He saw restaurants, stores, and fountains. Evan knew the landscape was barren. When you drove around in Virginia, you were surrounded by trees and could not see that far. During the daytime he knew he would be able to see a very long distance here—no trees to block or hide anything.

At the hotel, Mr. Z waited in the car while Evan checked in. Neither spoke. The routine was always the same.

The room was typical for a low-priced hotel. It smelled musty and had the air turned on full blast. Evan sneezed and turned off the air.

"Stinks like beer, sex, and smoke."

He put his bags down and took off his suit jacket and fake glasses. Then he removed a money belt from his waist and counted out three thousand American dollars. He handed it to Mr. Z. Now they could do business.

Mr. Z pocketed the money and opened his duffel bag, revealing its contents. "Everything you asked for," he said.

Evan first pulled out the pistol, an H&K .40 with four extended ten-round magazines. He had an older model at home with updated sites. He checked the action and tossed the weapon onto the bed. "Good work," he said.

Next he took out a brand-new H&K FP6 tactical semiautomatic shotgun and an assortment of boxes of ammo. Evan tried to conceal his enthusiasm, but he could not help it. He was a gun nut and had a collection that many would envy. He inspected various nonlethal and lethal rounds, like high-punch beanbag slugs, rubberized buckshot, and twelve-gauge buckshot. "Very good, Mr. Z. I didn't expect the exact models I asked for, especially new."

"*Señor* E," cautioned Mr. Z, "Juárez is very dangerous. You won't need the nonlethal rounds."

"Never know," said Evan, smiling.

"Don't be caught by police with guns, *Señor*. You know they are illegal in Juárez." Mr. Z smiled at the ridiculousness of the statement. Handguns where illegal in Mexico, yet who did not have one?

Evan ignored him and looked over his tools, which included three smoke grenades and three XM84 stun grenades. They each weighed about thirteen ounces and would blow your eardrums if too close. Evan had really good hearing protection. He picked up a metal, retractable police baton and some pepper spray and unfolded a Federal Police uniform. "This won't work. I'm too old to be a patrolman," he said, tossing the uniform aside.

"Sorry, sir. You can be plain clothes…maybe a detective," suggested Mr. Z.

"I'll keep it. The jacket will do." Evan looked through an assortment of flex cuffs and found the stun baton he had asked for. He also had a fake cell phone that he had brought. It also served as a stun gun.

"Juguetes agradable, no?"

Evan nodded and continued looking through the gear. "OK, here it is, but this bulletproof vest looks a little small."

"Mexicans are not usually your size, *amigo*," said Mr. Z. "But I got you extra-extra *grande*."

Evan stripped off his shirt and put on the vest; it was a little snug across the chest but would work. *A class-three vest; good,* Evan thought. *This will stop rounds from a nine millimeter up to a forty-four, and even a seven-sixty-two.*

Mr. Z seemed to read his thoughts. "The cartels use a lot of high-powered weapons, *amigo*. The *Cuerno de Chivo* and other automatic weapons."

Evan nodded. *Cuerno de Chivo,* which translated as "goat horn" was the slang term for an AK-47. "Better to have some bruises than be dead," he said. He'd had his ribs cracked and a lung bruised while wearing a good-quality vest.

Evan was satisfied; he pulled $1,000 more from his money belt and stuffed it in Mr. Z's hand. He was now down $4,000 of his brother's deck money. He would have to eat cheap while he was here. "Give me your cell," he said to Mr. Z. "I am putting you on call for the next forty-eight hours in case I need anything. Do you drive?"

"I usually just get things," protested Mr. Z.

"You like money, Mr. Z?" asked Evan.

"*Sí.* But I like to live even better. Would rather not. I do better getting things. That is my job."

"Safe house?" asked Evan.

Mr. Z smiled and held up the cash Evan had given him.

"I got more. Get me one in a nice area." Evan peeled off another hundred-dollar bill. "A down payment," he said. "You got a motorcycle and an SUV like I asked?"

"*Sí. Yo la he hecho a ti esta noche,*" confirmed Mr. Z, producing two sets of keys and forged registrations for both vehicles. "I give you big discount for old times' sake."

Evan smirked and peeled off another $1,000. "Been here an hour and already broke," he said.

Mr. Z looked at his fistful of dollars and bit his lip. "*Gracias, amigo.*" He smiled. "I got you some maps, addresses—Gustavo's Grocery Store. The brother, Armando, he is old and in poor health. Here's a picture."

"Perfect," said Evan, reaching for the packet of information.

"You rescue a kidnap victim? You freelance now?"

"I never told you why I was here, Z."

Mr. Z shrugged. "I no nosy, *amigo*; you know that. Only, I go into the store and do some looking around; I *comprar* a soda, and *su hermano* tells me about the kidnapping. Says one of the men involved may be a policeman. That is the word on the street. Armando was a well-liked man and respected by many on both sides of the law."

"*Gracias. Buen trabajo,*" Evan said flatly.

"*No hay problema.*"

"And the laptop?" Evan asked.

Mr. Z dropped another bag on the bed. "No charge for that. The agency left it behind. It can only get me in trouble."

"Cool," Evan said and smiled. "And I know how to use it. *Adios, amigo,*" he said as Mr. Z slipped out the door.

Evan organized his toys, hiding them as best he could. While he waited for room service, he showered and reviewed the facts he knew. The seven or so major cartels in Mexico had sliced up the country into territories. Some had formed an alliance known as the Federation. Two cartels in Juárez were in a bitter turf war, and the police and army were trying to intervene. In 2009 alone, Juárez had 1,986 murders. The police had no control. About half the police were corrupt, and the other half were terrified of having their families killed. More often than not, when a cartel hit man was killed or captured, they turned out to be an ex–police officer.

The Mexican Federal Police—the Federales—usually wore black ski masks to protect their identities when in public. Cartel hit men or *sicarios* had shown up at funerals of fallen police officers or soldiers on more than one occasion and killed the families of the deceased. On the evening news, you could see the latest lineup of drug dealers being posted next to masked police. The victories were a mirage. Mexico was pretty much a narco state.

Evan had read about drug-cartel killings now being posted on YouTube. Recently, a gang member's face had been melted off with acid and his still-living body dumped across the border. The Mexicans knew that the Americans would provide first-class medical care for free. Evan also knew it was not uncommon for corrupt police to escort tons of cocaine to the border. Most arrests were the result of a rival cartel ratting out their competition. Drug revenue was estimated around $20 billion a year. The cartels' gang networks even extended into the United States and were particularly influential in prisons.

It seemed ironic to Evan that an American recreational drug user might unwittingly finance rape, torture, and death perpetrated by cartels while at the same time vehemently professing to be antiwar and anticapitalist to the point of chaining himself or herself to the White House fence, screaming, "No blood for oil!"

Ordinary Mexicans were caught in the middle—family-loving, law-abiding people trying to scratch out a living. The economics of their lives was depressing. You could make $10 a day at a maquiladora. Or you could make $400 a week working for a drug dealer.

From an intelligence-gathering standpoint, what made any operation successful was developing networks and relationships with people who would help your cause. Bribery and payoffs were still the strongest motivators. Evan knew that he could not pass for a native and that he had to assemble a network quickly, which meant taking risks that he would normally never take. But in this situation, he was willing to sacrifice stealth to speed.

As he ate his room-service dinner, he considered what he planned to do and how to go about it. "OK, show time tomorrow," he said aloud. He caught himself speaking in English and laughed.

CHAPTER 7

Let's Make a Deal

Mexico City, 2200 Hours

Nathan Rock, founder of Dark Cloud, felt his BlackBerry vibrate. He stepped away from the command center where his team was watching and listening to events unfold. Roger was still posing as bait and waiting for the next contact with the kidnappers. And a second Dark Cloud team was tracking the money as it was moved to a warehouse.

The situation was tense but not out of control. Nathan had turned over supervision to Reo, his second in command. When Nathan mentioned that if Manuel died, it might make Roger more enthusiastic about the Dark Cloud cause, Reo had agreed that both he and Nathan would do nothing but watch as the operation unfolded. Nathan considered Reo a yes-man and an ass-kisser, someone he could manipulate. This made him useful. If Reo weren't in a secret relationship with the president's chief of staff, he would have never gotten this close to Dark Cloud. Nathan was not above blackmail in order to get his way.

Standing at the far side of the Rosas' game room that had been turned into a command center, Nathan looked back at his men. He had to admit that without Reo, Dark Cloud's money and secret political connections would have never have come to fruition. "Keep your friends close but your enemies closer," he muttered.

The president's chief of staff had a beautiful, cold wife, who was a popular TV news anchor. Nathan had met her at several social receptions and found her both off-putting and extremely desirable. He had resolved to have sex with her before he left this miserable country. How could her husband get angry? He was seeing a man.

Nathan's eyes narrowed as he pulled his cell phone from his pocket. He was suspicious about every person on his team, but he kept it to himself. He knew every member of his team, yet only a handful of people really knew him. He opened an e-mail from Francisco and waited for the encrypted message to download. *Why must they contact me for every freaking thing?* he thought as the photo from Juárez came into focus.

"Holy shit!" he yelled, glancing up as soon as he realized he had spoken aloud. Several people rose from their seats or looked at him.

"OK, boss?" asked Reo from across the room. Some people laughed; others kept working.

"Yes, yes. Get back to work. Reo, can I see you a moment?" Nathan stepped into a hallway where the two of them could be alone. He felt his skin flush and took a deep breath, willing himself to stay calm.

"Yes, Nathan?" Reo touched his arm the way a concerned woman might.

"You are in command. I have to go to Juárez."

"What? Nothing's going on in Juárez, Nathan. The action is here!"

Reo was a little over five feet tall and had thick, perfectly groomed hair. His nails were manicured, and he wore a custom-made suit. Reo reminded Nathan of the pretty-boy lawyers who could be found at any of the restaurants on Capitol Hill. Reo seemed harmless enough, but he was shrewd and ruthless.

"Is something wrong?" Reo asked solicitously.

Nathan turned and placed his hand on the shorter man's shoulder. He smelled like aftershave lotion, and Nathan suppressed a sneeze. "This man." He showed Reo the photo on his I phone. "I worked with him about eighteen, maybe twenty, years ago. He is in Juárez."

"And?" asked Reo.

Nathan replied, "And…I can't get into it right now. You handle this operation as planned. I've got to find out why this guy is here."

"Good guy or bad guy?"

"Not sure, Reo. That's why I need to find out why he's in Mexico," replied Nathan. "If he's working for the cartels, we have to take him out."

Reo's eyes widened. "So he is not a friend?"

Nathan shook his head. "The word *friend* is relative. Depends on why he is here. The fact that he is meeting with a man we have under surveillance with intentions of recruiting is highly disconcerting."

"And if he can be used?" Reo asked as he smiled and looked at Nathan.

Nathan turned away, dismissing Reo's naïve suggestion. Evan was too dangerous to control. He also would ask too many questions.

"Be back in a few days. Tell everyone that we are still meeting at the ranch. No leaks!"

"Fine, fine." Reo pretended to not care but was clearly hurt that he was not included in this little bit of intrigue.

"Sorry, Reo, really," said Nathan in a placating tone of voice. "I'll call you in the morning or once I get in the air. I have to call the airport, get the plane ready. OK? Forgive me? I am just freaking out a little." He felt like he was talking with his third ex-wife, emotional but dangerous and scornful. He had always changed his prose depending on whom he was talking to.

"Of course!" said Reo sympathetically. "Go, Nathan. We'll be fine here."

Nathan smiled and squeezed Reo's shoulder. "Thanks, pal. I really need you to watch over these clowns."

It was raining again. Roger looked at his watch. He had been waiting for hours with no place to sit. He was wet, and he was hungry. "OK, we aren't getting anywhere," he said.

"Just act natural." Mia's tired voice crackled in his ear.

"Act natural? What does that mean, lass? Is that the same as when the doctor tells you to breathe normal?"

"You make no sense, Roger."

"Stop talking. I got a van slowing down," he whispered.

A yellow customized van rolled to a stop near Roger, its brakes squeaking and engine idling as if it needed a tune-up. Traffic was still heavy despite rush hour being over.

"Freaking van looks like it was stolen from the '70s," Roger said. He spat and stared at the occupants. The city street lights illuminated the area well enough for Roger to see. He was exhausted.

The driver was skinny, and the one who got out of the passenger side was fat.

The passenger was breathing heavily, as if he had just climbed a flight of stairs. Roger sized up him up: Hispanic, in his twenties, about five feet eight and close to 300 pounds. He kept pulling his pants up, but his bulging belly forced them down again. His heavy breathing told Roger two things. One, the kid was too fat, and two, he was not adapted to the altitude, so he was new to the city.

Roger glanced quickly at the driver, who seemed nervous and twitchy and wore mirrored sunglasses, despite it being night.

Roger had another thought. The men who had orchestrated the kidnapping and the attempted hit on him were not bottom-rung amateurs like these punks. The men who had grabbed Manuel were professionals with military or law-enforcement training.

"Get in, gringo!" said the gangster.

"Piss off, wanker," snarled Roger. "Shoot me if you got the balls. I want proof of life!"

"Don't get in the van, Roger!" Mia spoke in his ear.

"Manuel, where is he?" Roger asked.

"He OK, gringo. Get in."

"I want the real kidnappers—the Scorpions—on the phone, and a proof of life!" Roger said, quickly.

The fat man paused and took a step back. "Screw you! Get in the van. No wait."

He pulled a cell phone out of his pocket and tried to make a call. "Crap, no signal!" he yelled to his driver friend, "Paco, you got a signal?"

"No...wait...Do now," the driver shouted back. "That's weird—like all of a sudden." He laughed crazily.

"OK, we'll do proof of life," said Roger. "Then the second money drop. I've been out here all evening. My feet are sore, and I am hungry. I am not in the mood for your amateur show!"

The side door of the van slid open, and a skinny, twenty-something white kid with long red dreadlocks wearing a dirty T-shirt and ripped jeans motioned him in. The fat one was breathing heavily, and he had beads of sweat on his forehead. He leaned heavily against a lamppost.

"Where is Manuel?" asked Roger.

"Stall him, Roger. We're watching you from above. Have to make sure you're not being watched," Mia's smooth, hoarse voice whispered in accented English. In any other situation, he would have thought she had a sexy voice. He could listen to her all night, except right now.

Roger looked up. "I am in a city with twenty million people. Everyone's watching." He swore under his breath.

"Get the hell in!"

Roger spoke to himself. "If I'm gonna die, I'll take them with me." He got in the van slowly and crouched in the back. The van stank like sweat and weed.

"Here." The skinny white guy handed Roger a cell phone while the fat one climbed back into the passenger seat. The entire van groaned and creaked as he dropped down. The driver turned on a Mexican rap station and pulled into traffic and drove quickly out of the nice part of town.

The white guy handed the gun to the driver and then reached for a machete. His eyes were wild as if he had been on meth for days. Tattoos swirled up his skinny arms. Roger counted seven piercings in his face, lips, and cheeks. He watched Roger, nervously.

Roger spoke into the phone. "Who is this?"

"Roger! Roger! Help me. Don't give in to these animals!" It was Manuel's voice, trembling as he tried to stay calm. Roger knew it wouldn't take much to break him.

"Son, you'll be OK. Have they hurt you?"

"Yes!" Manuel started crying like a child.

Roger went from being choked up to seething in anger in a second. He was still a kid as far as Roger was concerned.

Before Roger could speak again, the phone went dead. "No service." He wondered if Dark Cloud was jamming the signal.

The white guy snatched the phone from Roger. Dreadlocks, flopping around like a snake, pointed the machete at Roger and snarled, "He's OK."

"I have to go get the four million dollars," said Roger flatly.

The van moved down a one-way street to an intersection. The driver stopped at a traffic light and began to load a pipe with weed. The driver smoked his bowl, oblivious to any onlookers, and handed it to his obese partner.

Not good, Roger thought.

"First of all, it's seven million now," said the skinny white guy, "because you killed two of our boys. And second of all, you won't be delivering it."

"I won't?" asked Roger.

"Nah, you gotta die, you fuck. That's the price—your life for his." Everyone laughed except Roger.

The fat guy in the passenger seat let out his smoke with a loud laugh that turned into a strangled cough. "You stupid fuck, screw that little *puta* boy!"

"You'll never get paid," said Roger calmly.

The fat man in the passenger seat turned around, aiming a .357 at Roger. "Bull. Lie down on your face!"

Roger narrowed his eyes and looked at the gun. He was past his tipping point and about to snap.

"We do this all the time, you idiot. They always pay!" taunted the skinny white guy.

"Ha-ha, your life ain't worth shit!" said the fat one. "They pay, you see."

Everyone laughed again except Roger, mainly because he was now looking from his perch in the back of the van through the driver's window. Something even more odd than the three punks grabbed his attention.

The van was still stopped at the light. Through the driver's open window, Roger watched a large black Ford Expedition pull up next to them and pause. *Too obvious*, he thought.

The tinted window on the passenger side of the Ford slowly rolled down, and for a second Roger thought he saw a short-haired girl wearing a baseball hat. She was ducking.

Then he understood.

"Duck, Roger." Mia sounded calm and sexy in his ear, like she was telling him it was time to be kissed.

The sounds and smell of exhaust and the busy city seemed to recede. Horns began to honk, and somewhere in the distance, tires squealed.

Roger backed up.

The white guy with dreadlocks lunged with the machete, and the fat Mexican tried to get a clear shot. "Move so I can shoot."

Roger recognized the zip-like *pop* of a silencer and knew that it came from the SUV. He grabbed the skinny guy's dreadlocks and the arm holding the machete. The left side of the driver's head exploded, sending brains and a red spray into the air. There was the smell of gunpowder, pot, blood, and sweat.

The fat guy fired the .357, but the bullet hit Dreadlocks in the shoulder and he screamed, "Ah, fuck!"

A second round from the SUV hit the skinny Mexican driver in the face, and he crumpled. The exit wound made his cheek look like a juicy watermelon. The van began to roll forward slowly into traffic. Roger calmly wrenched away the machete and shoved it down the skinny white guy's throat. Dreadlocks stopped moving.

Horns honked, the light was green, and cars drove around them, oblivious to the situation.

"Get out of the van, Roger," Mia said urgently.

Roger started to open the van's side door when he saw a solid-looking man in a ski mask open the driver-side door. The masked Dark Cloud operative held a long pistol with a silencer under his jacket.

"What took you so long?" grumbled Roger, wiping blood off his face.

The masked man chuckled and reached into the rolling van to yank the gearshift into Park. The van jolted to a stop.

"You have an odd sense of humor, Roger," he said. "Help me move this, *amigo grande*."

Cars continued to honk and weave around the parked van.

Roger helped the Dark Cloud operative drag the body out of the driver's seat and pile him with his fat friend on the sidewalk. Operational security was blown at this point. Both men were breathing heavily and cursing at the weight of the two younger men.

"Like moving a freaking walrus," Roger said and groaned. "What if the police show?" Roger asked the Dark Cloud operative.

The operative paused to rip the mask off his sweaty face. He produced a police badge, which he quickly shoved back in his pocket. "Federal Police. That better, Roger?"

"Aye. Now I feel freaking safe," Roger shot back sarcastically. "Ye know my name. What's yours?"

"We got to go!"

Within a few minutes, Roger and the man, whose name he still did not know, were speeding down the street, cutting off cars and sideswiping trash cans until they had gained some distance.

"How much time do we have before the kidnappers figure things went wrong?" Roger asked.

"Not sure. Is the Explorer still behind us?"

Bracing himself, Roger looked out the rear windows of the van. The seat was soaked with blood, and he cursed. "I'd better not catch something from this fuck's brain matter!"

"They behind us, Roger?"

"No. Slow down," ordered Roger. "And what's your name? Tell me, or I'll start calling you Zorro or something worse."

The Dark Cloud operative slowed the van, turned into an alley, stopped, and said, "We have to wait for them." The man lit another smoke and blew a large cloud into the van. "Name is Carlos," he said, wiping sweat from his face.

"We should call them. They may be lost."

Carlos laughed and fixed his eyes on the rearview mirror. They waited in silence for a few minutes with the engine running.

Carlos began to speak in decent English, like someone who'd picked it up, not learned it formally. "We have three chase vehicles. They'll make sure we are not followed." He rolled down the window and tossed out his Lucky Strike. "They are jamming cell phones, about three square miles' worth, so even if people witnessed the little show back there, they will not reach anyone for a while. This buys us time."

Roger nodded. "You got some bank to get that kind of technology," he said.

"*Sí*. The Americans give it to the Mexican military, and we steal it before they sell it to the cartels," said Carlos. "OK, they found us."

Roger laughed and asked, "Now what?"

"We ditch the van, *amigo*, and then track our money. We have two live ones captured at a safe house."

"Manuel?" Roger asked as he and Carlos got out of the van and stood in an alley watching three Dark Cloud members pile out of the SUV. Roger repeated his question. "Manuel?"

Carlos spoke slowly and deliberately. "There are things going on behind the scenes. I can't answer too many questions about our methods. I already gave away a little."

Roger looked around at the scene and just shook his head. "Hell, you guys saved my life."

An hour later Roger and the three Dark Cloud members were sitting in a black, armored truck that had probably belonged to a cash courier service at one time. He was cramped, hungry, and smelled bad, but he was pleased to be sitting. He watched Mia and two slender men hunched over laptops. She wore a headset and stood over the men as they worked. The only light in the rear of the truck came from the computer screens.

"Never been a computer person," mused Roger.

He was amazed at how much technology had spoiled and changed the whole nature of warfare. With the right gadgets and computers, anybody could be an effective killer or spy or just eavesdrop on someone. He closed his eyes for a second and thought back to the massive radios he used to carry on forced marches in cold, wet Scotland. He favored the practice of training as if you had none of the high-tech crap, and then you would appreciate it more. The Romans had conquered the known world wearing sandals and marching around with no GPS.

"Have you found Manuel, or did we blow the whole damn operation?"

Mia looked at him and frowned. She was about five feet one and not intimidated by Roger in the least. She was athletic and voluptuous at the same time. Usually a woman was one or the other. Roger was not attracted to skinny, wispy runner girls. Roger stopped staring at Mia and started to repeat his question.

She put her finger to her lips and whispered, "Stop talking, Roger. We're busy."

"*Lo siento*," Roger mumbled.

The money had been tracked to an auto-body shop on the outskirts of the Narvarte neighborhood in the central-southern section of the city. Roger had been in this part of town before. It was safe enough during the day, depending on how you acted. His favorite meals came from street vendors and small, crowded cafés along the narrow, busy streets. All windows in Mexico City had bars across them, yet people would leave their bikes unlocked and let their dogs roam free. The neighborhoods reminded him of old pictures from the 1950s but with more color.

His stomach growled, reminding him how long it had been since he'd eaten.

"Roger!" Mia said urgently. "Two SWAT teams are going in." Then she swore. "Why are our men doing security?" She spoke in English for Roger's benefit.

"I thought this was your operation?" he asked.

"It's complicated, Roger. Politics and turf wars in the city." She spoke with exasperation. "They want to be on the news. We don't."

Two police SWAT teams entered the warehouse, and a small firefight began. From what Roger was able to understand, the Mexican Federal Police had either inserted themselves into the Dark Cloud operation or were invited. Either way, it was over in a few moments.

Roger closed his eyes. The stress and pace of the last twenty-four hours made him feel as if he were submerged in the deep end of a pool. His mind began to process the events. He had survived being attacked, had been escorted from a hospital by what can only be called a highly sophisticated mercenary group, and then had been woven into their plot to rescue the boy he had come to Mexico to cook and care for.

"They found him. He's OK."

Roger rubbed his eyes, which burned from lack of sleep. "Thank God."

CHAPTER 8
The Hombres
of Walmart

February 15, Juárez, Mexico, 0800 Hours

Evan woke up. He felt as if he had just swum to the surface from miles beneath the ocean. He gasped for air and felt his heart pounding. He stood up and looked at his hotel room. For a second he felt shock—where was he? He was sweating and began to calm his breathing.

"I need a drink."

The distant *pop* of machine-gun fire made Evan jump, and he cursed.

Evan washed his face and remembered that he was in Juárez, Mexico, with a job to do. He turned on the TV. He hated silence, and he hated being alone with himself.

He walked to the hotel gym, adjusted his iPod, and thought about his loose plan. Contact Armando's aging brother and make himself known to the kidnappers as someone who is terrified and willing to do whatever they say. Acting like a badass or a hotshot negotiator in his position would just freak the kidnappers out. They were expecting a normal person to deliver the money, preferably the maid.

Evan started walking and then jogging slowly on the treadmill. He ran over possible scenarios in his head; many of them did not end well.

He hoped to just give them the money and get the old man. He was willing to pay twice as much but was not going to offer that up easily. He just hoped these guys were idiots and not pros. Pros would have never picked Armando in the first place. Evan kept the kidnappers in the idiot category.

Francisco and Miguel pulled into the parking lot of the hotel where they had seen Mr. Z drop off the big American late last night.

Francisco slowed down and let Miguel out of the green F-150 pickup.

"Go watch the lobby. Text me when you see the American."

"Raul from Team Two should be leaving his room. He will meet you and give you a report."

"*Sí*, I could not sleep last night. Did I tell you how much I hate surveillance?"

"Only about a hundred times, Miguel. My back is killing me from sitting. You are young, my friend. They have coffee and breakfast. Don't be spotted."

"Whatever." Miguel took his briefcase and paper and walked across the parking lot to the hotel.

Francisco placed his cell phone, walkie-talkie, and binoculars on the seat next to him. He picked up his magazine and looked through it once he was parked.

His phone rang.

"*Hola?*"

"Nathan here."

"*Sí?*"

"Any news?"

"No. Nathan, we must talk."

"We are talking. What?"

"Well, quite simple. We have three teams of two people. Only six guys."

"You can add," Nathan said sarcastically and then sighed. He sounded annoyed this morning.

Francisco hated sarcasm; he hated arrogant people even more.

"You have us spread too thin, Nathan. You want us to watch this man. I know nothing about him. No plan. You also want us to watch and possibly grab Gerard and watch Mr. Z. We are tired, worn out. You need to either make a decision or fill us in."

There was a long silence. Francisco could tell that Nathan was getting angry.

"You must remain flexible."

"We need a plan."

Again the standoff.

Francisco was tempted to just make a decision and forget the American.

"Francisco, look, I apologize. Let me lay it out like this—Forget Mr. Z."

"OK, Gerard?"

"Team Two and Three are going to resume surveillance on the store. I just landed and can only send two more as backup. Gerard is my first priority. I want him taken as he is leaving for the airport. You, I want you to watch the American. I may want to speak with him. I just don't know how. I know he is not on vacation. Watch, wait!"

Francisco burned his lip on his coffee and cursed. His back was aching from an old bullet wound and a car crash years ago. He shifted in his seat and thought about what to say next. Nathan Rock spoke first.

"His name is Evan. He was a shadow warrior for the agency."

"And?"

"And he is mentally unstable. He did things in Colombia. He is unpredictable, smart, and can be, let's say, dangerous. He worked for me. Last I heard he was fired; nasty fellow."

"And big," Francisco added. He had to admit the big American scared him. "He knows you, Nathan?"

"May not remember me; however, I have to establish two things. One, is he here with the American government, and two, why?"

"I don't have the time to figure that out, Nathan, with all due respect. Gerard is a valuable target. He is sloppy and has a very false sense of security."

"Yes, we get Frenchy!"

"Then forget about this Evan person, Nathan!"

"He could be an ally or our worst nightmare." Nathan sounded stern.

Francisco doubted that. The American was only one man and not bulletproof.

Nathan spoke again. "Humor me. I can tell you more; believe me, there is more. Treat him as an enemy until you know."

"Engage him? Talk to him? If you know him, we can be frank."

"And you can get killed or expose something and draw attention to us. We don't want heat."

Francisco spoke. "Fine, boss. We will follow him. If my other two teams need me though, when Gerard's mission goes down, I am forgetting about your friend."

"Fine." Nathan sounded reluctant and knew better than to push the point with Francisco. "Watch him just till the other operation goes down."

Francisco smiled. "Thank you."

Nathan hung up.

Francisco's walkie-talkie clattered; it was Miguel.

"He is on the move. Carrying a motorcycle helmet."

"Can you make it back to the truck?"

"Try."

1000 Hours

Evan walked through the hotel lobby carrying his backpack and a motorcycle helmet. He was feeling jet lagged and still a little sluggish—entirely unmotivated.

He paused near the front desk and spoke briefly with a pretty, young desk clerk.

"I don't want anyone going in my room today."

"*Sí, señor.*"

"Coffee?"

"The café, sir." She smiled and pointed across the lobby toward the café.

Evan nodded, got some coffee, and looked around the lobby. He watched businessmen chat at wooden tables and hotel employees sweep floors and empty trash. Evan paused for a second and watched a small man in a business suit who was looking straight at him. The man looked away.

Was he watching me?

Evan finished his coffee, tossed the foam cup in a trash can, and walked outside into the murder capital of the world. The sun was shining, and the street was packed full of morning traffic. White school buses painted with green stripes served as public transportation. He observed VW bugs, BMWs, and motor scooters. On every corner there were people moving about, some in business suits chatting on cell phones and others in old cowboy hats and jeans. Even in this more upscale section of Juárez, he could spot the division between those who had money and those who had nothing.

Now I know where all the old VW bugs go when they die.

He recalled an article that he had read years ago stating that one in ten cars in Juárez were stolen from the United States.

Evan mumbled to himself, "Why go to Afghanistan."

He made sure his H&K .40 was truly concealed and scanned the city. His bulletproof vest constricted his breathing a little, and he began to sweat.

Evan found the motorcycle that Mr. Z had left for him in a far corner of the parking lot. The bike was an older BMW model with chipped paint and a few dents—most likely stolen from Texas. Evan sat down, adjusted the mirrors, and fired up the engine.

He eased into traffic and went around the block a few times to see if he was being followed. Once satisfied, he zoomed off in the direction of Armando's brother's grocery store.

Private Hangar, Juárez International Airport

Nathan sat at a small desk in the rear of a white Gulfstream V. The plane was in a private hangar owned by an oil executive. The plane had been washed, repainted, and outfitted with new tail decals within hours of landing. Nathan had built a network with some of Mexico's wealthiest business owners in his fight against the cartels. No one spoke as he and five of his team members looked at a map of Juárez. Laptops, cell phones, police scanners, and an assortment of coffee cups littered the makeshift operations center.

"OK, we stick with our original plan. Gerard has two men with him, and they have gotten comfortable and lax, to say the least."

Nathan looked at his men, who had pulled off such snatch-and-grab missions hundreds of times over the years. Each man had at one time been a member of Mexico's elite Air Mobility Command.

"Boss, the People's Market is in a busy part of town; the police response time is my only worry. I also am not comfortable with managing five kidnapped girls; if our intelligence is sound, they are drugged. We can leave them and call the police, but my team is not rescuing them. Getting Gerard alive may be an issue."

Nathan sighed. "I have confidence in your abilities and in your planning of this. This is your show. I have pulled two men off Gerard task force to watch someone else. I have another person of interest that we may have to make contact with. Could complicate things," Nathan said quietly.

"We need all hands, sir. You have a plan for this other person of interest?"

Nathan stood up and felt his stomach turning; he was more concerned about Evan's appearance on the scene than anything else right now. His team knew he was distracted.

"We have to snatch Frenchman at the People's Market. If not, the second option is the airport."

The leader of his assault team opened a Coke, shook his head, and spoke up. "The airport will be difficult. Well guarded, too open. Fine if we want to just pop him, but we need to trap the little rat, corner him!"

Nathan stood up and walked away from his team. He went to the back of the jet, turned, and said flatly, "You guys know what to do. Just do it. I have to be alone for a moment."

The shooters from Dark Cloud looked at each other perplexedly and then got down to business preparing their gear.

Evan arrived at the grocery store and parked on the sidewalk. This part of town was a different world from the area he had just left. Gang signs were spray-painted on empty storefronts. Abandoned cars, lost people, and trash lined the street. He observed empty lots with rusted fences, houses with bars, and convenience stores with shoppers going about their business. It was hard to believe that just a few miles away was El Paso and an entirely different world.

He walked into the small grocery store and pretended to look around.

"Can I help you?" An elderly lady with weathered skin and facial hair approached him.

"Gustavo?"

She looked at him and nodded. Evan noticed that she only had three teeth. "Follow me."

Gustavo was sitting among piles of paper at a desk that was probably as old as he was. He had the twitch of a man who had Parkinson's.

"*Sí?*"

"Don't get up, sir."

Evan put his hand up and tried to find a place to sit. A pregnant cat appeared, looked suspiciously at him, and then left.

"I am Evan. I am here on behalf of your niece."

Gustavo looked relieved and terrified at the same time.

"Hell of a cannon there." Evan nodded toward the gun.

"*Uh*-huh." The old man coughed as he spoke. He had the permanent wet rattle that many elderly smokers get. His English was excellent.

Evan offered his hand.

"You are an American?" Gustavo asked suspiciously.

Evan nodded. Gustavo had a firm handshake. "*Sí.* I need you to tell me everything."

"They contact me on this phone." Gustavo pointed to a sparkly orange cell phone on his desk. The phone looked like it could have belonged to a teenage girl. "They tell me—'When you have money, you call.'"

"Then what?"

"They say nothing else."

"They gave you that phone?"

"*Sí, sí*. Young boy on a bike brought it few days ago. I am poor. Why they do this?" Gustavo had fear in his eyes. He was helpless.

"Gustavo, I am going to be frank. Chances are we will give them the money and never see your brother."

Gustavo was visibly crushed but not surprised by Evans words. Hearing the truth was always much worse.

"I…I know. All my life I work hard, my brother works hard, but some, these animals, they no work—they just take!"

Evan nodded. "Put suits on them and a teleprompter in front of them, and we call them politicians. Same thing." Evan smiled, trying to lighten things up.

Gustavo nodded.

"It's like this everywhere." Evan pulled out a can of Skoal and packed a dip. "We play their game tonight, and then I am out of here. Look, I am really sorry, but don't give up hope, OK? We will try."

"That's all I have, Evan."

"This is probably not going to end well. I am sorry."

Gustavo acknowledged Evan's statement with a nod. His eyes looked bloodshot, dry, and tired.

"My city. People are fleeing. It is a war zone. When I grew up, it was a different place. My family, we have been here since father opened in 1912."

Evan stared at Gustavo and let the man talk. He suddenly wanted a drink and then wanted to skip across the border and go home.

Gustavo went on for twenty minutes, talking about growing up in Mexico, working, and watching his large family grow up, reproduce, move on, and die. The cycle continued for generations—some good stories but many bad. People here were just like anywhere else; they loved their families, food, and culture.

This old guy does not deserve this. Who does? Evan let his mind wander.

The phone rang. The ring tone was a Britney Spears song, and Evan almost laughed.

"Answer it."

Gustavo tried to hit the buttons and was unable to. Evan helped him and put the phone to Gustavo's ear. The old man's face drained of color, and he looked as if he might pass out.

"Y-Y-You...*señor*—they want to speak with you."

Evan bit his lip. He had just gotten his first piece of intel: they were watching the store.

"Hola?"

The voice on the other end spoke choppy English. "Who the fuck are you?"

"The man with your money. I don't want any trouble. I just want to pay and return Armando to his family."

"I said who the fuck are you?"

Evan paused. He had to play weak and submissive, no games. He really hated when people cussed like that. He tried to sound scared and let his voice crack as he spoke.

"I am a friend of Armando's daughter. She is in the hospital, sick, sick with grief. Do you have a daughter?"

"Shut up. You have the money?"

"Yes."

The voice paused. Evan walked to the window of Gustavo's office and looked outside. He did not expect to see anyone, but he looked anyway.

"The girl was supposed to come."

"She is too sick, I told you. I want her to see her father. What do people have besides family? Please, I will do whatever you say."

Evan tried to personalize as much as he could, then paused. "Can I just pay you now?"

"Shut up! You talk too much."

"OK, you are the boss. I am sorry. Just scared that's all. Look, we can work this out."

Gustavo put his head on the desk and visibly checked out.

"Think I am stupid, eh?" the voice asked.

The phone went dead.

Evan put the phone down and looked for a trash can to spit in.

"They hang up?" squeaked Gustavo.

"Just wait." Evan moved some dusty books and files off a stool and sat down. "Where's a good place to eat around here?"

"What?"

"Food, I will need breakfast eventually. Breakfast tacos—that's what is in my head."

"Oh, um, Maria, my sister. She…she has a place. I…I can tell her that you are coming. I c-c-can't eat."

Evan frowned. He hoped he was not insulting Gustavo by talking about food at a time like this.

"Gustavo, my friend, you must eat something, drink some water, stay focused."

"I have not eaten in two days. I throw up."

"I am not asking—you need to eat something."

Gustavo nodded.

Evan left him alone for a second and walked out into his grocery store. He found a jar of peanut butter and an apple and returned. He put the items on the table. "Eat."

The old man could not unscrew the peanut butter, so Evan helped him.

"Look, Gustavo, I will do my best. I am going to ask you a question, very serious."

"Y-Yes?"

"If I have an opportunity to kill these men."

"No!"

Gustavo dug his finger into the peanut butter. "Can you cut the apple for me, *señor*?"

Evan pulled out his Gerber and sliced the apple into small pieces.

"Evan, who are you?"

"A friend. The less you know, the better."

"You...you deal with men like these before?"

Evan admitted, "I have killed many men like these."

"Does it make you feel better?"

"Never."

Gustavo frowned. "Revenge is the Lord's business. Forgiveness, it can free you."

Evan nodded. "You are right, Gustavo."

"I have three sons who died to violence. They were not innocent, Evan. Like you, they were hard, had hard hearts."

Gustavo dug out more peanut butter and ate.

"I will do what I can. Understand?" Evan said calmly.

"God is my only comfort."

Evan nodded and considered Gustavo.

The cell phone rang.

"My father had a similar outlook, Gustavo."

"Where is he?"

"Dead."

"Then his pain is gone. Your father knows the truth now. Remember he is watching you."

Evan looked at the phone. It kept ringing.

"The pho...phone?"

Evan answered it. *"Hola?"*

"Shut up and listen."

A different voice spoke this time. This one stayed in Spanish and was deeper and more self-assured. Evan figured he was the leader.

OK, so I know there are at least two of them, Evan thought.

"Five o'clock, Walmart on Ejercito National. You park near the bus stop. Wait by the pay phone. We call you."

The phone went dead.

Mexico City, Manuel's House, February 15, 1200 Hours

Manuel's household was, emotionally, on the complete opposite side of the spectrum as the day before.

Roger was relieved and thankful that Manuel was alive. He tried to step back and just observe the family as they allowed the floodgate of emotions to flow. Roger wiped a tear from his eye and quickly looked around to make sure no one noticed. He was prepared to play it off.

Roger headed to the kitchen for a beer. From a safe distance, he drank his beer and noticed Mia smiling at him. Her eyes were red, and she took an offered tissue.

"Roger, why you hide?" she asked in English.

Roger shrugged and drank his beer.

Mia walked over to Roger and examined him with a sassy smirk. "You talking to yourself? Come to the group!"

Roger winked and held up his beer. "Beer is over here. We aren't an emotional lot."

Mia reached up and grabbed his cheek with her tiny fingers and shook him slightly. "You are not so tough."

She spoke as one who had authority in such matters, possibly the youngest child with older brothers, Roger guessed. She was the type who touched or grabbed whomever she was speaking to.

"Your beer is leaving." She giggled, took his beer out of his fist, twirled, and walked away.

Must have taken ballet as a child, Roger thought.

As offended as Roger was as a Scotsman to have his beer taken, by a woman no less, he did respect her sassy spirit and was thankful that she was not in the demanding business mode of earlier.

Roger joined the group.

Victor, Mr. Rosa's detective brother, was speaking. "The doctor says he will be fine. You all leave the country for a month or longer."

Roger nodded and looked at Mr. Rosa, who was holding his son's hand. He faced his brother. "I have a business to run! I can't leave."

"*Sí!* You can. It's called delegation. Life is more important. You have others to manage, I know!"

The two brothers stared at each other for an intense moment.

Manuel stared at the ceiling. The living room became quiet.

"I am not running!" Mr. Rosa blurted.

"All due respect, sir, these men, the Scorpions, they will come now with a vengeance. I believe they allowed us to retake Manuel; it was a test, a message," said a short, well-groomed man with a deep voice and glasses. He seemed to have some authority in Dark Cloud.

Mr. Rosa was defiant and puffed out, as if he was defending some wall in some ancient battle.

Then the general spoke up, and the battle plans changed. "*No!* My family has been through *enough!* You take my grandson from here!"

No one spoke for a minute.

The wife backed up her mother-in-law with a look, and the troop withdrawal began.

'Mazin' how they do that. Same everywhere. Roger drank his beer and looked around, trying to cover up his ridiculous smile.

The minute hand on an ancient grandfather clock was deafening. Roger had never noticed how loud the thing was before.

"Ladies, we go to our villa in Barcelona. My cousins can manage the business. My decision is final. OK?"

It was an approval and capitulation with a slight nod to his wife and mother.

"Great decision, sir."

The casual conversations and doting over Manuel returned, and all was *pacifica y maravillosa*.

"Can we speak? I have someone you need to meet."

Roger followed Mia, quite willingly, back to the bar by the kitchen. She went to the fridge and got him another cold Dos Equis.

The short man with glasses and a deep voice held a glass of wine. Roger had not seen him enter the house. He spoke to Roger softly, like a noble man might speak to a Viking.

"Allow me to introduce myself. I am Reo; I'm in charge while Nathan is gone." He looked at his watch. "In a few hours, Nathan is going to take down a major player in the Scorpion gang. He is in Juárez. We must all go into hiding after this happens."

"What?"

"Roger, let me be blunt. Gasoline is about to be dumped on a blazing fire. They will come after us and the Rosas."

Roger looked at Mia. She nodded and pinched his bicep. "Listen to him."

"OK, what is going on?"

"When we get to our training area, we will wait for Nathan and other elements to arrive. We have a major plan to reveal. We must stay on schedule."

Roger observed and nodded. He was more concerned about the Rosas right now.

Reo finished his wine and smiled at Roger. "It's a bit much to take in, I admit. This is a job offer, Mr. McDuff."

Roger almost coughed up his beer.

Mia rubbed his back. "Don't choke old man."

"Me? Job offer?"

Reo looked up at Roger. "My associates will fill you in on the contract and retainer bonus. Please don't feel pressured. This is dangerous. This is big." Reo raised his eyebrows with amusement at Roger's shock.

"Aye, so ye can't find a cook that can break limbs?"

Reo laughed and shook Roger's hand.

Mia punched him in the arm with annoyance.

CHAPTER 9

Blue-Light Special

Juárez, Mexico, 1300 Hours

Evan rode his BMW motorcycle the four miles through impoverished streets, past vacant houses and empty lots, to Walmart. His mind was racing. Evan drove up and down the busy street near Walmart, making a U-turn and observing the surroundings. The intersection with Walmart was just as busy as any street in the United States. Restaurants, liquor stores, auto-body shops, and a 7-Eleven lined the opposite side of the street. A large concrete median divided the road. Evan began to see the brilliance in the site selection. The kidnappers had picked a busy, open place for the exchange. They could sit virtually anywhere and watch him. More importantly, police would be hesitant to storm a busy area. Civilian casualties would be huge.

Evan drove his bike into the parking lot of the Walmart and took an immediate left. He parked near the left side of the store, which faced the street. The store was packed. Evan parked near the crowded bus stop and observed the lone pay phone. He turned off his bike, removed his helmet, and packed a dip. He spent the next thirty minutes watching people and seeing if anyone was watching him.

OK, I will play your game, he thought.

Evan watched a white-and-green school bus pull up to the bus stop. No one paid him any attention.

OK, so they will call, and then it will begin.

Evan pulled out his Android phone and plugged the hotel's address into the GPS. He was only four miles from his hotel.

He watched families with children, businessmen, and people who looked as if they had just been working in a factory shuffle into and out of the Walmart. He looked at the Sam's Club and suddenly felt an urge to shop.

Evan's Android rang and he jumped.

His brother was calling.

"Hola?"

"Como estas?"

"Sigo vivo. Hand-off tonight."

"Anything I can do?"

"Pray."

Evan hung up, put his helmet on, fired up his bike, and zoomed off.

Nathan sat alone in his jet, drinking coffee. His team was gone, his pilot and copilot were out in Juárez having lunch. He was nervous and kept listening to updates from his men in the field.

No one knew where Evan was.

Nathan cursed. He feared that Evan was working for the CIA and that maybe he was out to find and kill him. He had hoped that the unstable agent was dead.

"What the hell are you doing here, you bastard?"

Nathan had not confided in anyone about his fears and thought hard about how to either kill Evan or weave him into his bigger plan.

Nathan thought about the consequences of the CIA being on to Dark Cloud; would they interfere?

Nathan stood up and clicked on a surveillance photo of Evan getting on a motorcycle.

Nathan heard his secure satellite phone buzz and jumped for it. It was Reo.

"Yes?"

"*Hola*, boss!"

Reo sounded upbeat and cocky. Nathan did not like him much but was glad that he had him on his side.

"Report, Reo?"

"The team is evacuating. The Rosa family is en route to the airport. They are leaving the country."

"Good. At least one thing is going right!"

"Aw, what is wrong, boss?"

"Where to begin?" Nathan complained. "We have lost the man who was running the submarine deal—died when an electrical fire broke out. Key component of this operation."

"How's the sub?" Reo asked, unconcerned about the death.

"Fixable. We are behind schedule."

"We can use one of our other operatives, sir. We will have time at the base to sort this all out.. Tanya is still behind enemy lines. She will present another issue."

`Nathan clicked through photos of Evan and felt his blood pressure rise.

"Does Tanya know her man is dead?"

"She will, sir. She is a key player in this. I have confidence that everything will go as planned."

"Bullshit, Reo. Your optimism is not helping."

"Aw, boss, c'mon, cheer up. You will have Gerard!"

"True."

"And the American?"

Nathan chewed on his lip. "Don't have time to worry about him. Evan is his name. If he is CIA and here for us, we could be screwed. Can't kill him. They will send more."

"Nathan, I have never heard you like this. Are you OK?"

"No!"

There was silence for a few moments, and Nathan began to feel foolish; he was losing control.

"Sorry, Reo. I think we are going to pack it up, get Gerard, and haul ass. We have much to do. We need someone to take over the submarine deal. What was his name? Gotta break the news to Tanya."

"His name was Ivan, Russian gentlemen."

"Yes, deal with it later." Nathan picked up a small bottle of Bacardi, opened it, and poured it into a Diet Coke.

"Nathan, I know you. You are obsessing over this Evan guy, this American. C'mon, you are a chess player; think!"

Nathan drained his coffee. The little bastard, Reo, was figuring him out. "Continue, Reo."

"So what if he is CIA? Maybe he is not. What if they help? Remember *The Godfather*?"

"What?"

"Love American movies, Nathan. Remember the famous line: 'Keep your friends close, but your enemies closer'?"

Nathan clicked on another surveillance photo. This one was of a man whom both he and Evan knew from the past. This photo bound the two of them together and could prove as tempting as a queen left unguarded.

"Andre Pena!"

"Sir?"

"Andre Pena. He was released from a Colombian prison one year ago. He is here now working for Mario and the Eastern Cartel!"

"I don't follow you, Nathan."

"You are brilliant, Reo! Andre Pena. The bomb maker who killed Evan's family! He is here in Mexico!"

"Well?" Reo sounded pleased.

Nathan stood up and then sat down. He looked for his walk-ie-talkie. "Reo, I have to go."

"Yes, sir."

"Get everyone to the safe site!" Nathan felt his heart race and his mind sharpen. "*Every defeat is an opportunity.*"

Evan looked around his hotel room and got into character. He spoke out loud to himself after he turned on the TV.

"OK, here it goes. You guys want to play games? Fine."

Evan turned on the laptop that Mr. Z had given him. He hooked the kidnappers' sparkly pink cell phone to it via a USB cable. Next he removed a small, collapsible satellite dish from a bag and made sure he had a decent connection. Within five minutes the cell phone's call history was on the screen, and he was looking at a real-time map of Juárez, complete with cell phone towers and a series of numbers.

"Got you, bastards."

He triangulated where the kidnappers had called from and narrowed it down to a city block. They had most likely called from one of several businesses on a local street named Rancho El Becerro. The technology was not new; police and intelligence agents had been able to locate a cell phone, turn it on, and eaves-drop for years. He located the phone and turned it on. He heard nothing but saw a tiny triangle marking its location. The phone was in a building, and within a moment Evan was able to isolate it to within fifty meters.

"People's Market corner of Rancho El Becerro. A conve-nience store, eh?" he asked and made some more adjustments. He now had the call history of the phone he was listening to. He used the phones call history to locate it's most recent calls and then tapped into those as well. Within five minutes Evan saw circles representing twelve cell phones spread out over Juárez.

One was across the street from the Walmart, and the others were ten to twelve miles dispersed.

Evan sat down for a moment and grabbed the room-service menu. He ordered a big meal of skirt steak and vegetables with a few bottles of water.

After his lunch, he heard his first cell phone conversation; it was a man speaking with his wife.

Evan switched from phone to phone until he was back at the convenience store. Suddenly, he sat upright.

He grabbed a pen and some paper and made notes. He was listening for two voices he would recognize. Suddenly, he heard two men speaking. It was unmistakably the kidnappers.

Evan put on some earphones and tried to isolate the voices. He listened intently for about an hour and wrote down some names. No one was mentioning anything about a kidnapping or any code, but they were using their names. He paused and began recording the conversation for later.

"*Got* you!" Evan said and smiled.

"Juan, Juan, relax! You do as planned, *sí?*"

"I understand, but we must move him now. I cannot have him here when the crazy Frenchman comes back. You no get him. He…he—"

"I get it!"

"Paco, I am not comfortable with this. You being a cop will not make a difference. If he comes back for his girls and finds we are running our own operation, he will go crazy. I have a good job here."

"Coward. Fine, fine!"

"We must move him."

"Then move him! Let's take him somewhere else."

Evan could not catch much more and cursed. The phone sounded muffled now, as if it were in a pocket.

Evan now knew the name of two kidnappers: Juan and Paco. One was a cop, and they seemed to be in fear of someone.

"Who is Gerard? A rival gang?" Evan isolated the signal. It seemed to be moving. "So you are scared? You are moving Armando?"

Evan waited about ten minutes and watched the signal move and then disappear within the store. "No signal? A large storage room?" Evan seemed satisfied. They were more scared and preoccupied with this Frenchman character than with Evan. "Good."

Evan lay down and placed the laptop on his chest. He listened and half watched TV. He switched from phone to phone and listened to unrelated conversations. At least one of the men had a nagging wife. The other kidnapper, Paco, seemed to be in charge. He was the cop with the dirty mouth. He was obsessed with texting several different females about various X-rated topics.

Evan decided he would play the game and stick to his escape route. The men spoke briefly about the easy money they were about to make and gave Evan the impression it was their first time doing this.

Evan called Gustavo and gave him clear instructions. He hoped the old man listened.

"Look, you need someone with some wits about him to be ready to drive you and your brother across the border. I am going to give you some cash, but you must leave."

"You are not going to take us?"

"I might, but this is plan B. If I get your brother, then you both go; if not, then just you go. Either way, we are parting ways."

"I would feel better if you drove us!" Gustavo sounded animated and in better spirits than earlier.

"I plan on it."

"*Sí*, I trust you."

Evan spent the next hour looking over maps on his computer. Once he was satisfied, he called his brother.

People's Market, Rancho El Becerro Street, Juárez, 1400 Hours

Dark Cloud's surveillance Team Two consisted of two highly skilled shooters named Raul and Sanchez. They had been given instructions to watch the market and be prepared to storm it once Gerard was inside. Team One was still trying to find an American named Evan, and Team Three had eyes on Gerard at his hotel a few miles away. The men didn't say a thing as they watched a Juárez cop and the man they knew as Juan, the store manager, escort a blindfolded, elderly man out of the side door and force him in a car trunk.

"What the hell you think is going on with these idiots?" Raul asked.

"Either a sex thing or an execution thing," Sanchez answered.

"Gotta love this town. I am going to report it to Nathan," Raul said.

"Team Three says Gerard has not made a move yet. Guess his truck is still not fixed," Sanchez said and shook his head.

"We will need to move when he shows—too obvious right now."

"Fine."

Walmart

Evan parked the black Ford Bronco in a parking space near the pay phone at Walmart. Evan rolled his windows down and listened to the traffic. He spat out of the window and looked at the bag of money in the passenger seat. He drummed his fingers on the barrel of his shotgun, which rested on his right knee. He looked for a good radio station and glanced at the seat next to him. "Wish I had extra hands."

He found a Mexican *poca* station and left it on. He adjusted his Bluetooth headset so he could overhear any conversations from the cell phone that he had pinned as belonging to Paco, the kidnapper cop. He did not want to look at his computer screen or even open the laptop. He knew they were watching him. All he could do was wait.

Evan looked at his watch, got out of the truck, and walked to the pay phone to wait for the call. He took the duffel bag of money.

"They could be anywhere," he said out loud.

He knew they had moved Armando but was not sure where at this point. Evan realized how foolish this whole endeavor was. *This is exactly why a whole team is required to do something like this, idiot*, he thought.

Evan stood next to the pay phone and shook his head. His stomach had a knot suddenly, and he wondered if he would survive this night. He was scared, and he was glad.

"If you aren't nervous, you are definitely screwed."

The pay phone rang. Evan grabbed it—it smelled like smoke and tequila. He put his headphones down around his neck.

A bus squeaked and hissed as it stopped at the bus stop.

Evan watched a crowd of people close in on the school bus. He heard a backfire, a police siren in the distance, and a group of young girls laughing.

"Listen, *idiota!*" It was Paco's voice. He sounded tense. "We are watching you. We kill you if you get stupid."

"I just want Armando. Please, don't hurt him. His daughter, she is—"

"Shut *up!* Stupid American! Give the money to the lady in the white cowboy hat. She on the bus!"

Evan looked around the streets and behind him. His stomach tightened, and his eyes narrowed. "What?"

"You have about ten seconds. The bus, *idiota!* Right in front of you!"

The last passenger had just gotten on, and Evan followed.

"*Señor?*" the bus driver asked; he had one hand on the handle to close the door. The bus driver looked bored.

"*Uno minuto!*" blurted Evan. He scanned the passengers, who were settling in their seats, adjusting groceries, and herding children. He spotted a short, round girl in her twenties; she wore a low-cut dress and a massive cowboy hat. She and Evan locked eyes. He held up the bag.

"*Señor! Usted tiene que pagar!*" the bus driver said.

"Shut up!" Evan snapped.

The girl stood up and moved. She grabbed the bag and went back to her seat.

Evan left the bus and sprinted back to the phone. He saw a police car pull smoothly into the parking lot. It parked a few spaces away from his truck.

Crap, if the spotters see this cop, I am screwed.

Evan tried to get a glimpse of the cop as he picked up the dangling pay phone. He was breathing hard from the stress and told himself to chill.

"OK?"

"Bus six—your man will be on it unless we sense something up. Then he die."

The phone went dead.

Evan stepped away from the phone and looked at the police car. It parked about one hundred yards away. Evan watched a female cop get out of the car. She went into Walmart.

"*Can't believe this!*"

Evan walked back to his truck and sunk into his seat. He wondered if he should try to track the calls and find Armando or wait. Evan rubbed his eyes and opened a bottle of water. He felt like everyone in Juárez was watching him. He decided to test the kidnappers. He put the Bluetooth back on.

Evan started the truck and began to drive slowly through the parking lot. Instantly the sparkly cell phone rang, and Evan answered, "Yes?"

"Where the fuck are you going? I am going to kill the old man!"

"I was just going to go find a bathroom. I am nervous—I must pee."

"Hold it. Go back to where you were. Do something like that again, I kill you and the man."

"Yes, please, please don't," Evan said and smiled. He tried not to overdo the pitiful routine. *I am going to kill you losers*, he thought.

He parked in a different spot this time, facing the bus stop and road. He was helpless now, and if they double-crossed him, at least he knew where to go to find them.

Nathan felt sick again. He looked at the reports and picture surveillance from his three teams. Team One members had once again let Evan slip through their fingers. They had seen him return on a motorcycle and then nothing all day. Miguel had lost his patience and had the hotel clerk call his room. He was gone.

"You idiots! You did not want to follow him anyway, so you let this happen! Do this again and you are fired!"

Team Three had reported that Gerard's henchman had picked up his van, and they were now eating. Gerard and his thugs were joined by ten young men.

"I hope all these guys don't go to the store together."

Nathan called Team Two. "Frenchman is now with a total of thirteen bad guys. Could get ugly."

"Got it, boss. We watched an old man get shoved into a trunk by a Juárez cop and another guy at the People's Market. The store is empty; we could go in, set up an ambush."

"Hold that thought."

Nathan practiced some deep breathing and was about to eat his untouched lunch when his phone buzzed. It was Team One.

"Nathan! Nathan, we got him!"

"Who?"

"Evan. You won't believe this, but, but—" Miguel was talking in a hurried tone, almost giddy.

"Slow down! Let me speak with Francisco."

Nathan rushed to his laptop and tried to bring up Team One's position on Google Maps.

Francisco began speaking. "We were on our way to the People's Market, stopped by Walmart—*he* was there!"

"Who?" Nathan asked

"He was talking on a pay phone. We watched him. He gave someone on a bus a bag like he was in a hurry. Making a payoff out in the open! Boss, he is in some kinda trouble!"

"W-Where?"

"*At the Walmart!* Aren't you listening?"

"Why did you go there?"

"Water, smokes, sodas. It...it doesn't matter. He is waiting on something! This guy is not a spy, trust me!"

"You are watching him now?"

"Yes, he is doing something, can't tell, in a Ford Bronco."

Nathan smiled and then frowned.

"He is a block away from the People's Market?"

"At the Walmart!"

"What the hell!"

"Boss, we are going to go talk to him."

"What? *No! No!*"

"Boss, we have been doing this bullshit all day. This guy is acting erratic. We talk to him and then drive over to the People's Market. If you know this guy, we will ask him to meet with you."

Nathan paused. "I don't know."

"Boss," Francisco reassured him, "we will just talk. Friendly, casual, see what happens, feel him out."

"Be careful." Nathan thought about what Reo had said. "If the conversation goes well, put him on the phone with me. Just feel him out—do not come across threatening. He may be on a job."

"Boss, I got this. Whatever he was doing, he is done now." Francisco sounded very sure of himself.

"You get one shot. Go for it." Nathan hung up the phone.

He had to make contact eventually. It was now or never.

"Why is he so close to my objective?"

Walmart

Evan got one final fix on the cell phone belonging to Paco before it went dead. He assumed the battery was dead since he could not activate it. The kidnappers were ecstatic about their money and had spoken briefly about how to spend it. Evan became worried that they may just kill Armando.

"We can put the old man on the bus now, Paco. We can't drive around all night with him in the trunk. He is old!"

"Juan, you are too attached to the old fuck! We dump him and move on!"

"That was not the plan!"

Evan's heart raced when he lost contact, but fortunately, he was able to turn on Juan's phone. Smartphones were the greatest gift to snooping government agencies. GPS enabled, video, e-mail; you could hack it all, given enough time.

"I don't think that is right. We should take him to the bus stop."

Evan heard a third kidnapper's voice in the car. The background noise made the voice sound muffled, but he could make it out.

"Drop the fucker off now!"

"Fine!"

Evan plotted the transmission and realized it had moved back to Rancho El Becerro. *They are going back to the store?* Evan mused.

The kidnappers seemed to answer Evan's question as he thought it.

"We can drop him off as soon as I get a case of beer and my charger," Paco said.

"Then we free him," Juan said. "We cannot stay long at the store. Gerard, he may come soon!"

"Frenchman, Frenchman—shut up, Juan! Won't take long."

"Free the man—split the money."

"Sure, sure."

Evan's mouth felt dry, and his heart rate picked up. Something was wrong; he could hear it in Paco's voice. Paco seemed like a lone-wolf type who did not like his fellow kidnappers. While he seemed ruthless, they seemed weak. Whatever was about to go down at the store, Evan could tell at least one of the kidnappers was worried.

"Who is Gerard?" Evan asked himself.

Evan started his Bronco, took off his earphones, and closed the laptop. He had to act fast; if his hunch was right, this was the end. His adrenalin shot up to his ears, and he felt sick.

"People's Market!" Evan blurted.

Evan eyeballed the traffic and scanned the streets for cops. Rush hour was in full swing. He bent down to put his computer on the floor and his black backpack on the seat. He stared at his backpack. He had spare magazines, zip ties, and pieces of duct tape neatly torn in strips stuck to the outside of the bag. It was impossible to go into combat without duct tape. This was just a fact. Evan felt for the round-canister flash-bangs and smoke grenades.

"Blind assault, no plan, no backup, and why am I doing this?" he whispered to himself as he drew his Smith & Wesson M&P .40 from his ankle holster. Evan liked to have all of his toys in reach. He wished he had eight arms. The shotgun was on the backseat in a black canvas guitar case.

He had moments to drive less than a mile through traffic.

Then the unexpected happened.

"Excuse me, *señor*, can we speak?"

The voice was in English. Evan thought *cop* before he even looked up.

Several things happened at once, and as Evan pieced them together in his mind, he realized that two men had just got the drop on him. They could have shot him but did not.

Evan kept his cool close and his weapon closer and smiled. He glanced at a handsome man in his midfifties who was placing his hand on the passenger-side door. They moved like two cops, crouching and approaching him in his blind spot. Cartel members would not have wasted that much effort. Evan saw the hint of a concealed holster on the one who had spoken.

"My name is Francisco, *señor*. Can we talk?"

The second man walked up to the driver's side. He moved in a way that made Evan insecure. This man was younger, and Evan instantly recognized him from the hotel. *This guy was watching me this morning!*

"Are you two cops?" Evan slid the safety off his weapon. He always kept one in the chamber. What was the point of having a gun and not being ready to use it.

"No, *señor*." The older one spoke in English and smiled not unlike a salesman.

Evan's heart rate picked up. If there was one thing Evan hated more than politicians and lawyers, it was salesmen—except firearm dealers—they were OK in his book.

"Are you two going to give me Armando?"

Evan figured he had pegged them as part of the kidnapper racket. Maybe these two were cops on the take. They certainly were more sophisticated than the idiots he had been listening to.

Their reaction surprised and then confused Evan. "Who?"

He now knew he was in trouble, and wasting time.

"We do not know Armando. Sir, please. You are holding a gun, and we are not threatening you. We just want to talk."

The younger man tried to grab Evan's steering wheel as Evan fired up the Bronco.

"Please, sir, do not drive away!"

"Wrong move!" Evan said flatly. Evan raised his weapon slightly and stomped on the accelerator.

Both men backed off.

Tires squealed, horns honked, and people screamed.

Evan bounced the Bronco across the sidewalk, scattering pedestrians. He plowed through the intersection as the light turned green and cut off half a dozen cars in two different directions. Evan felt the rear end of his Bronco fishtail as a Mercedes smashed into his bumper. He floored it. The bumper came off. He bounced across the median, knocked a guy off a motor scooter, and accelerated down the less crowded side street marked Rancho El Becerro.

Evan was going about forty miles an hour when he hit the brakes. The Bronco squealed to a stop with two wheels on the sidewalk at the corner of a building. The engine began to smoke and rattle. Evan smelled rubber. He pulled a black ski mask down partly over his face as if it were a hat. He cut the engine and checked the mirrors. No one was following him, yet.

A few locals stared at him and then turned to walk in the opposite direction.

Evan put on his backpack, slung his guitar case, and moved quickly toward the corner of the building and then paused. He looked around. No one seemed to pay him any attention. He spotted several vehicles—vans, pickups, and delivery trucks—parked on the street. A group of teenagers were smoking next to a 1980s Datsun pickup, and an old man was locking his bike up to a light post.

Evan frowned. He tried not to think about the two men he had just fled from or how they fit into the big picture. He would sort out the details later.

"I am a sitting duck out here; I gotta move."

Evan scanned the street one last time and rounded the corner. His Smith & Wesson was reholstered. He suddenly wished he had his assault rifle. The shotgun put limits on his range and accuracy.

Surveillance Team Three sat uncomfortably cramped in the back of a stuffy black van. The sound of a soccer game had lost its appeal when the stranger arrived.

"You see that?"

"*Sí.*"

"*Que esta pasando?*"

The three members of Team Three were already on edge, and this new twist complicated things. The team had been watching the People's Market for hours, and they had witnessed kidnappers stuff an old man in a trunk, drive off, and then bring him back a few hours later. Now a large man with a guitar, a tactical black backpack, and an attitude was loitering around the building.

"This man, he is not a Scorpion."

"Is he here to settle a score? What should we do?"

The men spoke quickly among themselves. The van grew very quiet before the leader spoke up.

"If the assault team does not make it before Gerard, he will waste this fool. Only problem is, we have no element of surprise. I am calling Nathan. We have to cancel the operation."

The assault team that was supposed to have been there hours ago to set up and snatch Gerard was now stuck in traffic less than a block away.

"I am calling Nathan. We have to be ready."

Evan rounded the corner and spotted an older-model Cadillac with Texas plates, an Obama sticker, and a Coexist sticker on the chrome bumper. The trunk was open, and the engine was running.

"Someone in Austin must be missing a Cadi." Evan laughed to himself and spat on the sidewalk.

The sound of gunfire cracked from inside the convenience store and then stopped. He counted about eight quick pops.

"It's now or never," Evan said to himself. He felt a wave of anxiety and fear and then a hint of foolishness as one particular thought took hold in his brain: *Killed in Mexico, in a convenience store. What the hell?*

Evan checked the street again. The people where leaving, vanishing into shadows or doorways. Evan watched the teenagers, who had all been happily talking, drop their cigarettes and mota at the same time on the sidewalk, grind them into dust without a word, and walk away.

Evan pushed open the door of the People's Market and quickly moved inside. The door was heavy glass with bars and was covered with stickers.

He had two very simple objectives: one, kill the kidnappers, and two, find Armando and escape.

"Only problem is how."

The smell of gunpowder hung in the air. The remains of what must have been a huge fish tank were scattered on the floor. Evan made sure to avoid the glass, small rocks, and flapping fish. He moved down the slick aisle at a crouch, trying to avoid the carnage of fish, produce, and tortilla chips. He was near the cash register. The windows of the store were covered in posters of half-naked females Evan paused and stepped over the body of what he assumed was one of the kidnappers. Two Glock 19s lay near him. Evan shook his head; he was not a Glock man.

The idiot must have been trying to shoot it out Hollywood style, with two weapons. "Looks like the only thing you killed was a bunch of fish and some cans of soup," Evan whispered to the corpse.

"*No, Paco, No! Please,, don't do it!*"

Evan had a split-second field of fire as he regained his balance. He had not been spotted yet. He peered around the aisle and watched Paco, who was considerably thicker than the other two kidnappers. Evan guessed he probably had a love affair with 'roids. Paco looked unbalanced. He had massive, swollen arms and a barrel chest on top of two tiny legs. He wore his Juárez police shirt unbuttoned to his waist and was pointing a .357 at his fellow kidnapper's head. Paco was unconcerned.

Evan stepped into view, his shotgun pressed firmly into his shoulder, ski mask down, dip in his lip, and finger firm on the trigger. "*Fiesta ha terminado dónde está Armando?*"

Ramon Miguel Velacruz was the surveillance team commander. He and his men were armed with silenced M-4s and the sidearms of their choice. He himself had bought the weapons in bulk in Texas and had paid a decent price. Right now, he had a critical decision to make. Ramon had three opposing forces meeting in the same spot. If he were Catholic, he would have crossed himself and prayed.

The ski-masked man had entered the store to deal with the kidnappers; who knew who would come out on top in that disaster? Nathan had told him that under no circumstances was he to kill the large man in the ski mask; he was to bring him in alive.

The second, more pressing dilemma was that an armored, red Humvee had just pulled up in front of the store and was off-loading about ten members of the Scorpions. They were armed with an assortment of AK-47s and handguns. They showed no concern about operational security.

A white van pulled up behind the Humvee, driven by a man they recognized.

"Gerard!" Ramon said.

They watched as Gerard gave orders to his men to stay put, lit up a cigarette, and then disappeared out of their sight around the far side of the store.

"He is going around the side and down the alley; there is a fire door in the back where he can gain entrance. The guys in the red Humvee must be acting as security," one of Ramon's team members commented as he racked a round.

It was contagious, like a yawn. Everyone locked and loaded and clicked off their safeties.

"Ramon?"

Ramon cursed, crossed himself anyway, and reached for the handle of the van's sliding door.

"OK, here is the plan," Ramon said and then paused.

Everyone stopped breathing for a second and muttered a collective, *"Esto no es bueno!"*

A black Chevy Silverado belonging to the assault team pulled up behind Gerard's white van, blocking it in. At the same time, a green minivan, which was also part of the team, screeched around the corner and stopped next to Ramon's van. It stopped in the middle of the street, effectively blocking off any escape on the block. Everyone had a look of surprise.

The Humvee and Gerard's van were now caught in the middle, and so was Ramon.

"The assault team is here," someone said sarcastically.

Ramon's blood pressure pounded in his ears. He knew what was inevitable at this point.

Their eyes met, and Evan recognized the vacant, almost inhuman, look of an empty vessel posing as a human. He had seen hundreds of men just like Paco, from Afghanistan to Somalia. They all had one thing in common: they just did not care.

Paco kept his finger on the trigger and looked right at Evan. Juan was on his knees, pleading.

"No, *amigo mida*. I have all the money!"

Boom! Evan and Paco fired at the same time.

Evan bit his lower lip. "Oops, too slow," he muttered.

Juan's head exploded and sprayed Evan with brain matter and liquid. Paco took buckshot to the chest and face and collapsed, burnt and riddled with tiny holes.

"What the hell is going on in here?"

Evan heard shouts behind him now from out on the street. He took off his backpack and raced to the entrance of the market. He could see forms and shapes through the windows and knew what was about to take place.

"Now that's a Mexican standoff!" Evan spat Skoal on the floor and unzipped his backpack. He started tearing duct tape and stretching trip wire. "I need an avenue of escape!"

Within thirty seconds he had locked the front door, moved a chair in front of it, and set up a trip wire for his flash-bang and smoke grenades. "That might slow someone down, or just catch the whole place on fire and kill all of us!" Evan muttered to himself.

He picked up his backpack and ran to the back of the store.

The shooting outside started.

Pop! Pop! Pop!

"What the hell is going on?" Evan looked around the store. He figured either two cartel groups were having a turf war, or perhaps the police were involved somehow. Were the two men at Walmart trying to warn him? Was he caught in the middle of something massive?

Evan heard men yelling outside and the sound of automatic gunfire. He knew the fog of war all too well and figured if he kept moving, he could use it to his advantage.

"Help in here!"

Evan heard multiple pleas from down the hall. Most were female.

Evan looked down the store's hallway toward the emergency exit. There was a thick metal door that served as an entrance to a beer cooler. Evan bounded over to it and examined a chain and padlock. There appeared to be a broken dead bolt, so someone had drilled and attached metal rings into the doorframe and door so a chain could be fastened. Evan knew third-world engineering when he saw it and was glad.

"Armando?"

"Sí, sí, ayuda estamos aquí!"

"We?" Evan shot the padlock off the beer cooler with a breach round that he was saving in his breast pocket.

The breach round was great for these closeup jobs of six inches or so. They did not ricochet. The round's red plastic case was packed with powdered zinc, which burned hot and fast. He rested the shotgun against the wall so he could use both hands to remove the broken chain and lock.

At precisely the same time that Evan realized he needed his backup weapon, the fire-exit door burst open with a loud bang. For a split second, Evan and a wiry, bare-chested white man looked at each other. Evan noticed the man's huge, colorful tattoo of a Scorpion covering his lower torso. He wore aviator glasses and stank like booze.

"Stealin' my bitches?" The man held a gold-plated .45 by his side and began to raise it with one hand as if he were in some cheesy 1970s movie.

Only gangbangers and nonshooters shoot with one hand, Evan thought as he sprang forward.

The flash-bang and smoke grenades suddenly exploded, rocking the front of the store. The building was being breached. Men yelled and cursed, weapons fired, and glass shattered.

Evan charged like a freight train at the younger man and caught him by such surprise and ferociousness that his eyes almost popped out of his head. Evan slammed his left hand under the man's chin, rocking his head back and almost lifting him off the ground. Evan grabbed the man's rising wrist with his right hand and yanked it straight up so that the .45 fired twice into the ceiling. In less than a second, Evan's leg swept and barreled the man through the emergency exit and into the alley.

The firefight outside became fiercer, and Evan heard another flash-bang somewhere out on the street.

The white guy with the Scorpion tattoo was nearly knocked unconscious when he bounced off the pavement. Evan twisted and broke the wrist as he stomped on the man's face. He accented each stomp with a stream of expletives. The man stopped moving, and his eyes rolled back in his head. Blood, teeth, and drool poured from his face.

"Put you where you belong, you piece of crap!" Evan squatted down and lifted the limp gangster up to his chest and then over his head and slammed him into a putrid, fly-infested Dumpster.

Evan kept cursing as he ran back to the beer cooler. He had one clear avenue of escape, but not for long. The shooting had stopped, and he heard a car alarm, loud voices, and dozens of police sirens. The store was filled with smoke, and it began to drift outside.

Evan ripped open the door of the beer cooler. He now had his own .40 in his hands.

"*Thank you, thank you!*" multiple voices chanted in English and Spanish.

Evan experienced a cold shock as he walked into the beer cooler. The cold air went straight to his aching bones and chilled the sweat on his body. He was in no way prepared for what he saw.

"Armando?" Evan whispered. He tried to catch his breath.

An old man with greasy, matted, long gray hair and an out-of-control beard sat drinking beer while leaning forward on a crate. Armando was hugging a thick moving blanket to a huddled harem of shivering women. They were terrified and cold and wore orange jumpsuits.

"*Praise God!* My sweet ladies, you see, Armando told you he will take care of you! No fear! This man, he is our savior!"

Evan was speechless. He lowered his weapon and shoved it in his waistband. He watched the crying girls huddle close to their ancient friend. Evan could hear the coughing, cursing, and stumbling of men in the hall and knew they were coming. He knew it was over; he could not possibly escape with six people.

"What is going on?"

"A beer, *señor?*"

Evan just shook his head and closed his gaping mouth. Of course he took the beer. "Only in freaking Mexico!"

Evan turned slowly around to see what was going to happen next. He knew whoever came through the open door, friend or foe, had him outgunned and would not be happy with his booby traps. He was beat.

He coughed from the smoke, drank his beer, and rubbed his face.

When they came, Evan gave no resistance. He faced six angry, armed men, none of whom wore police uniforms. Evan was still in shock at seeing Armando surrounded by his girls.

"Who the heck are you guys?" Evan held his non-beer-holding hand up and smiled and then added, "It's Mexican night. You guys bring the chips and salsa?"

No one except Evan was smiling. They were not amused but furious and clearly understood English.

"Is your name Evan?"

Evan assumed they were not cartel members or he would already be dead. They were also not police. And they knew his name.

"Maybe." Evan looked from the terrified girls to Armando and then to the men with automatic weapons. The assault team began to lower their weapons as they processed the surroundings. They looked puzzled.

The smoke was dissipating. The whole scene grew strangely quiet, and Evan could only hear the cooler's compressor.

Evan was confused; they had not killed him, and for that he was relieved.

"I came to rescue Armando. Are you cops? How do you know my name?"

No one spoke.

Then Evan saw *him*.

A man in cowboy boots and khakis stepped into the beer cooler. His boots crunched broken glass and ice, and he held a napkin over his mouth to block out the smoke.

Evan opened another beer offered to him by Armando, took a drink, and shook his head. "What next? Juggling midgets?" he said in English this time while casually reaching for his can of dip.

"Hi, Evan. Enjoying Juárez?"

"Hi, Nathan. Want a beer?"

CHAPTER 10

Trust Me—I Used to Lie for a Living

Juárez, Mexico, 2100 Hours

A large warehouse stood at the north end of Gonzalez Airport in Juárez. The hangar was owned by a businessman. Evan watched and admired a yellow Gulfstream 550 jet. He sipped a Diet Dr. Pepper and watched as crews in white jumpsuits moved large rolling stairs up to the tail portion of the plane. They had just finished power washing the plane and were now placing magnetic strip decals and new tail numbers. Different crews were placing Pelican cases with what Evan assumed were weapons and equipment underneath the private jet. The smell of aviation fuel, mold, and heat filled the air. Evan loved airports; he liked the smell, the noise, and the sound of jet engines. Activity filled the hangar, and everyone moved with a purpose.

Evan stood still and finished sipping his soda. He felt like the kind of guy that people didn't like but didn't have the guts to deal with. He would occasionally catch a dirty look or scowl turned his way. He could read their lips and their body language from across the hangar.

Evan yawned and felt exhaustion creep into his bones. He glanced at a section of the warehouse that had been designated as an aid station. From what Evan observed, there was a doctor and perhaps some medics bandaging and picking out shrapnel and stitching up minor wounds. No one had been seriously wounded, but his stunt with the glass door and grenade had shredded people's exposed skin and damaged their eardrums. Fortunately, the assault team had worn enough body armor and protective gear to stave off most soft-tissue injuries. They had annihilated the gang members—caught them in a crossfire and shot them to pieces.

Evan had been allowed to sit in on the after-action report and put all of the pieces of the puzzle together.

Dark Cloud shooters were supposed to ambush and assault the People's Market to snatch and grab Gerard. Evan admitted that he chucked Gerard into a Dumpster, effectively keeping him safe from getting snatched.

"Oops, sorry. Had no clue who he was." Evan shrugged. His cavalier attitude seemed to infuriate many of the operators.

Evan had no regrets; he was just glad he had not been killed in the cross fire.

He was tired, dirty, hungry, and sore.

The police finally arrived, quickly whisked Armando and the girls away, and provided cover as Dark Cloud escaped.

He knew that later the police would claim a major victory on crime by stating something to the effect of, "Today we rescued five kidnapped girls and a Mexican national, blah, blah…"

Evan finished his soda and looked for a trash can. "Now what?"

Evan had given Armando the pile of cash that his brother had given him and strongly told him to take his brother and leave Mexico. Armando had said something that had stuck in his mind: "God has protected you."

Evan had said his good-byes and quickly called his brother to say mission accomplished. He felt a gnawing ache in his stomach when he failed to mention this character Nathan from his past.

"I plan on coming back tonight, different flight from Armando. The police are protecting him. I seemed to have caused a little mess down here. Explain later."

Evan had been sitting by himself, just thinking and staring.

A thick, serious-looking gentleman, midthirties, approached Evan from across the hangar. He was wearing a San Antonio Spurs hat, jeans, and a T-shirt. He had an MP5 slung over his back. His bushy beard reminded Evan of the Taliban.

"Sir?" the man said.

"*Que?*"

"Mr. Nathan Rock, he would like to speak with you. He is in the plane." He spoke excellent English and seemed tired, almost bored.

Evan looked around. "Sure, sure."

"This way please."

Nathan Rock sat reclined in a wide-armed swivel chair in the rear of the G550 aircraft. He reminded Evan of someone who was trying to play president in a miniature Air Force One. Nathan's eyes were closed, and he had a wet towel draped over his eyes. A woman in her midthirties massaged his shoulders.

"Ouch! Not that deep."

"You are tight, *señor*. Your neck, shoulders very stiff," she said.

Evan stood still for a moment and tried to think of something smart to say but refrained.

The shooter with the beard asked Evan if he needed anything to drink.

"Water."

The shooter tossed him a plastic bottle and left.

Evan sipped on his water and waited for the masseuse to finish. Once she left, Evan sat in another swivel chair and spun it around to face Nathan, who still had his eyes closed.

"Nice gig you got here, Nathan."

Nathan kept his eyes closed and did not move. He was aware that Evan was there but made no move to acknowledge him.

"Been what, fifteen…eighteen years?" Evan said.

"Something like that. Who's counting."

"CIA in the business of rescuing old men who have been kidnapped by bottom-rung kidnappers?" Nathan saids with a little contention in his voice and still did not open his eyes.

Evan could tell he was scared and trying to play cool and in control. Evan knew enough about Nathan to know he suffered from migraines, the result of being OCD and a perfectionist. Evan thrived on everything always being out of control and having an uncontrollable variable. He expected it.

Nathan, on the other hand, was in a constant war to control everything. If he could micromanage raindrops, he would.

"So I stumbled on your little operation. Dark Cloud, eh?"

"And completely screwed up snatching a high-profile cartel member."

Evan shrugged and looked at the calluses on his hand. "So grab another one. They are everywhere down here."

Nathan laughed, but was not amused. He removed the cloth from his head and faced Evan with bloodshot eyes. His face looked puffy and much older than his years.

"You still never answered me, Evan."

"I can give you that, Nathan. You followed procedure and did what I would have done. You watched Mr. Z, and as a result you found me."

"Evan."

"Answer is no, like I said. I really did come down here to do a payoff."

"To get back your brother's maid's father?" Nathan looked amused.

"Sometimes the truest things are the craziest," Evan said.

"Can't argue with that," Nathan countered.

"I could give two shits rather you believe me or not. Thanks for the lift to the airport and the free health care. We'll call it even for all the illegals my tax dollars support." Evan stood up, stretched, and yawned. "I got to roll."

Nathan sat up and held his hands up in a submissive posture. "Wait, come on, have a seat a minute. Your flight doesn't leave for about four hours."

Evan sensed there was something else going on and did have the time to kill. He really was hoping to get a massage from the attractive masseuse. Nathan spoke quickly in a soft tone trying to lighten the tension.

"Look, after reviewing the cluster that happened today, I really doubt you are working for the CIA. No way you would ever do such a thing by yourself. That's not even remotely a mission that—"

"Thanks for the validation. What else?" asked Evan.

"OK, here it is. You got a job right now?"

Evan laughed and almost choked on his Skoal. "Knew it. You want to offer me a job?"

"Seriously," Nathan pleaded.

Evan shook his head slowly and said, "Nathan, your shooters out there will put one in the back of my head the first chance they get."

"You really did not know. Just a crazy coincidence, Evan."

"So this guy you call Gerard, how high is he?"

"Top-tier enforcer for the cartel's military wing. The Scorpions are all contractors from other countries and defected Mexican special operators."

Evan nodded his head and shrugged. "Mmmm, guy looked drug crazed to me."

"He's a high-value target anyway. I can't get into the specifics of what I have going on, but we have something big coming down the pike."

"And out of the blue I show up, and you want me?"

Nathan sighed with exasperation. Evan was happy that he had a hand in the return of Nathan's migraine.

"You really aren't making this easy."

"I am consistent."

Nathan laughed and shook his head. "I need a guy who can speak Russian, knows Spanish, and has been to Cuba. I need someone who can pose as an arms dealer. A guy who knows a little about subs."

Evan looked out the window. "I'll call you if I meet any."

"OK. Look, I haven't seen you in what…twenty-something years? I know you and your team never liked me, and I know you blame me on some level for the unfortunate things that happened in Colombia. I can only ask your forgiveness for being a prick. I am sorry for the past. Could we have used better security to protect them? Moved them into our compound? Yes! But we did not. The higher ups, not me, made that call."

Evan held up his hand and remained calm. "Let's not go there."

"Fair enough."

"You need a Cuban-Russian arms dealer?" Evan suddenly looked at Nathan. This sounded familiar to him.

"One who specifically knows something about submarines," Nathan answered.

Evan cocked his head and narrowed his eyes. He looked skeptically at Nathan as if he were the big bad wolf at grandma's house.

Evan spoke quietly, almost in a whisper. "Ivan Romonov?"

Nathan smiled broadly in acknowledgement. His teeth looked white and sharp. "It worked in Colombia—why not here?"

"You are taking a mission that I created and pulled off, what, a few decades ago and repeating it with the Mexicans?" Evan was honestly perplexed, amused, and dumbfounded all at the same time.

"Copying is the best form of flattery, Evan."

Evan looked at Nathan and spoke more to himself than anyone. "Ivan Romonov, the Russian-Cuban engineer who was trying to get the Colombians a real Soviet sub? That operation? Only one Ivan—what a character. I put that whole thing together. I helped put that prick in prison in Moscow. The sub sank off the coast of Cuba before we could seal the deal."

"True, but how many high-profile drug dealers did you drown? Mission accomplished."

"No, really, Nathan, it sank on its own. I did not sink it."

Nathan laughed. "Whatever. You were quite infamous for that. Killed some of the biggest players in Colombia and changed the whole dynamic!"

"I didn't." Evan felt uneasy and changed the subject. "So you need someone like Crazy Ivan to pull off a bait and switch?"

Nathan smiled mischievously. "Well, I have always said, if you are going to run a carbon-copy mission, do it right."

"You said that?" Evan asked suspiciously.

"Well, I'm saying it now—bear with me. Yes, I copied one of your missions. I even salvaged the actual Soviet sub off the coast of Cuba. Most importantly, I bought Ivan's freedom and hired him."

Evan's jaw dropped. "What? You *what?*"

Nathan laughed. "You heard me."

"*Unreal*, Nathan! That guy was a jerk. He should be in prison!"

"You should be in prison too. Hell, so should I!"

"That's beside the point, Nathan. *Wait!* You said you need a Russian…um, what happened?"

Nathan frowned but was not sad. "He met with an unfortunate accident. He got electrocuted while fixing the sub. We still have it and were supposed to sell it in six weeks. This sale, I believe, was big enough to bring the bigwig Mario himself to the scene."

"Mario? You mean the current richest drug-cartel member in the world? The guy no one has seen in ten years?"

"The very same." Nathan smiled. "Dark Cloud's mission is to destroy his cartel, make them inept, broke, and just plain dysfunctional."

"So smaller cartels can take over and start a new, bloodier war? Just like in Colombia when Pablo got wasted? C'mon, Nathan, you know how this shit will go down. Even if you get this guy, nothing will change."

Nathan nodded in agreement. "Not my problem, Evan." Nathan leaned forward and spoke quietly. "Elements in the government and business have some personal issues with Mario. Normally, the attitude is 'keep the cash coming,' and let they us make some token busts, like when you have a crop of weed that has been hurt by parasites…We will take that. This way the gringos can justify their own law-enforcement operations and ultimately pay us." Nathan paused and drank some water.

"Only, Mario does not play nice. He wants to rule over the other cartels, bring them together, and be their CEO. This, of course, terrorizes the state and the political class. They want things to stay the same. Easier to deal with little fiefdoms than a unified front."

"Narco insurgency. You're talking narco state," Evan said flatly and spat in his empty soda can.

"Yes."

"And?" Evan asked.

"And Mario sends a hit team to the president's niece's *quinceañera* to show the president he can get to anyone."

"OK." Evan was listening more intently now.

"The hit team is led by another character whose identity I will not get into. He is known for kidnapping wealthy elites' children. Just was dealing with his handiwork in Mexico City, in fact, before you showed up."

"Sorry to spoil your party," Evan said, rolling his eyes.

"The hit team manages to get past the security detail and tortures the president's niece and wounds several others." Nathan paused and stared through Evan for a second as his eyes lost focus. "It was very sick what he did to her. I will leave it at that. In the end, fifteen police and security people were killed in the raid."

"Revenge," Evan muttered.

Nathan shrugged and inspected his fingernails. "Something like that."

Evan stood for a moment and stretched and yawned. He had heard enough. He could skip the massage. "Sounds like you got a busy couple of days. I am going to roll."

"Two more things...no three."

Evan paused like an impatient teenager. "I need to go. Being around you is too dangerous."

"Three things and then you can go. My guy will drive you to the terminal. You can think about it and call me if you change your mind. Four hours to think about it."

"Three things. Go."

Nathan grabbed his MacBook Pro off the floor and placed it in his lap.

"OK, number one, I need you to get inside, sell the sub—you know the damn thing as well as Ivan. It was your baby. I need you to do your thing and get me this bastard!"

Evan shook his head. "One down."

"OK, OK, two, Andre Pena—he's working for Mario. No one knows why. He was allowed to walk out of a prison in Colombia."

Evan's eyes got wide and he stared straight through Nathan and then at the computer. He recognized Andre Pena. He was older, but it was him. Evan stared at the man who had blown up his wife and child. Evan felt his blood heat to a mild boil.

"Piss off!" Evan grabbed his water bottle and began to walk off the plane. "I want my bags and a driver now!"

"Wait, wait. The third thing, Evan!"

Evan held up his middle finger and walked to the steps to exit the plane.

"Two million dollars in cash. Evan? Evan!"

Evan paused.

CHAPTER 11

The Zoo

Tetlanohcan, Mexico, February 16, 0800 Hours

San Francisco Tetlanohcan is a tiny mountain town with a population of about ten thousand in the Mexican state of Tlaxcala. Mexico City and its pollution lie two hours to the west.

La Malinche, or the Lady of Green Skirts, is a massive, dormant volcano with an elevation of 14,636 feet. The mountain serves as the town's one and only skyscraper.

Four miles outside of town, tucked away down a long, one-lane gravel-and-asphalt road, sat the entrance to a working ranch. The nondescript entrance was marked with a large rusty iron gate with faded writing.

Roger stood on a new, wide wooden deck that served as a second-floor balcony to a new stone-and-wood building. He sipped his coffee and glanced out over the thousand-acre estate. The sun rose slowly and dissipated a fog that was clinging lazily to the ground. He had overheard that the morning temperature would be forty-five and then climb to seventy in the afternoon. Roger looked out over acres of trees, crops, and a small herd of alpacas that huddled near an old fence.

"Sleep well?"

Roger jumped and turned around to see Mia and her sister. They were dressed in shorts and hiking boots, ready for their hike.

"Yes. You shouldn't sneak up on people."

"You shouldn't be so easy to sneak up on," Mia teased.

"Beauty has that effect on me, darlin'." Roger nodded at the two younger women.

"Nice here, yes?" Mia said quietly.

"How far are we going to hike? I am not in great shape, so don't lose me," Roger pleaded.

"Only one way to get in shape." Mia laughed.

Roger nodded and finished his coffee. "What is this place?"

They had arrived late last night under cover of darkness.

"The Zoo, that's what we call it," she said.

"And?"

"By tomorrow we will have about one hundred operatives. Everyone is assigned a room and a team. In two days training starts. We have indoor ranges, kill houses, outdoor ranges, and facilities to conduct our training. Only rule is, we do not venture off the property, and we don't clump around in large groups," Mia replied.

"Interesting out here isolated, I see. Can we go into town?"

"No. When Nathan arrives, we will get our orders. Secrecy is very hard to maintain."

"Thought I heard helicopters last night," Roger said.

"*Sí*, airfield about a mile that way." Mia pointed out toward the mountains.

Roger spoke and asked his most important question, "Are they going to feed us?"

Mia laughed. "Yes, we eat then hike. I will show you the obstacle course."

"Great," Roger mumbled. He figured he would just follow her lead, since she seemed to be not only well respected but pretty much known by every one. If Roger had learned anything from his life in the military it was to figure out when chow was and who were the people that could get things done. Mia was a go-getter like Roger, and they hit it off fabulously.

CHAPTER 12

Training Wheels

Huejotsingo Airport, Puebla, Mexico, 1000 Hours

The jolt from the landing gear caused Evan to drift slowly to the surface of a dream until he reached that place where he consciously knew he was dreaming but was unable to stop the reoccurring events. He drifted back to sleep. His brain gained altitude while his subconscious continued to perseverate over the same thought: *violent, bloody death.*

It was 1994 Columbia. A big band played its version of "Carita de Angel," a classic from Cuban composer Bebo Valdes. The piano, horns, and soft rhythm of the female vocalist did little to soften Evan's mood. On any other day, he would have sat at the bar and drowned himself. Evan paused for a second to listen; he felt like he had been here before.

"The angel of death is the only one here tonight," he muttered.

Evan adjusted his clip-on tie, put in a dip, and pushed his way to the back of the packed restaurant. No one paid him any mind as he moved past well-dressed, busty young women who stuck to gangsters and politicians like static cling. Music, smoke, and the loud voices of drunks who had lost all sense of personal space raised Evan's angst. He hated crowds. A bar was a bar no matter where you were. He stood in Cartagena, Colombia, in a restaurant once owned by the former Pablo Escobar. Anyone who was on the top of the food chain in the underworld had at one time made an appearance here. Armed guards, corrupt cops, and generals felt safe here.

"Have to be suicidal to pull off a hit in this place," Evan said to himself. He paused to spit in a potted plant.

No one noticed, and he smiled.

A large man with a scar down the side of his face stepped in front of Evan and held up a thick hand. The man held a wand like you'd see at the airport. He stank of cigars and whiskey.

Evan sneezed and spoke rapidly with great excitement. "Excuse me—allergic to smoke."

"Who are you?" The man was a few inches taller than Evan and quite thick and fat.

"Here to wish a happy birthday to Andre Pena's son, Miguel. Wow, who are those babes? Is that a soap-opera star?"

The man kept a steady gaze on Evan and placed his free hand on his hip, presumably on a gun.

"Yes, that's the soccer-player's wife…What's his name? She was a porn star." Evan spoke and turned his head sideways as if in deep thought. "*Oh* yeah, now I see it."

"Get lost!"

"And the blonde?" Evan asked as he peered past the bodyguard.

"Who are you?"

Evan was about to answer and then turned to sneeze again. "Excuse me, name's Miguel also. His dad sent me. I only got about five minutes; then I gotta leave." Evan looked at his watch.

"Well, more like four and half now."

Evan laughed and looked past the bodyguard and at the table where Miguel Pena sat sandwiched firmly between two intoxicated ladies. The married ex-porn star grabbed an ice cube and put it down Miguel's shirt. Evan sized up Miguel's two body-guards, who sat unmoving at the edges of the circular booth. One on each side. They were staring at Evan with their right hands in their jackets.

"Look," Evan began, "time is ticking, my friend. I must give him his present."

"I check you first. What you carry? Put your arms out!"

"Sure, sure." Evan held his arms out and let the man give him a thorough pat down and scan. If he had had a gun or a weapon, the man would have found it.

"Your hand...what that?"

"Inside joke. Night-vision goggles. He will understand in a moment. Go tell him Miguel is here. Gift from Daddy."

The man looked at Evan.

Evan watched the bodyguards watch him.

The blonde had disappeared under the table. Miguel was holding the edge of the table, a shocked look moved across his face.

"You give to me."

Evan glanced at his watch again. "Here." Evan gave the man a wad of one-hundred-dollar bills and smirked when his eyes lit up. *That easy to sell out. Amazing*, Evan thought. "Go get Miguel and me two Margaritas; you keep the rest. I'm just going to give him these goggles and then I'm outta here! Hate all this smoke!"

The man took the money, crammed it in his pocket, and bit his lip. He looked at Evan and the night-vision goggles and shook his head.

"Hurry up, weird one!"

"Oh, I will." Evan checked his watch and grimaced. "Two minutes. Shit." He put the night-vision goggles on his head so they sat up high on his forehead. He walked up to the table, smiled, and placed his hands flatly on its surface near a lonely steak knife. "*Hola*, Miguel! I am Miguel too. Got a present from Poppi!"

"Who the fuck are you?"

The two bodyguards began to stand.

Evan looked at his watch, the table, and the young blond girl who was trying to climb back into her seat. Her hair was a mess, and her lipstick was smeared. The married ex-porn star was staring at Evan. She was gripping the table as if they were on a moving boat and she needed to steady herself.

"What the fuck is on your head?" she blurted with the eloquence of a drunk.

"It's a punch line, bitch!" Evan said.

"Fuck you. Kill him, Miguel!" the blonde said.

Evan heard his wristwatch alarm chime. He smiled, picked up the steak knife, pulled the night-vision goggles over his eyes, and ducked.

Boom! Boom!

Evan sat up with a jolt, wide awake. The plane landed roughly. He was horrified, in hindsight, at how easily he had killed Andre Pena's son fifteen years ago. He had slit the man's throat with no more thought or compassion than he would have given to stepping on a spider. He felt nothing. No happiness, no sadness, no guilt.

Revenge was a lie, a dead-end alley, and this was no game. He had killed this man, and others, like a dog. Death did not ease death.

His head began to throb, and he felt an anxiety attack drawing over him like a curtain. "Pull it together." Evan closed his eyes and prayed that he could just lose his memory. His brain felt stuck, like the accelerator of a race car. "Forget. Screw guilt. It's just a feeling."

Nathan's voice brought Evan fully back to the reality he had been trying to hide from. "Sleep OK? You look like a train wreck!

Stay behind; you and I will drive out together. Got stuff to chat about." Nathan smiled at Evan and patted his shoulder, as if they were best pals.

"Sure. Need to sleep for a few more weeks," Evan said.

The Dark Cloud team was to meet for the first time in nine months. Nathan had reason to be careful. One traitor could end all their lives.

"Don't trust any of these people," Evan muttered to himself.

Evan stood up slowly, stretched, and listened to the Mexican mercenaries discuss mundane things such as *futbol* and a variety of interests. They grabbed their assortment of backpacks and duffel bags and headed off the plane. Plastic cases and other equipment was off-loaded from underneath the plane and loaded onto trucks with the names of bogus companies. The mercenaries piled into any number of vehicles ranging from cars to SUVs. No one would notice any of them; Evan nodded approvingly. Staying hidden was the only way to stay alive.

Dark Cloud had about two hundred employees. Any one agent could spill enough information to expose and kill them all. Evan knew drug cartels would attack and obliterate police stations, army barracks, and any other target they felt threatened by. They would pay millions to political candidates and law-enforcement officials, who would turn a blind eye.

Evan had his own theory of why Mexico was a mess and, on a larger scale, why the whole world was screwed up.

"Sir, are you OK?"

Evan complained and sat up. "Got a migraine, that's all."

"I'll bring you a drink."

"Thanks, I appreciate that."

"The altitude, sir—it gives headaches."

"Reality and memories give me headaches."

Forty-five minutes later, Nathan and Evan parted ways from the flight crew and got into a heavy, bulletproof 80s-vintage Toyota Land Cruiser.

Evan placed his weapon on his lap. He had on a baseball hat and dark sunglasses. He put a dip in his mouth and got into business mode. "You got a serious group of operators here."

Evan watched two men open the hangar doors so they could drive out into Puebla, Mexico.

Evan waved at them, and they ignored him.

"You got no idea how corrupt it is here," Nathan began. "A few months ago, some American CIA operatives with diplomatic plates were sprayed with bullets from Mexican Federal Police. Still investigating that one. Do you remember seeing in the news about US consulate workers being chased down and shot? Gangsters don't care."

"Evil is man's only consistency," said Evan. "Same everywhere. In Afghanistan we train and give supplies to Afghan police who turn around and sell it to the Taliban."

"Mexico is not Afghanistan. It's wealthy, well educated, and one of the richest countries in the world, which makes this whole thing that much scarier," Nathan said flatly. "We are dealing with a culture, a religion, and a cult of the narco and a government that is impotent. This is a very different enemy, and one that no one wants to talk about. Ever see the American media do a three-week story on the drug cartels? No."

Evan agreed and said, "I know. Colombia was the big player back in the day. Course we haven't helped with our neat little drug-flying operations."

Nathan ignored Evan. He knew that Evan had worked undercover as a pilot. "Fuck Colombia. That was the '90s, Evan. Back then the Mexicans were a joke. They were players, sure, but now they are moving out, expanding. They call the shots. They aren't just a pass-through point like in the old days. Mexicans are in Colombia and half a dozen European countries. They have this country by the balls. The drug war was a joke."

Evan did not cover up his annoyance and replied, "And once again, Americans are devoid of all responsibility."

"What a way with words, Evan."

Evan shrugged. "What a way with life. Legalizing it ain't going to make organized crime vanish. No, they will just change tactics, diversify. I got my wife and child killed playing this game; lately it has been haunting me more and more, as if it happened yesterday."

"You need to talk with someone," Nathan said.

"Ha! Would love to—and do what? Cry? Hug? And then what?" Evan said.

"That's not what I mean." Nathan sounded annoyed.

"I liked the violence. I miss it. Some people deserved to get wasted; some did not." Evan rolled down the window, spat, and then rolled it back up.

Nathan gripped the steering wheel and checked his mirrors. He looked a little nervous and frowned. "You're not really all there, are you?"

"Maybe," Evan said, seriously considering the question.

"Look"—Nathan tried to sound as diplomatic as possible—"we got set up. There was a leak eighteen years ago, and that's what led to her death. The Colombians, for whatever reason, wanted to keep Pena, so they stashed him in jail."

"Their death was revenge for the Pablo mission," Evan said flatly.

"We all failed you." Nathan fidgeted and was both nervous and sincere.

"I lied to them and broke the rules by getting involved and marrying a local," Evan said flatly. "My arrogance and belief that nothing could happen to me led to their deaths."

"It was horrible, but it's past," Nathan said.

"Not to me. The older I get and the more free time I have, the more I think," Evan said.

"I need you to focus on this job, here and now. If you can't handle the speeding train that you are about to get on, tell me now," Nathan said.

"I can," said Evan.

"Kinda hard to do our job if we don't trust," replied Nathan.

Evan looked out the window.

Nathan changed the subject. "Some people said that when you left Colombia, you really did not leave."

"Uh-huh. People say all kinds of shit. Some people say that it was not the Colombians who betrayed my team's identity. It was political—it was someone on the inside," Evan said, staring at the growing urban area.

"Inside?" Nathan asked.

"American," Evan countered.

"Bullshit!" Nathan slowed down and honked the horn as they hit traffic.

"Whatever. I did leave Colombia, took my month leave, parted with family, and I have never looked back," Evan lied.

Nathan said, "And all of Andre Pena's adult children were executed, one by one. Crazy coincidence while he sat in prison helpless and got taunting letters."

"Life's cruel, huh?" Evan said.

Nathan grinned but was not being humorous. "Where did the agency send you after Colombia?"

"Eastern Europe mostly. I did enough damage in South America for a decade, I guess. Nine eleven happened, and then it was trolling for terrorist cells in Europe and Asia. Identifying networks; setting up sting operations; buying weapons, drugs, whatever. They are big drug users. Good revenue."

"And?" Nathan prodded.

Evan quipped, "And? You want my résumé? I retired before I could be fired, about three years ago. I am basically a has-been—what do you want?"

"I want you to be Ivan, sell the sub, get me close to Mario."

"OK." Evan shrugged as if Nathan was asking him to get a beer or something similar.

"I need your A-game, not your 'I feel sorry for myself' game," Nathan said.

Evan chuckled. "Nothing like some honesty."

"Shit is going to heat up!"

"Got it. Once we kill off these kingpin drug dealers and get our suitcase full of cash, then what?" Evan mused.

"Not our problem." Nathan chuckled.

"My ass," Evan said bluntly. "We create a void, and another cartel steps in. Most likely, whoever hired you is representing some other cartels!"

"The government hired us."

Evan laughed, cursed, and spat out the open window again. "Like I said, another cartel!"

"Let's talk about Ivan." Nathan changed direction again.

"OK. Talk." Evan pushed his baseball hat down low over his eyes and leaned back in the seat.

"His girlfriend doesn't know he is dead yet. You will have to work with her."

"A warning?"

"One of many. When we get to the Zoo, we will split up into teams and cells. The briefing process will be long and painful, but I need you to be locked on."

"You embarrassed of me or something?" Evan chuckled.

"Jesus. No. Well, I don't want to be…Some of the stuff you say," Nathan said.

Evan smiled. "Got it."

Evan played with the radio now and tried to find some decent music. "Fine, I can play Ivan. But I do it my way. If you are going to plagiarize one of my old missions, we may as well do it right."

Nathan nodded and agreed. "Fine, but his girlfriend, she is unstable."

"So am I. His girlfriend is just going to have to deal." Evan chuckled.

"OK." Nathan did not sound convinced.

"Uh-huh. Talk to me about Andre Pena." Evan changed the subject again.

Nathan nodded. "You are in no danger of being spotted by him. We believe the cartels bought his freedom. Americans, of course, found out after the fact. He is here, and we believe he is working with the Scorpions at one of their training facilities."

"Training facilities?"

"Hundreds of them. All of the cartels now have paramilitary assault groups. Soldiers defect from the Mexican army at about a hundred a month. Anyway, they train new recruits in explosives, hand-to-hand, and close-quarter battle. Used to be just Mexican special operators—now it's trained killers from all over South America. The Scorpions have a few European and Israeli guys. I will get into that later."

Evan nodded. "Pablo hired former SAS commandos and Israeli commandos to take out FARC guerillas. Paid professional soldiers."

"Some of the cartels have an army of about ten thousand. Evan, the words *criminal insurgency* are being whispered around the Pentagon, but it isn't politically correct."

"Of course not. Don't want to lose the Hispanic vote, especially if we ever had to help Mexico. No, this country is pretty much overrun."

"Some think it's heading our way, up north," Nathan said flatly.

"We can just give them back California and call it a day." Evan laughed.

"I can give you all the info on Andre when we do our brief."

"So, kinda weird that me, you, and Andre Pena are all in the same country again. Freaking coincidence," Evan said.

"Or Providence," Nathan snapped.

"That's what I am afraid of," Evan mused.

"We gonna stop for a little coffee in Puebla, talk, and then make it to the Zoo."

"You're the boss."

Nathan drove fast and aggressively, like a drug runner or a cop trying to get out of a bad neighborhood.

Traffic slowed as they approached Puebla. Neither man spoke during the twenty-minute drive into the city.

Evan stared out the window and let his mind once again drift into a tangent. *Nothing has changed.* He figured that the extreme poverty in some places was how class warfare, resentment, and the romantic idea of Marxism was used to attract people to the notion that they were being screwed and cheated and that some cosmic fairness could be achieved if they would just let some different dude run their life.

Evan thought about the irony. *In the end, nothing changes. Whether you call someone a king, president, dictator, furor, emperor, or boss, the willful are going to rule over the will-less.*

Evan watched the city around him. People were going about their lives just like anywhere else. He watched a pregnant teenager talking on a cell phone while pushing a baby stroller. A cop coming out of a store smiled. A line was forming at a corner taco stand, and Evan felt hungry.

"Ah, here it is." Nathan pulled right off the street into a parking space facing a Starbucks.

Evan shook his head. "Really? Starbucks? All the local culture around here, and you want a freaking Starbucks?"

Nathan laughed. "Intel pickup, my friend."

"Oh."

"Stay in the car. Watch my back."

"You got ten, and then I am coming in and getting my latte."

Nathan replied with exasperation, "Fine, Evan."

Evan sat in the passenger seat while the truck idled. He tuned in a Mexican weather station and looked around the strip mall. He spotted a Papa Johns, a Burger King, and a few other stores that he recognized.

"Amazing. Our contribution to the world. Lots of junk to buy. Or, hell, we'll give you Walmart and pizza; you sell us meth!"

Evan watched Nathan go to the bar and order a coffee. A very attractive woman in her thirties who had been reading a newspaper at a tiny round table approached Nathan and gave him a hug.

Evan smiled. "How sweet. Now hand off—oh, sloppy—just like a cop!" Evan watched her press a thumb drive attached to a key into Nathan's hand. "Mmm, is that a key to your apartment?" Evan strained to get a better look at her.

She wore a knee-length business skirt and a sleeveless, white blouse. Her arms were muscular and her calves firm.

"Fake boobs, aerobics queen, and, oh, married. Ha!" Evan shook his head. He noticed her wedding band as she rubbed Nathan's back with a slow methodic stroke that ended with an inappropriate squeeze. "Nathan, you are still a dog!" he accused.

Evan watched them talk for about five minutes while Nathan waited for his fancy drink to be made. Once Nathan got his drink, the two made their way outside and sat at a table, knee to knee, holding hands and chatting like two schoolgirls.

"That's my cue." Evan turned off the truck, tucked his weapon in his waistband, and pulled his sweatshirt over the grip. He put on his sunglasses and opened the door and held it for a group of young people. They smiled, and he smiled back.

What are you up to, Nathan? Evan mused as he got his tall latte with an extra shot. He placed a Splenda in it and watched the two lovers talk. Nathan was either really into her or he was pretending very well. They held hands and kissed, and then she got up, and they parted ways.

Both Nathan and Evan watched with great respect from two different vantage points as she made her way into the parking lot, got into an unmarked police car, and drove off.

The drive through Puebla out into the country was uneventful. Once they were clear of the city and on Mexico Highway 150D heading toward the distant, dormant volcano La Malinche, Nathan spoke.

Evan was so busy thinking about a plethora of things, from Mexican women to what kind of snow blower he should buy, that he did not realize Nathan was talking. "Sorry, Nathan, zoned out. What did you say?"

"I said she just gave me a two-gig thumb drive full of tasty information. She works for Mexico's elite drug task force. Most all of her colleagues work for various cartels."

"And?"

Nathan smiled. "I guess we will see."

"See?"

"Just more information on Mario and his hangouts."

Evan watched scrubland and flatness give way to hills and pine trees as they approached the mountain. "That your girlfriend?"

"No, no, just a friend," Nathan said.

"She looks friendly," Evan said.

"Her husband and two kids were tortured, drenched in gasoline, and burned alive because of her job. Happened five years ago."

"Shit!"

"She still wears her ring."

"That is horrible. Wow!"

"The guy you threw in the Dumpster, Gerard, he raped her first."

"Wow, I feel like crap now. I should have snapped his neck!" Evan said.

"You will have your chance at redemption. That's why my team is so pissed at you. They have history with that evil bastard. Tracking him for a while."

"Where is Mario?"

Nathan shrugged. "She says she has something big. Will have to see."

"I want to look. If I am going to be in on this, I need transparency."

"Fine, that's fair," Nathan conceded.

"Where are we?" Evan asked.

"This is the only town near the Zoo. It's San Francisco in the state of Tetlanohcan. We travel down the equivalent of a farm road, until it dead ends. The gravel road stretches to the right and left for miles and almost circles the whole volcano."

"Why did you name it the Zoo?" Evan asked.

"The owner used to have a mission outreach and petting zoo. He is old now and lives in Australia," Nathan answered.

"How fitting." Evan rolled down the window and hung his arm out.

"You know, Evan, the Tlaxcaltecas Indians were the only group to resist the Aztecs. They are a fierce, independent people."

Evan nodded in agreement. "Yes, and they originally aided Cortez. Didn't work out too well for 'em in the end."

"Oh, your negativity. Sometimes you sound like—"

"Someone who sees only the miserable side to people?" Evan finished.

"Yes!"

"There is a reason."

They were driving down the lonely farm road to where it branched into crushed gravel in either direction. The two divergent roads stretched and curved till they disappeared out of sight among the pine trees. Evan smiled at the majestic mountain in the distance.

"Nice, huh?" Nathan seemed proud of himself.

"Yeah."

Evan and Nathan drove off-road for about thirty meters into the woods. They drove on a trail covered with compacted bushes and grass. The trail began to turn into a narrow gravel road.

"See? This entrance is completely hidden from the road!"

They drove up to a tall, black iron gate that was framed by two large stone walls. A new chain link fence connected with the walls and stretched out into the woods, encompassing the estate. Evan was impressed by several pairs of deer antlers over the entrance.

Nathan rolled down his window and typed in a code on the keypad. "Security still has to clear us."

The two men waited in silence until three men in jeans and cowboy hats approached from within the compound. All three men were scruffy with large tattoos decorating their arms and necks. One of the gate guards had a shotgun, and the other two had AK-47s. Safer to look like a narco ranch than a bunch of clean-shaven military contractors.

The gate swung open, and the men waved politely.

"Hey, boss."

"*Hola.* The others arrive?"

"*Sí*, all is set."

"This is the newest member of our team: Ivan." Nathan pointed at Evan.

Evan returned the obligatory head nod.

Once they were cleared, Nathan drove through the gate.

"Welcome to the Zoo, your home for the next six weeks."

Part 2

CHAPTER 13

The Love Boat

Gulf of Mexico, Five Days Later

Ten miles off the coast of Veracruz, Mexico, sat a 198-foot yacht known simply as the *Happy Mermaid*. The megayacht had high sharp lines, dark windows, multiple decks, and a crane arm that hung off its stern like a massive lobster claw. From a distance, the yacht resembled a floating, futuristic resort. Brilliant eco-friendly glass, solar panels, and polished, shiny rails encircled the yacht. The massive yacht boasted its presence with a subtle message to other vessels: *I am bigger and more expensive than you—now move along!*

When this megayacht was released in 2008, it caused such jealously among the world's elite that a Russian billionaire commissioned a German company to make one even bigger. Mario promptly threatened to blow the Russian's yacht out of the water if it ever got to close to Mexico. This caused the Russian to install an antimissile defense system.

Mario leaned against the polished stainless-steel rail of the top deck and swirled his glass of Macallan fifty-year-old Scotch. At $10,000 a bottle, Mario savored every drop: the color, the aroma, and the smooth burn that oozed down his throat.

Ocean spray, sunlight, and the smell of oil caused him to close his eyes and breathe deeply. "Liquid art," Mario said, slurring his words.

The billionaire opened his eyes and looked at his guest, like a sleepy cat. A short, nervous bald man in an Italian suit sipped his Scotch and tried not to cough. He was not a drinker, and it was still morning.

"Sir, I...I—"

"Please, please, call me Mario."

"Yes, sir, um, Mario, I plead with you and hope that my question or request does not offend you."

Mario smiled and held up his hand.

The man finished his Scotch and gulped in fear. Mario's guest was an executive with Mexico's state-owned Petroleos Mexicanos, or PEMEX, a $415-billion-a-year business. PEMEX is the second-largest state-owned oil company in the world.

"Yes, I know what you want to ask, and the answer is yes."

"Oh, sir, thank you!"

Mario snapped his fingers and waited for Jorge Valdez, the head of his elite paramilitary group known as the Scorpions, to approach. Jorge was never far and leaned against the rail. He looked amused at the oil executive and then frowned with some pity.

"Jorge, put the word out. No one touches the pipelines in the gulf!"

"Yes, boss."

Mario continued. "One hundred million last year was lost to pirates, who illegally tapped and stole oil from your pipelines. No doubt gangs who are losing revenue, primarily because they are poor at smuggling."

"Anything else?" Jorge asked Mario, clearly bored.

Jorge never took his eyes off the oilman. Jorge did not need to disclose to Mario how he would handle it; this was his realm.

Typically, he would just grab some rival cartel members or street people, take them to a warehouse, video a confession, and then have their heads cut off. It was effective and worked. Jorge loved YouTube.

"Take him home. Use my helicopter. He can send my payment in the next few days."

"Boss, I have to take another passenger ashore, so that works fine."

Mario nodded. "Yes! The computer girl. I want to speak with her before she leaves. Get this prick out of my site, and send her in!"

The computer girl had a real name, and it was Tanya Mendes. She was cagey, grumpy, and made no attempt to be social or nice. Tanya was an agent with Dark Cloud and had effectively hacked the ship's computers under the guise of repairing them and creating a secure mainframe and network for Mario's organization. Tanya Mendes, whose real name had changed so many times that it was no longer of any consequence, was born to a Japanese father, who had been a computer-software designer, and Brazilian mother, who had been a linguistics professor. Tanya had inherited both the shrewd brains of her father and the distractingly good looks and language ability of her mother.

By age twenty-eight, Tanya was working for the Brazilian intelligence service Agência Brasileira de Inteligência, or ABIN.

Her ability to troubleshoot and manage computer systems had made her quite valuable in the technical division. Nothing had ever been ideal or great in Tanya's life, but she had managed to struggle through and carve out a niche for herself.

When her father was murdered quite randomly one day while crossing the street, she came completely unglued. A few short weeks after his death, her mother went into seclusion and committed suicide. Tanya had nothing left. Her life spiraled out of control. She had always lived with her parents, and although not superclose, they had been the foundation that had held her predictable world together.

The story of her father's death went as follows: He was crossing the street on his way home when he crossed in front of a large SUV belonging to a Brazilian drug kingpin, whose name was now irrelevant in her mind. Tanya always forgot their names after she killed them. The kingpin's sixteen-year-old girlfriend, who had just finished snorting a few lines of cocaine and performing a sex act, asked quite whimsically, "Honey, if you want me to do that again, kill that man right there."

"That one?"

Tanya's father was shot in the head and then run over by a fifty-three-year-old man on a dare from a teenager.

Tanya cupped her hands over her head and breathed deeply. She shut out the years following her revenge and the new career that she had stumbled into. She had changed her name and country about ten times. She was now Tanya Mendes and was on a mission to cripple organized crime where it hurt most—not by killing the members; no, that was like killing roaches. They just came back. She destroyed them from within, financially.

Tanya was not *playing* a loaner; she was one. She preferred computers to people. Ones and zeros to conversation. She had designed and downloaded perhaps the most sophisticated virus she had ever made to date. The only ingredient left in her scheme was to hook up the ship's computers to the Eastern Cartel's network. A stolen satellite dish from a warehouse in Veracruz had halted her plan.

Tanya sat with her backpack in her lap and sipped coffee. It was midmorning, and she knew Mario was having his breakfast Scotch with an oil executive. She looked out at the sea and thought about her computer virus that she dubbed Centipede.

The virus, if infiltrated, would grow over the next few weeks and provide her with piles of data, passwords, account numbers, and virtually any piece of transmitted information, to include tapped cell phone conversations. Tanya had modeled her virus after the Flame virus, which was written by the CIA and Israel to infiltrate Iran's nuclear program.

Tanya still had fears that the program would be discovered.

"Computer girl!"

She was dozing when a gravelly voice barked her name.

"What?" She stood up and tried not to sound scared. "Time to go?"

"In a minute. Boss man wants to speak with you first."

"Um, OK. We taking the helicopter or boat?"

"Bird."

Tanya felt flushed, and her stomach tightened. She hated to fly, and she hated the water. Flying over water was the worst of both worlds.

"Shit!" Tanya stared defiantly at Jorge.

She disliked most people. In her mind, she would assign people an animal identity. Only a select few were privy to this information. Tanya had chosen a great white to describe Jorge. He had pointy, sharp teeth, a pinched face, and beady, brown eyes. His grin was never happy and was almost cannibalistic. He terrified her, and she loathed him. A tall man stood next to the solid, short Jorge and regarded her as a crow might look at a bread crumb. She bit her lip. This man's face looked badly beaten; his arm was in a sling, and by the wire holding his sneering grin together, she could tell his jaw was broken.

"Get the number of the garbage truck that ran over you?" Tanya blurted before she could stop her self. She had a nasty habit of speaking words as they popped into her head, which had cast her as rude and blunt.

The man sneered and tried to say something.

"This man is Gerard. He is my assistant."

She shrugged and tried to cover up her comment. "Hope you feel better," she said.

Tanya walked past the two men with her backpack. She knew playing scared would cause these men to prey on her. She preferred to be hated; they stayed away.

"Mario is that way!" Jorge pointed up a flight of steps, and she went up two at a time.

Tanya made it to the top deck and steadied herself as the yacht pitched and moved. She watched Jorge the Shark and the tall, thin, broken man with prison tattoos climb the stairs behind her.

Frenchman, huh? Tanya thought. *You look like a tattooed rat or a buzzard, tall and lanky. No, you are dubbed the Flying Rat.*

Tanya watched Mario approach. He seemed to be in a great mood this morning. Tanya hated mornings.

"Still a little seasick, my dear?" asked Mario.

Tanya nodded and backed away from the railing. The salt spray stung her eyes, and the rising sun made her squint. She could not stand sun in her eyes. "Don't like boats or water."

Mario walked onto the deck and greeted Tanya with a hug.

"How long to fix the computers?" Mario asked with a kind smile.

"Once the satellite is here, no time. My team, I need my team to work for a day or so, and then we need to work at your headquarters."

Mario laughed. "This is my new headquarters. I want a mobile business, and I want to run it anywhere."

Mario held up his hands. "Not a computer person—just make my business run. In six weeks I am having a birthday party. I am buying a new and very big toy! My sons will be there. I want you around for my birthday party."

"Happy birthday, sir. You know I don't do parties." Tanya stared at the deck of the yacht.

Mario ignored her. "My sons, they handle the books, the logistics. You must speak with them and their tech staff."

"Be glad too, sir," she lied.

"Will you be back by then?" Mario looked concerned.

"Yes, sir."

"The police, the government, they have been cracking our systems. We are too old fashioned. My payoffs to the governments on both sides of the border are eating into my profits, gas prices, planes, ships, unions. And with the economic uncertainty with that socialist up north, people aren't buying as much."

"Efficiency can save money, sir. Your business is like a bucket with so many holes."

"Smart girl. All of Mexico wants a piece of my pie! My sons, they say, 'Father, you must catch up with the times.' Ha! Back in my day, all you needed was this!"

Mario pulled a gold-plated Desert Eagle .44 out of a custom-leather holster on his hip. The grip was a beautiful blue polymer of some kind with a picture of a nude Mexican girl. She admired the holster too, which Mario had made with his own hands. He was obsessed with the old macho days of the cowboy and the age of the classic smuggler—he thought he was the reincarnation of Jesús Malverde.

Tanya hated guns but was always intrigued by the artwork and design of Mario's latest toys. He seemed to have an endless supply of such custom weapons.

"Both of my sons have their MBAs. They have men working for them with PhDs in economics, science, engineering, blah, blah. Me, my dear? A sixth-grade education."

"And you're the boss, sir. Education ruins a good mind."

Mario smiled and winked. "I like you, computer girl. You are bold—odd but bold."

"Say what I see, sir."

"Help them make my empire secure so I have something to leave for my family. These idiots are robbing me blind!" Mario put his hand on the railing and stared out at the ocean.

"No problem."

"I am buying a submarine." Mario smiled. He gripped the rail with both hands. He had tossed the empty glass overboard like he did every morning.

"Sub?"

"You will be here for the party. I want you to install computer-tracking systems on it."

"Yes, sir, but you know I hate—"

Mario raised his hand and waved it in the air, "Yes, yes, computer chica, you hate people, waves, boats, helicopters, the sun, and I am not surprised to hear that you hate subs."

Mario seemed charming for a second and smiled at her, like an old uncle who knew much more than he let on.

Tanya allowed herself a shy smile and brushed a wild hair away from her face. She looked at the sky and then looked away, embarrassed.

"Ah, there is someone in there! You are a pretty girl, computer girl. A smile like that, and you hide it! Rough, but there is a beautiful girl in there. You come to the party. I want people to see the smile. I want to see you happy, even if it's for a second and no one is looking, ha!"

"I will be there and will only step on that floating deathtrap if you go first!"

"Deal!"

"I must go, sir."

"Yes! Yes! I have a meeting in the mountains today with some government official, some mayor—more handouts, more payoffs! If only I could deport all these deadbeats to North America!"

Mario clapped his hands and raised his voice. "Jorge! Get my computer girl to shore. Anything happens to her, I will see bodies blowtorched!"

"Yes, boss!"

Tanya let Mario see a smile again, quite by accident, but this time she felt no guilt. Even if it was a killer sticking up for her, it did feel nice to be treated special.

CHAPTER 14

Dope and Change

Veracruz, Mexico, Two Days Later

Jorge Valdez loved the morning. He leaned on the railing of his balcony and gazed out at the Gulf of Mexico. A slight breeze was stirring as the first traces of color and light began to illuminate the horizon. He closed his eyes and took in the faint salt and oil smells of the gulf.

"How many fisherman and smugglers are out there right now?"

He heard the annoying laughter of sea gulls. The city was still asleep, and for an instant, Jorge felt almost peaceful. As soon as he realized he was calm, the acidic tension returned to his jaw and shoulders.

"Why do I feel guilty? Certainly all great leaders have felt uncertain. But betrayal is yet another thing."

From his penthouse in Veracruz, he had a great view of the seawall and port. Comacho Avenue snaked for miles along the crowded beachfront.

Jorge knew change was inevitable, just like hotels, strip clubs, and North American chain stores. He had seen the improvement from millions of invested dollars into the surrounding communities.

"Veracruz has grown up, changed, and so have I!" He spoke to himself and spat over his balcony. Jorge decided to say what was on his mind out loud. He had to hear the words. He had to believe them in order to make it real. He massaged his face with both hands and inhaled deeply for a moment. "Mario must die."

He looked out at the ocean and knew that on an emotional level he felt guilt. He owed everything to Mario, but on an intellectual level, a survival level, Mario was a relic. In Mario's day you did not ship one hundred tons of mota in a shipment, and you did not own cargo ships, planes, front companies, lobbyists, or fake organizations that preached open borders for the people so you could move your product. Mario did not understand the big picture of an increasingly global world of geopolitics and economics. No, Mario still thought it was the old days of killing and making payoffs to ship products. Turf wars, technology, media, marketing—it had all changed, and Mario had not. Jorge set his jaw and said it again: "Mario must die!"

He saw himself as a visionary, a revolutionary, and not unlike great men who had come before him in history. Men who had changed everything. Jorge was about to change everything, but not out of some lofty ideology, politics, or self-anointed greatness. No, he was a realist. Jorge would let his followers be the ideologists, the believers, the dumb wind-up toys that would do his bidding.

No, Jorge was far more practical. "I want to be Caesar!"

Jorge's vision was to develop a union of cartels. This union would share profits, combine recourses, capitalize on regional assets, and divide the country up into boundaries. The turf wars were ultimately bad for business and had claimed far too many lives, lives that could be spending money.

The "United Cartels" would exercise tremendous political and financial power to accomplish three things. First, they would back politicians who would bring their business out of the shadows to legitimize the selling, manufacture, and distribution of their product.

Emotional media campaigns had been running in the smaller outlying radio markets and newspapers, showing how drug violence was caused by its illegal status. False stories aired of mothers turning to the cartels to avenge the deaths of their sons, who had been wrongfully killed by military or counternarcotics police.

"If corn were illegal, people would kill to buy or sell that too!"

Jorge, of course, had no connections on paper to any of these groups. If Mario found out, his head would be on a stick. Outside the borders, Jorge had already secretly funneled millions into front groups in the States that advocated for legalization and open borders; this would pave the way for the legal shipments of his product. It may take years to break through with mota, but eventually it would pave the way for bigger cash crops, like cocaine and designer drugs. Locally, Jorge had spent millions giving clothes, books, and computers to school children. He had even followed the example of Pablo Escobar by building apartment buildings and a soccer stadium. Some cartels offered dental plans to workers and free housing for families. Jorge knew the details would take years to iron out, and like all revolutions, there would be blood and pain.

The dumb masses were always the easiest to persuade. The bread-and-circus concept had worked in ancient Rome, and it still worked today.

Second was the most difficult: Jorge had to persuade the other cartels to stop the turf wars, the killing, and begin protecting the people, even if it was a facade. He called this the Robin Hood phase. The cartels would appear to be the protectors of the people and portray the police as incompetent. Jorge had already seen this happen in several regions where kidnappers or rapists were released from the police and then snatched by gang members, publicly tried, and executed.

Jorge felt the stab again. Five of the eight cartels had agreed to his plan, and they all had the same demand: "Mario must die, and then we are in."

The third phase would be to isolate and destroy all opposing politicians and critics and to silence the media. He was not interested in ruling the government or making laws. He just figured an impotent puppet who refused to harass his business partners would create a more peaceful society and ultimately lower costs.

Jorge's plans may take years to cultivate, and he may not even live to see the final product, but his legacy as a good farmer would bear fruit.

First, he would honor his cartel relationships by killing Mario. The next round of assassinations would be much more grand and could possibly start a war if not handled properly.

Jorge had hired Andre Pena, a Colombian explosives expert, for this purpose. When the bombs had done their work, Jorge would announce that they were the work of Mario and that he, Jorge Valdez, would put an end to the violence once and for all.

"Mexico needs to be fundamentally changed, our children need to be safe and free to pursue their passions, enjoy their rights, blah, blah…"

Jorge smiled at the bullshit that could be shoveled down the dumb masses' throats. "Power to the people," and all that garbage.

The media would report it, or else.

The politicians and generals would agree, or else.

"Caesar." Jorge laughed.

The Mind of Jorge Valdez

Oaxaca one of the most biologically diverse states in Mexico. Four million people spread out over 36,214 square miles. Oaxaca is located on the Pacific and southwest side of the country—warm and tropical along the majestic coast where cliffs drop off suddenly into the sea. The interior of the state rises up with green and rocky cliffs with steep valleys. Agave for mescal, mangoes, coffee, and bananas are the main agricultural crops. The Zapotecs are the most numerous of the indigenous Indian tribes.

Jorge was half Zapotec. He grew up surrounded by a strong, closely knit family on one of the larger estates in the countryside. His grandfather, father, and all six of his brothers and two sisters were fiercely loyal to the family business. In the 1940s, his grandfather started growing and harvesting agave, which he used to produce several different types of mescal. Over the decades, the small operation turned into a lucrative estate with its own internationally distributed label. The distillery, shipping, and distribution had been a family affair, and all hands were involved. The company had modernized with the times. He had cousins and sisters who did the marketing, website design, advertising, and sales. His brothers and he managed the fields and day-to-day operations. Jorge had a head for numbers. He could motivate workers, settle disputes, and get things done when others were ready to throw in the towel. Jorge's early life as a member of a family-run business would later come in very handy when he met another man whose father had a much more lucrative family-run business.

When Jorge met Mario, everything changed.

Jorge left home for Mexico City at age twenty-one to enroll in college as a political science and history major. His parents figured he would get this need to be educated out of his system and then come back to the estate. No one could imagine the cascade of events that was to happen and the bizarre 360 that Jorge would take in his life.

After college, Jorge became an officer in the Mexican army. After a few years, he tried out for the elite Air Mobility Command, where once again his natural leadership style and no-nonsense way of getting people to comply accelerated his career. He was not obsessed with status or rank, just leading and being the best. He chased left-wing guerillas through the jungle and did battle with the narcos who were splitting Mexico apart. He did not consider himself a crusader but a staunch Mexican Nationalist. He loathed politicians and had some sympathy for dissidents and the underdog. He hated Marxists. Jorge cross-trained with US Special Forces and made a name for himself as a hardened leader. When Jorge turned forty, the political winds began to change. Army officers began to get hung out to dry by a new administration for abuses and various crimes that were at one time overlooked by the government. Such crimes included killing and torturing communist revolutionaries, narcos, and anyone else deemed an enemy of the state.

Jorge had three significant life-changing events during that year that would give him a complete paradigm shift. The first was when he was introduced to Mario by a retired fellow operator who was now leading a security firm. He was amazed at how open his friend was about his criminal activities, as if it was normal and perfectly OK. Jorge had spent months hunting for narco kingpins based on DEA and government intel. He had sent his men on multiple dead-end missions where they marched and hacked their way through the highlands of Sinaloa, taking out labs and doing snatch-and-grab operations.

In hindsight, Jorge realized he was being vetted for recruitment. He never told his superiors or anyone that he had met Mario, one of the most wanted men in Mexico. On his second meeting with Mario, his entire world was turned upside down. He accompanied his retired friend and Mario to a multimillion-dollar mansion high up in the beautiful hills of Sierra Madre. A swimming pool, a driving range, and even a private landing strip were carved into the hillside. Jorge was entertained by American and European hookers who made more in a weekend on their backs than he made in a year. He was amazed at the openness and decadence at Mario's parties. By the end of the night, when Jorge was exhausted by alcohol and the youth of the exotic call girls, he mustered the courage to speak with Mario.

"How do you do it? How do you evade detection? I have teams of men who fly around looking for you guys. But here you are. No one could miss this palace!" Jorge did not bother to contain his amazement.

"My friend, when the Mexican military or government gets a little pressure from the gringos at the DEA, they tell me. I donate one or two acres, or maybe even a shipment, and sometimes I give them rivals." Mario laughed and grabbed Jorge like a brother and spoke close to his face. Tequila and cigar smoke lingered on his breath.

"My friend, listen to me. This is a big game we play. We pay money to the politicians to sell a product that everyone in America wants. As long as the product goes north and the money flows south, they stay off our backs. You want to catch the organized criminals, you turn your guns on the politicians! Ha! We have been farming for generations; they made it illegal, *not* us!" Mario smiled and wobbled a little in his chair.

"You work for me, and you will see how the real world works. My father, he tells me stories of how the American government could not buy enough heroin from us at the beginning of World War II. We helped the war effort, ha! They treat us farmers as criminals, and they use men like you as chess pieces."

Mario had a unique way of smiling that made people feel as if they were having their minds read.

"You and me, we both come from farming families. You know how to work for a living. Politicians, they produce nothing! You have my respect, and if you need something, you call!"

Jorge never forgot their conversation and became more disillusioned by the month as he saw politicians and police take credit

SILVER, LEAD, AND DEAD

for drug busts and then show up at rival narco parties to get blow jobs by teenage prostitutes. *Norteamericano* drug-war money kept pouring in. Sometimes equipment, like body armor, night-vision goggles, and weapons would "accidentally" get lost and end up in the hands of el narco.

Then one day, Jorge's father and sister were kidnapped. His family refused to contact the police at first and paid ransom three times. The kidnappers broke contact and were not heard from again. The payoffs were bankrupting the business. The police were backlogged and did not want to pursue it beyond three weeks. Jorge gave up hope when his father's finger and sister's bloody underwear were delivered with a fourth ransom note. Jorge remembered the day when he finally crossed the line and reached out to Mario. He was cynical enough and had experienced enough to believe that the police were somehow involved.

What do you do? Accuse them and ask for their help? Jorge had thought.

Jorge recalled the response that his retired friend had given him a few days later over the phone. "Take leave for a few weeks. Stay close to home, and stay in touch with the police. Do not let any family member leave the ranch, and, my friend, arm everyone. Keep the guns hidden but nearby."

Jorge knew as a soldier that something was going down. He carried on as close to normal as he could. He kept his weapons handy and hidden. He secretly made an escape plan for himself and the family.

Then things got weird.

The media reported the discovery of the torsos of local police officers and possible criminals dumped in public places: parking lots, police stations, banks. Some type of cartel turf war was suspected. One morning, the heads of three well-known criminals were tossed through the window of a house belonging to the chief of police's mistress. The heads had been melted with acid. Jorge's case was suddenly a priority.

Jorge's family members were returned. Mario paid for them to be treated in a private hospital in Mexico City while the dust settled in Oaxaca. Jorge watched in amazement over the next few weeks as the newspapers began publishing anonymous articles about police corruption and gang activity. Police chiefs resigned, officers went to jail, and politicians fled the country.

Mario had sent Jorge a very strong message: "No one messes with me. Join me and see how the real world works!"

CHAPTER 15

Operation Crazy Ivan

Six Weeks Later

The Isla de la Juventud, or Island of Youth, is Cuba's second-largest island. The 850-square-mile island sits south of Cuba and closer to Mexico. Relatively undeveloped, it's surrounded by beautiful white sandy beaches, emerald-green waters, and brilliant coral reefs. The island's claim to fame was as a notorious prison.

Evan had seen the prison in person as part of a tour many years ago under a different passport. It reminded Evan of a bird cage. Presidio Modelo once housed Fidel and his brother. Once Castro seized power from the dictator before him, he began stocking the prison with his own enemies, many of whom had financed his revolution.

"What comes around goes around."

Evan wondered if the morons in the States who were funding its destruction would ever end up in a similar prison. *Probably not. Just get a reality show*. He frowned and then refocused himself before a tangent over took him.

Evan watched the waves and thought back to the last six weeks at the Zoo. Evan and Roger had dubbed Nathan the Zookeeper because, as Roger so eloquently put it one night over a few beers, "The man can shovel shit like the best of 'em."

Evan liked Roger from the beginning. He was a stand-up guy, a warrior, and always had an angle to get a great meal. Priorities were in the right place.

Evan had confided in Roger that he had known Nathan from the past and, without getting into specifics, partially blamed him for the death of someone close.

Six weeks at the Zoo had reminded Evan of an all-star team of musicians getting together for the show of their lives. Dark Cloud was made up of some of Mexico's top intelligence officers, special-operations instructors, shooters, gadget men, and private-sector engineers. Evan participated in the breaking-in period of all day and night ruck marches, obstacle courses, range time, and flying time. Dark Cloud had several aircraft on loan to them from various businessmen around Mexico, including a Black Hawk helicopter. Everyone, no matter what his or her job, had to feel some pain and sweat.

Nathan turned over the training schedule to a Mexican who went by the name of the Shot Glass, presumably because of some sordid story from his past. He was blunt, fair, and had a nasty scar down his face, which Evan admired.

"I know you bastards have already proved yourselves, or you would not be here. We have all been working for the last year but most of us never together. Pain, misery, starvation—that is the glue that will bind us! So today, you are all back in basic training and will be treated like prisoners. The cartels will not be so nice."

He was ruthless and unforgiving and did his best to get the team to solidify like concrete. It worked.

None of the 150 men and women of Dark Cloud needed to be taught *how* to do their job; they just needed to be reassured that they could rely on the man or woman next to them if they had to be switched out.

"Each tool in the toolbox needs to be identified. The best tools for each job will get used. Nothing personal. Deal with it!"

Shot Glass had said flatly as men panted, sweated, threw up, and cursed.

Evan was just pleased he could keep up with those who were fifteen years younger than he was. He knew he was being watched. He made sure no one was watching when he popped his Motrin and cursed his aches.

Dark Cloud was split up into Green Team One and Green Team Two. The two teams of direct-action operators were each subdivided into three fifteen-man squads called Alpha, Bravo, and Charlie. Each team was autonomous in the respect that they gathered intelligence, did surveillance, and took part in mission planning and executing based on direction from the Brain, or command group. Evan admired the simplicity and bare-bones essentials of how things would operate. No politics, no red tape, no one creating some worthless job or procedure so he or she could look good on paper or justify a meaningless existence.

There was no deadweight or petty pissing matches. Get in, get out, and stay alive to get paid. Both Green Team One and Two had ninety soldiers, most of whom had formed their cliques and habits from prior military service together. Most of them had been operating with Dark Cloud over the last year. The largest group of Dark Cloud personnel were behind-the-scenes people, the get-it-done men and women: logistics, safe-house procurement, getaway cars, transportation, money, weaponsmiths, pilots, computer and surveillance techs. Most of these men and women were technical people who had regular day jobs in law enforcement or intelligence and merely subcontracted in secret to Dark Cloud. These assists were spread out over key geographical areas around Mexico. Only a few of them were at the Zoo.

Nathan had created a small-scale, private-sector assassination squad. Nathan's intelligence network was quite vast too. He had secret sources in all branches of the military and law enforcement. Every person on the team knew that one betrayal could bring down the whole house of cards. Nathan never shared where the money came from or who the highest accountable person in government was.

Evan was one of the spies, or talent, in Green Team One, which was now going to be commanded by Roger since the previous commander had died in a helicopter crash. Evan had overheard some slight grumblings when Nathan announced Roger as being the commander.

Much of the grumblings had come from Roger himself. "I don't know the language, politics, or culture as well as these men. One of them should lead."

The other squad leaders had initially been resentful and had their doubts, but things were worked out. Roger had served a career with the British SAS, which demanded serious street cred.

Roger was also very down-to-earth and did not pull any punches. "Look, men. This is yur show. You run yur squads however ye want. I will handle heat from above and get everything we need to survive and manage. You know this land better than me. It's yur freakin' fight. Just don't play games."

From that moment forward, Roger was welcomed as one of their brothers. He could also cook better than anyone in all of Dark Cloud. Warriors had to eat. They did what he said, and it all worked out. Alpha Squad was commanded by El Coyote, or Daniel, Bravo Squad was commanded by Joaquin, and Charlie by Luis.

The team's nickname was the Chupacabras. Green Team One's area of operations consisted of the gulf regions from Coahuila to Quintara Roo. Evan was impressed to learn that Green Team One had spent several months last year creating a network of small, self-sufficient bands of vigilantes. These vigilantes would rally and protect each other's farms and properties from cartel members and from the roving bands of men who would kidnap girls as young as nine and sell them into the sex trade.

"Our little monster we created is now growing on its own across Mexico!" El Coyote had explained to Evan and Roger over a case of beer. "We have empowered and armed civilians to form their own cells. They attack cartel convoys and publicly hang bands of men who used to steal their wives and children. It is not without cost, but they are a thorn in the sides of the cartels out where the police refuse to go!"

Green Team Two was led by Oscar, a quiet, unassuming man who was half German. He was proud to admit that it was a German, whom he was related to way far back, who had emigrated to Mexico in the 1800s and started a brewery that now sold one of Mexico's finest beers.

He was hands down the best sniper out of anyone in Dark Cloud. He had competed in international special-forces competitions and had an impressive number of kills. Green Team Two's squad leaders were Pablo, Alpha Squad; Juan, Bravo Squad; and Gustavo, Charlie Squad. Gustavo was obsessed with the game Call of Duty.

Green Team Two's area of operations was predominately the Pacific side. They conducted operations from Sinaloa to Chiapas, which was a region so dangerous that the Mexican army rarely ventured there. Green Team Two had some fairly impressive success with creating vigilante cells as well. Last spring, one of their cells disrupted a train owned by a group that was transporting young immigrant women kidnapped en route from El Salvador. Evan was not shocked to hear that the young girls would work as slaves in the field harvesting crops during the week and then work as prostitutes at bars for the field hands on the weekends. The girls were branded like cattle with a hot poker.

"Evil," Evan said.

The vigilante cells created by the teams had helped form a generous network of both intelligence-gathering and direct-action assets to conduct clandestine missions in hostile territory. The vigilantes had no clue what Dark Cloud's greater agenda was nor did they care. They got their money, supplies, and training. Everyone was happy.

Reo was Nathan's right-hand man and man servant, as Evan called him. He reminded Evan of a termite with glasses and legs. At five feet one, he had an air about him that left you feeling as if you were shorter than he was.

"I have never been looked down upon by such a lil' fella," Roger had grumbled after their first meeting.

Reo was extremely smart, well connected with the Mexican establishment, and reminded Evan of the sniveling little snarky lawyers that he had always wanted to choke to death when he was standing in line at Trader Joe's in Virginia.

Then there was Tanya.

Evan had met Tanya just prior to her going back on board Mario's yacht. His impression of her was mixed. She was strikingly inelegant yet beautiful. She had the hard body of a CrossFitter with the attitude of a female parolee. She regarded Evan as a caveman and was visibly angry that he was acting as her former boyfriend's replacement.

Evan was introduced to her under his cover name of Ivan the Cuban-born half-Russian citizen. He was to work with her undercover to seal the submarine deal dubbed Operation Crazy Ivan. Tanya had successfully planted a computer virus within Mario's computers and had a position as his lead IT person. She explained that Mario's organization was mixed about buying the submarine.

"His sons, who are *all* named Mario by the way, and Jorge, his head of security, are dead against it. They say it will draw attention," Tanya had said flatly.

She was a mix of Japanese and Brazilian, which afforded her a luxurious blend of features. She was hard when engaged with people and looked vulnerable and aloof when no one was watching.

"Mario will have his screeners meet you a minimum of three times before you are allowed to meet him. He has perhaps fifteen or so doubles that he uses as surrogates at times. I will tell you how to spot the real Mario."

"How do you know that you are dealing with the real one?"

"That's my job," she had said flatly.

"So you don't know?" Evan had pressed. He refused to walk on eggshells around her like everyone else did. "There has not been a picture of Mario since he strolled out of a maximum-security prison ten years ago," Evan finished.

"Play the game," she had countered coldly. "I will be given your picture and fingerprints and will be assigned to look you up. It's SOP." Tanya handed Evan a thumb drive on a black nylon necklace. "Don't lose it."

"What is it?"

"Everything you need to know about the sub—specs, history."

"Basically it's an ad?"

Tanya looked past him as if she were talking to a wall. Evan started to wonder if she were on some kind of medication; her eyes did not look right.

"Yes. You can look at it, but do *not* download it. That will activate what's hidden inside. Encourage the bad guys to download it onto their own computers. Get it?"

Evan took the thumb drive and put it around his neck. He regarded Tanya and Reo. *Where the hell did you find these two, Nathan?* he mused to himself.

"Your last screening will be on the yacht, with Jorge. That's a problem. He is a mystery, even to me."

Evan recalled the details of the rest of their conversation. Tanya may have been a cold fish, but she was excellent at recalling and relaying details. She filled in information about Mario's superyacht, his staff, the key players among the Scorpions, and where the ship's heavy weapons were. Sources had indicated that the *Happy Mermaid* had antiaircraft capabilities. Part of his job was to confirm the ship's defenses. Tanya knew nothing about guns, so she was little help. Evan thought back to the conversation several days earlier and put the pieces together in his mind. He spoke quietly to the waves and wondered what was beneath the surface in Mario's world.

"If the *Happy Mermaid* has the firepower, they say an assault on the open sea will be nearly impossible and suicidal. Then there is the politics of the deal; Mario's sons do not want to buy the sub, yet their father does. Is there resentment? Is there division? If she can figure it out, more is beneath the surface. The sons are heir to the throne. Why not take father out and have the empire for themselves?"

Evan saw the lights from another boat off in the distance. He continued speaking out loud to himself.

"Then there is Jorge Valdez, the ever-paranoid security chief and head of the paramilitary army for Mario's cartel. Mario would rely on him to sniff out any fissures, unless he himself is more like a shark and smells blood in the water. He may just kill them all and take over himself...How loyal is he?"

Evan knew from intelligence reports that Jorge Valdez was ruthless, ambitious, and formally educated on military doctrine. He was no doubt smarter than Mario and his sons. Would Jorge Valdez ever turn against Mario? "I have to figure all this out," Evan said to the wind and waves. The last several weeks had been a blur, and now here he was, alone, talking to the sea.

Evan spat over the side of the rusty 133-foot Mexican salvage vessel and sipped a cup of burnt black coffee. The boat moved up and down, gently spraying white foam into the wind. The ship had a diesel-and-oil smell that reminded Evan of a gas station.

The time was 0312, and Evan knew they would soon be at their lonely grid coordinate in the middle of the dark gulf. The distance from the port at Cancun to their GPS point was 220 miles. This watery marker was still twenty miles off the coast of the Island of Youth and was well outside the interest of the US Navy, Cubans, and US Coast Guard. Evan had been assured that their cover story as a salvage vessel would hold water, so to speak, from any prying eyes. Evan shivered from the wind and spray of the gulf and thought about the irony of what he was doing. He finished his coffee, packed another dip inside his lip, and leaned over the rail again. He wished he had brought a fishing rod.

"Why do things seem to move in cycles? History, mistakes, and bad dreams?"

"Talkin' to yourself, lad?"

"Hey!" Evan jumped. "Wow! You snuck up on me."

Roger leaned against the rail next to him and stared out at the gulf. The constantly shifting waters were illuminated by a half-moon, which was tracking across a cloudless sky.

"Have you slept at all since we left, lad?"

"No. Too much on my mind," Evan said.

"Sorry to hear that," Roger replied.

Evan chuckled. "My mind is too active to sleep—like these waves, always churning. Just feeling nostalgic, I guess, or maybe a bit moody. We are all going to die doing this job."

"Well, lad, you're a bit of an optimist, aren't you?"

Evan shrugged and did not answer.

"Why you here, Evan?"

Evan deflected and spoke to the waves. "You know, in October 1962 during the whole Cuban-missile-crisis thing, there was a Soviet submarine, a Foxtrot class B-59. The subs were escorting shipments of supplies to Cuba when they were intercepted by the US Navy."

"And?"

"Well, two of the commanders on that sub wanted to launch a nuke at the United States, thinking that the war had started... One disagreed and averted a nuclear war."

"Thanks for the history lesson. Why a sub?" Roger asked.

Evan smiled, shrugged again, and then carefully answered. "He wants a bigger toy. Economic standpoint. You're right—it's stupid. The sub makes one voyage and probably gets impounded. On the other hand, he can deliver ten times the product in one shipment as a disposable sub and make up the cost of buying it twice in one load. Only problem is, the US Navy and the US Coast Guard will spot that thing first time it gets anywhere close to the coast. He should know this. The Gulf of Mexico is the most monitored body of water anywhere."

"Disposable sub? What are ye talkin' about?" Roger asked.

Evan rubbed his jaw and stared off into the distance as if he were reading something in the waves. "Bear with me. The sub Mario is buying is a vastly upgraded version of a Foxtrot-class submarine, it was registered as a B-36 and in 1993 was supposedly sold for scrap. Well, it wasn't. The Soviets frequently sold off their old inventory and created a paper trail to cover it up. This made American snoopers feel better. The now-dead Ivan worked with me to bribe politicians and government types to let us take it off their hands. That's all I can get into. I got a history with the late Ivan. Trust me—he's better off now than if I were to get ahold of him...But I digress. This old hunk officially can reach about sixteen knots on the surface and fifteen below. With the upgrades and modernization, it can reach about twenty-two knots with your fingers crossed. We could get from Cancun to Florida, which is roughly four hundred miles, in less than twenty-four hours. Of course, logistically you would have to unload your supplies at sea into some speedboats and pray you could do it before the US Coast Guard blasts you. This sub is huge, Roger, two hundred ninety-four feet long—almost as big as Mario's yacht. It's great bait for an egomaniac. Now the disposable narco subs that have been growing in popularity over the past decade or so are made of wood and fiberglass, are about ninety feet long, and can't dive like a real sub. They hang just under the surface, which makes them hard to spot…Only problem is, the navy is making their detection devices more sensitive, which does not help the Foxtrot. It may do OK diving deep, but when that thing surfaces"—Evan laughed and spat—"you will see the coast guard and navy freak. Now, the advantage of a narco sub is that you use it, off-load near your target, and then sink it. They are cheap to build and carry four to twelve metric tons of cocaine. Of course, the big drawback is that same four hundred miles takes sixty-six hours. The upgraded Foxtrot could off-load about three times that."

"Wow. How would they off-load?" Roger asked.

"Launch it through the torpedo tubes attached to rubber boats or floatable containers. Attach the cargo to the sides, and release it beneath the surface. You have to have a well-coordinated pickup operation. Surfacing the sub is a no-go."

"Unreal. Who makes these narco disposable subs?" Roger asked, fascinated.

"Colombia, Brazil, Ecuador. They estimate that about thirty percent of the drug flow comes from subs. They make them in the jungle, and some have gone as far as Spain and Italy. It's business innovation—love the free market."

Roger laughed and pointed at Evan. "You need some new hobbies, son, like cooking, chasing women."

"True. Don't judge."

"You hungry?"

"Born hungry."

Veracruz, Mexico, Three Days Earlier

Evan inspected the bottle of water carefully, opened it, and took a drink. He had little trouble relaxing, given his circumstances.

He stared at the blue oval pool and out at the beach where it met the gulf. The smell of salt and Coppertone teased his nose.

Evan sneezed and looked at his watch.

The Hotel Fiesta Americana sat on the Gulf of Mexico in Veracruz and provided safe, temporary seclusion from the underlying crime and subculture of death. Evan pretended for a few moments that he was on vacation. He smiled at the pretty twenty-something Mexican bartender. She wore an I love New York shirt that was two sizes too small and was far from modest.

"Any food, *señor*?"

"*No, gracias.*"

Evan watched the pool for anyone who was watching him. Other than flirtatious young couples and a few elderly Europeans, the pool deck was bare. Wind chimes tingled in the breeze from where they hung on the bamboo-and-pine half-shelter of the bar. The bartender went back to texting near the cash register, and Evan settled briefly into a relaxed posture. He pulled his straw cowboy hat down over his eyes and pushed up his sunglasses.

"Don't get too comfortable, lad." His earpiece crackled, and he grinned.

Roger and Green Team were watching him from the balcony of one of the rooms high overhead on the eleventh floor. There were team members in the lobby and in front of the hotel.

"Anything?"

"Aye, Tommy is in the lounge heading your way. Took a cab. A couple of thugs in suites are drinking beer inside at the bar. They aren't trying to cover up watching him. We got your back. Just stick to the plan, eh?"

"We'll see, Roger. I like to wing it occasionally."

"That's what I am afraid of."

Evan unbuttoned his Tommy Bahamas Hawaiian shirt to get a little air and packed a dip.

OK, remain calm. The plan was for him to make contact with Tommy, who was their direct link to Mario. Tommy wanted reassurance that he would be protected and not double crossed if he got Evan into the inner circle. Nathan had warned Evan that Tommy was a little paranoid and not altogether there.

"He's nuts," Evan had concluded. "Great." He wasn't sure how he was going to play it with Tommy. Evan daydreamed for a minute, back to dealings with Russian mafia types like Ivan, right-wing guerrillas in Colombia, and Afghan commanders.

"They are all the same. Everyone's got an angle, and it's usually money, power, sex, goats, or all the above."

He had traded any number of conveniences to the world's scumbags for information. When it came to getting stuff, everyone was a capitalist.

Evan spat in his now-empty plastic water bottle. He watched a man in his early seventies walk over to his table with the swagger of a movie star: chest out, grinning, and hand extended. He was wrinkled and tan with his gray hair in a long ponytail. He had tiny mirrored, round sunglasses that hung down on a large nose. Evan ignored his hand and just waited for him to sit down.

The man smelled of booze and cigarettes. Evan assumed by his yellow-tinged eyes and bowling-ball belly that he was probably a drunk with some liver disease.

"Ivan, huh?"

"Yep."

"You don't look freaking Russian. You're what—a Puerto Rican?"

"Cuban Russian, one parent of each. You wanna talk in Russian, Spanish, or English?"

Tommy ran his fingers through his thick hair. He looked nervous and fidgety but confident. He clicked his fingers in the air and spoke in perfect Mexican Spanish. "Two tequilas. Bring my bottle under the counter."

"How long have you lived in Mexico, Tommy?"

"Too damn long. It's getting crazy—time to move! Give me a second."

Tommy answered his buzzing cell phone. The Mexican bartender gave Tommy a gentle kiss on the cheek and set the bottle and two glasses on the table. Evan watched her return to her perch at the end of the bar, where she continued to text and watch TV.

Evan smiled. "She's gotta gun too, eh?"

Tommy stopped speaking for a second. "What?"

"The girl. She's what—your daughter? She's got a piece under the bar, huh?"

Tommy concluded his quick phone call and set his phone on the table. "Yes. One of many lovely children I have. She is my little Carla. She watches out for me."

Evan watched Tommy take two shots and then pour one for Evan. Evan slammed it and savored the warm, smoky burn.

For a few moments the two men stared at each other. Evan heard laughter, loud music, the backfire of a car in the distance, and maybe even the *pop pop* of a nine millimeter somewhere in Boca del Rio.

"The ground rules before we begin?" Tommy blurted.

"Sure."

"You got a team here watching us?"

"Of course. They are also watching the thugs at the bar who are watching you, Tommy."

Tommy smiled nervously and lit a cigarette. His hands shook briefly as he began his personal nicotine-and-alcohol treatment to calm his nerves.

"Look, Ivan, or whatever your name is—I got a lot to lose here. The guys inside at the bar, they are the real deal, Mario's screeners. I can get you to them. You make it past them, and we go see this bucket-of-rust sub." He sucked on his cigarette until it glowed. "This whole game is in your court. I can't make you any guarantees. But let me be clear."

Evan turned to watch a beautiful, full-figured South American woman walk past with a toddler. "Tommy, the deal was, you get me access, and you toe the line. Stick to the script. I get you out of here no matter what the outcome."

"Unless we are riddled with bullets, Ivan."

Evan nodded. "No kidding. You seem like a wreck; you're nervous, you're shifty, and you're an open book. You betray me out of some fear to save your ass, and you and your girl, maybe even your pet Chihuahua, disappear."

Tommy laughed, more like a nervous expulsion than anything. "I hate pets."

"Figure of speech."

"Whatever."

Evan looked critically at Tommy and realized that the man was just simply insane. Years of adrenaline highs, drug binges, and who knows how many women.

"Now that we got the 'we don't trust each other' speech out of the way, let me fill you in on where I am coming from, Ivan." Tommy slammed another shot and lit up his fourth cigarette.

Evan braced himself for another rant.

"I am sixty-nine years old. I came to Mexico in 1987 after doing six years on a twenty-year stint. Technicality. I got out, headed down here, never looked back."

"That explains why you dress and act like Don Johnson, still stuck in the cocaine '80s." Evan laughed.

"Screw you, youngster. Happens to lots of guys—they lose time in the joint, get stuck in an era. Anyway, I flew drugs, guns, whores, and other stuff for the CIA. As long as I played by the rules, they didn't care what the hell I did on the side. I flew for Mario's dad too. We had a big fleet of planes." Tommy seemed to stare backward into the nostalgic era of another time that was really not quite as pristine as he imagined it at the time.

"Back then commies were the threat. Hell, now they are running your country! Surprised they ain't putting Bible thumpers in camps yet! Drugs were quick cash, and there was a code, you see. Governments took their payoffs, freedom fighters got their guns, flag wavers got to sing, and *bang*." Tommy brought his hands together in a clap as if he were wrapping up a sermon at a gun show. "American apple freaking pie and cash for everyone!"

"Your mouth, Tommy." Evan looked around and frowned.

"Screw you."

"Then what happened? So you ran drugs and weapons for the agency. So what?"

"Then the fuckers set me up."

"Cry me a river, Tommy." Evan spat into his bottle.

Tommy was slowly getting unglued. Evan was seriously having doubts that he could trust him.

"I sat in prison for six years in Florida. I knew if I spoke, they would take me out. I was scared to eat or drink anything 'cause of those mind-control drugs they use…Same shit they did with that movie-theater shooter and that nut up in, what, Connecti—"

"Focus, Tommy." *Dude's crazier than I am*, Evan thought, not sure if he was impressed or worried.

"When I was free, I came back down here to *mi familia*, Mario Jr. He accepted me into the casa, and I picked up where I left off."

"Happily ever after?" Evan prodded.

Tommy's eyes narrowed, and he leaned forward. "Basically, I can smell a fucking spook a mile away." Tommy held up his fingers in quotation marks and mockingly said, "*Ivan*." Tommy stood up and gripped the edges of the table.

Evan glanced out of the corner of his eye. Tommy's daughter had produced a sawed-off shotgun and laid it on the bar. Tommy waved her off. No one seemed to notice.

"You're a spook, Ivan. You ain't even old enough to have been in Cuba when the real shit went down! You're a 'Rican for all I know. You probably can't find Russia on a map!"

Evan chuckled. He could tell Tommy was having half a dozen different conversations at once, spurned by years of disconnected brain synapses. *No, drugs don't affect your brain.* Evan's mind drifted.

"Tommy, what's your angle? So you hate the government, the CIA—who doesn't? Hell, you haven't been in the States for a while. They canceled *Miami Vice*, by the way. You got to do this my way, Tommy—trust."

Tommy just kept talking right over Evan, as if his lips were not moving.

"You working for them, and you gonna leave me high and dry. Vietnam and half a dozen other freaking countries and hundreds of people have been left out to dry by the agency. The whole nine-eleven thing was—"

"*Stop!*" Evan put his hand over Tommy's mouth.

Tommy froze in fear and sat back in his chair, deflated.

"Take a breath, Tommy. I don't work for the agency. I am here as a mercenary. No rules, just this." Evan pulled a roll of one-hundred-dollar bills out of his pocket and smoothed them out flat on the table.

Tommy started breathing again.

"The great equalizer, Tommy. This is why I am here."

Tommy stood up and then sat down. He looked emotionally exhausted. He suddenly drank straight from the bottle, grabbed the stack of one-hundred-dollar bills, and slid them into his cargo pocket. "I want five passports, five different countries."

Evan replied, "Done."

"Me, my daughter, and my new wife."

"Congratulations."

Tommy lit his eighth cigarette. His fingers were trembling. "She lives in Italy. Was an Italian stripper, had a car crash last year, and is now born again. The life *or* her—that was her line in the cocaine. She wants a family and to disappear."

"She pregnant?"

Tommy smiled but not a happy smile. It was more of a grimace of fear. "Yes, gonna have a girl. All ten of my kids are girls. Carla, she's the only one who will talk to me. Only one I know."

"Something is still working, clearly."

"I think if I get away from this life, I can seek forgiveness, start over. Be a real man." Tommy rubbed his hair and looked at his fingers.

"How long you got?" Evan asked flatly.

Tommy looked at him for a second and then answered with great clarity, as if they were suddenly having a serious, adult conversation. The paranoia was gone. "Doctors say about a year."

"OK."

"Understand my angle, Ivan?"

"Loud and clear."

"OK. OK, Ivan, I am sticking to the script that your boss sent me. Knew you from a Russian job."

"Good boy. My team is going to pick up your Carla. Tell her to chill. She is going to a safe house, just in case."

"OK." Tommy suddenly reemerged from deep thought as an in-control Don Johnson persona. He stood up, made to move away, and then paused. "You know, there was a rumor back in the late '90s that several drug cartels of the Colombian persuasion were going to purchase a vintage Soviet sub. Heads of three cartels went to the bottom of the sea, helped paved the way for one cartel to take over—some say, to be controlled by the CIA."

"Conspiracy theory, Tommy." Evan shook his head and dismissed Tommy's words with his hands as if he were clearing a cloud of smoke.

Tommy laughed. "Yeah, hell, you're too young to know about that. Probably bullshit."

Evan nodded and smirked smugly. "Total bull."

Evan and Roger finished breakfast in silence. Evan enjoyed a cup of real coffee, savored it, and set the cup down.

"You know what's funny, Roger?"

"What?" Roger poured more boiling water into his French press and watched the time as the hot water met with coarse Colombian grounds.

"Here I am, an American playing a Russian, eating the best Mexican food I have ever had, made by a crazy ex-SAS Scotsman off the coast of Cuba. How 'bout that for multiculturalism?"

Roger checked the temperature of his coffee, pressed the press down, and poured a strong black cup in his "Don't back talk the chef" mug. "Aye, you like the steak, eh?"

"We ever go back to that ranch to train, and I am firing the cook and putting you in the kitchen."

"Too isolated out there. You should learn to cook. You eat enough!" Roger teased Evan.

"Takes too much effort. Guess just like any skill, you got to practice. My ex-wife, she could cook. Wouldn't even let me boil water. Said I did not do it right," Evan said.

Roger laughed. "Aye, we would have gotten along. I am a little particular about everything in the kitchen."

Evan laughed and thought back to Veronica and her spicy Colombian temperament. The angrier she got, the cuter she got, which always spun any scenario out of control. She got mad, and Evan wanted to have sex. God did have a sense of humor with his design of women and men. Evan continued, "Veronica, she used to spend hours prepping and cutting and talking a million miles an hour to her friends on the phone while she tasted, weighed, and did whatever it was she did. I stayed away when she cooked. The kitchen looked like some kinda special-ops command center; important, strange stuff went on in there."

"Sounds like a beautiful Latina."

"Kitchen looked like a war zone when she was done. I used to say, 'Jesus, Veronica, you don't have to use every appliance and pan in the kitchen for every meal.'"

Evan finished his breakfast of marinated skirt steak and eggs with peppers and onions. "Not that I complained, don't get me wrong. She used every weapon in the arsenal for every battle, no matter how big or small. I reaped the rewards, and I washed the dishes. That was the deal. More coffee?"

Roger nodded and poured Evan another cup of coffee. "And the way you eat, lad, you probably kept her busy."

"True," Evan agreed.

"What's your story? Why Mexico?" Evan asked.

"I wanted a change. I wanted away from the cold and the rain. I wanted something more remote. I like Latin women and the food they cook," Roger answered.

"Can't argue with you there. Other than Scotch, castles, and sheep, I can't think of much else about Scotland that I like," Evan said with a smile.

"Oh, you're a freakin' comedian. Don't bite the hand that feeds you."

Evan looked at his empty coffee cup and frowned. "You got a point, Roger."

"No, really, I came over here to explore. Needed to get away from all of the reminders of a miserable, drunken past and childhood. Can't retire and live in Scotland. I have two ex-wives there and another ex-fiancée in England. Hate the British, anyway. The French are either gay or rude, and I have had a wee bit of trouble there with the ladies too," Roger said and shook his head.

SILVER, LEAD, AND DEAD

"Had a bad thing with the fiancée of a police chief while attending cooking school in Paris."

"Sounds familiar. Mexico is like the drain in the sink of the world. Anyone who is running from something ends up here eventually, spiraling," Evan concluded.

"You definitely are not right, my friend," Roger said and refilled Evan's cup but only halfway. "You're cut off."

"*Hola, buenos dias.*"

Evan and Roger turned to see a short figure standing in the doorway. It was Daniel, or El Coyote, the other leader of Green Team One. He wore black leather combat boots, camouflage cut-offs, and a green bathrobe. His bare chest was covered in tattoos of Bible quotes and pictures of Mexican cowboys. El Coyote always had his custom-made AR-15 with him. He unslung his rifle and lay it on the table. Evan admired El Coyote's weapon. He had a red-dot optical scope and laser sight and had switched out the upper receiver and bolt so that it now fired a 7.62 round instead of the 5.56.

"You could deer hunt with this thing," Evan said, smiling and picking up his rifle. "Mind?"

"No, not at all." El Coyote was always smiling and liked to attempt telling jokes in English. His English was horrible, but he was learning. Evan would ofton poke fun at Roger's accent by telling him to learn English from El Coyote.

On the first day Evan had met him, they were on the shooting range. He had tried to impress Evan and Roger with his English.

"I show you boys how we Mexicans lick ass."

Evan had about choked on his dip, and Roger doubled over laughing.

"Did you hear what he just said?" Roger said and laughed.

El Coyote had looked offended and held up his hands. "*Que es problema?*"

"It's *kick* ass, not *lick* ass!" Evan said.

El Coyote was an outstanding marksman, so he got a pass. From then on they stuck to Spanish.

"I did not sleep so well, kept feeling sick. The patches, they did not work for me," El Coyote said and groaned.

"How much time do we have?" Evan asked.

"The ship's captain told me that within one hour we should be there. He has been in contact with the receiving team. The sub, he says, is having trouble with its diesel engine." El Coyote frowned. "They need another part."

Evan cursed. He had cleared the AR-15, removed the upper receiver, and was inspecting the bolt. "We just left freaking Acapulco. Why the hell didn't they tell us before we left? We came out here to fix their electrical problems, and now they have a new problem? We can't very well let Mario's guy know that the sub doesn't work!"

El Coyote shrugged. "We don't tell him anything. Everything works fine."

Roger grumbled. "Evan's right though. If we would have known earlier, we could have brought out some parts!"

"We can wing it," Evan said.

El Coyote poured the last of the coffee into a plastic mug and frowned at the two men. "We have another problem: Mario's man, he is a retired Mexican naval officer. He knows submarines. How can we fool him?"

Evan put the weapon back together, put the thirty-round, curved-style magazine back in, placed the weapon on Safe, and put it on the table.

"You should see my custom AR at home. You'd love it. I have a Beowulf fifty-caliber upper receiver and bolt."

"Evan?" Roger spoke as if he were trying to speak to someone in another dimension.

"OK, sorry. We let Mario's guy see what we want him to see. We tell him we are upgrading the engine, making it faster. We don't say anything unless he asks. We can tell him there will be a delay. Too easy. Worse comes to worse, I shoot him."

Roger ignored Evan's last comment. "Aye, we will keep him sidetracked. Ye better go wake up the cargo."

Evan looked at his watch. "OK. We do everything like we rehearsed."

Evan made his way below by himself. The team had agreed that Mario's observer was to see as few of them as possible and only when necessary. Evan and Tommy were to be the only actual faces that he saw, and anyone else was to wear a ski mask and remain quiet. Roger was the only one who was forbidden, for obvious reasons; his accent and size made him stand out.

Evan adjusted his H&K .40 in a nylon tactical holster attached to his thigh and then unlocked a steel cabin door.

"*Hola*. Get up!"

A short, fat man with a beard lay snoring on a mattress on the floor. His clothes were folded neatly and placed on top of his shoes.

Mario's observer wore a blindfold, and despite having his hands cuffed and chained to a ring on the floor, he snored loudly as if he were comfortable.

"Wake up!" Evan tore the man's blindfold off and uncuffed his hands. "You sleep OK?"

The man sat up, rubbed his eyes, refocused, and looked at Evan. "*Sí*, I always sleep best when at sea. How long I been asleep? Did you drug me? I no have slept that good in years!" The man laughed and moved to get up off the bare mattress.

"No, just tequila," Evan lied.

Evan handed the man a cup of coffee.

"Yes, yes, no offense taken. Where is the sub?"

Mario's observer rubbed his wrists and stood up. He was short, confident, and still had an air of superiority about him. He acted in control despite his situation.

"You were in the Mexican navy?" Evan asked flatly.

"Yes, how you know this?"

"Intelligence is our business. Took your fingerprints and picture while you slept. Same thing you did to me, screening."

"Captain Miguel, retired. Good coffee. Then you know I am wanted all over Mexico?"

"Yes." Evan changed the topic. "You brought a computer with you?" Evan pointed to a Pelican case that held a laptop and power cable.

Captain Miguel nodded and sipped his coffee.

"Here is how it's going to work, Miguel. I give you this thumb drive. It has all the stats and dimensions of the submarine, what it can carry, and how it's been updated. You can look over it until we get there." Evan handed him the virus-laced thumb drive.

"I can keep this, Ivan?"

Evan responded to his cover name. "It's yours. When we get to the sub, we take you topside, meet with Tommy, and then go for a tour. After that, we give you a satellite phone, and you call Mario. Keep it brief. You can transmit pictures with our camera."

"Fair enough. You men are serious about not being found, eh?"

"We have been in business for many years, Miguel. A submarine is a big toy to hide—and expensive."

"I need to shower, brush teeth before. Is that possible?"

Evan took the empty coffee cup and nodded. "Yes, we can do that. I will be back in ten minutes with stuff to shower. In one hour we will be at our destination."

CHAPTER 16

Sunrise Near Veracruz

The *Happy Mermaid* moved through the waters off the coast of Veracruz, Mexico, without a care in the world. Only essential staff was on board, with the exception of Tanya and her team of computer technicians. They had finished their legitimate job of installing an encrypted Wi-Fi system and updating the ship's computers to an encrypted network, effectively allowing Mario to stay in touch with the inner workings of his business anywhere. Mario's sons could now handle the money laundering, bank accounts, and legitimate and illegitimate business with ease. Shipments could be tracked, payments could be made to government officials' Swiss bank accounts, and private e-mails of Mexican law enforcement could be hacked.

Tanya looked at her watch and cursed. She could see the dim light of morning creeping into her cabin through the tiny oval window, or porthole. She stood up, stretched, and closed her laptop.

"They are up to something."

She had been up all night with her team, reading through encrypted e-mails and financial records until her eyes had hurt. They were careful to not openly or loudly discuss what they were doing. Tanya was certain that her cabin was clean of bugs and microphones; they had scanned it, but one could still not be sure. She had been given the freedom to move almost anywhere on the yacht unbothered, but she chose to stay close to where she was working.

Tanya was actually quite proud of her team and had really moved Mario's billion-dollar drug-shipping business into modern times.

Tanya showered and readied herself for the morning. She really did not like to allow herself to be happy for too long, but she could not help it. She alone now had almost complete access to every detail of Mario's operation. If information was transferred electronically, she could find it. That being said, only about 39 percent of his massive empire was online. He wasn't running an Internet business; he was running a cash-for-drugs business. Business was done mainly in cash and face-to-face. He had hundreds of subsets of people who took care of distribution, sales, and enforcement. Mario had several dozen warehouses hidden along both the Gulf and Pacific coasts that were rumored to be stocked with cash. The grand total was a staggering number in the billions. The seemingly fragmented, disjointed process of business was actually brilliant. You could not destroy a drug empire by taking out one distributer or even the top dog himself. The whole operation just kept moving, and many in the organization, especially on the bottom tiers, had no idea whom they were working for.

Tanya ran her team much the same way. They gave her the puzzle pieces, and she put them together and shared just enough to let them know they were doing a great job. Some on her team had been with Mario for as long as ten years and had switched sides out of a promise for a new life. Tanya was thrilled with the power that she had accumulated for herself. She did her best not to draw attention to that fact and did her best to hide it, but the fact was, she could wire millions to herself from Mario's secret accounts no matter how secure. The virus she created, Centipede, was like a nuclear bomb to computer systems. Tanya actually felt kind of sad. She knew everything she had worked so hard to build could be destroyed in a few hours. She recalled the conversation that she had with one of her teammates.

"You know you have to turn over the keys to Nathan eventually. Give him the password," Sebastian had told her. He was one of the younger, yet smartest, members of her team. He was savvy and shrewd, and he loathed people as much as she did. The other members of her team seemed cliquey and she felt as though they really did not care for her.

"Once the virus is launched, Tanya, no one steals anything from Mario. Nathan could steal it all and then destroy the evidence, leaving us nowhere."

"Screw him," she whispered.

Tanya closed her laptop, locked it up, and left her cabin. She had much to think about.

She had joined Dark Cloud six months ago with her boyfriend, Ivan. Nathan had bought his freedom from a Russian prison. He and Tanya had agreed to a one-year contract. Tanya was a member of Ivan's gang of computer hackers and underworld arms dealers. They had made millions until their betrayal and arrest.

Three years she had sat in prison in the cold mountains of Siberia.

"You should be grateful to me, Tanya. Ivan wanted you free, and I arranged it. You and he are a package deal. If anything happens to him, you still must pay your debt."

Tanya grimaced at the words spoken by Nathan just weeks before Ivan died from a fire on the cursed Russian submarine. Nathan had tried and tried again to seduce her, implying that if she did not comply, she could go back to prison.

JAMES GARMISCH

Tanya made it to the top deck of the yacht just in time to see the orange ball of the sun begin to rise. She thought for a long moment about the convoluted e-mails she had just read, the funds hidden in front groups routed through false identities. She thought about her own betrayal and her many enemies who would love to find her. Ivan was a manipulative liar. Dark Cloud was a suicide mission, and now some overgrown ex-spy was trying to fulfill Ivan's original mission. Tanya stared at the horizon and for a moment forgot about her fear of the water. She had the capability of stealing millions of dollars and vanishing.

Knowledge is power, she thought. *Jorge Valdez wants to kill Mario and overthrow the Mexican government.*

Her hands shook at the magnitude of what she had just thought. She was not sure how he was going to do it yet or if it would work, but the implications were clear. Months of sifting through data and analyzing bits of seemingly unrelated information had brought her to this conclusion.

She yawned and leaned on the rail of the yacht. She thought she saw some dolphins in the distance.

"Good morning, Tanya."

Tanya felt her heart skip a few beats and the color drain from her face.

"We meet again."

Tanya reached out a trembling hand. "Yes, Mr. Valdez."

"Jorge," he corrected. "Come eat breakfast with me. You are the computer-security expert, yes?"

"Uh-huh."

His charming smile did little to comfort her. She felt as though he could see into her.

"Think you can help me with something? Seems that we have a hacker."

190

Off the Coast of Isla de la Juventud, 0730 Hours

The whole ocean looked different now that the sun was up. The ocean was a dark blue-green with white-capped peaks, and the sky was a brilliant blue. No clouds were in sight.

Evan stood on the deck, leaning against the rail of the rusty salvage ship. A breeze chilled his bald head. Miguel looked up at him and cupped his eyes from the sun.

"How do we get on board?"

Evan spat and pointed to a ladder that was being hoisted overboard by two masked members of Green Team. They had AK-47s slung across their backs.

"Is he going to make it?" Miguel pointed at Tommy who was still heaving over the side of the ship.

"Tommy, you going to make it?" Evan spoke in English.

Tommy, who was wearing cutoff shorts, blue deck shoes, and a red suit jacket from the '80s, shook his head. "You two go ahead. I…I can't go inside that submarine." Tommy slumped against a large spool of wire that probably weighed a thousand pounds, took off his sunglasses, adjusted his long hair, and opened a new pack of Camels.

"Fair enough. Stay here." Evan went over to his team members and spoke quietly in Spanish. "We won't be long. If any unwanted guests show up, do as we planned."

"*Sí.*"

The biggest concern was that a plane belonging to the Cuban air force or a ship might spot them.

Evan, Miguel, and the two masked members of Green Team climbed over the rail of the salvage ship and began the slow, precarious process of climbing down the rusty ladder to the deck of the sub. Evan was the first to reach the deck of the Cold War–era sub and helped Miguel gain footing. The sub seemed to pitch slightly but seemed steadier than the salvage vessel since most of its weight was below the waterline.

"OK, we have to hurry. It's daylight, and we don't like to stay surfaced too long."

"Can we take it for a drive?"

Evan shrugged and made it to the hatch, which led below deck. "Up to the ship's captain. We are going to dive, I believe, and stay out of sight for a while. You'll get the complete tour."

Evan hoped and prayed that the sub would not be spotted. They were well outside of Cuban and Mexican waters; however, it was satellites and planes he was worried about. The States had the technology and resources to spot them even though they were a tiny spec in the middle of nowhere.

Tanya tried not to show her hands as they would not stop shaking. She had been hungry when she first got up, but now she felt sick.

Jorge sat across from her, eating an omelet and toast. The *Happy Mermaid* had a formal dining room on the third deck that opened up to a wide, covered outside-dining area with brilliant wood decking and custom-made glass tables. She was always amazed at the brilliance of Italian designs. Leather, wood, polished brass, and hand-etched glass made Tanya feel as if she were among royalty on the floating palace. She heard laughter behind her and turned to look toward the stern of the yacht. Two naked girls, teenagers perhaps, got into a hot tub with a muscular man whom she recognized as Blaise. *Flying Rat*, she thought.

"You said *hacker*, Mr. Valdez?"

Jorge laughed and sipped his orange juice.

"Yes, yes, not really. *Saboteur* is perhaps a better term. One of the many cats that lounge around on this floating strip club knocked over a glass of water on my computer. Fried my keyboard. Can you fix it?"

Tanya relaxed, smiled, and started breathing again. "Where is it?"

"I'll have it brought to you. It still turns on, but..." Jorge spoke to her in an easygoing manner, as if they had known each other for years.

He was a very handsome man with an intensity that made you want to stand up straight and speak clearly. He reminded her of a shrink, and she had seen many. His eyes dissected her, evaluated her.

"After breakfast I have a meeting. I will have one of my men bring it to you. I need it fixed in three hours."

"You going to shore today?" she asked, trying to turn on her charm. She was not a naturally charming person, so when she did smile or flirt, it usually caught men off guard.

"Yes." Jorge looked past her now and began to stand up. She knew he was watching the acts taking place in the hot tub.

"Excuse me." Jorge began to head toward the commotion on the lower deck.

"Can I ride with you when you go ashore?"

"The yacht is pulling into dock tonight, needs some supplies—some mechanical problems as well. Can you wait?"

"Mechanical?"

"Engine related, very boring." Jorge did not wait for her to say anything else. He walked away, down the ladder, and to the hot tub on the deck below.

She turned to watch him briefly. Jorge was talking to Blaise Gerard. She assessed the body language and realized that it was not a good conversation.

Tanya turned back to her coffee. She thought briefly about the cold prison in Russia, the snow, and solitary confinement.

"What are they up to? I have to get off this boat. That bastard Nathan. I have no choice; I have to tell him."

Tanya thought about standing naked in the snow, shivering next to other female inmates. The first one who shivered or fell over would be the night's sport. The eyes of the leering guards were more like wolves' than men's. Gerard reminded her of the same sort of sadistic animal. Jorge was more like the Flying Rat's game warden than boss. She wondered if Jorge could contain his men.

"I need to hack Jorge's files. Is this a trap? Or is this an opportunity?"

Tanya had a sudden urge to run away. She needed some courage.

The tour of the sub went unexpectedly well. The power worked, and the engine and computer upgrades seemed to be online.

Evan and the crew had a quick meeting and decided to come clean about more of the sub's faults than they had intended. Fortunately for Evan and his team, the Mexican navy did not own submarines; therefore, Miguel had never even been on one. Unfortunately, however, he seemed to know everything about electrical engineering and diesel engines.

The afternoon sun was directly overhead by the time they had ended their cruise in the sub and reboarded the salvage vessel. Miguel was allowed to photograph the sub and was given access to a satellite phone from which he could speak with his superiors.

Evan met with Roger and Tommy in the kitchen. "So glad I never joined the navy," Evan began. He sipped water from a plastic bottle and sat on a wooden stool. "That freaking tin can makes me claustrophobic. It's noisy and, well, just sucks."

"Well, what's the verdict?" Roger asked and groaned.

"It's going to take about three days to get this beast up and running. We have to move it somewhere closer to Mexico and get some parts to finish up the repairs. Me and you and a few guys have to get up to Veracruz by tonight."

Roger looked at his watch. "Not going to happen, lad. That's a long haul."

"We leave soon, we can make it. Tommy and I have to meet with Mario's money guy. They have a crew flying in to pilot the sub once the deal is made."

Roger looked concerned and said, "That's not how we discussed the whole thing going down. If we lose control over the sub by turning it over to a crew, then we lose our opportunity to smuggle our team onto his yacht."

Evan shrugged. "Then we change the plan."

"Evan, we don't have any support—just a team of about thirty men. If we start breaking this thing up, it could get ugly."

Evan considered the original plan and conceded. Roger was right.

Tommy spoke up for the first time today, surprising both Roger and Evan. "You two talk like freaking cops."

"Go ahead, Don Johnson. What's your plan?"

Tommy ignored Evan's smart comment. He nodded, ran his fingers through his hair, and adjusted his flowered silk Hawaiian T-shirt. Tommy was broad shouldered and bony.

"Drug dealers are, above all else, paranoid and always looking to pee on trees. They want to control the situation and keep people off their game." Tommy picked up an apple, bit into it, and chewed loudly. "Mario has never done business with you. He is going to try and move the date up like it's urgent and then change the location. If he gets his crew on the sub, you guys will lose a chance."

"OK. Keep talking. You make sense when you're sober," Evan said flatly.

Roger said flatly with frustration, "Jeez, Evan, you always gotta say somthin' smart."

"Who said I was sober?" Tommy laughed. "No, you guys gotta change plans yourself, a minimum of three times, and then go back to your original plan."

Roger and Evan looked at Tommy and stopped talking.

"Follow my lead. Let me talk to Miguel," Tommy said. He acted in charge, so they went with it.

"We have to get the sub to shallow waters, regardless—hide it and work on it," Evan said flatly.

"True," Tommy admitted.

Evan spoke quickly with some stress in his voice. He was feeling the effects of sleeplessness. "The sub's captain and chief engineer say they need about eight hours of work. They have a place with overhead cover, seclusion, and access to docks just south of Quintara Roo. There is also an island that they party at near Cozumel. This might be the place to meet for the sub hand off."

Tommy said, "Let me do the talking. Trust me."

Evan finished his water, stood up, snapped his fingers, and pointed at Tommy. "Fine, let's chat with Miguel. You got the helm. Roger, turn course toward Veracruz. We can roll in by tonight. The sub can move out on its own to its concealed location."

"Fine. I hope you two know what you're doing. I'm gonna call Nathan, give him the plan, at least as it stands now."

CHAPTER 17

Under the Wire

Tanya packed her duffel bag, careful to put her computers and other equipment in the proper zippers. The only positive thing that had come out of her time in prison was that now she was a neat freak. Every piece of clothing, every wire, every piece of paper had to be just right. Tanya, at one time, had been a slob, buried in piles of stuff. Now she was a minimalist packing nothing that she could not throw in a bag and run away with.

A knock at the door made her jump, and she cursed. "Hold on."

Tanya took a small thumb drive and placed it securely in her bra. If she had the opportunity, she would infect Jorge's computer or download anything interesting.

"Wait!" she yelled as the knocking got louder.

She looked at herself in the full-length mirror and adjusted her peach-colored tank top to be less revealing. Looking at her jeans, she frowned. No matter how much she ate, she seemed to keep losing weight; her pants were too loose.

"*Hola.*" She opened the door and froze. It was not Jorge as she had expected. "You," she blurted out. She was glad she did not say, "flying rat."

He looked her up and down and leaned against the door-frame as if he was exhausted. He was wearing a computer bag across his bare shoulders.

"What are you doing here? Where is Jorge?"

He stank of cigarette smoke. Tanya hated smokers.

"He told me to bring it. He's got business to attend to."

Tanya took the offered bag and walked to her desk.

Gerard stayed in his spot with the door open. "Tanya, can you do me a favor too?"

She shrugged and opened Jorge's laptop and laid it flat on her desk. "Depends. Do you know if he turned it off and on?"

Blaise shrugged, uninterested. "He said some of the keys don't work anymore. He tried drying it with a towel."

Tanya removed a portable keyboard from her backpack and plugged it in via a USB port. "Tell him to use my spare keyboard for a day or so. Transfer his data if it does not get better."

"Fine, fine," Gerard said.

Tanya grabbed her hair dryer, turned it on low, and methodically used it on the laptop keys.

"Tanya, can you do anything with this?"

She ignored the flying rat until she was done using her hair dryer and had packed Jorge's computer back into its case.

He had tapped his foot for five minutes.

"OK, now, what do you need?"

Gerard handed her a grainy photograph that looked as if it had been folded up in someone's pocket.

"A print-out picture? Really, I need the digital file." She handed him the case and studied the picture. She could not recall the last time she had seen an actual photo on paper.

"I can get it. This is from some contacts up in Juárez." Gerard spoke slowly through his stiff jaw.

Tanya stared at the picture for a second and then almost gave herself away with a gasp. "What do you want me to do? This is a faraway picture of some idiot at a Walmart bus stop." She bit her lip. To her it was unmistakably Evan, or Ivan, but fortunately the quality made it unclear.

"Are these two the same guys?" Gerard handed her a second picture from his pocket. The subject in this picture was wearing a ski mask and holding a shotgun.

"Can't tell," she lied and shrugged. "Looks like some big moron at a bus station, too far away to tell. And then what…A guy robbing a convenience store? Both men are large and wearing similar clothes."

"This guy was involved in an ambush on my crew and me."

"So? Send me the digital files, and I will see. Really though? Like can't you find someone else in Mexico to do this?" Tanya began to speak rapidly as if she were annoyed and insulted. "I have tons of work to do!"

"Sorry. I just got it yesterday. Pictures were e-mailed to me. You are here. I was just figuring you could—"

Tanya paused and shook her head, exasperated.

"OK, forget it." Gerard clutched the bag and turned to leave.

"Wait! E-mail it to me. I will work on the pictures when we have a connection. Currently, we are in a blackout—no signals, no coverage. Give me a second to write my e-mail."

Evan listened intently as Tommy the professional smuggler submerged himself into his element. First he told Miguel that the deal was, with great regret, probably not going to happen; a buyer from South America wanted to buy the submarine and was willing to purchase it as is. Tommy threw up his hands, acted very sorry, and then left the deck. Evan stared at the waves and the sea gulls in disbelief for a full hour. Miguel made a few phone calls. He looked flushed.

What is this idiot doing? Evan thought.

Forty-five minutes later, Tommy had a humble yet heated conversation with someone on the satellite phone. Evan assumed this someone was Mario. Tommy used "Yes, sir," and "No, sir," many times before finally breaking into a broad smile.

"OK, OK," Tommy agreed.

Tommy handed the phone back to Miguel, who looked confused, and then left the deck of the swaying salvage boat. Evan turned to follow Tommy when Miguel called his name.

"Ivan, wait, *señor*. My boss, he wants to have a word."

Evan adjusted his sunglasses.

"Sure." Evan took the phone and answered, *"Hola?"*

A deep voice in surprisingly courteous Spanish responded. "To whom am I speaking?"

"Ivan."

"I am Jorge Valdez, Mario's chief of security. Listen, Tommy just brought up a matter that I believe we can resolve."

"Not sure what he told you, Mr. Valdez," Evan said truthfully.

"The sub is in a bad state of disrepair and will take a few days to fix. My man Miguel confirmed this. How many days to make it functional?"

Evan paused for a long second. "About three days."

"And Miguel said you are not willing to change the location of the exchange. May I ask why?" Jorge said.

Evan felt his pulse quicken and thought about what Tommy had said: these guys always changed their minds. They had to confirm that Mario and at least one of his sons would be there at the purchase. The entire flimsy plan depended on this.

"This sub cannot easily be hidden, and we were under the impression that a demonstration of sorts for your boss was part of the deal," Evan stated.

"Once we purchase this sub, where are we to keep it?"

Evan shrugged. "I would build a covered dock somewhere remote, an island maybe?"

"And you have other buyers or potential buyers?"

"Yes."

Evan listened to silence.

"Can you meet tonight at about eleven, Veracruz? The *Happy Mermaid* will be in port. It too is having mechanical problems. Join us for dinner. We may have a location for the exchange."

"I don't have any nice clothes, Mr. Valdez."

"That's fine. We will discuss the details. May I speak to Miguel?"

Evan handed the satellite phone back to Miguel, went inside the ship's cabin, and climbed a ladder up to the observation deck.

Tommy looked at Evan and smiled. "This is the game we play, Ivan."

"Is Mario going to be present?" Evan asked.

"Yes. This sub sale is the centerpiece for his birthday party. Everyone will be there!" Tommy said with great confidence.

"Hope you're right," Evan said.

Tommy nodded. "They will still have the advantage, Ivan, no matter where we meet. Then there are the ship's guns."

The salvage ship had changed course and was steaming full throttle back toward the direction of Mexico.

"I hope that piece-of-shit submarine makes it to Mexico before it sinks!" Tommy laughed.

Evan ignored him and left. He needed to find Roger and work out their game plan for the evening. They also needed all of Green Team One to meet them in Veracruz and set up several safe houses. Evan looked up at the sun for an answer.

"Another day with no sleep. I should have just stayed retired."

CHAPTER 18

Battle of Chapultepec

Nathan sipped probably the strongest coffee he had ever had in his life. It was thick, full of resin, and had just a hint of cinnamon that burned his lips. He hoped the caffeine would jump-start his heart and perhaps mind into some sort of brilliant breakthrough.

He waited.

"You know, Nathan, this is the Chapultepec Castle. It is tied in with the Mexican-American War." Reo cleared his throat and began pointing at the magnificent walls and courtyard just outside the castle.

"Amazing that men marched all the way from the coast to get here. Ugh! The elevation, the bugs. How did they endure? And yet no one remembers even why or how the whole thing began. I mean, who can really tell you? Men died, and for what? I mean to Mexicans, yes, the Americans were invading, but why?"

Nathan looked at his watch. He spat a fine coffee ground onto the cement and watched a group of pigeons congregate, mindlessly pecking at nothing.

Nathan's security detail looked relaxed yet alert. They were professionals, and as such had no delusions that they were invincible, bulletproof, or safe.

"Reo, your man, he is late."

"He is on Mexican Standard Time, my friend. Shall we go in and look around?"

"No, been here many times."

"You know, the American generals Robert E. Lee and Ulysses S. Grant fought here. Ironic, yes? Of course they were not generals at the time. They marched up here with Major General Winfield Scott from Veracruz, where they landed back in 1847. Dawn, September twelfth, to be accurate, they began—"

"Reo! No offense, but really I am not in the mood for a history lesson. It's over. I know the marine corps hymn came from this miserable place high up on this hill. We leave in five minutes."

Reo frowned and suddenly reached in his pocket; his phone was buzzing. "Speak of the devil." He looked at the screen. "He is here, traffic. Be patient." Reo smiled like a schoolboy who had used his professor's own words against him.

Nathan finished his coffee, dropped it in a wastebasket, and then waited for his contacts to arrive. He was not feeling optimistic. Nathan had been meeting with a representative named Roberto for nearly a year. Roberto was the liaison between the anonymous private-sector corporations and the small sect of Mexican officials who had originally hired Dark Cloud.

Jorge Valdez stood in the center of an oval, carpeted room in the bottom of the *Happy Mermaid*. The oval room served as Mario's situation room. Jorge thought, with a twinge of guilt, that it was now the room where he was plotting Mario's demise. Jorge had several situations coming together at once, and as a good battlefield commander he would use each one to his advantage. First of all Mario Jr., Jorge's oldest son, an arrogant prick with an MBA from UCLA, was on his to approve of the purchase. He was the money man of Mario's operation. Nothing major was purchased without his approval. Mario's youngest son, also named Mario, went by the nick name of Little Mario. He was usually jet setting around Europe schmoozing and paying off police and high-ranking officials. He would also be at the sub deal and birthday party. Jorge knew that Mario Jr. was not a fan of the sub sale, but conceded that it would happen to please his father. Jorge needed the sub deal to succeed as well—it would serve two purposes. One, it would further divide the Mario and anti-Mario loyalists. It was a decadent purchase that would only draw attention to their organization when seized by the police. Two, the location of the sub purchase would be the perfect backdrop for the annihilation of hundreds of enemies, Mario included. Again the guilt.

Jorge had decided weeks ago where the location of the sub purchase would be. It was even better now that Tommy had mentioned it. Jorge was familiar with the old smugglers game of "we have another buyer" or "we need to switch locations." In the end, everything would workout in Jorge's favor. His army was ready.

"Boss?" Gerard asked. He had been saying something that Jorge had missed.

Jorge focused on the present and sat down at the table and rearranged three satellite phones, a cell phone, and an iPad. He breathed deeply and looked up at Gerard. He was the only one who called Gerard by his real name.

"Gerard, the answer is this. Though I do appreciate your perseverance in investigating the ambush in Juárez, I need you to drop it. No doubt an informant or rival gang was involved. Those amateur kidnappers no doubt brought down unwanted attention." Jorge looked regretful and waved his hand in the air. He did not want to crush Gerard's spirit but had to be firm.

"You are my best man. I need you to help with this operation. If you can investigate and still be here mentally and physically, by all means do it. But this operation…" Jorge thumped the desk. "This operation will redefine Mexico!"

"Yessir." Gerard seemed satisfied and sat on the table.

The sound of a helicopter made the glasses and table vibrate.

"Mario Jr. is here," Jorge said.

Nathan, Reo, and an unattractive, heavyset woman named Carletta sat at a small, uncomfortable steel table in chairs that were equally uncomfortable. Nathan offered up his chair to the middle-aged woman when he realized her chair rocked as if one leg was too short. Birds surrounded them, the sun was lazy and low, and now two separate security details were pacing quietly in the distance. Nathan locked eyes with Carletta. She was weathered, cultured, and tough. Her eyes were shrewd and her hands firm as she laid them flatly on the table. Nathan heard a siren off in the distance, which was then muffled by a jumbo jet.

"Nice to meet you too, Carletta. I am not quite clear why Eduardo didn't make it. This is a little odd. Should I call the secretary to the president?"

"No. No, Nathan. Eduardo met with an unfortunate accident." She frowned.

"What?"

Nathan and Reo looked at each other. Nathan held up his hand to calm down his shooters, who were beginning to close ranks. "What kind of accident?"

"Nathan, we are pulling the plug on Dark Cloud."

Mario Jr., his two bodyguards, and two politicians whom Jorge knew quite well entered the room quietly. Jorge smiled broadly and waved toward the comfortable chairs, which were pulled halfway out, just so, for his guests. Jorge knew things about the two politicians that Mario Jr. did not know. For instance, they were on board with his designs to destroy Mario's empire and blame it on the cause of a major political assassination.

"Sit, sit, my friends. Mario, how is your father?" Jorge paused.

Mario Jr. was not smiling. He was clearly annoyed at something and puffed up as if he had some sort of agenda to present. "Where the hell is the booze?" he grumbled.

"Here. Are you OK?" Jorge moved to reach for a glass but was shoved out of the way.

"I'll get it my damn self!"

"That is one," Jorge said quietly to himself. He smiled on the outside, yet began to boil within.

Mario Jr. was in one of his moods, which meant that the evening was going to be long and unpredictable. Jorge sat down once everyone was settled and then decided he too would get a drink. He poured a small glass of mescal and settled down at the head of the table. Mario Jr.'s two bodyguards stood near the door, and Gerard placed himself near them. Gerard, like Jorge, had a deep distrust for anyone else with guns—even if they were on the same team.

"Mescal Disgusting, tastes like urine." Mario Jr. paced around the room like a mad cat.

"You know, my friend, that my family has been making this brand for generations. I take that as a bit of an offense. It is an acquired—" Jorge began.

"Oh, sorry, did I hurt your fucking feelings?"

Jorge smiled and folded his arms as he spoke diplomatically, "Shall we get down to business?"

"There is no business. We are not buying the sub, and I am on to you and your friends. How about that for business?"

Jorge stopped smiling, took a drink, and placed his glass down quietly.

Gerard put a toothpick in his mouth and slid the tips of his fingers into the waistband of his jeans.

For a second, Jorge and Gerard locked eyes. True warriors never had to speak.

All was settled.

Nathan could not speak for a full minute. He watched the pigeons and tourists sputter around aimlessly going to-and-fro. He checked to make sure his phone was on Vibrate and then placed his sunglasses firmly over his eyes.

"You are serious?"

"The political winds are changing, Nathan."

"To whose favor?" He chuckled.

"That is to be determined," she said.

"You are getting scared," he stated flatly to Carletta.

She refused to get on the defensive and smiled, like a warm grandmother who had just busted a child for stealing cookies. "Some are."

"Explain." Nathan felt his blood heat up and his heart begin to pound. For an instant, she reminded him of the type of bureaucrat that used to just make decisions without knowing any of the details; or was she just a puppet?

"I will, Mr. Rock, but—"

"Where is the secretary to the president? That's who I want explaining this whole thing to me. You see, this is not my first rodeo, as we say, and this is the first time you and I have met."

She frowned.

Nathan watched his bodyguards watch her bodyguards.

Reo was texting someone and then abruptly stopped. Reo never stopped texting. He looked up at her and spoke. "You are jamming our signal. I know who you are. You work for the CNI. We have met before in a social setting."

"Gentlemen, look, we approve of what you are doing. It is just that things behind the scenes are changing. People are getting nervous."

"And greedy?" chimed in Reo.

She smiled and said nothing.

"Talk. Can I get you a drink, some coffee?" Nathan asked, trying to improve the deteriorating situation.

"No. My time is short, so allow me to get to the point," she said.

"Certainly." Nathan had changed his demeanor now and was smiling on the outside, yet boiling on the inside.

Carletta settled into a smug yet sweet tone and began speaking. "It took us a while to figure it out, but you are quite brilliant. While your soldiers were building up little vigilante cells and intelligence networks around Mexico, they were also establishing the whereabouts of Mario's cash warehouses. You built a trusted human-intelligence network in places my agents won't even go! Now, on to business. In the last six months, Dark Cloud has cost our conglomerate of private backers and government officials a substantial sum of money. We have seen a few arrests here and there, the discovery of a kidnapping ring of gringo whores being sent to the Middle East, and the release of Andre Pena, the notorious bomb maker, from prison and his arrival into Mexico. We have invested millions in what? We have flown you and your warriors around Mexico and helped you purchase a base to train, and yet what have we seen?"

She paused and looked exasperated. "Mr. Rock, now you want to buy a submarine? An elaborate trap to kill Mario and his sons? This is madness. We let you go with it for a while, yet now it is just out of hand."

Nathan ignored her and interjected a quick question. He locked eyes with her. "You are giving me economics. More importantly, have you told anyone about the warehouses?"

"No."

"You mentioned politics?" Nathan probed.

She nodded and conceded his point. "Yes. Our biggest back-er, whom I cannot name, is withdrawing. He is standing to make billions in a deal with the *norteamericano* political class, some type of telecom deal that I cannot get into."

"Go on," Nathan said. He was trying to keep his voice low but was losing.

"He cannot be connected with us any longer. The press cov-erage of our war and the fallout and destabilization of the bal-ance when Mario dies? It cannot be predicted and may make us—"

Nathan interjected, "No, allow me. You're getting pressure from the *norteamericanos* to hush up your drug war because it may hurt the political classes. This is your country! I have seen what these morons do to other countries."

No one spoke for a full minute.

Carletta spoke first.

"We have no more cash. You have cost us a few million al-ready, and many of our members are withdrawing and getting cold feet." Carletta shook her head slowly with sympathy and blew smoke from her nostrils. "The house of cards is collapsing, Nathan."

Nathan looked at Reo, who looked at the table. She contin-ued trying to sound like the rational one.

"Now, you want us to pay off two hundred million for a submarine? Something that will certainly attract huge attention from the United States when it gets caught? Can't afford the cost or the embarrassment."

Nathan leaned back in his chair and spoke. "So there it is. So you go back to prearranged drug busts—cartel leaders selling off their rivals so you can parade them in front of cameras." Nathan shook his head.

Carletta was not smiling anymore and stood up abruptly. "I think our conversation is over, Nathan Rock. Go see the sights up here, learn some history about old empires." She waved her hands around at the castle, smiled, and gathered her purse.

Nathan panicked and for the first time in his life threw all his cards on the table in desperation. "What if I tell you I can kill Mario and his sons and bring down his whole organization in about three days? You can replace him with whomever you like—that's your business. We pay for it all ourselves, and I make *you* rich!"

The grandma smirk went away, and Carletta now just looked like a greedy bitch. "You bluff."

Nathan laid it all out on the table for her, hoping something would stick. He knew he could find her angle. She was, after all, a government employee.

"My men are about to get Mario, who you people could not find for the last ten years. I have a team on the inside that has hacked into his computer systems, infiltrated, and gained access to every electronic form of payment that Mario owns." Nathan stood up to face her.

"You lie," she said.

"Bullshit, lady. This is my world. I have access to all of the pouges...maybe even you, that are on his payroll. I can steal him blind, billions; empty his Swiss accounts; expose and embarrass. I also know where his warehouses are! You need a fleet of C-130s to haul the cash away. That's my ace in the hole! Now, you can watch the Mexican government burn it in a huge bonfire and giggle in front of the cameras, or you can stuff your pockets!"

Carletta's eyes got wide. "You were saving this gem, this information, for what—blackmail?"

"Insurance!"

"Insurance? You are shrewd, Nathan."

Nathan cracked his knuckles and sat back down. "Have a seat, Carletta."

She sat and looked at him sideways in disbelief.

"I want information and any resource I need up front," Nathan said. "Dark Cloud is still a go. The Mexican navy is still a go!"

"My cut?" she asked bluntly.

Nathan reached out and gently squeezed her hand. "My dear, what's a few billion between friends? Now let me tell *you* about empires!"

CHAPTER 19

Hunger Pangs

Veracruz, Mexico, 2100 Hours

Evan felt grim, worried, and a little annoyed all at the same time. He was hungry but did not want to eat, tired but could not sleep. Something puzzled him, but he could not place his finger on it. He thought about his dog, the snow, his brother, and what his brother would say if he knew what Evan was up to.

He thinks I am on vacation, or does he really know better?

Evan thought about the money that Nathan was going to deposit into his bank—the freedom it provided and the chance to start over off the grid in another country. He thought about conspiracy theories, Nathan, and Andre Pena. Why did his wife have to die, and why, after all these years, was he thinking about it again?

Evan suddenly wanted to flee, to just get out of Mexico and disappear. Truth was, he had no home to go to. He had a dog and no money. He could not even legally drive.

"Evan, what the hell are you doin' in there, lad? You ain't got no hair to wash!"

Evan was back in reality. He stood in the shower in a rented six-bedroom house that sat on a waterway near Veracruz. The house came complete with a three-car garage, a pier, and a small, screened-in indoor swimming pool. He was also sure that they were not the only residents in the neighborhood living in a house with no furniture.

"Sorry, just thinking!" Evan yelled over the running water.

"It ain't good for you!"

Evan dried off, got dressed, and left the bathroom. It was dark outside and a little chilly, and the house felt cold as well with no furniture. Drapes covered the many windows, and the only light Evan could see was from the buoys and other houses on the causeway.

"OK, can we start with a once-over now that the princess is out of the shower?" Roger grumbled.

Evan sat down Indian-style on the hardwood floor. Some sat, and some leaned. Evan realized that part of Green Team Two had joined his team, bringing the crew to about forty people. Equipment in the form of computers and Pelican cases with weapons were piled in the living room. Among the new arrivals, Evan recognized the cute, short Mexican woman with a sweet yet feisty attitude. She seemed to be quite fond of Roger. He recognized some of the drivers and surveillance types whom he had met at the ranch. All in all, Dark Cloud was vastly outnumbered by the various cartel armies and corrupt police who populated the landscape.

Roger clapped his hands. He stood near a dry-erase board. "Listen up. We're going over it one more time, lads. Sorry, but we got some slow folks and new arrivals, so let's get it straight. Yes, we are all tired, and we'll eat in a bit."

"I am only here for the food," Evan added.

No one laughed for once.

"OK, Evan, you and Mia and Tommy, of course, are to meet the boys who will take you aboard the *Happy Mermaid* here, where they suggested." Roger pointed to a map of Veracruz that was taped to the wall.

They were meeting near a hotel in the northern part of the city, right across the street from a marina with a long pier.

The *Happy Mermaid* would most likely be anchored out in the channel.

"You guys will be escorted out to the yacht. Anything happens, and you're on your own."

"Great," Evan said with mock enthusiasm.

"You guys know what to do. Mia, be discreet with planting electronics. I am not sure if they sweep for bugs. We got a team in a room in this hotel here. It should be high enough to pick up your communications till you go inside."

A stocky Mexican with a full beard and wearing an Everlast hoodie spoke. He only wore gym clothes. His name was Joaquin, and he was a fierce warrior and devout Catholic whose grand parents had fought in the Cristero conflict. He had a quiet, calm voice. "My guys are there right now and can confirm that the yacht is anchored. They have a Zodiac boat that has come ashore twice and returned to off-load people. One of the individuals it off-loaded, named Sebastian, looked like a member of the computer team. No sight of Tanya!"

"Sure?" Mia asked. "She was supposed to come ashore and give us an information drop."

"Looks like no one else is leaving the ship. Another puzzling thing too is that there is no helicopter. We have good intel that the helicopter left this afternoon to go to the ship, yet it never came back and is clearly not there. Must have whisked off somewhere else," the man with the hoodie explained.

"OK, let's move on," said Roger.

"Evan and his team make their deal, plant their bugs, and hopefully identify ships armament. If we catch up with Tanya, great; if not, we will go from there. I want a team following Sebastian."

Roger looked around the room. "If all goes according to plan, which it never does, we will have an arrangement for the sub hand-off and a purchase. We have to get Tanya or someone from her team to confirm that the computer virus is active. Regardless, Mario and his sons go up in a ball of flames in a few days. If Tanya was successful, then we all get a major bonus when Nathan divvies up Mario's wealth, like he promised."

Evan smirked and raised his hand. "Can I add something?"

"Sure."

"Keep your finger straight and off the trigger until you are ready to fire, and don't aim at anything you don't intend to shoot. Kill them all. That's all. Call me when the pizza gets here!" Evan got up, packed a dip, grabbed a magazine from one of the team members who was in the middle of reading it, went back into the bathroom, and locked the door.

No one said a word.

CHAPTER 20

Sebastian was terrified.

He had dealt with computer hackers and identity thieves all over the world. For years, he had lived in half a dozen different countries off refund checks from the US IRS for people who did not even exist or who were dead. Sebastian had never even set foot in the States but had wanted to. He had met Tanya in a café in Rio and had signed on with her team and then eventually Dark Cloud. Nothing had prepared him for Mexican drug cartels. He had heard stories of their rituals to the drug-smuggling saints and sacrifices to cults. He'd heard of them raping migrants from El Salvador by the hundreds, burning people alive, melting people in acid, chopping heads off and putting it on YouTube, and even kidnapping school buses full of children in order to sell their organs.

Sebastian did not have even one tattoo nor did he like to drink. He was not a fighter or brash. Now here he was surrounded by four large, by Mexican standards, men who could kill him with their bare hands. He tried not to shake or talk or be so obviously scared. Tanya had given him a micro SD card that held about one gig of data. It was carefully wrapped in plastic and hidden in his tube of Chap Stick.

"If you can make a call, stash this and tell them where it is. Do not get caught. If you do get caught, drink this. It will kill you quickly and painlessly. Being raped and tortured could take hours; this will be seconds."

Sebastian could not stop thinking about the small vial of allergy medicine that was actually poison or the Chap Stick that had enough condemning data on it to collapse Mario's organization and drain him of close to a billion dollars.

Sebastian clutched two plastic bags full of clothes and necessities from Walmart. It was nine fifteen at night, and he was waiting in a crowded Mexican restaurant by the seawall and marina. The four men who were with him were decorated with tattoos that were all very different yet told the same morbid stories of death, rape, submission, and dominance.

"Fat Man!"said one of the gangsters who had identified himself only as the Turtle. "You going to get drunk before we go back. Loosen up, white boy!"

The Turtle was short and wore a sleeveless T-shirt that said, "Your university sucks" on it in English. He had a full set of gold-and-diamond-studded teeth.

"I...I don't drink, but you pick." Sebastian regretted his comment as soon as he said it.

"Don't drink? Don't drink? What are you, gay?" The Turtle got real close to Sebastian. His eyes were glazed, and his breath stank. "You scared?"

Sebastian sat at the small table in the crowded restaurant and clutched his bags. "Yes."

"Hey, Paco, Monkey, the white boy is scared! Bring a bottle of tequila. I knew we should have brought that little tight-ass girl instead, huh?"

"Frenchman saving her for himself!" One of the gangsters laughed.

The gangsters all spoke English and had mannerisms as if they had been educated by rap videos.

Sebastian watched a well-dressed man brush past the crowd and into the bathroom. He was talking on a cell phone and avoided eye contact with the gangsters. The crowd seemed to be clearing out of the restaurant, afraid of its bold new inhabitants.

Sebastian suddenly had an idea and took a deep breath. "I have to go to the bathroom."

The Turtle sat across from Sebastian, putting a beer in front of him. He stared at him for a long second and then shrugged and spoke. "So what? Go, freak!"

Sebastian stood up. "Watch my bags?"

"Get the f…Yes, go!"

Sebastian separated himself from the table and quickly walked into the bathroom. He breathed deep and tried to calm his nerves. He first contemplated asking the man with the cell phone to call the police, but the ramifications of that would be too difficult to sort out. He had heard of a story recently of three teenage girls who had been raped by cartel members down by the Guatemalan border. They had escaped and sought out the local Mexican police for safety—only, the police were owned by the cartels and turned the three right back over to their captors. They were burned alive.

"Excuse me?" Sebastian's Spanish was very proper, and he was sure that he had an odd accent because Mexicans always looked at him funny when he spoke.

The man in the suit who had just been talking on his iPhone was washing his hands. He looked up. "*Sí?*"

"I am planning a surprise party for my friends and am supposed to call my friends to show up, only I forgot my cell phone."

The man looked uneasy for a second and reached for some paper towels.

"I know this is weird. Men don't usually talk in bathrooms. Could I use yours, make a quick call in here? I cannot call out

there. It will ruin the surprise!" Sebastian pulled out a one-hundred-dollar US bill.

"You are not a fag, are you?"

"No." *My God, why do people keep saying that?* Sebastian thought
as he handed the man the money and took his offered phone.

"So, Ivan, what's your story?"

"Too many volumes to even begin, sweetheart." Evan looked
out the window of the taxi as it sped through the streets of
Veracruz on its way north to the hotel.

Tommy was in the front seat, talking a million miles an hour
with the cab driver. Evan barely noticed the malls, billboards, people, or restaurants. His mind was trying to slowly ease into character.

"Short version," Mia said with impatience. "They say you are
unstable, not cut out for this."

"Who are *they*? Someday I will find them."

Mia laughed. "Roger trusts you, and I think you're OK. Let's
just watch each other's backs in there."

"Sure, honey."

"You gonna call me honey all night?"

"No, sweetie," Evan quipped.

"Shut up." Mia laughed and punched him in the arm.

"So are you up for this?" she asked.

Evan nodded. "We are going to have our hands full, extract-
ing Tanya, making a deal with Jorge, and trying to plant devices
on the yacht."

"We will be fine," she said smoothly. "We will just follow the
script. But don't call me sweetie or honey!"

"One thing worries me, Mia."

"What?" she asked.

"Andre Pena. What if he shows up? And, for that matter, what
if the real Mario shows up? On that note, what if I am recognized

from the Juárez operations? Sometimes I think Nathan wants me set up."

Mia whistled and looked at her nails. "That's like three things—pick one."

"Getting recognized," he said quickly.

"Intelligence puts Andre Pena somewhere in Mexico City. They think he is involved in some recent political bombings. The real Mario has been spotted in about three different places throughout Mexico. Of course that's common; he has doubles. No reason anyone should recognize you from Juárez."

Evan packed a dip in his mouth and smiled. "Angel, you familiar with the word *snafu?*"

She looked puzzled. "No."

"That's my life verse. I should have a sign that says, 'Keep back one thousand feet.'"

"You need professional help, sweetheart," Mia said and laughed.

Sebastian quickly made his phone call in the bathroom to a number provided to him by Tanya. He explained to an answering machine what time it was, were he was, how many people he was with, and where he was making the drop. He then added that he was terrified and wanted out now.

"They are going to kill me!" he whispered into the phone.

Sebastian was done with this mission, he wanted out.

He spoke quickly in English. He began to sweat with tension as he said bye to the man with the phone and then went into a bathroom stall. Sebastian felt his heart pounding as he stuck the Chap Stick underneath the toilet tank with some adhesive that he had hidden in his shirt pocket. He dropped the empty container of Dermabond and quickly bent down to pick it up from the tile floor. The Chap Stick was secure.

Three things happened at once that just about caused Sebastian to have a heart attack.

The door burst open, and he heard the Turtle's voice. "Hurry up, Fat Man! Food's getting cold, and we gotta go!"

He had also dropped his suicide liquid into the toilet. When he had bent over, it had plunged into the water.

"I am coming!" Sebastian cursed and left the stall and started to leave the restroom.

"Wait!"

He froze, terrified that death was coming. "Yes?"

"Wash your hands, Fat Man. You're sick!"

The Turtle held the door for him and waited till he was done.

Roger set down a large bowl of beans with rice and chips topped with guacamole and homemade pico de gallo. He went to retrieve his coffee.

The men at the makeshift safe house were grateful as always and devoured anything that he made like locusts. They kept the fact that he wasn't Mexican and could cook Mexican food quiet.

"Hey! We got a situation." Miguel walked into the room wearing a wireless headset. He was holding a cell phone and had an iPad mini in his arm.

"What you got, lad?"

"We have contact with one of Tanya's team."

"Sebastian?" Roger growled.

"Yes. Using some guy's phone in a bathroom, sounded hysterical—he dropped off our intel in a bathroom. Got the address!"

Roger stood up and grabbed his radio and then he looked at the map with the other team members, and within a few moments, they had a plan. The only problem was that they were spread thin.

"We got six safe houses in this area and about seven parked cars set up for emergency evacuations." Miguel spoke rapidly and pointed with his pen at the map of Veracruz. "Problem is, Teams One and Two are converging on the area up here where Ivan and Mia are going. Most of our other assets are at the hotel as well."

"So it's just us?" Roger asked.

"Yes. We can triangulate the call; we have the number and location," Miguel said.

Roger began to feel nervous as if something was about to go wrong.

"Gentlemen," Joaquin began, "my team suggests we rescue Sebastian. Snatch and grab. They may take him back on board, or kill him. They recognized some of his escort. They are errand boys, unstable and show-offs. Not pros, which you know makes them shifty."

"Shit!"

"Here, you see over here!" Miguel pointed on Google Maps and then moved over to point at the map on the wall.

"Well, holy shit. Sebastian is about a block away from us! Let's go get him. We can't wait!" Roger walked to a large plastic box, opened it, and grabbed a folding stock MP-3.

No one spoke for a second.

"Roger, you have already been spotted by these men once, back in Mexico city."

Roger shrugged. "That was weeks ago and hundreds of miles ago. Scotsmen are a dime a dozen around here. I need to get out the house. You guys stay here." Roger pointed to Miguel and Francisco.

Joaquin nodded and put down his cup.

The two men strapped on bulletproof vests and loaded up weapons and ammo. Joaquin pulled on a Federali Police uniform, just in case.

"You drive," Roger grumbled and headed out the door.

Evan and Mia pulled up to the hotel, tipped the cab driver, and got out.

"Here we are," Tommy said quickly as he lit up a cigarette.

Evan looked around the empty parking lot, the marina, and the hotel, which towered over them. There was a traffic circle in front of him with a light traffic and pedestrians walking along the seawall. Evan thought for a moment that this could be a romantic venue if it wasn't for the fact that he was about to meet some of the most hardened killers in the world.

"Here they come," Mia said.

Mia squeezed Evan's arm and pulled him toward a pier that jutted off from a private marina landing. Only a few small boats were moored at the pier, and other than two teenagers talking on their scooters and an old man fishing, the scene was fairly empty.

Evan looked up at the hotel and hoped that he was being watched by his team. Not that it would do any good. *No communication, no weapons, no nothing—this is it.*

Mia seemed to read Evan's thoughts and walked close to him to stay warm.

"Here." He stripped off his Windbreaker and gave it to her.

"Thanks."

Tommy, Mia, and Evan moved down the wooden dock and watched a fairly large, flat-bottomed party boat pull up to the end. Six well-dressed men in their midthirties jumped off and held the mooring lines. They did not bother tying up the boat.

"Tommy?" Jorge waved and yelled.

Tommy waved in recognition and smiled. "*Hola*, Jorge. We going to party out on the town first or what?"

"Not tonight, my friend. Have some sad news and some issues."

A well-built man in his fifties stepped onto the pier and waved for Tommy and his friends to come close. They did as told. Evan sized up Jorge Valdez and his men in a matter of seconds. His henchmen were not your poor gangsters from the slums or rejects from the prisons that were so often used as hired guns by the cartels. These men had shifty eyes, deep intelligence, and seemed awkward in suits, like special-forces operators who had to wear their uniforms once a year.

These men were undoubtedly the Scorpions.

"Ivan, this is Jorge Valdez," Tommy said. "Jorge, this is Ivan and his secretary, Mia."

"Come aboard, and let me offer you a drink." Jorge guided his guests over to a tiny glass table and pulled the chair out for Mia. He then sat down at its head and motioned for Ivan and Tommy to sit. "Bring the lady some of my wine. I have a vineyard in Italy, sweet and smooth like you." He smiled at Mia and squeezed her hand.

"Tommy, I know what you drink—pretty much anything, like a vulgar American. You, Ivan, you are hard to peg. Half Cuban and half Russian, eh? Mojito or vodka? I can tell a lot about you by what you drink." Jorge smiled. He let the back of his hand slide across Mia's breasts ever so smoothly as he reached for an ashtray. "Excuse me. Sorry."

"That's OK. They are big and get in the way."

Jorge about choked and began to laugh. Evan was impressed. By not being too prudish and having a good sense of humor, she had won him over.

"I prefer mescal," Evan said flatly. What he really wanted was a rum and Coke and a dip.

The drinks were served, and the boat gently began to move away from Veracruz until the streetlights began to shrink and glimmer and only a white-foam wake glowing in the moonlight connected them to land.

"Jorge, you said you have bad news. The sub deal?" Tommy started.

Evan nodded and thought, *Good, don't waste my time. Get to the point.*

"No! No, my friend! The deal is on. I was visited by Mario Jr. earlier today, and he said we can pay you for it." Jorge suddenly frowned. "Unfortunately, he and the helicopter he was flying on never made it back to shore. We suspect they crashed, weather or mechanical problems."

"That's horrible! Mario must be upset to lose a son!" Tommy said with sincere sympathy.

Jorge drank his mescal and looked out to sea and then back. His eyes did not blink, and he smiled. "Yes, terrible. I told his father that his son wanted the sale to go on as soon as possible. He would have wanted his father to have this big toy for his birthday. We will celebrate Mario Jr.'s life and Mario Sr.'s birthday on the same day this year."

"We can wait, Jorge. My God!" said Tommy.

"No, no. We will talk on board. Mario will want to speak with you, both of you. I think the sale is best, and we will have a big party when we deliver it. This may be what he needs."

Tommy looked around the boat and at his hands and then drained his glass.

"Let's have a toast to Mario Jr.!" Tommy exclaimed.

"Yes!" Jorge agreed.

Sebastian settled into the backseat of a black Humvee with cushy leather seats and tinted windows. He could not find the seat belt, and when he could not figure out what to do with his hands, he just folded them in his lap.

The Turtle sat next to him smoking a cigarette while the other gangbangers sat in the front seat. The music was so loud that

Sebastian could barely think, and the smoke made him cough. The Humvee moved out into traffic and started heading back north toward the marina.

"Hey!" the Turtle said. "Turn it down."

The music went off, and Sebastian listened to the conversation between the three men.

"Take a side trip to the garage."

"We got to get back, bitch!"

"After we do a little something."

"We just ate. You gotta shit already?"

"You got the blowtorch in the back?"

"Always."

Sebastian suddenly realized this conversation was scripted as if they were purposefully building him up for something. He realized he was never going to leave the Humvee alive.

Roger and Joaquin parked on the curb at the intersection of Xicotencatl and Francisco Javier Mina and casually walked into a tiny glass-front café that had seen better days.

"In my opinion,"—Roger spoke in English, which is what Joaquin insisted he speak in—"the places that look like dumps like these are usually the best."

"True. Fish tacos to go are their mainstay, but everything is excellent. Been here years ago."

The small café had a single glass door, which was propped open with a milk crate, and a glass front, which afforded a view into the restaurant. There were about five cheap plastic tables, which were occupied, and a wooden counter with a cash register on top.

Roger immediately realized they had missed Sebastian. "He is not even in there!"

"This is the place. Our backup should be here in about ten minutes."

The two men walked into the café, and all motion seemed to stop.

Roger about knocked over a well-dressed man who was talking on an iPhone. "Excuse me." Roger was about to let the man walk politely by when Joaquin seized him.

"Back inside!"

Roger stood half in the door and half on the street, his MP-5 ready, not really caring right now that they were completely blown cover-wise.

Joaquin quickly held up his Federali identification and let his MP-5 hang on its shoulder holster. He spoke in rapid Spanish. "This is a police matter. Stay calm, but *put that phone down!* That's better. No one move. We are looking for a short, fat Australian. He's white. He would be with four men he should not be with!"

No one spoke for a second. Roger eyed the well-dressed man, who was looking a little gray.

"That man was talking to the narcos. We know who they are!" A pregnant teenage girl behind the counter spoke up. "He was in here with the Turtle, who comes in here every week or so. Scares customers, but tips well if I show him some smiles."

"Go on."

Roger watched the tables. People seemed to be ignoring them and going back to their eating. They didn't touch their phones or text anyone. Roger felt foolish for not having the equipment to jam signals; however, that probably would not matter anyway if someone on the street spotted the police. Lookouts for the cartels were everywhere.

"Sir, excuse me!" the well-dressed man said.

Roger looked at the well-dressed man whom he had stopped at the door. He took a step back into the café and sat down on a stool. He seemed to be sweating. Roger nodded.

Joaquin looked critically at the man in a way that made Roger uneasy. Roger figured that Joaquin probably was a real cop; he handled himself just like an asshole.

"Talk!" Roger said.

"I was in the bathroom, and this gringo gave me one hundred dollars to use my phone. He said it was about a surprise party. I thought he was gay at first, but he was nervous." The man paused to pull out a cigarette and light it with shaky fingers. "I came out, bought a pack of smokes from Maria there." He pointed at the pregnant teenager. "I laughed and told her what happened."

Maria, who was overly enthusiastic, chimed in. She was short and not ugly, but one would have guessed she was much older. "The narcos overheard him! That's when they left. Grabbed the fat white guy and took off in their truck! I knew they were mad. I think they were kidnapping him. The Turtle works for the Gulf Cartel, gangster wannabe!"

"Shut up, Maria!" A customer stood up. "You and your family are dead talking this way!"

Roger pointed his weapon at the young male who had suddenly stood up. He was skinny, and his pants had to be constantly pulled up.

The teenager started talking again.

"I don't care! We all know! They took that man out of here. The police never do anything around here. I was raped last year in his brother's garage. Said he would change my oil for free! Liar! No police ever did a thing—*laughed at me*, said I begged for it 'cause I have no money. I have a job! Screw all of them. Curse them all!" She began to scream hysterically and cry.

A few customers tried to stand up and comfort her, but she would have none of it. She just screamed and confessed all of the wrongs that had been done to her.

Roger could not understand much once she started yelling. They just talked too fast, and Mexicans had a particular way of putting things.

"Roger, go into the bathroom and find the item. We got seconds, not minutes!"

Roger cursed and lunged through the small café and into the urine- and beer-smelling bathroom. He almost ripped the toilet from the wall until he remembered to lift the lid from the tank. He found the Chap Stick container and shoved it in his pocket.

Maria was still screaming hysterically about relatives, friends, pets, anyone she could think of who had been wronged by the cartels or police. To her they were one and the same.

"Roger, let's go!"

Roger was about out of the café. He was breathing heavy and then paused. The girl was crying now with half a dozen people around her. The skinny boy with the loose jeans had fled, presumably to call the bad guys.

Joaquin honked the horn and beckoned him to hurry up.

Roger looked back at the girl and then grumbled, "Hold on!"

He took off his ski mask and then reached in his back pocket and pulled out two wads of bills, which every member of Dark Cloud had for emergencies, like bribes, transportation, or basic escape-and-evasion tactics.

"Get out of my way!" Roger parted the small, tanned people with his massive hands and put his hands on the girl's shoulders.

She was sitting now, wet hair sticking to her face.

"Take this and disappear, sweetheart. It's about two thousand. Vanish!" He spoke in English, not even thinking about it, and then turned to leave.

"Thanks. Thank you! You're not the police?"

Roger got into the Suburban and fought with his seat belt as Joaquin floored it.

Tanya was finishing her last set of push-ups and pull-ups on the top deck of the *Happy Mermaid* when she noticed the small party boat unload its passengers. She felt a burn in the pit of her stomach. She should be ashore right now, free with her whole team. Veracruz was only a mile swim. She could make it, but if they discovered her, she and everyone else were dead. The *Happy Mermaid* had a well-stocked gym that was glassed-in and afforded a panoramic view of the ocean and Veracruz. She could watch who came and went and get in a workout. She never worked out during daylight for fear that the muscle heads, the Scorpions, would be grunting and farting and staring at her. Tanya grabbed her towel and wiped the sweat from her face.

Sebastian, I hope you make it. She felt a twinge of guilt at having sent him bogus information, but her deep distrust of Nathan and practically everyone had given her cause to be paranoid. Tanya had given Sebastian all of the detailed inner workings of Mario's organization—names, accounting information, tax documents, business documents, legal documents—information that would make any law-enforcement officer or prosecutor. Over a hundred politicians, police, and other criminals would go away for life with such evidence.

Tanya started hitting the heavy bag now with some oversized gloves left by one of the muscle heads. Her shoulders were tense and her jaw set.

Nathan will be pissed, but he will have to rescue me, she thought, *and negotiate.*

Tanya had changed Mario's passwords and account information on half a dozen different bank accounts and had the contact information rerouted to her. By the time Mario, or anyone,

SILVER, LEAD, AND DEAD

figured out that half a billion dollars was slowly being dribbled away, she was hoping to be long gone.

Tanya took off the gloves and thought about Dark Cloud. She had to figure out a way to make sure the workers got their share and that Nathan would be cut off and screwed, yet whom could she trust, and how much time did she have? Nathan had suggested that if anything happened to the real Ivan, her boyfriend, he could take over in the sexual department. "You killed him. I know it."

"Hey!"

"Ahh, crap!" She spun around to face Gerard.

"Sorry to scare you. Jorge wants you to come join us for dinner. I have Susan here. She can loan you some decent clothes, a dress."

Tanya crossed her arms over her chest and felt very self-conscious of his eyes. *Why did men have to stare so much? It's like they forget what boobs look like and are afraid they will never see them again!* she thought. "No choice?"

"He would consider it rude. He wants you to meet a man."

"OK. When is Sebastian coming back? He was getting shampoo and conditioner for me!"

"You can use mine," Susan said with a Barbie smile. She was young, perhaps twenty, and appeared to be an American-born mix, probably from Trinidad or Haiti, and white. She was beautiful and dumb.

"OK, fine. Sebastian—where is he?"

Gerard shrugged. "Haven't had the time to check on him. But I will."

Evan and Mia made themselves comfortable at a large oak table set up in a circular dining room surrounded by glass and screens. The table was set for twelve with brilliant china and crystal that

Evan guessed had cost thousands. Evan drank from his glass and had it filled instantly by one of the six waitstaff who stood encircling the table. There was a slight breeze in the air, which caused some of the wind chimes to tingle and the waiters to close the sliding glass doors. Evan was starting to feel hungry and wondered what was for dinner.

"Nice dinner cruise, huh?" he whispered to Mia.

"Yes. No doubt. Look at the pictures on the wall. Mexican presidents, American film stars, and a few senators."

"From both sides of the border," Evan commented.

Mia whispered. "Empty helicopter pad. Wonder if Mario is coming to this meeting?"

Evan shrugged and watched guests filter into the room, shake hands, nod, and look for their names. Jorge entered with his six bodyguards, and everyone stood.

Evan again sized up this new set of bodyguards and came to the same conclusion: these were the professional shooters. Evan never forgot a face, and he instantly recognized one of the slimmer-build henchmen. He seemed stressed enough that he must be in charge of something.

Frenchman, he thought.

Mia squeezed his hand and leaned close to whisper in his ear. She smiled as if she were saying something funny but was instead quite serious. "The guy whose jaw you broke, Gerard, he is there. The other man next to him is the man who organized Manuel's kidnapping. His name is Yuri."

"Guess they outsource their best psychos. Getting Europeans to do the jobs Mexicans won't do," Evan mused.

Mia rolled her eyes and pinched Evan in the arm like a sister. "You are such an ass," she said through the clenched teeth of a fake smile.

Evan shrugged and watched her stick a thumbnail-sized piece of tape underneath the table. The transmitter was good up to two miles and could transmit for twenty-four hours. He wondered how many other devices she had already planted.

Roger and Joaquin had just finished doing a quick recon of the garage from across the street when Team Four arrived in a white Toyota Land Cruiser.

"One entrance on the side alley. There's a fire door in the back that opens to an empty parking lot surrounded by the other buildings. Locked with a chain," Roger whispered into his radio.

The leader of Team Four was named Munoz, and he had belonged to an elite team of the navy before jumping ship and joining Dark Cloud. "We can blow the door off the hinges, and you guys can toss a flash-bang in from the side door. We need about six seconds," Munoz said quickly.

Roger looked sideways at Joaquin and nodded. The blinds were drawn on the garage, and the lights were out. Loud music could be heard inside the garage, undoubtedly to muffle whatever was going on inside.

The Turtle regarded his prisoner with a smile. He loved it when they screamed, yet this one was so scared, and he had not even done anything yet. He had Sebastian tied firmly to a wooden chair with duct tape over his mouth. Tears streamed down his face, and snot ran in rivers from his nose. He had his men hold the fat man's hands as he secured them to the arms of the chair with a nail gun.

"Blowtorch next. Now, who the hell did you call on that man's phone?" The Turtle ripped the tape from Sebastian's mouth and waited for him to stop sobbing. "Stop it! Stop it! I have raped teenage girls that have cried less than you, ha!"

His friends laughed.

The Turtle put the muzzle of his .357 to the top of the man's head and looked back at his three friends. Two of them were smoking joints and trying not to laugh. The other two looked bored and played with their guns. No one was watching the doors or the windows.

The Turtle suddenly saw a shadow cross by the bottom of the heavy wooden door into the garage.

"Hey, Paco? Did you lock the door?"

"Huh?"

That's when the chaos began.

Boom! Boom!

The initial explosion behind the Turtle scared him so bad that he squeezed his trigger, blowing the top off Sebastian's head.

He cursed and brought his gun up but could not see. Something was in his eyes.

"Police!" someone yelled.

Smoke, controlled fast *pops*, and another deafening explosion all seemed to blend together. The Turtle felt something powerful slam into his body as he spun and fell. He saw boots and his friends being shredded by bullets.

"Wha—"

Someone placed something hard into the back of his head and spoke calmly in a funny accent. "Lights out, shit fur brains."

Pop.

Roger stepped over the kid who used to be the Turtle and looked at his watch. He dug his hearing protection out of his ears. "You were not kiddin' about six seconds!"

"I never kid with time, *amigo*," Munoz said flatly as he let his weapon dangle on its sling and put a piece of gum in his mouth.

"Roger, Sebastian is dead!" Joaquin yelled.

"Crap! OK, mates, strip these scum of their identities, cell phones. Leave the bodies as they are. Torch the place."

Nathan got the phone call as he was just getting out of the shower. Sophia, a prominent Mexican socialite and activist handed him the phone as she walked past him, naked and smiling. "For you, sweetheart," she whispered. She went into the shower and closed the door.

Nathan shook his head. He hated it when others answered his phone, but for her he would make an exception. Nathan put on his bathrobe and sat on the corner of the large bed. Sophia had been helping him work out his frustrations for the past few hours in the penthouse at the Hyatt Regency in Mexico City. She had also provided him with some dirt on Carletta.

"*Hola?*"

"Roger here."

Nathan paused and felt the tension creep back into his neck. "Any word from Tanya?"

"No. Bad news though. Sebastian—"

"Who?"

"One of her computer-geek friends. He was taken ashore by the looks of things to do some shopping and return to the ship. He dropped off the computer data but got made in the process."

"What?"

"He's dead."

"The computer info? Witnesses?"

"Taken care of. We lost a man, you prick!"

Nathan reached for the remote. The soccer game was on, and he wanted to catch the last half. "Terrible. Just terrible. Where is Tanya?"

"Still on board," Roger said.

"Get the computer intel to me ASAP. Clean up the mess. Secure Tanya if possible," Nathan said.

He could hear Roger's pause.

"Can you make sure Ivan, or Evan—what's his name—gets off the boat alive?" Nathan hung up and cursed out loud to the room. "I need my money!"

Carletta worried him. If he did not give her a little something soon, she would surely pull the plug on Dark Cloud, whatever that meant. Would she leak their identities to the cartels?

Andre Pena drank the last of his margarita and leaned against the rail of the top-floor balcony of Jorge's penthouse. Jorge had given him instructions to keep out of sight and make himself at home. Andre looked out over the city of Veracruz, the busy streets, and the calm gulf, which stretched out to the horizon. He had a lot to think about and considered the path before him. "I will need a lot of supplies for this operation."

He went to his computer and composed an e-mail to Jorge describing the materials he would need. In the last five months, Andre had set up six training camps around the most obscure parts of Mexico for Jorge's private army of commandos. Most of these men had military training in explosives, yet he took them to an entirely new level: making a bomb without a massive budget and constructing and planting IEDs and VBIEDs. He had instructed the men on how to read the enemy, what their SOPs were, and how their love of laws bound them up to the point of paralysis. In a few days, he was going to construct his masterpiece.

Mario's birthday party would be at a private beach house belonging to a prominent Mexican politician. The assassination of such a large group of politicians would launch Jorge into his new order, as he called it.

"To the new Mexico. Home of President Jorge and the Narco Party!" Andre Pena laughed out loud and walked back outside. He looked off in the distance and could see the flashing lights of fire trucks weaving through traffic, miles away.

"Should not play with matches!" He laughed.

Gerard took the small Zodiac ashore with Yuri, who mainly worked with his own crew in Mexico City. The Scorpion bosses called their groups cells, and they were dispersed throughout Mexico's territories or plazas. The turf wars had heated up in the past few years, creating so many military groups that Gerard could not keep them straight.

"Can't stand dress-up parties like that!" Yuri exclaimed. He had a thick Russian accent and was fluent in Spanish and French.

"It's about time to get out of this freaking country, Yuri!"

The two men bounced along over the dark, oily waves, heading toward the shimmering city lights. The water smelled like fish, oil, and stale mud.

"Jorge's going to get us killed with this taking-over-Mexico thing. We really need to pull in all of our troops. Mario's loyalists will go berserk when he gets taken out." Yuri spoke.

"I told him this. He says he has the three other cartels backing us. We will have to kill thousands over the next few weeks, quickly and quietly, after this whole thing goes down."

"Sounds like the bloody Russian Revolution." Yuri laughed.

"Or the French," Gerard corrected.

The two men rode along in silence for a few moments, feeling the spray on their faces.

Evan listened to Tommy give the sales pitch as the dishes were cleared. Mia had gone to the bathroom and had even taken a tour of the yacht with one of the other girls at the dinner party. Mia played her part as if she were famous. She greeted people with smiles, shook hands, gave hugs, and listened with intensity to Mexico's upper elite go on about their ungrateful children in schools in the States or their villas in Europe. Evan watched her with respect and amusement. He kept to himself and took advantage of the free wine and food that he would normally never touch. Evan watched the body language of Jorge and the politicians as they ate and talked. Evan had a feeling that Jorge was not a fan of the sub but was going along with it with enthusiasm. Too much enthusiasm.

"So, Ivan, where are you from?"

Evan looked at Tanya and smiled, pretending like he did not know her. "All over. Mostly grew up in Europe as a child."

"Amazing. Ever been to Brazil?"

"Yes."

Evan pretended to listen as she spoke to him about useless, empty bits of small talk. He wondered where Gerard and Russian had stolen off to. Evan really wanted to walk around the deck of the yacht.

Tanya moved close to him. She was clearly uncomfortable in a dress that fit too big in the chest and waist. She pressed a napkin into his hand and then stood up. "I need to get some air. Be right back."

Jorge nodded and smiled. Jorge seemed to be her self-appointed protector and kept an eye on her like a father might watch his daughter among a group of young boys.

Evan read the napkin under the table: "Meet me in five."

"So, Ivan, can you agree to the terms that Tommy has set out here" Jorge asked.

"Yes."

"Good."

Jorge stopped talking to a man who Evan swore was a news anchor on a local TV station. "Ivan, be honest. Will you be able to deliver, let's say, the day after tomorrow?"

Evan drained his glass and paused as if he were really thinking about his answer. "Moving everything forward a day will be a stretch. This island you speak of, if it has a deep-water channel and a large-enough dock, mmm, we can make it work. You will need to build something to protect the sub from prying eyes from above."

"Will do."

"Well, I tell you what, Jorge, since the sub still needs some work, I will have my men bring it to your island, and they can just work on it there. I will give you a maintenance contract and crew for the first year, and they can train your men. I want you to be successful. I also want to train your men properly. I am very particular. There is an art to loading supplies from a submerged sub. Lots of details to work out."

"Yes, yes. Mario has men who will be all ears when they meet you. Me? I am not an engineer, but I know they are here somewhere!" Jorge laughed and looked around the table. He even looked under the table. A woman in her midthirties jumped as if she had been touched.

"Jorge! You dirty old…"

People laughed.

Evan smiled on the outside and wished he had a flamethrower. He drank more wine and began to have sinister thoughts.

"I will knock a cool six million off the price since I am delivering something early and not in perfect order. I have my reputation," Evan said across the ongoing conversations, as if he were doing friends a favor.

Tommy's eyes got wide, but he nodded with approval.

Jorge sucked on his cigar and grinned. "If only Mario Jr. was here. Well, his father has given me the go-ahead. Our navy expert, whom you took to see the sub, has said it's a good boat. Looks like this thing has undergone a ton of upgrades."

"Definitely," Evan agreed.

Jorge smiled. "You are honest. I like that."

Evan nodded and spoke. "I don't blow smoke. I have to hit the bathroom. Need some air too. Mind if I walk around the yacht? I admire its workmanship. I am guessing that the engine and hull were made in Germany and the finishing touches were done in Italy."

Jorge nodded with approval. "You know your yachts. Modeled after a Russian billionaire's. Mario did not want to be outdone."

Evan smiled. "Need an antimissile system?"

"Ha! No, but we have antiaircraft capabilities." Jorge laughed. The alcohol had loosened his lips, and for that Evan was thankful.

"Amazing!"

"Later I show you, huh?"

Evan stood up and gave Jorge the thumbs-up. People loved to brag about their toys, even if they belonged to someone else.

"Be right back."

Evan made his way to the men's room. The drinking part of the dinner was in full effect, and Evan knew that they were all buddies now.

He went into the one-room bathroom, locked the door, and turned on the light. He waited for the knock and let Tanya in. She was quite beautiful and did not look like such a bitch right now.

"What's up?" Evan asked.

"Sebastian?"

"Huh? Don't know."

Her breath smelled like wine, and she drew close to him and whispered, "You hate Nathan?"

Evan could sense that she was scared, and even if she was just being nice for that reason, he still felt bad for her, crazy or not. "Of course."

"Then I trust you," she said.

"Huh?" Evan felt confused, if not concerned.

"I need a friend. I need an ally—really. Nathan is not what he seems. This mess here, it is not what it seems." Tanya moved closer so that her lips were next to Evan's chin.

"Go on," Evan whispered.

"I think Jorge had someone killed today on the yacht, someone important. There was cleaning with bleach, and I overheard some maids talking. Carpets being removed, bloody towels."

"OK."

"Jorge is planning something. Me and you need to talk, but don't share this with Nathan. I have looked at his e-mails; he is planning a coup or something. Don't know how yet."

"What else? Hobbies, girlfriends?" Evans asked, his mind was working to build a profile on him or anyone they could use.

Tanya thought for a long second. "Has a hot ex-cop-turned-real-estate-agent girlfriend in Boca del Rio. Penthouse, likes to travel. Been to a place called Virginia Beach a few times."

Evan's throat went dry. "How do you know?"

"I am a hacker, Ivan. He has a redhead in some place, a town where they dress like old colonial England. Saw pictures on his computer."

"Williamsburg?" Evan asked.

"That's it! I can't get much else. They have turned off the Internet. I gave Sebastian some damning evidence! Now, I should have just kept it. I could have slipped it to you. If I could turn on and use my system, I could tell you everything."

Tanya paused and took a deep breath. She seemed to be on the verge of tears.

Evan felt awkward but tried to be sweet. He felt bad for her. She was over her head. "I had no idea we would meet, babe."

"I have to tell you something—promise not to deceive me," she said.

Evan felt as if he were talking to an irrational high school girl; was she playing him, or was she coming unglued? "Promise. But I need to know about the ship's weapons. We have to get you out of here tonight."

"Can't...Look, when I leave this boat I will have to go to Mexico City; we have one more job to do for Mario. Hook everything up to his servers—at that point everything goes live. After that, I get debriefed by Nathan. That's what really scares me."

"Why?" Evan was confused.

"You have to protect me from him!"

Evan gave her a hug and kissed the top of her head. "It's going to be OK. Promise. I got your back. Call or text when you're done. Nothing's going to happen."

She sniffed. "Sorry. I am crying like a bitch, Ivan." She took a deep breath and then unloaded the burden that was troubling her. "I just stole a billion of the dollars that Nathan was going to steal. Hid it from him. The accounts are in my head. I moved it all. Nathan doesn't give a shit about the police intel—it's about the money."

Evan sucked in his air and let it out slowly. "Wow."

"I have to escape once I am done in Mexico City, before or soon after I debrief. He will figure it out eventually."

"Why?" Evan asked. "You just stirred up a hornets nest. Text me when you are done; I will see what I can do. I need time to think."

"Ivan, I got my reasons. He was never going to split the money with Dark Cloud. I am going to! No time to explain but I need an ally."

Suddenly, a knock at the door made them both jump.

CHAPTER 21

Safe House

Roger made it back to the safe house after midnight. He was tired and confused, and he had a headache. No one spoke on the ride home. Sebastian's death was just the first in a long line of deaths that they knew were coming.

Roger, Joaquin, and now Francisco and others from Dark Cloud were assembled in the safe house's living room.

"One of you has to take this to Nathan back at HQ," Roger said and held up the micro SD card. "Any word from our surveillance teams?"

"Yes. Evan, Tommy, and Mia are being dropped off. Sounds like they had a good time—drunk as hell!" Francisco added.

Roger ignored the underhanded jab that someone had had a good time. "Crap. We have to access the fallout from this Sebastian thing. Make some calls, get connected with our contacts with local law enforcement, get the ears and eyes out." Roger opened a bottle of water.

Joaquin spoke up. "Roger, we have to get the word out there that the whole Sebastian thing was some kinda gang hit, a fluke. They won't likely make the leap that the sub sale or Sebastian or some conspiracy has any tie to them. We can call and have some of our crime bloggers put the word out there."

Roger shrugged. "Do what you think is best. Something about all this just doesn't sit right. Bring Evan in the morning. Have him and the crew stay in a hotel tonight. Can't afford to have him be traced to us. We bug out in an hour, split up, and then reroute at the next safe house at zero six hundred."

Roger looked at the Chap Stick with the computer data and shook his head.

Boca del Rio, Veracruz, 0200 Hours

Gerard and Yuri were having a hard time standing without swaying gently on their feet. Both men were exhausted and had ridden around for the past two and a half hours with various lookouts and police who were on their bankroll. Anyone who was connected knew that the city belonged to the Eastern Cartel and the Scorpions, though sometimes turf wars did come knocking.

Yuri sat on a brown desk in the middle of a warehouse that housed stolen merchandise, ranging from cars to microwaves and occasionally young El Salvadoran female migrants who acted as bonded sex slaves during their long, painful journey to the States.

"What's the deal?" Yuri had taken his shirt off and lay his Glock 22 on the table. Two young, topless girls kneaded his shoulders.

"Poor thing, you are so tense," one girl said.

"Yes, this life is stressful, my sweets."

"Can you take us to *Norteamérica* soon?"

"Yes, soon. My back really hurts sooo much. Oh, that's nice!" Yuri closed his eyes. He loved massages; he had chronic pain from a parachute accident years ago with the Russian army. He heard a loud noise, like a door sliding open, and then multiple footsteps. Yuri watched Gerard and three policemen walk past a brand-new forklift and into the center of the warehouse. Gerard had a badly beaten young man with him. His hands were tied behind his back, his shirt was gone, and his pants could hardly stay up.

Gerard pushed him so that he fell to his knees. He seemed to crumple into a ball of sweat, blood, and grime.

"Who's this?" Yuri asked, too tired to care.

The police officers headed toward the large refrigerator and beer. "One of our little lookouts. He saw the whole thing and let Maria, the bitch who runs our café, run off. She cleaned out the cash register. Took one of my guns too," Gerard said and kicked the boy. "Will this night ever end? Bring me a beer!"

Yuri sat, still enjoying his massage. He spoke pitifully to the teenage girls who were kneading his back. "See what I have to go through? The stress? Always dealing with these criminals!"

"Poor thing."

"Awwww."

They kissed him gently.

"I could not make it without you two." Yuri sighed and snapped his fingers. "Sweetie Uno, get the man a cerveza!"

Gerard stood over the boy, looking tired and annoyed. Yuri smelled smoke, sweat, and body odor.

"You stink, Frenchy. You been in a fire?"

Gerard drained his beer and looked at his friend. He always got a kick out of how, no matter where Yuri went, he ended up having females do things for him.

"Yes. The Turtle and his four idiots, they were all shot, stripped of their phones and IDs, and burned. The man Sebastian, who they were torturing for some freaking reason, was dead too! Whole place torched."

"Police?" Yuri asked.

The three police officers shrugged and laughed.

"Word is, they were raided, some rival gang, professional-military style though, flash-bangs, breaching charges. Boys never knew what hit them."

Yuri pointed his gun at the sobbing boy. "Him?"

"He has a story you may be interested in." Gerard sunk into a chair that was brought to him.

"Speak." Yuri commanded.

The boy opened his mouth and began his tale, between sobs, of the two men who raided the restaurant. "And when they left, the big gringo...He was big, like a giant with a beard and long hair, funny accent, not *norteamericano*. I spent my summers in Texas. The white people up there no speak like that."

"What did he say, look like?"

"I tell you, big like a giant! He gives Maria a pile of money before he leaves. The other man was dressed like a cop. They drove a nice Ford Explorer."

Yuri raised his hand, and the boy stopped talking. "Got it. And then you let Maria empty the safe and steal my gun."

"I could not stop her. Please understand, she had the crowd on her side!" the boy pleaded.

Yuri shook his head, raised his gun, and shot the teenager between the eyes.

Everyone jumped, and for a second it got real quiet.

"That really did not help my headache," Yuri moaned. "But I could not handle the little thing's whining!"

Gerard ran his hand over his sweaty, bald head. "That man, he is the Scotsman. I tell you, the same man involved in the Mexico City rescue of Manuel Rosa. Now tell me I am making stuff up! The man in Juárez at the airport, he is the one who beat me up. *All* this is connected, Yuri! Someone is playing us! That computer freak had something these people wanted, and he was on our yacht. You with me? Am I just imagining this?"

Yuri looked at the Boca del Rio police officers. "I want surveillance tapes. I want a picture of this man. No, Gerard, you are not mad."

"I am going to bed." Yuri stood up and snapped his fingers. "Ladies!"

CHAPTER 22

Lead Rules, Blood Pools

Veracruz, Mexico, Monday, 0600 Hours

Evan woke up the next morning on the floor. The members of Dark Cloud had splurged at a local sporting-goods store and bought folding chairs, a card table, sleeping bags, and mats. Evan had two things on his agenda: a call to his brother and a run.

He began walking up the narrow sidewalk toward the gulf. He felt a slight breeze and heard the distant, mournful cry of a ship.

Evan thought about the meeting with Jorge, who actually was a charming guy if you could get past the murder and mayhem.

The sub deal would go down on a private 550-square-acre island north of Cancun. The island boasted a deep-water dock and sturdy seawall. The island was owned by an Old World, politically connected family.

Nathan had arranged for military support with the Mexican government. Evan had his doubts that they would show up.

"That thing is going to be spotted," he had informed the cartel members last night.

No one seemed to care. Throwing money away was just no big deal.

The sub was technically Mario's at this point, and Evan just had to be on hand to deliver it tomorrow. Evan thought about the repairs, the service contract, and all the legitimate angles of the sub deal that could possibly delay the transaction. Evan had negotiated with Jorge to have a crew of his own men service and conduct the first run with the sub.

Jorge, however, was determined to hire a crew from Europe to handle the sub. "I am fine with that, but until they are vetted and hired, we will help protect your investment!"

From its new home, the sub could easily hide in the deep waters of the Caribbean. The sub could sneak behind Cuba and make its way to Florida. The trip would take about three days. The US Navy had made cutbacks on their detection capabilities but would still be looking.

Evan thought about the cover-up and denials from the Pentagon a few years ago when a Russian Akula-class nuclear-powered sub patrolled US waters for close to a month unnoticed. Some surmised that it was making a trial run to nuke American cities, which was part of the plan to cause a major catastrophe. The stealth submarine had caused serious waves among the elite bean counters. The American sheeple, of course, were too busy twerking and waving whatever flag was popular at the moment to notice that their walls were crumbling. "Idiots." Evan spat on the sidewalk.

The meeting on a private island near Cozumel was a better venue for conducting a military assault than the open ocean.

Evan looked over his shoulder and saw a man picking up cigarette butts off the ground and trying to smoke them. Evan fished for a five-dollar bill in his pocket and handed it to the man as he walked by. He thought about what Tanya had said for the hundredth time.

"Protect me from Nathan."

Evan had a distrust of Nathan, but what Tanya had said was far deeper: she had a paranoid hatred. It did not take Evan long to figure Tanya out. She pretty much hated or feared everything. She was unstable, yet had warmed up to Evan, perhaps out of fear that she had no friends. Sebastian was the only one on her team whom she had trusted. Evan sensed that Tanya was perhaps drawn to him because he was the complete opposite of her.

"Or she knows I am a sucker and will protect her, even if she is crazy," Evan muttered to himself.

Evan considered her statement about Jorge being in Williamsburg, Virginia. This disturbed Evan more than her stealing a billion dollars and then having the guts to admit it.

Evan thought about Camp Perry nestled on the York River. "Could there be a connection?" Evan muttered.

He felt his heart begin to pound and stuffed his paranoia. "No, can't be. But why not? Manuel Noriega was recruited by the CIA while he was in school in Peru. A slew of our enemies had been our friends before they were our enemies again."

Evan began to jog and now thought about fish bait. "I have to get her off that damn boat. She has the potential to collapse this whole house of cards if she is found out."

He was not angry at Roger for sending the computer data to Nathan. He just would not have done it himself until he had examined it. Something deeper was going on; he just could not put his finger on it. "Trust, but verify."

Evan decided he would not share her funneling of Mario's money to herself with anyone. He decided he could get a migraine trying to figure her out.

Evan ran for about thirty minutes as the pink-and-orange glaze of morning began to spread across the gulf. A breeze picked up, and he heard sea gulls and surf in the distance. He wondered what people on the other side of the ocean were doing at this exact moment. The truth was, the whole human race was pretty much equally jacked up.

"This world is a mess. Nothing new under the sun," Evan spoke to the wind. "OK, time to make the call." He looked at the phone in his hand and imagined what his brother would say. "Screw it."

Evan dialed his brother, and started to feel a little nervous, like a child who was about to get a scolding or tell his dad that he had just wrecked the car.

His brother answered the phone half asleep. "Hello?"

"*Hola*, it's me. How's my dog?"

"Huh?"

Evan took a deep breath and stared at the ocean. *Here goes everything*, he thought. "We gotta talk. Listen carefully."

Evan turned his back to the gulf.

Veracruz, 0600 Hours

Tanya ate breakfast with the remaining three members of her team. She did not like any of them. She tolerated them. Sebastian, she liked. He was dead.

Elian was a great programmer but had wandering weasel eyes and bad breath. Frank, the only one who defended everyone, seemed more like a girl. Star reminded Tanya of a dried-up old hippy on the lam who still had acid dreams of being a teenager. She had to rely on them if she wanted to ever make it off the yacht alive.

The *Happy Mermaid* sat motionless in the still waters of the early morning gulf. The sun was beginning to rise and chase away the last of the darkness. The ship's crew began to stir.

"Where does one find a job as a crew member on a drug dealer's yacht? I mean they can't like advertising in the paper. Do they get benefits?" Tanya mused in an attempt to break the ice and curb her anxiety, which was beginning to manifest itself through obsessive napkin tearing. Tanya was scared.

"I just want my phone back!" Frank stated.

"How can we get work done if we are kept in this Internet and cell phone blackout?" Tanya said.

"We have done almost everything we can do here," Frank continued.

Tanya tore napkins and cursed. "Would love to text Ivan, get an update."

"You like this Ivan guy, Tanya? He is, like, scary. Something in his crazy eyes." Star stared out at the ocean and spoke slowly.

"We have set up and rebuilt as much as we can. We really need to visit the Mexico City office and iron out any glitches," Tanya said, ignoring Star. She figured Evan was one of the few men evil enough to handle these cartel members. She wanted her phone.

No one spoke for a minute. The weight was still considerably heavy with the discovery of Sebastian's death.

Tanya looked at her half-eaten breakfast and felt sick. "We need a signal to finish up. Look, guys, Frank is right. We have to get off this boat. Swim, anyone?"

"Tanya, can you swim?"

"No."

"Like, um, someone has to, like, talk to them." Star spoke with the rhythm of a teenager, which Tanya found annoying in a woman of her age. Tanya could do without Star speaking at all. "Like, the whole point of us being here is, like, for upgrades and, like, proper satellite uplink things."

Tanya pushed away from the table and stood up. She felt slightly light-headed and queasy still. Tanya wanted to scream or stab someone. She was suffocating. She hated the ocean. She hated people. Maybe she was having a panic attack or an allergic reaction to all of the above.

"I have to get off this boat!" she said urgently and then changed the subject and her focus. "We have to make this seem urgent. We tell them there is a network problem."

"Fine." Frank looked at Tanya and frowned. He was concerned about her mental health; she seemed more and more unglued at times. "Let's act soon. You OK?"

"No. I need to go lie down," Tanya stated.

"They seem to like you better than us, but we will ask. Go rest."

Tanya held her hand up in a mock wave and walked away from her coworkers.

When Tanya was gone, Star rolled her eyes. "That girl may be brilliant, but she's a freaking basket case!"

Jorge Valdez took two Advil and drank his fresh-squeezed orange juice in a small, square glass. He was not as stressed today. Jorge sat in his cabin by himself and reflected on the events of the last two days.

"Are things going according to plan, or are they falling apart?" he said to the empty room.

In the last forty-eight hours, he had lost his temper and killed Mario Jr. His clean-up crew had successfully disposed of the body…and the helicopter. "No one can salvage and use old junk like Mexicans can." Jorge smiled to himself with pride. Mario's pilot had not even hesitated to join their cause.

"Silver or lead," Jorge muttered to the empty room.

Jorge had successfully pitched the lie to Boss Mario that his son was in favor of the sub purchase and had vanished in a freak accident. Mario had not asked for too many details, for he had never had reason to doubt Jorge.

"Betrayal for a greater cause. It still hurts, yet it is a burden paid for by many of the greatest world leaders throughout history. The ends justify the means."

Jorge was troubled by something else though. Did Mario Jr. know the details of Jorge's secret campaign across Mexico to create a narco state? Did he know about the bomb-training facilities? Jorge wondered if someone had leaked information. Thousands were involved in his lobbying efforts, from the immigrant-rights groups that he funded from DC to Texas to the media members who looked the other way.

"What does he know?" Jorge said to his cabin.

Jorge opened his computer and reread all of his saved e-mails. The small, private island, just north of Cancun, would prove an excellent place to set his trap: no cell signal and sketchy radio contact.

The real Mario had not been seen in public for weeks. He had been moving from safe house to safe house. Mario lived the life of a scared billionaire, in exile in his own country.

Jorge shook his head. "That is not going to be my existence. No! I will be legitimate, change the laws so that what I do is merely seen as the leader of a unionized labor movement. A great leader, unafraid!"

One of Mario's doubles had been gunned down in Sinaloa at a hotel just a week ago by Mexican marines conducting a raid. The government's disdain and tolerance of Mario had come to an end. Jorge hoped that his murder of Mario along with such a large number of politicians who had backed him, all in one event, would solidify a new deal with the government. An outright coup was, of course, impossible, but public opinion could be swayed so easily. The masses were stupid, and the politicians would prefer to keep their lives.

Jorge, through his liaisons, had already reached a sort of loose deal. He read over an anonymous, encrypted message that had sealed and paved the way for his future success.

With the target out of the way and the organization dismantled, you will be welcomed as a leader of the Union of Cartels. Laws pushing the legalization of your product will pass. The terms of our agreement are as such: you reduce drug-related violence by 45 percent, you have an agreement with the other members to reduce and eliminate human trafficking in accordance with our agreements with other countries, and you allow at least one substantial drug bust a year. All members of your union will be immune from extradition. (Compensation will follow, of course.) Final term is the protection and ceasing of the sacking of the state-owned oil supply. You will be given support of the law-enforcement and military branches of the administration to conduct such operations.

Jorge reread the e-mail message. He felt like Napoleon for a moment, outsmarting the dimwitted bureaucrats of his day. The more arrogant, bold, and outright crazy an idea seemed, the more likely it was to work, especially in today's world.

Jorge glanced at his watch and shook his head. He sometimes wished he could be in several places at once. Later today he would have to leave the yacht and meet secretly with some of the top members of his rival cartels.

"Yesterday's enemies are today's allies."

This final meeting would seal the deal and solidify the union and hopefully bring together an army.

A knock at his door caused him to jump.

Jorge cursed to himself and stood up. "Yes?"

"Sorry, boss. I know you do not want to be disturbed. I have a request."

He recognized Gerard's voice.

"Let me get dressed. Hold on!"

Once dressed he quickly opened the door.

Gerard and Yuri stood in the hall. Both men looked as if a night of drinking had taken its toll.

"Yuri, Gerard?"

"Sir. You gave us orders to not follow you today," Gerard said.

"Yes," Jorge said slowly.

"Tanya and her team. They need to finish their work. They want to leave and go to Mexico City."

"Let them! I can spare no one to protect them. They are Mario's concern."

Gerard looked disappointed and nodded. "Yes sir."

CHAPTER 23

Mr. Franklin

Mexico City, 0700 Hours

Nathan and Reo stood quietly in a large sporting-goods warehouse owned my Manuel Rosa's father. The orange glow of emergency lighting cast eerie, short shadows and created vast pockets of darkness throughout the facility. Rows of steel shelving reached to the ceiling of the massive warehouse. Forklifts and other equipment were parked in a straight line near a long, wooden table and lockers.

Five people stood staring at each other.

"This place is huge," stated Carletta, who was clearly in an upbeat mood.

Nathan did not reply. He watched the last stack of one-hundred-dollar bills zip through the electronic money counter. One of Carletta's men put a rubber band around it and shoved it in a massive duffel bag.

"How much you figure one million dollars weighs?" she asked smugly.

"About forty pounds," Nathan said without emotion.

She nodded. "I guess the CIA has flown enough of its money around the world that you would know that, huh? Weight fuel cost and so forth."

"Costs money to prop up the *turd* world and pay off dictators and petty midlevel bureaucrats," Nathan replied coldly.

Carletta's demeanor changed. "This is only a drop in the bucket of what you guys have cost the money backers."

Nathan looked expressionless at the money machines and avoided Carletta's eyes. "This is your first good-faith payment. You are forcing me to betray my men."

"Oh, bull, Nathan! You have been betraying your men all along. Don't pretend like you care about them. The whole Dark Cloud war is a farce."

Nathan shrugged. "No, the war is real. They just do not need to know my true purpose. I want them to succeed."

"Whatever," she said dismissively and finished. "Where is the rest of Mario's money, the cash stores?" she asked.

Nathan smiled without showing teeth. "Insurance, Carletta."

"No. Your option, Nathan, is to have the plug pulled altogether. I can have the Mexican navy say no to your operation with a phone call!"

"So you say."

"You think I am lying, Nathan?"

Nathan chewed on a toothpick and faced her. "The Mexican navy operation, it goes down without you exposing any of it or leaking any of it! Dark Cloud and the navy get to waste Mario, that's it. You don't care for him anyway, but"—Nathan pointed his finger at her—"your president, he wants results. He gets his results, I get my cash, you get yours, and I leave. Do you want your name attached to the operation's failure?"

Nathan felt anger rise in the pit of his stomach. He had always planned on stealing Mario's money. He had never planned on leaving his men out to dry. Such an act would not look professional. Carletta had set him up this way on purpose, to deflect from her.

"Nathan, it has long been rumored that Mario has, at any given time, about two to eight billion dollars in cash stashed around Mexico in certain warehouses. We have been looking for years, and now you have found them. I am a little skeptical and embarrassed."

"You're the Mexican CIA. You just were not savvy enough, I guess. Maybe too busy trying to milk the United States out of chump change," Nathan said smugly.

"I beg to differ. You have done the work for us. You are like the second wave of conquistadors," she said.

"And you were the first?" he countered.

"The cash is rightfully ours. You can have his online finances." Nathan calmed himself.

"We can work this out, and everyone can leave happy."

She wanted his prize. Nathan felt his blood pressure rise and fought the urge to shoot her on the spot.

Carletta was correct about one thing: Dark Cloud was a false-flag operation. Mario had to be destroyed so he could never pursue Nathan.

Reo and Nathan were the only two who knew where Mario's thirteen warehouses were. From the beginning, the billions in cash had been his main prize. Most of it had already been flown out of the country. The logistics of moving such a large sum and keeping it quiet was not easy. Nathan preferred not to let anyone else in on the scheme.

Nathan thought about the consequences of failing in his mission. The real purpose was to provide finances for his superiors' global operations. He had not even let Reo in on all of the truth.

"Failure is not an option," he whispered to himself.

"Carletta, you have ruined me, and you leave me with what?" She smiled and stared. "You are still leaving with millions!"

"You can have what you are after, Carletta, but I must have what I came after. My mission must succeed."

"OK," she said slowly. The corners of her lips rose in a smile.

Nathan spoke quickly and firmly. "*Only* when the navy operation goes down. When Mario is *dead* and my contract with the Mexican government and backers is complete. As that happens, I have men who are staged to steal the treasure."

"How?" She looked at him suspiciously.

"Logistics is my business, bitch!"

"I see." Carletta watched the last stack of one-hundred-dollar bills get stuffed into the duffel.

"Carletta, this is how it has to go down."

"*Fine!*" She waved her hands with impatience.

"Once Dark Cloud and the navy have completed the mission, I will give you what you want," Nathan said quietly.

Once Carletta and her entourage had left, Nathan turned to Reo. Nathan's face was red with anger. His eyes were intense and distant, like a battlefield commander. "We need to bring in Tanya and her team. Kid gloves come off. I need to know everything she knows and if she has spoken with anyone. Use whatever means necessary. She could sink all of us."

"Yes, sir. So far the data that she has sent is quite damaging to many important people in Mexico and beyond."

"That, Reo, is why loose ends are dangerous. Data and intelligence are only as good as the chess player who uses it."

"On it," Reo said.

CHAPTER 24

The House That Blood Built

Veracruz, Mexico, 1200 Hours

The tiny brick-and-wood house with bars and a scrap of yard seemed even more cramped than it had earlier. Thirty members of Dark Cloud had drifted into and out of the house over the course of the last three hours. The teams had been reduced to groups of two or three for the upcoming travel. One person from each group would check in with Joaquin or Miguel and get airline tickets, rental-car information, fake IDs, and hotel accommodations in Cozumel or on Isla Mujeres. The distance to Cozumel was about six hundred miles.

The men were split up over different flights so as to not attract attention. Weapons and equipment were going by truck.

Evan was feeling anxious again. There were so many what-ifs that he did not know where to begin. Murphy's Law was what he was most concerned about. Evan knew he was a magnet for bad luck and had a special place in Murphy's heart as a stepchild. He looked at his watch and wished that this whole thing would just be over.

"OK, listen up," Roger announced.

Joaquin and Miguel were handing out assignments. They would be the last ones to fly out this evening. El Coyote had left the previous night with a team to set up the next meeting place.

"OK, listen. So far today's report is pretty uneventful. Tanya and her team were allowed off the boat this morning. They were escorted to the airport by a detail of Scorpions and then released. They are currently being debriefed in Mexico City. Questions?"

"Yes." Evan raised his hand.

He surprised people by being serious and not making any off-the-wall comments. Perhaps that unsettled them more than if he had been bizarre.

"I got a text from her before she got on the plane. They have work to do still. Can we get her pulled out?"

Joaquin looked at Evan and shrugged. "That's Nathan's call."

Evan shook his head. "It's getting too hot. She needs to be pulled in."

"She is still on the job, Evan. Has business to attend to in the city, that's what I was told. Nathan said he would watch her and bring her in once it was safe."

"Fine."

"Nathan wants her first—that's the direction I got. We can call later. Does that work?"

If she is made at this point by the cartels, the whole mission will collapse, Evan thought.

Mexico City, 1200 Hours

Arcos Bosques stands out as a rather odd building. The two towers are thirty-six stories, making it one of the tallest in Mexico City. The massive office buildings are joined at the top by a bridge, almost giving it a look like a giant pair of pants. The buildings are situated in the upscale business district of Santa Fe.

Tanya and her team had just finished with the computer systems at Mario's nearby office. The office workers had been friendly and were a welcome change to the throat cutters they had been with for the last several days. She seriously doubted that any of them had a clue that their financial company was a front for a cartel. The team members had an early lunch and were now returning to their hotel suite at Aqua Bosques, a few blocks away.

"Anyone else jet lagged and just done with this whole thing?" Star asked and groaned.

Tanya agreed. "This is almost like work. When is our linkup with Nathan? I am done with these cartel-empire thugs!"

"We are done. We are getting paid! Let's celebrate back at my room," Elian said flatly in his creepy, monotone voice.

Tanya's phone rang, and she separated from the team. "You guys keep going; I'll catch up. I gotta take this."

"You coming to drink, right?" Frank asked.

"Sure, give me a minute. I have to take this," she said and separated from her coworkers.

Tanya paused outside the massive hotel. She watched her co-workers and shook her head. She hated it when people stood around in groups and texted.

"Evan?"

"Hey, just checking on you. On my way to the airport. You guys OK? You done?"

"Yes, going to meet that prick Nathan later. My team is being nice to me. Going to go drink a little before meeting *him* for a debrief," she said.

"Call me after you talk to Nathan. Our team has been trying to call him all day," Evan urged. He quickly explained to her how he believed things were going to heat up once their operation began. The Scorpions might add things up and send people for her. "Don't have to tell you that the data you guys have gathered is damning to hundreds of people on all sides of the law and border. People get edgy when billions of dollars are at stake," Evan said quickly, stating the obvious.

She sensed something else in his voice, an anxiety or maybe a warning. Tanya spoke her mind without filtering, as was her style. "Hey, I believe you do have a human side. Won't go as far as to say *sweet*, but not just a muscle head connected to a trigger finger. You are worried about me."

"OK. Interesting way to pay a compliment wrapped in an insult. Not the first time. Course I am concerned. You're OK for a computer geek. Tanya, call me later."

"Will do. Gotta go. Bottle of wine with my name on it!"

"Bye."

Tanya had hoped she could have met up with Evan before being whisked away to Mexico City, but it was not to be. Now she was on her own again and had to make some quick decisions.

I know you're watching, you bastards, Tanya thought to herself. She was certain that both Dark Cloud and the cartels were still keeping tabs on her.

"OK, let's go." Tanya rejoined her partners in crime and joined in their idle small talk about weather, technology, and gadgets as they rode the elevator up to Frank's room. They had finished lunch earlier. She decided she would allow herself to relax.

"Like tequila, Tanya?" Frank asked.

"In moderation. Prefer wine."

"We have wine," Star interjected as she dug in her massive purse for something. She was always digging, Tanya observed. She should have been a coal miner.

"Focus on the money. Remember that Pink Floyd song?" Frank spoke while putting himself in between Elian and Tanya. Tanya turned her head to avoid Elian's breath.

Frank's room overlooked the busy Mexico City streets. Tanya accepted her first glass of wine while she stared out Frank's window. The one thing Tanya did like was heights. She loved staring at activity from afar, as if she were looking into a fish bowl. The human condition was dismal, she realized, and she was part of it.

"I have a late flight back to the States. Never setting foot in this country again," Star began, still rummaging through her purse.

Tanya tuned out the chatter and just stared out of the window. She wanted to flee—get her money and go. She watched a jet climb in the distance—soaring higher and higher, pulling away from the city.

"I am flying out tomorrow, early. Disappearing forever," Frank said and groaned.

"Where to?" Tanya asked. She had not given any thought to where she would go, or with whom. She was alone again yet hated company.

Elian managed to slip up behind Tanya, lightly brushing his hips into her backside. He was obsessed with approaching her or staring at her from behind, avoiding her eyes.

"You OK? You're so quiet." His voice was deep and unconcerned, almost mechanical.

Tanya moved away from him. His breath was on her hair. She spun to face him, and he backed up, his eyes drifting over her and to the floor. "Strong wine. Can you pour me some more?" Tanya stepped away from him and moved back to where the girls and Frank sat.

"Sure."

Tanya knew in a day or so she would never see any of these people again and would not have to endure Elian's subtle advances or be so close to danger.

The stress of the job had been tremendous. When news of Sebastian's death reached her, she had sunken into an even deeper pit of paranoia. He was her ally. Though not strong, she could trust him.

Soon it would be over.

"Tanya, toast?" Star asked and giggled.

She accepted her wine and for a second felt shaky on her feet, as if a warm, humid breeze had gently swayed her. She began to not care about anything but caught herself.

"Um, um, 'K. To what? Throat cutters? Weasel men who deceive you? Piles of money and the people who—"

Frank raised his hand.

Star covered her mouth and suppressed a snort-like laugh. Elian put his hand on her hip. He reminded Tanya of Lurch from the *Adams Family*.

"Dear, I was thinking of something a little more toast-like," Star said.

Frank giggled.

"Like, um, to a job well done. To a leader." Star nodded and raised her glass. Her face was red as if sharing an inside joke. "We pulled it off, like, um, the big payoff—it's coming!"

Tanya moved away from Elian's hips again. Something suddenly struck Tanya as odd. They were all looking at her, as if waiting for her to say something, or was it something else?

"I have to use the bathroom. Be right back."

Tanya bumped glasses with everyone, then spun around, pushed Lurch out of the way, and stumbled to the bathroom.

"Nothing will matter soon. It will all be over," Star said as if she were singing a song. "You're creepy, Elian. Leave that girl alone."

Frank laughed. "I need some music. Where's my iPod?"

Tanya closed the door, locked it, and moved to the window so she could get a better signal. Her eyes were losing focus as she texted Evan. Her fingers began to feel like rubber. She sat on the toilet and braced herself. Was the bathroom spinning? The last time she felt this way, she was about to have surgery. She was slipping down a tunnel.

Tanya sent Evan a quick text and then took a picture of the hotel brochure and card, which had the address and room number, that sat on the back of the toilet.

"Tanya, you OK?" a voice asked, not too concerned and on the verge of giggling. It was Star.

Tanya looked at her phone and for a second wondered why she was holding it. Suddenly, she remembered and then erased the texts she had sent to Evan. Next she dialed emergency services, 604-1240, and spoke into the phone as quickly as she could.

"I…I have been kidnapped. I am Tanya, Tanya Mendes. Listen to me, I have been drugged. No, not on drugs, you idiot."

Tanya dropped the phone and felt herself slide to the floor. She could not tell if the thud she heard was the door crashing open or her head crashing downward. It did not matter, she figured.

"I am dying," she muttered.

CHAPTER 25

That Salty Taste

Isla Mujeres, 1300 Hours

El Coyote walked down the small pier and stepped onto the rusty fishing trawler that served as their floating operation center. The crew was still ashore gathering supplies, like beer and food, for tonight's brief. El Coyote was soaked with sweat and could hardly wait to have a cold beer. In less than twenty-four hours, he had secured a small warehouse where equipment could be stored as it arrived by ferry. He had made and inspected the sleeping arrangements for over forty-five men spread around the island and on Cozumel. Last night he had been in contact with the submarine's captain who assured him that the sub would be ready to pick up passengers at about four tomorrow morning. Getting men out to the sub in the dark would be the challenge. He was having issues with the Zodiac boats.

El Coyote went into his cabin and sat on his bunk. He was exhausted. He looked at his watch and cursed. "Not enough time!"

He had ten men out running various errands on the island.

"One mistake, and we are all dead," he muttered.

A knock at his door caused him to jump. He stood up looking for his pistol.

"Who is it?"

"It's me, *amigo*, relax!"

One of his men had returned. He had a smile on his face. "Good news, *amigo*, the navy is officially back on with the original plan. Tonight, at twenty-three hundred, an admiral will be here with his staff. They want to go over the plan for the assault tomorrow."

"Thank *God!* I thought the whole thing was off earlier. OK, when do they start bringing in men?"

El Coyote's friend shrugged and pulled two cans of beer out of a paper bag.

"They have been arriving over the last forty-eight hours. They never stopped. On again, off again, and so on—you know how the navy is!"

"Helicopters and boats, eh?" El Coyote took the beer, opened it, and drank half of it.

"Yes. Just make sure everyone is here tonight by twenty-three hundred."

El Coyote now had a new set of problems in his head.

"You think we can pull this off, *amigo*?"

"I hope so, or we are all dead."

"Still no word from Nathan. I'll text Roger, tell him things are a go."

Aeropuerto International de Vera Cruz Heriberto Jara, 1315 Hours

Roger checked his phone, nodded, and then shoved it in his pocket.

"The navy is playing again. The mission is a go. Meeting at twenty-three hundred." He read his text to Evan.

"Cool, always liked the navy—seagoing bellhops," Evan teased and clapped his hands.

Roger squinted in the intense sunlight and looked skeptically at Evan and Tommy. Heat was rising in waves from the landing strip, and a small shadow from a lonely hangar in the general-aviation section was quickly losing its shadow, inch by inch.

"C'mon, Roger, trust me!" Evan packed a dip in his mouth and winked. He placed a new pair of aviation sunglasses on his face, hefted his backpack on his shoulder, and cocked his head to the side. "What could go wrong?"

Roger looked back at the main terminal. The airport was small by any standard, and it was a stretch to call it *international*. A lone, white control tower rose over a one-level, white building.

"That's my plane over there. What could go wrong? Ha! I am looking at what can go wrong, and it is right here!" Roger pointed at Evan and shook his head. "You are talking me into some crazy scheme of yours. We got enough stuff going on, you wanker!"

Evan dismissed Roger with a wave of his hand. "I know operational security. Look, this is better. We get to keep our guns this way! *And* I get to be your pilot, *and* we have a bar."

"That's not helping my confidence, lad!" Roger cursed and turned to look at his plane, which was taxiing away from the gate.

"Oh! There she goes, and I could be about to take a nap right now, a little stewardess bringing me a water!" Roger declared, his anger rising.

Evan shrugged and looked over his shoulder.

Tommy was smiling and walking back in their direction. He gave Evan the thumbs-up.

"Roger, what time we got to be at the brief?"

"Twenty-three hundred. Why?"

"Well, it's six hundred miles to Cozumel."

"Aye, that's why I wanted to ride in a jet, not a twin-prop puddle jumper! *And* not with you flying!" Roger dropped his duffel bag and weapons case and pointed at the aircraft they were about to board.

Evan smiled and picked up Roger's bags. He walked backward, talking. "Roger, it's a Beechcraft 350I, top speed about three hundred fifty miles per hour. It's smooth. Tommy worked his magic to get it. I think it belongs to Mario's fleet!"

"What are you up to, Evan?"

Roger started following Evan, muttering under his breath. "I don't need a bar. I need sleep. I hate *small* planes!"

Evan shook his head and laughed.

Roger caught up to Evan just as Tommy approached. The sound of Roger's missed jet was deafening as it took off.

"OK, Evan, we are a go! Ol' Tommy still has his magic. The crew has her gassed up and ready. Full bar, and you're flying!"

"How long to Cozumel?" Roger asked and groaned. He felt his skin getting warm in the sun.

"Cozumel?" Tommy calculated out loud. "From Mexico City?" Tommy smoothed his hair under his hat and spoke. "Altitude, air speed—a good four hours. Take us an hour to get to the city from here."

"*What? Mexico City?* We ain't got time for a sight-seeing trip, Evan! We got a job—have you gone insane?" Roger growled and reached for his duffel bag.

Evan backed away, out of his grasp, and winked.

"Evan, you did not tell him that we are going to Mexico City?" Tommy turned and began to walk fast, not wanting to be anywhere near Roger's wrath. "Why didn't you tell him?" Tommy blurted as he walked quickly past Evan toward the safety of the plane.

"No need. You did. Come on, Roger! We're going to Mexico City first and then to Cozumel. We will still make our date with the admiral!" Evan picked up his pace and carried both their bags to the idling Beechcraft 350I.

"Evan!"

Mexico City, 1500 Hours

Tanya gasped for air and tried to scream. Water filled her mouth, leaked into her lungs, and burned her throat. Her hands fought against the ropes that secured her wrists so tightly to her ankles that she felt like a calf at a rodeo. Hands groped her naked body. They were going to rape her and then drown her.

Tanya suddenly felt the cold, wet bag being ripped from her head, her blindfold came off, and she was flung like a doll onto a bare, hard mattress.

She could now see the bathtub and the filthy mattress. She heard a train nearby and smelled cows, straw, and mold.

She was in a barn.

Tanya knew she was about to die.

"Ready to talk yet, sweetheart?"

Tanya rolled herself over onto her back. Her legs were folded unnaturally underneath her as if she were doing yoga. Her back and thighs began to cramp. She wished that she would suddenly die of a heart attack or a stroke, but she had no such luck. Her fitness was keeping her alive.

Tanya looked up to see three short teenage Mexican boys. They were bare chested, skinny, and hairless, with tattoos of Santa Muerta decorating their bodies. One of the teenagers had an eye missing and a large Mexican flag tattooed across his chest. The one who stood over her stank like sweat and weed. He had large studs in his lower lip and no bottom teeth.

She looked for the voice that she recognized.

She could not cry anymore and hoped things ended quickly. She thought about Siberia and cheering guards, and how she had blocked everything out.

"Ready to talk?" The boy with no teeth ripped the duct tape off her mouth.

She could not feel her hands or feet. "Kill me."

"*No*, you can live. *If* you help!" Reo stepped out of the shadows.

271

"Don't believe you."

"Fine." Reo snapped his fingers. "Get her some clothes, untie her, and bring her to the table."

The teenagers untied her and threw some clothes in her direction. They watched silently as she painfully slid on sweat pants and a sweat shirt. She was still barefoot and limped over to the table. Tanya felt her teeth clatter, and she could not stop shaking. She was not sure if she was cold or just terrified. Everyone around her seemed to be sweating.

"Sit," Reo said.

Tanya spat blood onto the floor and tried to steady herself against the table. She stood for a moment and looked at a MacBook that was connected to a twenty-seven-inch screen. She saw piles of paper and her own computer in pieces.

"We have the Internet. Log in, undo your bullshit. I am sure Mario has more than three million dollars. We estimate he has about two billion in his online accounts."

"Th-th...then you know he has warehouses stacked full of cash. Euros, pounds, and dollars, about two to seven billion. It's all in my report. How much freaking money do you guys need?"

Tanya coughed and began to feel her circulation come back. The pain in her limbs reminded her of thousands of needles. "Why...why did you do this to me?" She sat down and groaned.

Reo looked at her with pity. "Big plans require big money, sweetie."

"Who needs billions of dollars?" Tanya put her forehead on the table and her trembling hands on the wooden bench on which she sat. She reached into her mouth and wiggled loose teeth. Her nose began to drip blood.

Reo shrugged and divulged more information.

Tanya knew that the more he told her, the less likely she was to live. She did not care anymore.

"Tanya, it's like this: Dark Cloud was a false-flag operation. It was an opportunity to apply a formula, a business model if you will. Not perfect, but with some tweaking, it can be improved next time, somewhere else. Things like this require money."

"You're lecturing me on, what, corruption? You're...you're a hack!"

Reo dismissed her with a smug look and continued. "There are worldwide operations going on that are, well, just too complicated for your pretty little head to wrap around. Nathan has let me join his club, and we will follow our orders."

Tanya laughed sarcastically and pinched her nose to stop the bleeding. "I need some ice and a towel," she demanded.

Reo snapped his fingers and barked orders. "Paper towel, blanket."

"Reo, you really don't know Nathan, do you? He is going to sell you out just like you guys sold me out!"

"*Bull! You* betrayed us, Tanya."

"*Only* 'cause I don't trust you. You proved me right. Tell me, Reo, what do you know about Nathan?"

"I know he is part of something bigger than our narrow vision of reality. A global view that requires some eggs to be broken...A vision for a world without—"

"Cut the Che Guevara shit, and get to the point. I want my death quick, by the way."

"Strangulation or bullet?"

"Bullet!"

"Want to see it coming or not?"

"I want to do it."

Reo nodded and handed her a towel. He wrapped a blanket gently around her shoulders. "I respect that."

"Go on, Reo."

"Anyway," he continued, "we have work to do."

"I need a drink," she whispered.

Again Reo snapped his fingers. "Bottle of water!"

Tanya looked around the barn-turned-torture-chamber. The teenagers had grabbed a case of beer from a refrigerator, carried it out the massive, swinging doors, and placed it in the bed of a pickup. Tanya touched her swollen face and scanned the rest of the dusty barn. The bathtub that they had almost drowned her in was no more than a horse's trough. There were no animals, tools, or equipment, like tractors, in the barn, yet she smelled cows and pigs.

"What...what is this place?" She tried to stall.

"Some gangs specialize, just like any business. Specialization is the new normal and key to getting things done in a busy world. These guys"—Reo pointed with his pinkie to the teenagers drinking beer off the tailgate of the pickup—"they are cleaners. They get rid of bodies through a variety of methods. Sometimes acid, sometimes burning. Other times they cut them into little pieces and feed them to the pigs."

Reo was getting bored. He gestured to the computer. "Usually a pretty girl gets special treatment. I will spare you that, and we will choose the quick execution."

"Thanks."

"Your teammates have been spying for us, confirming that you have indeed been stealing and moving Mario's money around. That money, in the sum of a billion, needs to be rerouted."

Tanya shook her head. "It took me six months to hide it and move it. I can't do it in one night! The gangsters will get alerted, and their banks will just freeze the assets! Reo, just take your two billion, or whatever it is, in cash and fly. Kill me. Get it over with."

"Disable the Centipede virus, Tanya. Give me the account numbers of where you sent the money. Once I confirm it's there, we end this. I can transfer later. You gave us valuable information. Hundreds will go to jail! Now, we want our money."

"Give me the keyboard. I will do it."

Tanya felt her heart sink. She cherished her breath and the beating of her pulse. She looked around the barn and realized this was the last stuff she was going to look at. Her last breath was moments away.

"Try anything, sweetheart, and I will turn you over to the boys. They look good and drunk!"

"I have to stop the virus first." Tanya coughed and then began typing on the keyboard. She stared at numbers and websites and asked herself one important question, the last one she might ever contemplate: "Do I want to die quickly or slowly?"

Suddenly, the feeling came back to her feet, and a warm burn began to rise from her toes to her legs, stomach, chest, and then head. Tanya paused for a second and recognized the emotion. Anger. She could feel again, and she was angry. She stuffed the emotion until she needed it. Tanya began to look around the table.

"Crap!"

"What, dear, what?" Reo suddenly looked concerned.

"My thumb drive!"

"Your what?"

"Thumb drive."

"Your team said nothing about a thumb drive!"

"That's because I don't trust them. I am a hacker, Reo. I hate people!"

He nodded and did not challenge the statement. "OK, why do you need it?"

"You will see. It is like a remote for the virus. *Any* attempt to touch Mario's money or alter his accounts, or the accounts I set up, will erase everything. *And...*" She paused. "*And* unleash the virus into destroy mode. It could go global, technically, freezing everything. You and Nathan, of course, will be implicated. Whomever the hell you guys work for will be out of business—even worse if you have sent them." Tanya paused and stared at the screen.

"What? *What*, Tanya?"

"Have you or Nathan sent any e-mails to anyone?" She let out a laugh.

"*Why?*"

"This virus is like a cyber nuclear bomb, Reo! It goes everywhere, eats everything. Loves data. Yum!"

Reo paused and narrowed his eyes. He reminded her of a shrew or a mole, but she had him.

"You conniving little bitch!"

"You hired me 'cause I am the best. The Americans used a similar virus to cause a near-meltdown to Iran's nuclear facility. They got the concept from me! It can cause a financial meltdown to a banking system or a power grid. Bye-bye, money!"

"Then we renegotiate." Reo looked worried now. She had his attention.

"I get two bullets?"

"You get freedom. You go with me and one of the boys to get the thumb drive. Where is it?"

"In my hotel room."

"*Bullshit!* We searched the room!"

Tanya laughed sarcastically, as best she could with a bruised rib.

"Men searched! Every female knows that men can't find shit even when it's right in front of them!"

Reo bit his lip and glared at her. "Get yourself cleaned up. We leave in ten minutes!"

Mexico City, 1500 Hours

Yuri, a.k.a. the Russian, put eye drops in his eyes, drank a swig from his Monster energy drink, and placed his drink on the large oak office table. He looked squarely into the eyes of the terrified office workers.

"Look, let me explain myself. We come from different worlds. I live out there." He pointed out of the large window to the city beyond. The office building was nestled in the Santa Fe district of Mexico City and overlooked the odd building that looked like a standing pair of pants.

"The real world. I don't cross over into your world very often if I can avoid it. Understand?"

The Russian looked at the office workers—Mario's CPAs, MBAs, lawyers, and secretaries.

"I am tired. I just flew in from the coast. I am sunburned and hungry, and I need a shower. Now, I am only gonna ask one time."

The Russian reached in his pants and pulled out a large black hunting knife. He laid it flatly next to his energy drink. He loved scaring these people, having some fun.

"Where is Tanya? The short little computer girl? She's a cute, sassy little thing."

Yuri looked at each of the six people—three men and three attractive women who looked more terrified than the men.

"She w-w-was here this morning, sir."

Yuri smiled. "Good. Any idea where she went?"

"Sir." A young woman in a dress several sizes too small spoke up, very official sounding. She had beautiful brown eyes and jet-black hair.

Yuri shook his head.

"Sir, they spoke of going shopping and having lunch over there at the shopping center. The one you call Tanya, the others were plotting something against her. I heard them whispering, so I listened."

Yuri rubbed his jaw and looked thoughtfully at the young girl. "Yes?"

"They had a surprise for her in a room. I think they were staying in the hotel in the same building. One of them had a handbag from the mall. They really disliked her."

"OK. Good." Yuri reached in his pocket and pulled out a roll of one-hundred-dollar bills. "OK, I have a business proposition."

The girl started to cry.

"*Sumasshedshiy devushka!*" Yuri spoke in Russian and laughed. He corrected himself. "Crazy girl, listen, I am not going to hurt you. I will pay you to help me find Tanya. She works for Mario. I need to save her. She may be in danger, OK?" Yuri stood up and moved toward the girl. He handed her a one-hundred-dollar bill. "Come. What is your name?"

"Maria."

Yuri smiled and admired the contortions it must have taken to squeeze a full figure into her dress.

"Of course it is, Maria. I won't hurt you. Your looks and my money will make a great team. One hour, that's all I need."

"*Maria, no!*" One of the older women stood up.

The men said nothing.

"It's OK. It's OK. We will stay in public," Yuri said soothingly as if he were talking to a child.

Maria sounded shaky and began to cry. She put her hands over her face.

"Stop this! This will not work. *No* crying. I will give you money not to cry!" Yuri cursed and peeled off more bills and pressed them into Maria's hands.

CHAPTER 26

The Cuban Cowboy Way

Airport Parking Garage, Mexico City, 1500 Hours

Evan and Roger dropped their heavy duffel bags at their feet and crossed their arms. The weather was cooler up in Mexico City, and the air felt a little dryer. The parking garage was thinning out, and there were no cameras visible. The two men watched the black Toyota Land Cruiser park. The vehicle creaked as a solid, round man stepped from the vehicle. Mr. Rosa's brother Victor, the detective, emerged from the vehicle and approached the two men.

Roger stared straight ahead and spoke quickly to Evan, who was packing a dip in his mouth. "Still can't believe you didn't just come out and tell me that the lass had been kidnapped, you prick! I would have come. I am worried about her now. This whole mission could go down the tubes. Hope the lass is OK!"

"I know. I know you would come. The difference is you would have shown a level head and called a meeting and a committee and then assembled a team blah, blah." Evan spat on the ground and focused on Victor.

"And what's wrong with that, lad?"

"Too freaking long, Roger. Gotta keep this quiet. Do this the cowboy way."

"Aye, General Custard was a freaking cowboy, eh?" Roger replied and stuck his hand out to meet Victor, still never looking at Evan.

"Roger, you look as though you have aged. Evan, well you always looked bad from what I hear. I have news for you two."

"How is your brother?" Roger grumbled.

"Fine. They are in Spain."

"Good."

"There have been some strange goings-on. I had to do some digging, but, you know, that is what I do."

"Aye."

"First of all, you should be at the coast."

Evan shrugged. "*Sí.*"

Roger began, "It's a long story. We need to find Tanya or call off a massive mission." Roger raised his eyebrows. "Tanya, his girl."

"She ain't my girl! She ain't my type!"

Victor Rosa laughed out loud like a walrus.

"Ha! The last four women who I said were not my type, I married! Ha-ha-ha!"

"OK, you two, when you're done, we can get down to business," Evan said quickly and nudged his duffel bag with his foot.

"Aye, Evan sent you the text. Any leads?"

"Yes, this is what I do. Get in!"

Roger and Evan piled into the Toyota Land Cruiser and buckled their seat belts. Victor drove fast, very fast, and used turn signals as an afterthought, usually after he cut someone off.

"OK, listen, and listen good, *amigos!*" Victor began speaking rapidly.

The tires of the Toyota Land Cruiser squealed as they rounded the slow curves in the garage. Victor gunned the engine when he could. He spoke slowly as if he were on a Sunday drive at a racetrack.

"Nathan turned over a gold mine worth of data midmorning and then vanished. His whole administrative group, including Reo, all gone!"

"That must be the SD chip," Evan said.

"What kind of material?" Roger asked.

"Miles of names, facts, figures but, more importantly, politicians and cops. The fax machines are working overtime. We have about one hundred arrest warrants printed so far. After your operation tomorrow, they start getting served! We are not telling the DEA anything yet. They will want to make a miniseries about this."

Victor paid the gate guard and ran the stop sign that he was supposed to use to ease into traffic. Tires squealed and horns honked.

"My God, people cannot drive in this city! Couldn't they see I was coming? Look, listen. I got suspicious. Why would Nathan give us a treasure trove and then leave? He has a mission and men to lead."

"And?" Roger asked.

Evan closed his eyes as they almost hit a man on a bike who had the right-of-way. Victor plowed on, oblivious.

"Carletta," Victor said as if everyone knew her.

"Who?" Roger asked. He shook his head.

Victor continued. "The last person Nathan saw was Carletta, the head of Mexico's version of the CIA. She extorted him, and not out of a few million pesos. He sent us evidence before vanishing!"

"Wow, wait, slow down. She extorted him?" Evan asked.

Victor nodded and looked in the rearview mirror as he spoke.

"Sort of, if you can call taking money from a thief extortion. Nathan left the evidence trail framing her, but he made it clear that she was to be taught a lesson."

"You're kidding. What are we talking?" Evan asked.

Evan gripped the side of the seat as they ran a stoplight and swerved around a car that was changing lanes.

Roger just shook his head.

Victor continued speaking.

"A few billion. She threatened to blow the cover off Dark Cloud unless he revealed where Mario's cash stores were. Intelligence operatives have been looking for it for decades, and here comes this foreigner and does it! *Boy*, he pissed off the intel community. I just learned about all this hours ago, by the way. Your call and his behavior set my wheels to spinning."

"So Nathan decided to give her a cut, save face, and bail on us. Did he compromise us?" Evan asked, clearly worried now that he would die in a traffic accident instead of by a bullet.

"I don't think so. He went to great lengths on a recording to say, 'Oh, my men deserve the money. I need my honor, blah, blah…' He is gone. He had taken the money secretly months ago, I suspect. Only she did not know that. No one did! Guess he was going to bail after the operation." Victor kept glancing in the rearview as he spoke.

"*Wanker!*" Roger punched the passenger seat in front of him.

Evan laughed. "Dark Cloud was a joke—the whole time we were being vetted for a suicide mission. He just wanted the money. No wonder he kept us so busy." Evan reached in his pocket for a can of Skoal.

"My friends, we were all duped, but I look at the bright side: I am going to arrest a lot of people. Tomorrow, God willing, Mario will be dead, and one cartel will be weakened!" Victor said and shrugged as if the whole thing was no big deal.

"Two more will pop up," Evan said flatly.

Victor came to a jeering stop at a green light to let a beautiful, dark-haired woman pushing a stroller cross the street. Evan and Roger looked at each other.

She smiled, and for a second all three men were silent. Cars jammed on their brakes and horns honked. The light was green.

"Yes, my friends, that is what I call job security! Ha!" Victor said and then stomped on the accelerator once the female was safely on the sidewalk.

Evan almost swallowed his dip and spat quickly out the window. "Did you find Carletta? Reo? Any evidence of Tanya?"

"Oh, we found Carletta. No clue where Tanya is."

"And what did Carletta say?" Evan leaned forward as they entered the Santa Fe district in Mexico City.

"Not much, my friend. Throat cut in a warehouse on the outskirts of town, wads of hundred-dollar bills crammed down her throat and shoved in her clothes. Her bodyguards, all dead."

"And?" Roger asked, shaking his head.

"Sorry, that's it. Nothing to see," Victor said.

Evan let his jaw drop for a long second and stared out the window into the city. He was in a far wealthier part of town.

"Um, then why the hell are you driving around Mexico City if there is nothing to see?"

Victor hit his brakes, sending everyone lurching forward. Evan banged his head on the seat in front of him and bounced back when the seat belt caught hold. Victor smiled in the rear-view mirror.

"I did not mean there was nothing to see, my friends. We get something to eat, and then I take you to Tanya's last-known whereabouts."

"Any leads?" Evan asked. He nudged Roger, who just shrugged.

"We found her friends. All dead, in a Dumpster. One of them had Tanya's room key in her pocket—her wallet, cash, and jewelry!" Victor sounded excited. He clearly loved police work.

"What the hell is going on?"

Victor pulled into another parking garage. This time he flashed his badge, and the gate went up. "Tell everyone after me that this garage is closed! You only open the gate for me, understand?"

"*Sí!*"

Victor pulled into a parking space and scraped a brand-new Corvette with his bumper. He was unaware, and Evan said nothing.

Victor's phone rang, and he answered it. "Hold on. *Sí? Sí? Muy buena!*"

He hung up and turned around in his seat. "I am fat. You are young." Victor stared for a long moment at Roger and Evan until the full impact of his words sank in.

Roger was the first to speak. "Aye, Victor, you stay here."

"Good idea. I am going to get you two the best steaks you have ever had, guacamole so good that—"

"Stop, stop. Get it to go. Meet us back here," Roger said as he quickly got out of the vehicle.

Roger and Evan went to the trunk and retrieved their duffel bags.

Victor got out of the Land Cruiser and inspected the brand-new Corvette next to him. "*Dios mio!* What a shame. Some asshole scraped this poor man's car and had not even the decency to leave a note. People today. *Mi* mama is right: the world is collapsing!"

Evan stared for a second at Victor, with his duffel over his shoulder.

Roger grabbed Evan by the elbow and guided him away.

"Wait, wait! Take the room key! Tenth floor. I have an officer waiting up there for you. I call him, tell him you coming. I am waiting on a call, a sighting of men putting a body in a trunk not far from here. Then I get our food," Victor said, waving them off. He had other matters to attend to.

Evan and Roger waved bye and walked through the garage with their duffel bags. Neither man said a word as they entered the building and walked through the lobby to an elevator.

Roger reached out to hit the button, and Evan stopped him. "I need to use a bathroom. That drive…"

Roger nodded.

Tanya had never even considered smoking cigarettes until this moment so near the end of her life. Reo had let her sit in the passenger seat on the short drive into the city. No one spoke.

Tanya had done her best to clean herself up. She wore a baseball hat, sunglasses, and an oversized jacket with the collar up. She still looked as if she had been in a car crash. Her head hurt, and her anger still kept her warm. Reo parked on the street and looked sideways at her.

Two teenage punks sat in the backseat texting. A red Audi Q7 with three more teenagers followed close behind. She knew that they all carried weapons, and she had little hope of escape. When Reo figured out there was no thumb drive, she would die.

"You! Stop texting. Stay fifteen feet behind us at all times. If we get in trouble, start shooting. Not her. I need the thumb drive," Reo barked.

The kids nodded and put their iPhones away.

"Get out, Tanya. Don't be stupid."

"I have a twisted ankle, busted teeth, and a broken rib. I could not outrun you or a bullet if I tried. I just want this day over with!" Tanya pleaded. She was not above pretending it was worse than it was.

"Perform well, and you live," Reo snapped.

"We have to stop at the front desk, get a new room key—one of those card things."

"Yes, I know, honey. I have stayed in a hotel before!" he said.

Tanya, Reo, and the teenagers walked into the street entrance of the office building. Reo looked as if he belonged in the mall. The rest of them, including Tanya, looked as if they belonged in a homeless shelter. She had no expectations of surviving this day, but she still had hope.

Roger waited for Evan on the ground floor, just outside of the bathroom. He admired the magnificent architecture of the building, indoor palm trees, natural lighting, glass, marble, and the echoing sound of fountains. He knew he could never afford to shop in any of these stores, with the exception of Crate & Barrel. He watched the glass-enclosed elevator rise up into the building and stop on the second floor. The hotel entrance was somewhere on the second floor. Roger looked at his watch and then spotted a water fountain. Suddenly, his throat was dry. He took a step forward and almost collided with a young woman who was coming out of the female restroom. Roger paused and put his arms up to avoid hitting her.

"Sorry, sweetheart," he said in English and smiled.

She was breathtaking, and she almost caused Roger to lose his words. She had been crying.

"You OK, bonnie?" Roger frowned and touched her shoulder. One of the problems Roger had with being so tall was that he was afforded a vantage point that in some instances revealed too much. He tried to keep eye contact as she looked up and smiled. Her eye makeup had run down her cheeks.

"*Sí.* Oh, you are American?" Her English was basic and cute.

Roger felt suddenly weak in her presence. "No, lass, I am Scottish."

"Oh, really?" She looked puzzled. "You are tall!"

"Aye, I get that all the time."

"You play basketball?"

"No. You model?" He smiled.

"*Sí*, part time." She nodded matter-of-factly.

Roger laughed. "Of course."

She frowned.

"Whatever is wrong, sweetie, don't let it get you down. Man trouble?" Roger looked around for Evan.

"My name is Maria. Not man trouble. Monster trouble! *Comprende?*"

"Sorry, honey. Men usually act like monsters to cover up their little problems. Get what I mean, lass?" Roger winked.

She giggled and for a split second was free of her burden. She wiped her eyes with the backs of her hands. She squeezed his arm, sniffled, and walked to the elevator in the lobby.

Roger watched with great respect and then turned quickly away.

"Who were you talking to?" Evan came out of the bathroom wearing a black leather jacket that made him look a little stockier than he was. He had his duffel bag looped over his shoulder like he was going on a trip.

Roger could tell Evan was wearing a vest. He could also see the bulge under his arm and the strap from his tactical sling. "Lad, you could not be more obvious. Ye carrying the HK under that? What else you got in your bag?"

"Toys. Toys that make loud noises."

"Only insecure men need so much gear."

Evan laughed. "Let's go, wise one!"

Roger and Evan walked toward the elevator and waited.

The two men rode in silence to the second floor. Roger reached into his duffel bag and grabbed a full-sized XD .40 and shoved it in his waistband. He pulled his shirt over it.

"Does my gun show?" he asked sarcastically.

"Yes, and it makes you look fat!"

Roger was about to say something smart, but the doors of the elevator opened.

Yuri looked at Maria. She seemed perkier than earlier. He had been joined by four more of his henchmen as he stood in the hotel lobby waiting on her to return. None of them spoke. Yuri liked to use other Russians as his hit men and inner circle. Each Scorpion operator ran his own cells as he saw fit.

Maria waited patiently for a few minutes for the Russians to speak among themselves. They seemed to be planning. Suddenly, Yuri motioned for them to move toward the hotel elevator. "Let's go."

The five large men and one tiny girl crammed into the elevator. Maria felt very uncomfortable and tried to make herself one with the wall. She avoided eye contact and the chance of touching any of the men. Maria hummed a little tune. Suddenly, she giggled and then coughed to cover it up.

"What the hell is so funny?" Yuri asked.

"Oh, nothing, sir. Just someone funny I met."

"Want to share it?"

Maria chewed on her lip and shook her head. "No, it's kinda rude. But true."

"Whatever. What room are we going to?" Yuri asked.

"Tenth floor. Room 1025."

She tried not to look at Yuri's gross piercings or satanic tattoos. She also did not want her back facing him. The glaring eyes of Yuri's men made her feel sick and like less than a piece of meat. Yuri had voiced his unconcern with females, but these men were different.

"So who did you talk to? Did he flirt with you?"

"No, no, sir. He was an older gentlemen. Tall like a basketball player, funny accent, Scottish, he said."

The door chimed, the elevator stopped, and the doors opened.

Maria made to leave the elevator and paused. "You look pale, sir; are you OK?" She asked, not really concerned just curious.

Yuri walked slowly off the elevator as if he were in deep thought and none of them were there. Her words had jolted him like a few lines of cocaine. He leaned against the wall and put his hands up, as if trying to make the world pause for a second.

His men paused. Maria froze.

"Am I being paranoid? How many Scottish men can be in this town? In this country? Big Scottish men?" Yuri looked around and touched his knife. He had a .357 strapped under his leather jacket.

"Move!" He put his hand on the small of Maria's back and shoved her gently along. She was light like a paperweight. Yuri decided he would kill her or use her as a shield if he needed to. He wanted to locate Tanya and get out of the city quick. He cursed the fact that Gerard was without cell phone coverage. He spoke to his men in Russian.

"Look, I think we are being followed. Could be same stupid bodyguard from the Manuel operation and Veracruz. Sounds crazy, but bear with me. One of you stay at the elevator! If it's obvious, kill him. You two, go to the room!"

Tanya paused and took a deep breath. "Reo, look, I have a twisted ankle. I can't walk up any more stairs, and my ribs are cracked. I may have a punctured lung!" she lied and leaned against the wall in the fire-escape stairwell. Tanya wanted to take the elevator; it was more public.

Reo looked at the teenagers and then Tanya. "You made it five flights. That's admirable. Fine, we will take the elevator."

"I have to be able to make it, and I know you can't carry me."

Reo frowned and looked coldly at her. "You are a piece of work."

"And you are a sucker. Try calling Nathan—see where he is."

"He's busy."

"He left you."

"Shut up!"

Tanya opened the fire door and considered running for it. She was outnumbered five to one.

"Tenth floor, Tanya?"

"Yes."

"Elevators are all busy. We can walk, or I can turn Carlos loose on you!"

Tanya looked at the teenager. He just glared, vacant of human thought.

"Fine, we can walk, but slow."

Roger and Evan did a mental assessment of their gear and equipment and the day that stretched ahead of them. Evan had six thirty-round magazines for his submachine gun. He liked to tape two together facing in opposite directions. This way he could remove it, flip it, and slam it back in. This was not always the best technique, but it would serve his purpose today. He adjusted his bag, which was beginning to feel a little heavy. Forty-caliber ammo was not light. The struggle was always carry too much gear and not need it and be slow, or don't carry enough so you are light enough to run like hell, yelling, "Wish I had more ammo."

Evan spoke first. "I am hungry."

"Aye, me too."

Both men watched the digital numbers flash by slowly.

Five, Six, Seven...

"So, what's your favorite Mexican dish, and don't say Mia!" Evan teased.

Roger laughed and snapped his fingers. "You got me, lad."

Eight…The elevator stopped and a little old lady made to get on.

"Going down?" she asked.

"Honey, we are going up not down," Roger said politely and smiled.

The lady looked at him angrily, threw her hands in the air, and barked with a New York accent, "Why the hell not!"

She left. The smell of Ben Gay hung in the air. The doors closed. There was silence for a second, and then Evan spoke.

"Fish. I would say fish is my favorite."

"You don't say?" Roger asked.

"Definitely!" Evan finished.

Ding…Floor nine.

"You know, I won a recipe contest with my Balsamic vinaigrette salmon recipe," Roger said matter of factly.

Evan looked interested now. "Dude, you're making me hungry."

Ding…Floor ten.

The doors opened, and both men jumped.

"*Watch out!*" Roger yelled.

Evan and Roger both moved at the same time.

A short, stocky Russian thrust a .45 with a suppressor through the doors as they opened. The man made eye contact with Roger, cursed as he recognized him, and let go a string of Russian words that Evan did not care to translate.

Pop! Pop! Pop!

Roger pushed the man's arms up so that he shot into the ceiling while Evan charged low. Roger dove into the hall over the two tumbling men and away from the muzzle of the gun, which continued to pop rounds into the ceiling. Suppressors were not really that silent. Roger pulled his weapon out and moved to regain his balance.

Evan pinned the man's elbows with both arms and tried to move into a better position. The Russian kicked wildly and began to wriggle free.

Evan head butted the Russian as hard as he could and then twisted with all his might, swinging both his legs around the man's gun arm, causing it to hyperextend. Evan twisted the weapon away from his grasp and flung it. He broke the man's arm and then kicked him in the side of the face as he fully extended. The crack was loud.

The whole thing was over in seconds.

The would-be shooter screamed as loud as he could.

"He is warning someone!" Evan said as he removed his H&K from his ankle holster and put a bullet in the man's forehead. Evan held his weapon down and looked at Roger, as if this killing was just a tiny pause in their conversation.

"Aye, I think we need to move, lad!"

Evan stood up and checked himself. He stepped over the body, picked up his duffel bag and slung it, holstered his H&K .40, and pulled out his H&K UMP .40, which had twisted around behind his back during the brief wrestling match.

Evan liked to keep things simple. He could use the same ammo in both weapons if given the option. The UMP was a smart-looking submachine gun, compact with a folding stock, and it weighed a neat 4.96 pounds.

"You know, Roger, they really need to be more careful who they let in these places."

Roger looked sideways at Evan as if he had two heads. "You're not freaking right in the head, son!"

Evan was moving quickly down the hall now, his tactical sling tight, and his weapon out in front. "Let's go, Scotty!" Evan mocked Roger's accent, doing his best voice of Scotty from *Star Trek*.

"Now you done crossed the line, you little—"

The scream of a girl suddenly made the two men shut up and put their game faces on. They heard the *pop-pop* of a handgun and covered each other as they moved in.

There was no cover in the hallway, unless they kicked in a guest's door and hid inside.

A Few Moments Earlier

Yuri kicked the door to room 1025 open and burst in with his .357 held high. A uniformed Mexican police officer was coming out of the bathroom, and they locked eyes for a second. He never had time to react. Maria screamed.

Yuri shot him twice and dragged the screaming Maria into the room. "Shut up, whore!" He hip tossed her onto the bed and she rolled across it and onto the floor.

Yuri spun around and glared at his other three comrades.

They spoke in rapid Russian.

"You hear that?" one asked.

"Police?" another asked.

Yuri answered "*No!* They are coming! Cover the hall, right where it curves up there, move up. We take them down then head left to the fire exit. I don't want them on our flank!"

"Fine."

"I am going down to the floor below. You guys meet me. I will pull the fire alarm. That's our cover to leave!"

"Brilliant! Elevators will stop. People will flood the stairwells!"

Yuri stepped back into the doorway and watched two of his men creep with their handguns to the bend in the hallway. They took a knee and covered the hall.

Guests could be heard talking loudly in their rooms, and no one dared venture out into the hall.

Yuri knew that one of his men was dead and had a gnawing feeling that things were about to get worse. Yuri looked at

Nicholas, who was a large man with thick arms and a barrel chest. He had spent the last ten years in prison and was indifferent to life.

"Nicholas, good luck."

"I don't need luck."

Yuri grabbed Maria by the hair and dragged her to the fire exit.

Maria started screaming.

Yuri kicked opened the door into the fire-escape stairwell and was about to go down when the explosion happened.

Evan nodded to Roger, who plugged his ears and made ready. Evan tossed the flash-bang around the corner, took a knee, and held his breath. This was going to hurt.

Boom!

The percussion caused the fire alarm to sound, the sprinkler system to fire, and about half a dozen people in their rooms to start screaming. Doors were opened and then slammed.

Evan shook his head to clear his throbbing ears, spat on the ground, and tapped Roger on the shoulder. The two men burst around the corner, aiming low and searching out targets. Evan was not an advocate of spray-and-pray unless it was necessary.

Both Russians took rounds to the face and chest as they scrambled to regain their balance after the shock of the grenade. Wild rounds peppered the walls and ceiling. Hot shell casings bounced across the carpet.

Suddenly Evan felt a thump to his chest and stumbled. He lurched sideways. He knew he had been shot. He crashed through a door as rounds began punching holes in the drywall next to him.

"There's one more!" Evan yelled. "You OK?"

Evan assessed what had happened and within a few seconds had the information he needed and a plan. His ears were still ringing, and he realized he still had his earplugs in. Evan pulled them out. He had been hit in his vest by a round. They had killed two stunned shooters in the hallway. The flash-bang had left a nasty charred mark on the carpet and filled the hall with the smell of sulfur. Evan thought briefly about Camp Lejeune, Panama, and Colombia.

"Smells always bring back the fondest memories," he muttered as he checked himself. "Boots, fingers, toes." He grabbed his crotch. "I am OK, Roger!"

"I wasn't asking, wanker!"

The other shooter, wherever he was, was ready for them.

"We gotta keep the momentum!" Roger said.

Evan pied off the corner of the doorframe with the short barrel of his weapon. All was clear. He decided against a smoke grenade since the confusion would hurt him more than help. When civilians started to fill the hallway, the bad guys would have the advantage.

He gave a quick nod to Roger, who had crashed through a door on the opposite side of the hall and was using the doorframe as cover. Evan could hear females screaming inside the room.

"*Somos la policia, permanecer abajo!*" Evan yelled and began to move quickly, hugging the corner of the hallway, weapon and eyes acting as one.

Roger followed close behind, the side of his face stained with drying blood.

As Evan made his was down the straight hallway, he noticed a door open to his left; it was Tanya's room. He backed up and scanned the fire-exit door to his right. It had just closed with a click.

"We are sitting ducks out here. Either go in Tanya's room or go down the fire exit," Roger said.

Both men could hear hotel guests talking in their rooms; the fire alarm was deafening, and Evan knew it was a matter of time before the police and fire crews were storming the building.

Roger covered the open door to Tanya's room while Evan held up two fingers and counted down as he inched along the wall.

Suddenly, a large man burst from the room in a last-ditch effort to gain surprise.

Roger shot him in the head while Evan shredded his body with a quick five-round burst. The man stumbled forward a few steps, never squeezed his trigger, and collapsed at their feet with a thud.

"I think the idiot was out of ammo," Roger said after the man dropped.

"Some guys got all the luck, eh?" Evan said.

Without a word, they made sure Tanya's room was empty and then moved toward the fire door.

"I hear screaming!" Roger blurted.

"They went down the fire escape, reloading."

Evan switched magazines and dug out his last two grenades from his bag. He put a smoke grenade in one cargo pocket and a flash-bang in the other.

"OK, Evan, you getting a little carried away with your pyro. We gotta have a talk, lad!"

Evan pouted and then spat on the floor. He flicked sweat off his bald head. "I missed the Fourth last year—gotta make up."

Roger shook his head and coughed. "You're not right, son, really."

"Fine!"

Evan scanned the halls and stepped toward the fire-escape exit.

Yuri grabbed the screaming Maria by her hair and dragged her as fast as he could down the stairs. He was on the ninth landing and did not like the sounds he heard from above. He knew his crew was dead, and at this point he just wanted to save himself and get word to Gerard that he had been right all along. There was a conspiracy. His cell phone had no signal, and he cursed.

"*Zatknis!* Shut up!"

"Let go of my hair!" Maria screamed hysterically. She tried to fight him for a moment.

Yuri paused at fire-exit door nine, jerked her around, and punched her in the diaphragm. She crumbled to the ground, stunned and unable to suck in a breath.

Guests were filling the halls. He could hear nothing over the drone of the fire alarm. Yuri threatened anyone who stepped into the stairwell.

Yuri shoved his weapon into his waistband as he encircled Maria's thin waist and dragged her through the doorway to the ninth floor. He felt like a fish swimming upstream. Hotel guests were pushing against him as they bottlenecked and made for the emergency exits.

Yuri yelled at the top of his lungs as he loosened his grip on Maria. "*Retroceder!* Go back to your rooms!" Just for effect, he waved his .357 around and leveled it at no one in particular.

Yuri needed to use the crowd to his advantage. They could form a useful smoke screen, but he could not get bogged down in any kind of a hostage situation.

I have to get out of here and contact my crew! Yuri felt panic rise in his stomach.

Maria sobbed.

Yuri stepped back from the young girl, who was barely in her twenties. She was frozen in terror and was only going to slow him down.

"Go, Maria!" he barked. "Before I change my mind!"

Guests began to scream and push against each other, a fist-fight broke out, and he heard shouts from inside the hallway.

"There is no fire. Get back in your rooms, or I will kill you all!" Yuri left Maria and plunged through the crowd, pushing and slashing, his knife in one hand and pistol in the other.

The crowd dispersed and stampeded like cattle back in the opposite direction.

Yuri had only one thought in his head now: *escape and notify the Scorpions that they were being hunted.*

Roger and Evan made it to the landing of the ninth floor with a crowd of about fifty people not but a few steps behind them. Evan felt as if he were fleeing a sinking ship. People screamed and yelled and did all the things that you were not supposed to do in an emergency. Some people were stealing TVs and towels from the rooms.

Evan made it to the landing first and opened the ninth-floor fire-exit door for Roger. "I will be behind you. There is another fire exit at the far end of the hall."

Roger looked at Evan and shook his head. "Splittin' up is not a good idea!"

"Crowd control."

Roger looked at him for a second, shook his head, and went onto the ninth floor.

Evan yelled at the top of his lungs and tried to hide his weapon. "Listen, everybody, there is no fire! We are the police looking for a group of terrorists. Best thing you guys can do is quietly, calmly get down the stairs and evacuate." Evan stood by for a few moments and made sure that the slower ones were guided down first.

Roger made it a few feet down the hall when he spotted a girl crouched on the floor trying to use her cell phone. She was sobbing and shaking so badly that she could hardly hit the numbers. Her hair was plastered to her face, and her nose was running. She was the beautiful girl from the bathroom.

The fire alarm was still blaring, and the guests on this floor had begun barricading themselves back in their rooms. Some had fled to the other fire exit down the hall.

"Get up, Maria." He helped her gently to her feet and brushed her hair out of her eyes.

She looked relived when she recognized him.

"Still havin' monster troubles, darlin'?"

She nodded and looked at Roger's weapon.

"Where did he go?"

Maria pointed down the hall toward the other set of fire doors.

"Listen, Maria, I need ya to make it to the parking garage. First level, space 12A. There is a short, fat police officer named Victor Rosa. Tell him we are OK. You stay with him. Got it?"

She nodded, sniffed, and looked up and down the hall.

"You'll be OK." Roger turned and began to jog down the hall.

"*Wait!*" Maria called out.

"Aye?" He paused and turned around. Roger was feeling constricted by his body armor and was beginning to sweat.

"The monster?"

"Aye, don't ye worry 'bout him." He winked and gave her a nod.

Maria did as told. She watched the large Scotsman run down the hall and suddenly felt empowered. She sniffed and ran toward the door. As she opened it, she was face-to-face with another man—with a bigger gun.

He smiled and held the door for her. "It's OK! OK? Hey, you need to get out of here!"

Maria took off her remaining high heel and fled.

Evan let the fire door slam and spun around to sprint down the hall. His chest hurt where he had been shot, and his lungs burned as he ran. Adrenaline kept him moving.

Roger had just made it to the seventh floor landing and was turning to check the next set of stairs for any signs of movement when he saw the barrel of a handgun being held by the satanic, painted Russian.

Boom-boom!

Roger knew one thing about physics: every action had an equal reaction, and an object in motion tended to stay in motion. In the movies, they always showed someone getting shot and being thrown against a wall or something. If that was true, it would launch the shooter backward with the same force. Roger watched the muzzle flash and jumped. He thought about his father for a second and about the day when his father had finally shown him respect. The day his father hit him, and Roger had dared to hit him back. Now in hindsight, he knew that his father just wanted him to be raised to have a tough, fighting spirit, the bastard.

The bullets felt like hot pokers as they hit his vest and sent waves of pain into his abdomen.

Roger had not hesitated to leap down the four or so stairs onto the Russian. The Russian's weapon fired one more shot, and it burned the side of Roger's face point-blank just before both men crashed to the ground. Yuri's ankle cracked under the weight, and he tried to spin out of the way. Roger tried to move as fast as he could to clear the weapon from the man's grasp and bring up his own. The Russian was far quicker and rolled Roger over onto his back and came down hard with a knife in both hands. Terror, insanity, and death flashed in Roger's eyes.

Evan made it to the end of the hall in seconds. He ripped the fire-exit door open and burst through. He heard the shots and yelling. He leapt down the steps five at a time with his left hand gripping his UMP .40 and using the railing for balance. He made it to the eighth-floor landing just as the fire door burst open and two men barreled through. Evan had no idea who they were, but he guessed two things. They had been waiting just inside the door. Evan was at the top of the landing ready to go down when he was ambushed. His peripheral vision told him that Roger and the Russian were locked in battle on the landing below, and had now rolled down the stairs to the sixth-floor landing.

The yelling and swearing were at a hysterical pitch.

"*Shit!*" Evan cursed as he was caught off guard and side tackled. He knew there were at least two. The three men tumbled down the stairs with Evan mostly on the bottom. He banged his elbows, back, and knee, possibly on someone's jaw.

Evan emptied the last of his ammo into his assailant, who was swinging wildly. His heavy duffel bag was choking him and throwing him off balance. Evan felt a slash to his leg and realized he had been stabbed.

"*Die!*" his attacker yelled.

Evan heard the *pop* of a nine millimeter and the sound of bullets bouncing off the brick landing and walls around him.

For a second Evan about panicked. He was just on the cusp of being overwhelmed and underestimated by his enemy. The tide was not in his favor as he found himself on his back at the bottom of the stairs, using the dead body of what he now realized was a teenager as a bullet shield. Two more killers entered the stairwell and began firing wildly. No shooting discipline. They laughed hysterically and held their weapons sideways like gangsters.

A third kid emerged from the fire door at the top of the stairs with a machete. "Kill him already, motherfuckas!"

Evan used both hands to hold up the gangster's dead friend while he lay on his back. The kids did not seem to mind that they were wasting all of their ammo shooting their own friend in the back. It was a hysterically funny game to them.

Evan's wave of panic and glimpse of doom washed over him like a tide, but like any tide, they always come in and then go out. They always change.

The boys were done shooting and now started kicking Evan. One of them produced a switchblade. The dead gangster bullet sponge was dripping with blood from holes top to bottom.

"Just kick his ass. Reo wants him alive!" the gangster with the machete at the top of the stairs yelled.

Roger felt something hard hit the back of his head and he began to lose consciousness. Suddenly, he remembered where he was and what he was doing. He wasn't sure if it was the Russian's fist hitting him in the face or the back of his head hitting the floor that was causing his brain to see reality in waves. He heard fighting and shooting above him and hoped that it was Evan coming to his rescue. Truth was, Roger began to feel like he just did not have his edge anymore.

"You Scottish prick! You killed my men at the airport! You ruined my operation!"

Roger blocked the blows as best he could and went for a different tactic. He kicked upward and reached for Yuri's lame foot as he knelt down over Roger. The pummeling stopped as Roger grabbed hold of the man's ankle and foot and twisted. Roger was not sure how he had ended up on the floor again in the first place, but since he was down here, he had to grab what he could.

He twisted Yuri's ankle as hard as he could and first heard it snap then saw it twist completely around until it was backward.

Yuri screamed.

He hopped backward and away from Roger as quickly as he could. Somehow he got loose. The fight was gone from him. He made to escape. Roger used his hips and legs, rolled to regain balance, and got to his feet. He was far stronger than Yuri, and both men knew that if Roger got a good hold of him, no amount of training and quickness was going to overcome the angry, six-foot-four Scotsman.

Yuri lunged for the fire door on the sixth floor, opened it, and was gone, hopping and swearing as he fled. Roger was impressed that he could hop that fast.

"Evan, are you up there?" Roger yelled.

Evan rode the tide change and allowed the full fury of his pent-up anger and frustration with being in this country to overtake him. He remained calm and focused on the prize. For a brief second, something his judo coach had told him as a teenager in Japan burned into his mind. It sounded better in Japanese, he mused, but the logic was still sound: "The victory is already yours."

Evan waited until both thugs were on the same landing before he struck. He rolled quickly onto his hips, scissoring his legs, and pushing the dead body from him. He clipped the ankles of one of the gangsters, and he went down, his head and elbows hitting the wall as he lost balance. The one with the knife leapt on Evan and stabbed at his face. Evan deflected the shot away from his face. He ignored the blade. It burned through his cheek and ear.

Three, maybe four, things happened at once. Evan was not sure, but he was in control. The first gangster, who had lost his balance, sprung back up with the grace of a youngster. Evan trapped the knife arm of the second gangster and twisted to his left, then changed directions and stood up, twisting to his right, locking the gangster's arm and head down near the floor. The thug screamed.

The third gangster with the machete raised it over his head and leapt down the stairs.

Evan calculated motion, gravity, and confusion all in a split second. Hand-to-hand combat was like mental chess: "Consider fully—act decisively."

Evan stomped down hard on the straight elbow, bending it backward until it cracked and went limp.

"*Aaaahhh, perra!*"

Evan spun to his right and caught the body of the gangster midair by the elbows and legs. The idiot had probably grown up playing video games and thinking they were real. Evan let the thug's momentum carry him on his way down the stairs in a forward tumble and crash.

"Air is the best blocker."

Evan punched the first thug, who had sprung to his feet so quickly, once in the throat and twice in the ribs. The kid went down. He turned blue, and his eyes bulged. Evan did not want to leave his back exposed, so he grabbed the fallen thug's head, slammed it into the wall, and twisted his head till he heard vertebrae pop.

"*I kill you!*" The gangster with the broken arm tried to flee down the stairs, crying hysterically. He stepped on his friend, who had dropped the machete and was now trying to regain his balance.

"My leg, my back, something broken. Kill that motherf—"

Evan heard Roger's voice from somewhere below. "Evan, you there?"

Evan kicked, punched, stomped, and twisted the thugs until the fight was gone and they yielded to the inevitable tide of darkness.

Their video game was over. There were no second plays.

Blood was running down Evan's face. He cursed and leapt down the stairs, glancing at his watch. It had all been over in a few moments.

"Roger, you OK?"

Evan retrieved his UMP .40, put a fresh magazine in, and untangled his duffel bag from around his neck and waist.

"Yes! The Russian is getting away. He's wounded. So am I!"

Roger and Evan paused and looked over the stairwell. The sound of firemen and policemen making their way up the stairs was getting closer. The building was strangely quiet, and the two men looked at each other.

Roger made a suggestion. "Now would be a good time to drop a smoke grenade."

Evan smiled like a kid and pulled his smoke grenade and percussion grenade from his pockets. "Feeling lighter already." He was glad to lose the weight.

Evan pulled the pins on both his grenades and tossed them up the stairwell. Both men made it through fire door quickly as the grenades exploded. Smoke and the smell filled the building.

"That will keep them busy for a while."

Both men were covered in sweat and a mixture of their and others' blood. They stank like smoke and gunpowder.

The two men covered each other and moved into the hallway. That's when things got bizarre.

Yuri had backtracked and headed for the original stairwell. His foot burned and throbbed. He cursed and hoped he could escape. The elevators were not working, and hiding in a room would eventually lead to his arrest. He had to escape, and he hopped on his good foot as best he could. He made it to the fire door of the original stairwell and was about to open it when he glanced over his shoulder. He saw Roger and another man charging, as best they could, down the hall. He paused for a second and realized something.

"You're Ivan!"

Evan and Roger kept their weapons trained on the Russian as they closed the distance. Yuri looked at both of them in disbelief as they narrowed the distance.

"Now I get it. You guys are all part of some kind of plot!" Yuri said and reached for the door.

Evan spoke to Roger as he aimed at Yuri's head and placed his finger on the trigger.

"Roger, something I need to tell you."

"Can it wait?"

Yuri flipped off Roger and Evan and pushed open the door, preparing to hobble through.

Evan never had a chance to shoot.

Boom!

The back of Yuri's head came off in a shower of red. He stumbled backward for a second and looked unseeingly at the man who had just shot him from inside the stairwell.

"Take cover!" Evan yelled.

Roger moved to the right, trying to take cover in a doorway while Evan took a knee.

Evan heard a click behind him and knew within a second that he and Roger had just been outflanked.

"Crap!" Evan spat.

Roger looked at Evan clearly disturbed. He heard someone racking a shotgun shell behind him.

"*No se mueven!*" a voice yelled.

Evan and Roger froze in place. They watched a skinny white kid with no tattoos or piercings step over Yuri's dead body and into the hallway. He held a sawed-off shotgun. He had a meth smile with partially black gums. He wore a tie-dye T-shirt, ripped shorts, and Timberland boots.

"*Hi, boys!*" The snarky, familiar voice of Reo could be heard behind them.

Tanya looked in disbelief from her chair as Reo and two of his remaining teenagers escorted Evan and Roger into the empty hotel room, where she was duct-taped to a chair.

The occupants had fled and left the door wide open. Reo and his crew had spotted Evan, Roger, and the Russian's gang during their struggle. Using radios and quick planning, Reo had managed to beat them down the stairs and set up a hasty ambush. He had never suspected that Evan would kill most of his crew in the stairwell, but he had adjusted.

Reo smiled and breathed heavily. He looked at his two remaining gangsters and shook his head. "OK, we have to make this quick," Reo explained. "Jose, shoot this one first." Reo pointed at Roger.

"Did you get the thumb drive, Evan?" Reo asked between breaths.

Evan stood with his hands by his sides next to Roger. One gangster was behind them with a shotgun, and the other was in front of them holding Evan's UMP.40.

"No, didn't really look, Reo, you double-crossing lil' bitch. You know Nathan scammed us all! I notice he is not here. You're doing his dirty work again. Where is he?"

Evan grinned and mocked Reo. "The police say he is gone. Left you holding the bag. Must have taken him months to steal all that money, the planes, the logistics. Mmm, did he keep you in the dark, or were you in on it?"

Reo's eyes flashed with rage, and he jumped forward to slap Evan.

Evan laughed. "You hit like a girl—no offense to girls." He nodded toward Tanya.

"He has not left me!"

"He has, you wuss," Roger growled.

Reo pulled his cell phone from his pocket and backed up so that he was standing next to Tanya. She was duct-taped across her chest and arms to a wooden chair.

Reo was sweating heavily and looked concerned. He pressed his Glock 20 against Tanya's temple with his left hand and made a phone call with his right.

"Ever use a gun before, lassie?" Roger joked.

Evan heard voices in the hall and decided it was now or never to make a move. "Roger, you know about the Spartans, huh?"

"What?"

"Carry your shield, or go home on it." Evan turned around and faced the kid with the shotgun. He sidestepped so that he was protecting Roger's back and blocking the room. The kid stood partway in the hall. His eyes were glazed from a mixture of not enough sleep and too much meth. He had sores on his face from picking at scabs, and his fingernails were dirty and worn down.

"Turn back around, bitch!" the kid said.

Evan stepped forward slightly and spoke quickly to the gangster. "It's not too late to save yourself. Run!"

"What?"

The voices in the hall grew louder, and Evan knew it was now or never.

He heard someone down the hall yell, "There is a fire. Everyone needs to leave the building!"

For a second the kid was distracted.

Evan leapt forward and pushed the gun out of the way just as the kid squeezed the trigger.

Boom!

The buckshot went into the wall and floor. Evan yanked the shotgun from the kid's grasp and pistol-whipped him in the face with the stock.

The kid collapsed and gripped his broken nose.

"Get!" Evan yelled.

The teenager stumbled to his feet and tugged on his pants to pull them up as he ran.

"Hey you! Stop!" Evan heard more voices in the hall and spun back around.

The gangster in front of Roger squeezed the trigger, but nothing happened. The weapon was still on Safe.

Reo dropped his phone and shot at Roger as he backed up. The bullet went into the back of his last gangbanger by accident, and the kid went down without so much as a scream. Roger moved as quickly as he could to shield Tanya.

Reo aimed the weapon at Roger's head and stumbled, shooting into the ceiling. Tanya suddenly rallied energy, as if she had been storing it up for one last explosion. She stood up and charged at Reo, who had tripped over an electrical cord and was backed up against the window. He still had not hit a target, and he shot one more time. A bullet hit the TV set.

Tanya crashed into Reo with all the force she could muster. She used her legs and core to rip herself free from the chair and drive every ounce of her body into Reo.

Roger grabbed Reo's gun hand just as Tanya slammed him into the window.

The window cracked, the curtains came down, and the chair splintered.

Reo screamed.

Evan stepped into the hall to see who was yelling.

Roger helped Tanya get to her feet. She was remarkably calm.

Reo banged his head on a corner table and then struggled to get up. He put his back to the window. He looked shocked and beaten.

Roger put Reo's gun in his pocket and spoke over his shoulder to Evan, who was in the hall talking to someone rapidly. "Hey, lad, who are ya talkin' to?"

"Hotel security! They say we have to evacuate! There are terrorists or something in the building!"

Evan had closed his jacket and had no weapons near him. He stood in the hall and watched as a man approached. He was wearing a suit and carried a radio.

"I heard a gunshot, saw that kid. What is going on?" the security guard asked, clearly fearful for his own life.

Roger cursed and looked at the room. How would they explain all this?

"Hey, tell them to go to the tenth floor, room 1025!" Roger yelled.

"Wait here, lass!" Roger squeezed Tanya's arms and looked in her eyes. "OK, Tanya?" He handed her the gun and then pointed to Reo, who was leaning against the window, trying to stop his bleeding. Large cracks that resembled a spider web ran throughout the window.

Roger stepped out into the hall next to Evan and closed the door slightly.

The hotel security man looked suspiciously at them. "My God! What happened to you two? Are you OK?" The man began to speak into his radio. "I am calling police."

Evan stopped him gently. "No, no, we are OK. We were on the tenth floor when the shooting started! Then we came down here to my girlfriend's room to check on her. There are bodies in the hall, in the stairwell!" Evan pointed down the hall.

"You two need to come with me. The police and fire department are going floor to floor, making sure the building is secure."

Evan just now realized that the fire alarm had stopped. He spoke quickly as Roger looked up and down the hall. "Look, how do we get out of here, fast and unseen? We have someone famous with us, and, well, she can't be seen. We are actually her security detail. Famous American actress!"

The security guard looked confused and held his radio in his hands.

"Why do you look like you have been fighting? *And* I know you have guns. I have none." The man held up his hands. "The police have to say it's safe first. They are on the second floor still."

"I get it. We are doing our jobs, just like you! Mexico is an awesome place, and we want to come back. Look, our client, she is hysterical!"

"Um, I…I think you all need doctors," the guard said. The blood had drained from his face as he tried to process what he was seeing.

"Elevators?"

The security guard was in his midfifties and balding, and he had a worried, pockmarked face. He was a rules kind of guy, and anything outside of the box was new territory for him. Evan could sense his confusion and fear. The guard wanted someone to tell him what to do.

"We have rules, procedures. This is Mexico City, not the wild west. I…I—"

Roger pushed Evan out of the way and faced the shocked security guard. He held a roll of one-hundred-dollar bills under the man's nose, as if they were smelling salts.

No one spoke.

Suddenly, the security guard nodded, took the money, and pocketed it. Now he was back in his box.

"Oh! The staff elevator. Come with me, *amigos*. We go right out to the parking garage. No one see you." He smiled.

Evan smiled at the security guard and then glanced at Roger with concern. "Wait here."

Evan stepped into the room, closed the door, and moved quickly over to Tanya. She stood frozen, as if in a trance or in a dream state. She wasn't shaking, crying, or showing any emotion.

"WTF! Where did Reo go?"

Evan stepped past her and looked out the window. Hot, dry air and a breeze from outside had caused the air conditioner to kick on. Evan could see crowds of people and vehicles below. The smog and the noise of Mexico City invaded the room.

He put his hands on Tanya's shoulders. "What?"

"I pushed him," she said matter-of-factly.

"Wow. Tanya, honey, we gotta go!"

"OK."

"Now, what was this about a thumb drive?"

Tanya shrugged. "Made it up. Let's go."

Victor Rosa walked out of the Café de Mexico with enough food to feed an army. He had three plastic bags in his right hand and two in his left. He was talking to his fifth wife on his Bluetooth headset. He made his way through the parking garage and paused near his truck. There was a young woman pacing back and forth near his Toyota Land Cruiser, talking on a cell phone.

Suddenly, she hung up and looked at him. "Sir, are you Detective Rosa?"

"Yes."

"Glad to see you!" The girl was extremely attractive and looked as if she had just been assaulted.

"Honey, I will call you back. No, really I can't explain this one. Later."

Victor fished for his keys and hit the button to unlock his truck. "And you are?"

"Maria. Oh, look, here they come!" The girl pointed behind Victor.

He spun to look and then realized what was going on. He set the food down and watched in dumbfounded wonderment the sight before him.

Evan was carrying Tanya, who looked as if she had been thrown from a moving vehicle. Evan did not look much better, with a weapon slung over his back and plaster dust covering his face and head. Roger had more bruises and cuts than Victor could count yet waved cheerfully.

"Victor, this is Maria," Roger said. "We're taking her home." He pointed to the young lady who stood near his Land Cruiser.

Maria offered to take the bags from him and loaded them in the Land Cruiser. She was very helpful.

"Somebody scratched this Corvette!" Maria exclaimed as she opened the passenger door.

"We have to go, Victor!" Evan blurted.

The four people slowly and painfully got into Victor's truck without so much as a word. They all smelled like sweat and smoke.

Victor quietly got into the driver's seat. He had almost not noticed the fire trucks and police cars with the arrival of his friends.

"You two cause all this?" He waved his hand around.

"No, the Russian did. You better make up a good story to tell the media. Your cop is dead, Reo is dead, and there are a bunch of dead gangsters."

"I see, my friends." Victor considered what they said as he backed out slowly. "Quite a mess."

No one spoke as Victor calmly drove out of the parking garage, flashed his badge, and made it through the blockade of emergency vehicles. He waved at some of the group supervisors that he knew and drove away.

"Sooo," Victor started, "did Reo have anything to say?"

"Um, yes." Evan coughed. "He wanted to know who scratched his Corvette! Then he jumped out the freaking window!"

Roger tried not to laugh and squeezed his eyes shut.

Tanya spoke to no one and pretended to check her nails.

"You know, the smell of that food is making me very hungry!" Maria stated.

"Aye. Bunch o' comedians," Roger grumbled.

CHAPTER 27

"The Plane, the Plane"

Private Island Plutarco, 2100 Hours

Jorge Valdez was so glad to finally leave the *Happy Mermaid*. The ship was brought into dock alongside three smaller yachts at the island's concrete-and-wood marina. A sizable seawall had been built to shield prying eyes from the sea as well as for protection from storms. Jorge left the vessel feeling a little uneasy as his legs got used to land. He walked with his entourage down the gangplank to the pier and along the well-lit walkway toward the beach house. A small crowd swarmed them like celebrities.

"Just in time, Jorge. The party is well under way! Can you take us on a tour of Mario's yacht?"

"No! I am sick of that bucket. I need a drink and to be on dry land. Go help yourself."

"A submarine? Is it true? Mario is buying a submarine? How exciting."

Jorge paused and looked at the young thirty-something wife of one of the politicians. She was having trouble walking and had a glass of wine in her hand. She was wearing a bikini top that was too small and a silk wrap around her waist.

"Oh, yes. Let us get to the party, and I will tell you all about it!" Jorge walked arm in arm with the woman as her husband, who was decades older, went on board the yacht to explore.

"How many people have you told about our new toy?" He smiled as they walked.

"Oh, everyone knows!" She laughed.

Jorge squeezed her arm and smiled. "Well, I have something to show you. Let me get settled, and we can talk."

Jorge was thrilled that in less than twenty-four hours, he was going to kill half these people. They were an example of the bourgeois—

Jorge felt his phone vibrate as he walked. "Sweetie, you keep walking. I will catch up. I have to take this."

Jorge watched the young woman sway down the dock to the beach house. He hoped she did not fall off the pier. The large windows were lit, the ceiling fans could be seen inside slowly swirling, and guests gathered at the windows and pointed. The pool had floating candles and seemed quite still compared to the crashing waves behind Jorge.

"*Hola?*"

"I see that you are here."

"Ah! Mr. Pena, you have arrived. Now the games can begin, huh?"

"Been here for three days, posing as the grounds keeper. Come meet me in the kitchen. I will give you a rundown of my handiwork."

"As long as you don't blow us all up by accident." Jorge laughed.

"No, not planning on it. You ready for this?"

"I believe so."

CHAPTER 28

Click Click Bang Bang

Isla Mujeres Marina, the Fishing Trawler, 2200 Hours

Isla Mujeres, or Island of Women, was so named by the early Spanish settlers because of the many carved goddesses found around the island. The Mayans believed that the island had some significance to the fertility goddess.

The island sits eight miles north of Cancun and is one of the ten municipalities of Quintara Roo. The small narrow island is a mere 4.3 miles long and 650 meters wide. A narrow airport on the north end of the island allows small prop-driven planes or helicopters to land. Only about twelve thousand or so people, depending on the season, live and work on the island.

Tommy had flown the plane the last leg of the journey and landed it on the tiny runway, which was basically a strip of land down the center of the island.

Evan noticed two small Cessnas and two Black Hawks with the word *Navy* on the tail sections. "Looks like our guests are here."

The sun had set hours ago, but with the help of a full moon, streetlights, and the small lights from the airfield, Evan could see that the island was indeed as small as it had looked from his maps. Once the plane taxied, they exited and grabbed their gear. A Jeep Cherokee was idling and waiting. A member of their team helped them with their bags and gestured across the street. The sound of waves crashing against the coral and the sound of a moped was all anyone could hear. Evan smelled seafood and immediately suggested a quick side trip. No one argued.

The travelers were glad they did not have to walk far. It was less than twenty-five yards. The entire island shut down at night. Most of the tourists came over for day trips on the ferry from the mainland. Roger and Tanya had slept the whole journey. Roger was thankful that Victor had been able to locate a private doctor who was able to stitch and patch them up before the flight. The surgeon had given Evan a few stitches where his earlobe had been and treated his minor soft-tissue injuries. Tanya had been given a Valium, and Roger, a few shots of whiskey.

Evan, Roger, Tommy, and Tanya stepped on board the idling trawler and moved quickly down a dimly lit stairwell into a large, brightly lit galley. They were all exhausted and perhaps a little dazed. Tommy and Tanya went off to find a place to sleep.

"You two look like crap!" El Coyote said to Evan and Roger, laughing.

"We feel like it!" Evan smiled and accepted a cup of warm coffee. He felt a little light-headed and knew that the adrenalin was about to cut off. His eyes ached from being awake and from flying. His jaw and the back of his head throbbed.

"We stole a plane, killed some bad guys, rescued a girl, and had a few tacos. Questions?" Evan announced to the crowd, who had turned to watch the newcomers.

The members of Dark Cloud muttered and cracked jokes for a few seconds and then settled down.

A well-groomed man with short hair, weathered skin, and the intense eyes of someone who had been institutionalized in the military too long stood up. "I am Commander Thomas. I heard you men had an ordeal today."

"Yes," Roger agreed.

"I am glad you men made it back in one piece," Thomas began.

Roger and Evan sat down and turned their attention to the brief.

"Let's begin!" The commander sat down with his young officers.

Evan looked around the room through tired, droopy eyes. He finally felt like he belonged to this group. All forty-five members of Green Team One, known as the Chupacabras, were present. The whole team would stay on the trawler and serve as a quick-reaction force once the initial ambush was launched from the sub. Green Team One was still commanded by Roger. Fifteen men from Green Team Two's Bravo Squad were present as well. The other thirty men from Green Team Two were either on the sub or making their way to the island to hide out.

An officer with the navy's special-forces unit stood up and spoke. Some of the operators from Dark Cloud knew him, and the typical, friendly insults and jokes were thrown out there, at the annoyance of the vice admiral.

"OK, men. Please, no questions; no looking at your handouts. Everything should be up here." The naval officer tapped his head and looked at the men, who were crammed into the tiny ship's hold. The same brief had been given to the one hundred marines who would take part in the second phase of the actual raid. Time, space, and security made the logistics of the two groups being in the same location impossible.

"Situation is as follows: We have roughly one hundred adversaries on the island. Thirty to forty are members of Jorge Valdez's Scorpions. We expect them to be armed with submachine guns, hand grenades, and possibly RPGs. They will fight to the death!"

Evan smiled. He admired the guy's impatience.

"Mario's regular *sicarios*, they will drop their weapons and blend in, possibly take hostages to escape. No one escapes, though." The officer stopped and drank some coffee handed to him. "Thanks. Nowhere to go. Our surveillance from above has confirmed that there are at least two pickup trucks with fifty calibers mounted in the bed. We expect it to patrol the dock on the front of the beach house. The other one seems to be stuck on the east side of the island at the small dirt landing strip."

Evan eyed the aerial photos taken from either a high-flying plane or drone. He noted the long seawall and wooden-and-concrete pier that moored three yachts. The *Happy Mermaid* was by far the longest, at close to two hundred feet. The other two were a modest 75 to 120 feet. At the end of the pier were a series of steps that went down to a floating dock and a large canopy where the sub would slip into partial cover. He shook his head. How long would it take someone in the United States to notice the sub on a satellite photo?

Behind the five-thousand-square-foot beach house, with its magnificent palm trees, swimming pool, and outdoor decks with canopies, was a small golf driving range and tennis court. Evan doubted he would have time to get in a few rounds. He glanced at the long, straight, crushed-coral road that stretched half a mile to the smaller docks and protected marina. Evan noticed something he had not seen the last time he had glanced at the photos. He confirmed quietly that these were taken in the last twenty-four hours. The dirt landing strip had one small helicopter and a Cessna. A small fishing vessel and two small sailboats were parked neatly at a lonely pier, protected by the pickup with the .50 calibers. A large seaplane, or flying boat rather, sat plain as day. Evan peered closer at the plane and identified it as a Grumman G-111 Albatross. This plane could easily make it to the States.

"My ticket home?" he said to himself.

The naval officer in civilian clothes continued on with his brief. Evan packed another dip, listened, and realized he no longer felt sleepy.

"Without you men securing the boats and sub and, most importantly, neutralizing antiair defenses, our birds can't fly. The *Happy Mermaid* does have two such assets. The bow of the yacht does have the twenty-five-millimeter Mark 38 chain-gun system. It is hidden quite well below deck and can be raised via elevator. The operator is exposed. The stern has a slightly less sophisticated twenty-five-millimeter chain gun on a swivel electronic mount. It was installed incorrectly, and it would be difficult to hit any aircraft with it. Its main purpose would be protection of the rear of the ship from other boats."

Evan thought, *A well-trained operator could take out a few helicopters before getting blown into pieces.*

"Where the hell do these guys get these weapons?" someone joked. "America?"

"You can get anything on eBay these days," someone said.

Laughter went around the room for a second.

The naval officer refocused everyone and finished his brief.

"Anyway, the mission outline is as follows: One, capture, identify, and take out Mario. Two, secure the submarine and immediate docks. Three, secure the *Happy Mermaid* and take out its defenses. Four, secure this area previously identified as LZ one. The first birds will be fast rope teams here"—the officer paused to use a laser pointer—"and here."

Evan noticed that eyes were getting heavy, and a few heads were nodding. He looked at the flying boat again up on the screen. It was a tiny, grainy speck. *Awesome escape vehicle if crap goes wrong*, Evan thought.

"As I stated earlier, phase one concludes when Dark Cloud confirms Mario's death, neutralizes the air defenses, and secures the landing zone in front of the house. Phase two begins when the assault force arrives approximately five minutes after the smoke is popped. The front of the house will be assaulted by four Black Hawks. The teams will fast rope to the deck and take their positions. One team will fast rope onto the roof if clear. The second wave of birds should arrive three minutes after, along with the boat teams, who will reinforce and secure. The raid of the house will be the call of the commander on the ground. The whole operation will be a *navy* operation at that point. Hostages, securing the house, keeping the LZ clear will all fall under their command. Dark Cloud stands fast and prepares to evacuate. We expect to see some resistance, but as we have seen in the past, they usually throw down their weapons and then claim innocence."

A few short chuckles went through the audience.

"Civilians will be herded into the house and later segregated. Hopefully, Dark Cloud can accomplish this. There are about seventy civilians."

Evan looked around the room and spat in his cup.

The rear of the house would be secured by four UH 46s that would off-load the first initial wave of one hundred marines.

Evan shook his head and wondered, *Lots of confusion. Cornered bad guys with no hope are likely to fight to the death, or hide behind the politicians and guests.*

"Phase three begins when the boat teams land and surround the island. The total number of troops on the ground will reach close to three hundred, which maintains our desired three-to-one ratio."

Again, grumbles and head nods. Evan watched bottles of water being passed around and suddenly felt thirsty.

"I know it's getting late, but bear with me," the naval officer continued. "Once the house is secure and everyone is isolated and segregated, we move into phase four. All guests are identified, arrested, and transported separately from any surviving cartel members."

Evan went above deck where he could breathe and think clearly. The sky was lit by a full moon and brilliant stars that seemed to shimmer if you stared too long. The boat swayed gently as it rubbed against the rubber tires and pier where it was moored with heavy ropes.

He was not concerned with the navy's plan; he knew it. He was much more concerned with what could go wrong and what was going to happen after that. Could the navy get enough troops on the ground quickly enough? Who would be killed in the confusion? Who was going to leak the operation?

Evan thought again about Colombia, explosions, and how Andre Pena tied into this whole mess. Andre had been involved with an estimated thirty-five political bombings of candidates and government officials across Mexico. Intelligence reports had even placed him at four different training camps belonging to different cartels. Evan paused for a second and muttered to himself, "Is it possible that something bigger is going on here?"

Evan felt a migraine coming on. Something about the last few days really began to irritate him. This whole mission had too many moving parts, too many players, too many angles, and too much possibility of just plain not working.

"Can I join you?" Tanya asked shyly. She approached him from the left and leaned against the rail next to him. She appeared stressed and tired, just like everyone else. The tension was contagious.

"Sure. How are you feeling?"

Tanya shrugged. "Not great. Took some more Valium and a few shots of tequila. Thing is, I don't even drink. Feeling, um, mellow, but—"

Evan nodded and patted her shoulder. "The pain is real. Death is not a game."

"True. Why do we get affected by it so much? And yet the evil bastards who rape, steal, murder, and torture keep doing it with no remorse? No effect at all on them, but us, those with a conscience, we are tortured in here"—Tanya tapped her head—"forever."

Evan spat over the rail and nodded.

"They are effected—don't be fooled. The human capacity to justify evil, drown out the consequences, and even change the language so that good people are bad and bad people are good, it's all a crock. They just don't care, or they are too far gone. Are you going to be able to do this?" Evan asked bluntly.

Tanya looked out at the water for a second and did not answer right away.

"I don't want to, but at this point, I need to. I worked for six months to break into Mario's system, hack it, destroy it, and, yes, steal his money. Granted, I did plan on setting a good portion aside to give to the operators." She gestured to the men downstairs, who were now listening to Roger and EL Coyote present the last part of the brief. "I justified in my head that ripping off Nathan and Mario was justified, repaying their evil."

"Doesn't usually work that way," Evan said.

"I know."

"So you lost all of it?"

Tanya nodded. "Close to a billion US dollars. It's a huge sum to move and hide. All numbers on a screen, not real. No way I could have got to it anyway. Can't exactly withdraw it from an ATM or stop by the Swiss bank with a dump truck. No, I just wanted to ruin Nathan and get the money for the troops. I screwed it all up."

Evan shook his head. "No. Your instinct was correct. Nathan used you and your team to destroy his computer operations and isolate his assets. You just underestimated Nathan. You had a suspicion that he would rip everyone off. Well, he did!"

"But he tricked me at my own game," Tanya muttered. "I trusted my team, yet they spied on me."

"Tanya, look, Nathan has been at this game for twenty years. Don't sweat it."

Tanya laughed and seemed to sway a little. The drugs loosened her lips and spirit, and she was actually pleasant for a change.

Evan felt a little concerned for a second that she might start crying or throw herself into the sea, and then she relaxed.

"Tanya, everything will turn out OK. You did fine. Did what you had to."

Tanya's eyes began to grow heavy, and she wobbled a little. She was not going to remember much of their conversion later, but she had an easy clarity right now. "Evan, are you over revenge? Can you forgive? I can't."

Evan shrugged and watched her sway.

She lost all sense of personal space and got way too close, and he let her.

He changed the subject and decided to plant a seed in her thoughts, one that she would probably forget.

"Tanya if things go real bad I am going to have an escape plan. I need you to be with me."

Tanya laughed out loud for a second and then put her arm around Evan.

"OK, what is it?" she asked.

"I might snatch one of these guys...Mario or Jorge and take them back to the States. I can get a plane and protection from my brother. I still need to work some details out."

She had to stand on her tippy-toes to encircle his shoulders and pull him down to her level, where she whispered in his ear. "You, Evan, or Ivan, or whatever your name is, are so full of shit! You just make up stuff as you go along, don't you?"

"Pretty much. You can come with me if you want. Roger's in."

"Sure, let's kidnap someone who everyone wants dead. Why not the Mexican president? Let's grab him!"

Evan nodded as if thinking. "Is he supposed to be there tomorrow? Naw, I am more a target-of-opportunity type. I better get you to bed. You're about to lose it."

Tanya leaned against him. Her eyes began to grow heavy as if she were in that twilight stage of awake and sleep. "Thanks, I can't even remember where my room is right now. Help me get to bed. No kidnapping drug dealers, no bounty-hunter shit! Promise?"

Evan shrugged and picked her up like a child. "Promise. Won't kidnap anyone," he lied.

"Don't drop me."

"I won't; I need you."

Evan looked down at her. She was snoring.

Roger let El Coyote give most of the brief, primarily for two reasons: Roger's Spanish sucked, and even though all the members of Dark Cloud could understand English, they could not understand his Scottish accent. Most of the men had worked with El Coyote at one time in the special forces and had that bond. The mission, as all missions go, was simple on paper. Roger knew it would most likely go to hell once they hit the deck.

Green Team One, the Chupacabras, consisted of three cells of fifteen operators who would hide on the fishing trawler. Roger, El Coyote, Joaquin, and Daniel made up the leadership. Their mission was twofold: first, secure the dock from the *Happy Mermaid* to the submarine, and second, destroy the antiaircraft weapons on the *Happy Mermaid* as well as sink the yacht.

Green Team Two, Caballo Verde, also consisted of three fifteen-man squads named Alpha, Bravo, and Charlie. One squad would stow away on the sub. Its mission was to kill and isolate Mario's security detail and to allow the snatch team to kidnap Mario. The snatch team had three criteria in which they would evaluate Mario. First was through Tanya's face-to-face, second was through dental records, and third would be fingerprints. A positive identification would be reported to Roger, who would notify the navy. A false identification would mean that both teams would have to secure their respective areas and wait for the navy. The conventional wisdom was that if the real Mario did not go onto the sub, then he would be on the *Happy Mermaid*, in which case he would become Green Team One's problem. The other two cells from Green Team Two would not be on the sub; they would split up into smaller groups and hide along the beaches and other empty boats that they could consolidate when the shooting started and help secure the dock near the submarine. The terrain offered many rocky beaches, trees, caves, and even some abandoned fishing cabins.

A secure landing zone was the overall strategic goal. Even if finding Mario never happened, they would still have to make sure that the raid was able to take place. No one suspected that Dark Cloud could survive for more than an hour, worst-case scenario. They would be too outnumbered and outgunned, not to mention that there was no real cover once the shooting started. The guests would need to be herded into the house, and this again was Green Team One's job. The heavy guns and antiaircraft platforms had to be eliminated.

Roger waited for the brief to be over and then sat down.

"You looked worried, my friend. It will all be OK!" Joaquin smiled and sat down next to Roger. His English was fluent, like a native speaker. He offered Roger an opened Tecate and smiled. "Been years since you have done this sort of thing, huh?"

"Aye. I am a freaking cook now, a chef. Did not come to Mexico to get caught up in this shit." Roger drank his beer and cursed under his breath.

"Yes, yes. I was educated in Austin, came back here to fight for my country. You see, norteamericanos think we are all lawn-mower operators and clean-up crews! You know I can cook, but I am not going to be a manager at Taco Cabana just because I am Mexican!"

"OK." Roger nodded.

"Another thing that pisses me off is all the Mexicans that live in America and run around waving the Mexican flag—they're posers. Stay and fight! If you love your country so much, why did you run away? Stay in it. Fight for it!"

Roger watched him become animated and just nodded. "A man who knows what he wants. I'll drink to that."

Joaquin drank too and smiled. "I got a girlfriend in Texas—hot white girl. She and I, we get married after this." He laughed.

Joaquin gave Roger his beer and finished his story.

"Aye, lad, you got it together. I gotta get some sleep. Night."

"Good night, Roger. I need a few more, and then I sleep too!"

Roger winked, shook hands, and moved on. He could hear Joaquin switch over to Spanish and strike up another conversation with anyone who would listen.

Roger found Evan standing by the ship's rail, talking with Luis, who was a member of Green Team One, and Oscar, who was the leader of Green Team Two. The three men stopped talking sports and nodded at Roger when he approached.

Luis and Oscar said good night and left.

"How you feel?" Evan asked.

"Ah feel like you look!" Roger chuckled.

Evan agreed and went down the laundry list of minor injuries that he and Roger had accumulated before the actual battle had even begun.

Roger changed the subject. He reported to Evan what he had heard from one of their team leaders. "I have some reports from the island. My guys have made it to their objectives. There is apparently a huge party going on right now. They think Mario has arrived. Place is an armed camp. Helicopter landed not but an hour ago."

Evan nodded and looked pleased. "The yacht and mooring areas?"

"Looks like the sub has a parking space ready. My guys reported that they can swoop in from their hiding sites pretty quickly and even have good sniper positions. Most of the guests are staying in the house or at the pool. The rock star, Mario, has landed, I bet."

"Any word on the sub?" Evan asked.

Roger nodded and pointed out to the dark, oily water. "About a mile out there somewhere. Full moon will help us and hurt us."

The two men discussed the logistics of their actions later that night.

At 0330 hours, Evan, Tommy, Tanya, and the four other members of the snatch team would leave via a Zodiac and meet with the sub. They would get another few hours of sleep while the sub made the four-mile journey to the island, encircled it once to drop off the remainder of Green Team Two via the torpedo tubes, and then waited and eased into its new home at 0700.

Evan did not even want to think about the lives of the men; it was inevitable, yet not something you dwelt on.

"Any little slipup tomorrow, and we all die. The navy may abort landing if the situation on the ground is too crazy," Roger said.

Evan nodded in agreement. He checked his watch and stopped Roger from leaving right away. "Hey, on a serious note. Thanks for going on my half-baked plan today."

CHAPTER 29

Green-Colored Glasses

Jorge Valdez cursed out loud. He handed a fairly hefty night-vision scope back to Gerard and then started speaking quietly into an encrypted satellite phone. "He has arrived. The real Mario is finally here along with two of his cousins."

Cousins was the slang term used to describe Mario's look-alikes. Some of them were more convincing than others. One of his best and most entertaining cousins had been killed in Madrid two years ago, while on vacation, in a jealous love triangle between a female police officer and a popular teenage singer. Jorge had to chuckle when he recalled the details. Mario was furious that he had to make the rounds in the underworld and explain that he was not dead. It seemed that this cousin had become more infamous and popular than he had. Flowers still piled up on his gravesite at a *narcofosa*, or cemetery for drug traffickers. Some to this day still refuse to believe that Mario is still alive.

Jorge listened to the voice of the leader of another cartel and frowned. "Yes, I can tell them all apart. It's difficult, but you kill them all. Look, no matter how this goes down, I need to know I have support. I will have to hide for a while before I can re-emerge. I want you to make sure that your supporters are ready to act!"

Jorge accepted a glass of mescal from Gerard. The satellite link was very good despite their distance.

"I can do my part," the voice said. "Tomorrow, after this little show, there will be about fifty attacks around Mexico. I suspect that at least half of those will be mayors, police chiefs, and media personnel who are targeted to be killed. The rest will run. You control the media. I will cleanse. The Union of Cartels is looking forward to victory and complete cooperation from the government."

Jorge listened for a long moment and nodded.

"Before any rebuilding there must be destruction."

"Good night."

Jorge hung up and looked at Gerard. "Mario has brought more of his bodyguards than expected. Are all of our men here?"

"Yes. Mr. Pena is all set too."

Jorge looked visibly worried, like a coach before a Super Bowl. "Tomorrow begins a new era for this great nation."

Jorge smiled and slapped Gerard on the back. "*Don't* worry, my friend."

"And if media personalities do not cooperate?" Gerard asked.

"They find themselves in a vat of acid, ha!" Jorge chuckled and continued. "I have arranged for millions in charity to be given away over the next few weeks to show my loyalty to the"— Jorge used his fingers to make quotation marks—"people. Yes, as far as the people are concerned, the drug wars will end, the violence will cease, and we shall eventually become legal businessmen…Well, in a few years. I may not even live to see it all transpire, but, nonetheless, this is my legacy."

Gerard nodded and crossed his arms as if in thought.

"Brilliant. One question: what really changes—if I may be blunt?"

Gerard put the scope up to his eye and watched a group of men walk from a helicopter toward the house. Mario and his entourage moved slowly, like celebrities. Ladies swooned, and men bowed and shook hands.

Jorge answered honestly. "Nothing. Nothing really changes, except perception. People talk about the crisis for a few weeks and then lose interest. Perception, my friend, is everything. All of the cartels will work together until someone screws up, but, nonetheless, we are creating a perception. *You*, Gerard, are going to be rich and in charge of an army!" Jorge laughed again and finished his drink.

A breeze was picking up, and the two men stared for a moment from their perch on the top deck of the *Happy Mermaid*. The beach house was fully lit, and people could be seen moving in and about it, eating, and socializing. Jorge could smell food grilling and hear intermittent chatter.

"You know, boss, I am hungry."

Jorge nodded and was about to answer when his walkie-talkie crackled. There were no cell phone towers on the island. "Yes?"

"Jorge, sir, Mario wants to say hi to you. Will you join him to eat?"

Jorge shrugged. "Is the pig ready?"

"Sir?" The voice on the other end sounded offended for a second.

"The roasted pig, you fool! I have been smelling it cooking all day. In fact, it is my recipe. Is it ready?"

"Yes!"

The two men made it off the observation deck and down to the main deck and off the yacht. Four members of the Scorpions waited for them as an escort.

"Ah, you men look sharp! Tomorrow you had better be on your toes. Mario's thugs out number us."

"We can handle them, sir!"

CHAPTER 30

Gang Plank

Tommy prayed. He opened his eyes, looked out at the buoys and lights of the sleepy town on the Isla Mujeres, and prayed some more.

"Look, I know you heard me. This time just don't ignore me, please. You let me, my little Carla get out of this freaking…Sorry, sorry, I know I should not curse. At least save her! Keep her safe."

Tommy removed his fourth "this time for real" last cigarette from a plastic box and put it to his lips. His fingers trembled as he opened the flame of his gold Zippo. "Lord, this is also really my last cigarette!"

"*Tommy!*"

Tommy cursed and closed his eyes as a massive hand slapped his back. He smelled tequila, aftershave, and oil from somewhere on the boat.

"Hi, Evan." Tommy said and groaned, not attempting to cover up his disappointment.

"Sorry, know it's late. Looks like you dropped your smoke in the water! Sorry, dude; you gotta quit anyway."

Evan's voice was a little loud, and he steadied himself against a coil of cable on the fishing trawler's deck. "Wow, is the ship moving? Did we hit a storm?" he teased.

"No, you're wasted, Evan."

"That's what I get for trying to keep up with Roger."

"He's a little bigger than you," said Tommy.

Evan nodded. "OK, OK, Tommy. Look, I'm on my way to bed, and I just wanted to ask you one thing."

"Yes? Can you talk quieter?" Tommy asked.

Evan took a deep breath and checked himself. He regained control and spoke clearly. "Did you do what I asked?" Evan sat on a large spool of wire, folded his hands in his lap, and waited for an answer.

"Yes," Tommy said as if under duress. He was referring to a conversation he and Evan had had earlier about securing the giant seaplane for an escape. Evan claimed he had struck a deal with the admiral. Tommy was not sure if he should believe him or not.

Evan leaned forward and raised his eyebrows. "Aaand?"

Tommy removed a small device from his pocket. It was a tiny satellite-enabled texting device. Looked like a cell phone, yet sent texts only and could take pictures. "Carla is on the island, working as a server."

"What does she say?"

Tommy ran his fingers through his hair and for a second did not look as old as he was. Evan had finally annoyed him to the point that his confidence was bigger than his fear. *Anger does that.* Evan smirked to himself.

Tommy read the text from his daughter out loud:

Daddy, don't worry, doing fine. I have been here on many occasions. They don't let anyone touch US girls. They already got girls for that kinda thing. I made friends with the guy guarding the plane and smaller boats like u said. I can be on the pier when u say and do what u want. Wrapped around finger. LOL, XO XO.

Tommy shoved the thing back in his pocket and stared at Evan. "Don't get my baby killed. She has no clue how bad it's going to get, and you won't let me tell her!"

Evan frowned. "You know why! Ignorance is bliss. They can't get anything from her. Make sure she is fishing and at the plane the whole morning. Tell her what's going down when we get there—then and only then. Just as I told you."

Tommy looked shrewdly at Evan. "I am not stupid, Ivan, or Evan, or whatever. Been in the shit before, flew out of Vietnam with heroin and guns for the spooks with bombs going off, just never with my daughter before."

Evan shrugged. "That plane is our ticket home if we need it. I got clearance from the admiral to take it as a spoil of war and run once things go down. When the mission is complete."

"Or if everything hits the fan!" Tommy said.

"*When*," Evan countered and then finished. "We just don't want to get shot down. I also don't want your daughter anywhere near the house."

"How noble of you. She can't fight off any thugs who try to get it before us." Tommy spoke while he played with his lighter.

"I'll get there as soon as I can or Roger will," Evan said.

"Well, I am heading there as soon as we land. I have a suspicion about who owns that flying boat. Gotta make sure it's ready to fly."

Evan stood and spoke. "It's been a long, crazy day. Bedtime. See ya."

"Night, Evan—I mean, Ivan."

"Night."

CHAPTER 31

Scrambled Eggs in Paradise

The sun rose slowly in the east, as it had for thousands of years. The pink ball stretched its glow out across the terrain. The sun did not care about morning people, non-morning people, drunk people, or despised people. It always came, and it always shone light on the obvious. Night and day had been locked in such a long game of tag that neither knew who was really chasing whom.

Jorge Valdez and three of his henchmen, including Andre Pena, sat outside on the back porch of the beach house. The final guests had arrived late last night, putting the mansion at capacity. Jorge knew the list of VIPs, all of them on one side or other of the law depending on the day and who was handing the briefcase of cash across the imaginary line.

"Silver or lead?" Jorge spoke out loud with a chuckle.

"Boss?"

His three bodyguards looked up from their newspapers and coffees to listen to their leader. Without cell phones, and with the satellite-connected Wi-Fi turned off, guests had to read or use nonelectronic means to amuse themselves. This was preferable to Jorge. When did people ever just sit around and talk without staring like little monkeys at a screen?

Jorge sipped his coffee and smiled. His spirits were high despite being slightly hungover and drained.

"Silver or lead?" Jorge repeated. "You choose."

His men nodded. They understood the term. You can take a payoff, silver, or you can take a bullet, lead. Jorge motivated his aides like a good general.

"Listen to me. This is a great day. Do not worry!"

"Yes," Andre Pena agreed.

Andre wore a modest outfit and looked as if he could have been going to the beach or working in the yard. He kept a baseball hat down low over his eyes and expensive sunglasses low on his nose. Only a trained eye could tell that Jorge was wearing a bulletproof vest under his untucked Tommy Bahamas button-down. He wore cleanly pressed khaki pants with a custom-made leather holster. His weapon of choice today was a silver-and-gold Smith & Wesson handgun. It was a huge weapon that fired .50-caliber bullets. The custom etching and grips made it plain beautiful to look at and even more fun to shoot. Jorge had killed a grizzly bear with the same weapon on a hunting trip to Alaska.

Andre was clearly uncomfortable about being so blatantly in public and mingling with people he was about to blow up.

Jorge seemed to sense this and spoke calmly, "It is one thing, my friend, to hide in plain sight. It is another to sit near people who are merely walking corpses yet do not know it. Small talk with them, smell them, flirt with the senators' wives, talk soccer. Easy to watch a fireball in the distance, but meeting the soon-to-be-charred souls up close? This makes for a better time, huh?" Jorge smiled. He was calm this morning. His nervousness was gone and his anxiety dissipated. He was ready for the fight.

"I have no delusions about what I do, Jorge. I just prefer to not be around people. I will watch, yes. I always have. I have always studied my targets. I am at the stage of my life now where I like to teach others, the new generation, to make the bombs. This is my grand finale, a fireworks display to bring in a new era. No, Jorge, you misread me. The smell of bodies, it does not bother me. I am numb to it."

Jorge leaned forward and touched Andre's arm. "I did not mean you any disrespect. I just talk sometimes."

"None taken, Jorge. Since I have been here, the men I have trained at your camps have taken care of about seventy-five of your enemies. Pablo himself used to say, 'Have them fear you. Have the mention of your name cause them to pee their pants.'" Andre paused to put a strawberry in his mouth. "Your enemies, after today, will take notice."

Jorge nodded and smiled. "Andre, I hope you will stay in Mexico after this."

"No, no, I have to go."

"At least let me show you the Pacific side, where I come from, very rural, welcoming. Different world from all this."

Andre crossed his hands and considered for a moment.

The two men drifted off into conversion about the beaches of their respective countries, food, climate, and, of course, sports. After about ten minutes of friendly chatter, a girl in a bikini walked by the table carrying a fishing pole and a tackle box. She had a brilliant tattoo across her back of a leopard—the tail extended down beneath her bikini bottoms.

"Hey!" One of Jorge's men stood up. "Where are you going?"

The girl, who was thin yet still shapely, paused and removed the pink headphones from her ears. She wore large bug-eyed sunglasses and chewed gum. Jorge could hear some form of obnoxious rap music even at this distance.

She smiled very shyly and respectfully. "Good morning, *señors*. I am going down to the pier. It's quiet and away from everyone. I like to fish." She smiled, and everyone softened. Jorge's man sat down on the direction of his boss.

"Over at the pier?" Jorge turned to address the young girl.

"Yes, where that big seaplane is and the little boats. Great spot. Quiet." She shifted from foot to foot, swaying her tiny hips.

She was still too young to know the hypnotic effect that had on men, or perhaps she wasn't.

"Yes, she's OK. She can go." Jorge waved at his guards to relax and began to pick up his paper. "You are Carla, yes?"

The girl paused and, for a second, almost looked concerned. "Yes?"

"I know your father, Tommy. You should be proud of him. He has worked with us for years. You, I have seen too, working the tables. You work hard, my dear. You go fish! Anyone tells you otherwise, you send them to me!" Jorge winked at the girl and then waved her off.

"Thanks, sir." She turned and walked quickly away.

"So, Andre, you have any children?"

"Did." Andre looked down at his hands and pretended to be inspecting them.

"I have upset you?"

"No, no. A lifetime ago. My three sons were butchered by rival cartels, a notorious hit man named the Snake…It was years ago."

"Tell me. I like to know the stories behind people. I have never heard this from you."

Andre sighed. "Must I?"

"No, no, my friend, but that anger of being wronged, it is the fuel that you will need to make it through the day."

Andre shook his head. "Ah, you are good—a shrink by trade?"

Jorge laughed. "Only if you want to tell."

"I blew up a target, an empty car with dead bodies already placed thus so. A spectacle, a setup."

"A setup for you?"

Andre Pena nodded. "A setup for me and this hit man."

"The Snake?"

"Yes. I don't want to bore you. It is painful."

"Please tell me."

Andre Pena paused for a few moments, drank some orange juice, poured some coffee, and popped a grape into his mouth. "I was contracted to kill a man's family, his young wife and child. Only they would not actually be in the car. Other bodies were, already dead. The idea I guess was to make this man snap, make him think his family was dead. Only they were not even present. I did not know who this man was, only that his own people wanted him to snap. That was the rumor I heard years later. A mind game. Well, it worked. He snapped and killed my sons as if they were dogs. Sent me pictures and letters while I was in prison. Sent me an empty Skoal can with my boys' teeth. I don't believe that they quite knew what they were doing when they pushed this man over the edge. Once you start a maniac like that, how can you stop him?"

"Skoal?"

"A nasty habit. Tobacco that they spit. This is how I knew he was American, this Snake. Never saw him. Heard of him, his reputation, his involvement with Los Pepes. No one can tell how many murders he, or anyone, committed back in those days." Andre finished his speech as if he were talking into the past. His eyes grew distant.

"Pablo was a great man. He was brought down by savages such as these."

"He killed your family, yet you did not kill his?" Jorge asked.

"Yes, ironic," Andre said flatly, clearly uncomfortable.

"And you explained it to him?" Jorge leaned forward, fascinated.

Andre laughed for a second and looked away toward the peaceful ocean. He watched the girl in the distance sit down by the dock under the shadow of the massive seaplane's wing.

"Explain to a ghost? How?"

Jorge frowned and poured Andre some coffee from a silver pot.

"Well, I am sorry, Andre. Today let the memories go up in flames. It is time to let it go! I think, my friend, that you will find peace."

CHAPTER 32

Floating Cans

The Island, 0704 Hours

Evan had never wanted to join the navy.

He loved the ocean, he loved fishing, and he especially loved kayaking on the back streams and wild rivers of Virginia and West Virginia.

His brother had made fun of him when he had joined the marines: "Aha! Evan, you're going to be a bellhop for the navy. You're going to live on a gator freighter packed like a sardine!"

Evan shook his head and laced his boots. He barely slept with the thudding and whooshing and other strange noises on the sub. Evan had to concede that his brother was right; he did end up being on ships for long periods of time, flying his helicopters on and off.

Ships I can deal with, but subs? No way! Evan stood, folded his sleeping mat, and rolled a poncho liner.

"Morning!" Tanya said.

Evan banged his head on a pipe when he stood up. "Morning, Tanya. Ouch. These things are not made for tall people."

She reached up and touched his head and pouted. "That will leave a mark. Maybe improve your looks, eh?"

Evan regarded her for a second. She wore a zip-up green flight suit that was too big and a baseball hat that clearly had belonged to a male. "You seem perky this morning. Not hungover?"

She smiled and raised a plastic cup of coffee. "This and my new outlook."

"New outlook?" Evan smirked.

"Yes. Being negative is a choice. I have a lot to be thankful about. I could have been killed, and you rescued me. I still may be, but it's, well, out of my control. I can't be depressed, fearful, and angry forever," Tanya stated boldly.

Evan gave her a hug and then put his hands on her shoulders as if she was a child and he was leading her off to the playground. "Walk this way. Let's go to the bridge."

Evan felt uneasy with the noises of the sub and the odd banging sounds. "Did you change your meds or something?" he asked.

"Funny, ha-ha. No, did some cocaine, but that's beside the point. I just realized that these brushes with death, they are a test. My battlefield is with computers, but I can't hide behind them."

"Did you sleep at all?" Evan asked.

"Like a rock. Valium is great!"

"Liked it better when you were grumpy all the time." Evan complained, "I need about a week's sleep."

The oversized Evan and the undersized Tanya made it to the control center of the sub and tried to stay out of the way. There was nothing to look at but pipes, walls, and mechanical equipment.

Evan frowned. "Are we there yet?"

Juan, Team Two's Bravo Squad leader, and two men who seemed to know something about subs looked up briefly and then looked away. Juan, who also wore a zip-up flight suit, broke off from the men and came over to Evan and Tanya.

"We are here. Surfacing in about five minutes. You come with me. We will be the first up. The rest of the men will follow, just like we planned."

Evan nodded and turned to Tanya. "OK, cupcake, you better go hide in your rabbit hole with the snatch team. Just follow one of the loosely unlikely plans that we have devised. It will all work out," Evan said sarcastically.

Tanya looked pissed, then softened. "You can't get to me. But *cupcake*? Really? Not very PC."

Evan winked at her. "Neither am I."

She squeezed his hand and patted Juan's arm. "Good luck. Let's end this thing!" Tanya turned and disappeared down the narrow passageway.

"She's so pleasant this morning. She on something?" Juan asked suspiciously.

"Cocaine."

Juan nodded and smiled.

The sub made an awkward lurch, and Evan heard more noises that made him feel like he was in a teapot about to explode.

"Here we go," said Juan, who seemed amused that Evan was so uneasy.

Green Team One

Roger and El Coyote, Alpha Squad leader, looked at each other and then out of a tiny porthole from within the ship's cargo hold. Green Team One was packed in, not unlike fish. Fifteen men with body armor, a mixture of submachine guns, side arms, and various knives and machetes were crammed into this particular section of the ship's hold. Thirty more men were divided among two other such storerooms in the bottom of the boat. Roger picked up his coffee mug from where it sat next to an AT-4 and a box of hand grenades.

"OK. Show time," he grumbled.

El Coyote's radio cracked, and the room grew silent.

All members of the Dark Cloud assault team had radios with ear pieces and tiny microphones. Each squad had it's own frequency so that only those men could speak. There was also a frequency where just the team leaders could speak as well as one in which the whole assault force could communicate. Every man knew that when the shooting started, pretty much everyone was going to talk at the same time. Radio discipline was paramount.

"We are docking. Be quiet! They are boarding with about ten men, heavily armed." Someone outside alerted the whole squad.

The radio went silent. Everyone began to sit and get into a position where they could cover the heavy, locked steel door and not make any noise.

"They likely will search for a few. The sub will attract more attention," Roger grumbled.

"Hope you're right, *amigo*," someone said.

Green Team Two, North Point of the Island

Oscar, Pablo, and Gustavo lay prone, covered with netting and vegetation. They were a good two hundred yards from the edge of the beach house. From their vantage point, they could clearly see the beach house and pool with its nude swimmers and the docks with the *Happy Mermaid* and other vessels. They had watched in silence, ignoring the sand and flies. The ocean was just twenty-five yards behind them. The rest of their men were strung along the tree line of the beach. There was not enough cover to conceal them for long in the daylight, but hopefully they would not need long. They had been there before sun up, having been deployed from the submarine's torpedo tubes.

Pablo and Gustavo were Oscar's two squad leaders. Alpha and Charlie. Each squad had fifteen men and its own crucial mission. Oscar did a radio check with all his men. Everyone answered.

Oscar motioned for his men to fall back. They gently crawled and moved back into the scrubby brush, being careful not to move too quickly.

"OK, let's get into position," Oscar whispered. "The submarine is being tied up. The trawler is in place. Your snipers have my clearance once the smoke pops. We have to keep the gun trucks engaged so that Team One can clear the LZ."

"Right," Pablo answered. "You guys better get a move on. I scouted last night, and you have a decent amount of cover till you get to the rear of the submarine. They like to fish and drink and smoke over there near that canopy," Pablo said.

"What about that brick wall?" Gustavo asked quietly.

"It's solid, but the fifty-cal. will shred it," Pablo replied.

"Mmm," Oscar said, "Lets be ready for anything."

Oscar moved back into the shade, slowly like a snake. He was aware of every branch, twig, and rock. He was as methodical about the simple act of moving as a surgeon was about cutting. He spoke as quietly as a breeze. "One of those gun trucks will prevent anyone from exiting the submarine."

Alpha and Charlie had planted cameras and sensors to protect their own perimeter. There was barely enough vegetation on the rest of the island for cover, so once a force began to move, they had to commit.

Oscar and Alpha Team planned on creeping up the beach and helping secure the sub from the outside so that their people could escape. Bravo Team was on the sub.

Oscar checked his gear and was about to give the signal to move out when something caught his attention. Someone spoke over the squad radio.

"Heads up."

"I think they are coming right at us," Pablo whispered.

Oscar lay as close to the ground as he could. A large spider crawled across his legs. He ignored it. Two ATVs with two females and two men rode across the sand and scrubby brush from the edge of the gate that surrounded the pool straight toward Team Two.

"I think they are going fishing," Oscar said.

"We are in their spot," Pablo whispered.

Oscar looked back at the pier, where people were beginning to congregate and gawk at the submarine. People were spilling out of the house and coming off the yacht. He guessed that he was looking at close to eighty people, and then something caught his eye. "Crap!" he said.

Pablo, Oscar, and Gustavo froze and watched as four F-150 pickups with .50 calibers drove and parked in intervals around the long dock.

"That's way more firepower than the brief said!" Pablo said with frustration.

"They must have been in the garage. I had no clue they had four; that means they got six!" Oscar said.

Pablo cursed. He had counted two last night when he went on a patrol of the island.

The ATV with the unsuspecting fishermen was now almost on them. Oscar grabbed his knife and slowly pulled it from his leg sheath. His two men did the same.

"Gustav, call Roger," Oscar said. "Tell him there are four gun trucks spread out around LZ Mario."

"Why do they need that much firepower? They expecting a war?" Oscar spoke to his friends.

Oscar watched as the two ATVs stopped near the edge of the scrub, and the four occupants began to giggle and flirt and make their way to the beach. One of the girls seemed to have stepped on something and protested. One of the bare-chested sunbathers, a decently fit man with the body of a swimmer, picked the girl up and carried her. Oscar figured they were all in their early thirties, were married or dating, and were very comfortable with each other. None of them were armed. Well educated, no tattoos, and plenty of money. He was a master at sizing up targets.

"Get close. Zap them, and zip-tie them," Oscar whispered into his radio.

The four fishermen made it to the soft, white sand in the shade near the lightly breaking surf.

Oscar could sense something was wrong.

One of the women, a tall blonde who was wearing a suit she had probably worn at one time before she had had children, paused. She suddenly pointed in Oscar's team's direction.

"This is not good," he muttered.

CHAPTER 33
Caesar's Blues

Mario's Happy Mermaid

"The submarine! It is here!" The teenager jumped up and down gently by the window of Mario's spacious cabin. The silk curtains were drawn, and they could see out, yet no one could see in. Mario sat up in bed, staring past the naked girl and ignoring her youthful playfulness. He stared out at the island, the dock, and the large, black submarine, which was being guided in and tied to the pier. A makeshift canopy some two-hundred-feet long was slowly being pulled over it, suspended by a steel, cage-like structure.

"Good. Good. After breakfast and after my cousin takes a tour, after he sees the beast, I will go board it. I am depressed, my little chicas. Drink, fun, taste—all means nothing. I have it all, yet—"

A slightly older girl in her twenties climbed into bed and sat Indian-style next to Mario. She placed her hands on his large belly and handed him a glass. "Drink this. It will get you back in the mood. We will send you from here with a smile and ready to take on the world!"

Mario sighed as the young women squeezed his arms and tried to get his attention.

Mario just stared at the sub. "My tequila?"

"Yes," the teenager said, "and you can't have your clothes till you—"

"Chica, I am not interested. Get me my pants. I cannot stop thinking about my son and my misery."

The teenager walked over from the window and placed her hands on her narrow hips. She had a sassy, annoyed smirk as she swung from side to side. "It is no use. He is down in the dumps!"

Mario slowly got out of bed and let the girls dress him. The tequila tasted a little strange, metallic. "Even my tequila has no taste. Sex has no pleasure. And the submarine already bores me!"

The two girls looked at each other and shrugged.

Mario stood in front of the window and watched his entourage of armed killers mixed with the Scorpions walk toward the sub. He noticed the four gun trucks and shrugged. "Why must I always be surrounded by such paranoid men who think I need so many guns? Are we at war?"

He saw Jorge Valdez out in front, like a commander, extending his hand to a large man who Mario presumed was Ivan. Mario shifted from foot to foot. His body felt warm. He watched his cousin perform just as he would: shake hands, nod slowly, and walk with grace, poise, and the swagger of a king.

"I am up here like an impotent little king. I need my spirit back! This cousin of mine, he will steal my glory. He looks happy!"

Mario turned to the girls, who had gotten their clothes back on.

"Boss, you no look good."

Mario stared at the two girls. They sounded far away. Suddenly, Mario realized something was wrong. The room seemed to tilt, he felt his heart pounding in his ears, and his limbs began to feel useless and numb. He tried to talk, but his tongue felt like a sausage. Mario stared past the two concerned girls.

"Mario, you are scaring me!"

"Is this one of your tricks?"

The younger girl began to cry and rushed forward to help the stumbling Mario.

He suddenly saw six men appear like vapor behind the girls, yet even though he knew they could not be there, they were.

"You see that?" he mumbled and staggered.

"What?"

Mario looked at his hands. They were numb; he was having trouble getting words out and breathing was becoming difficult. "Am...am I...I having a...a heart attack?" Mario looked at his glass and then at the girls. "Wh-wh...who?"

The older girl rushed to Mario and helped him sit. Panic was in her voice. "Your son, he gave me the drink, moments ago in the hall."

"My son is dead."

"No. little Mario Your other son!"

Mario stared at the ghosts of men he had killed decades ago. They seemed to be growing and multiplying. His legs began to burn, and he tried to curse, yet nothing would come from his lips. He recalled a *narcocorrido* about an assassin dying and meeting his victims in hell.

"G-g...go...d-d...doctor!"

Jorge Valdez, Gerard, and Jorge's two other henchman, Julio and Samuel, stepped back as Mario listened intently to Ivan. Jorge was bored but tried to show interest. He hated the idea of going into that deathtrap. He counted Mario's bodyguards and cursed. He was outgunned by them. Where had the gun trucks come from? He saw young men, whom he did not recognize, manning the machine guns in the beds of the truck.

What is he up to? Jorge wondered why Mario had chosen to sleep in, not show, and let this cousin see the prize. "Is he on to me?" Jorge asked himself quietly.

Jorge turned to look at the beach house, which was a good hundred yards away. Scores of armed men, some looking like teenagers, leaned against the thick, white cinder-block wall that surrounded the house. The misfits were smoking and eyeballing the female guests with an open crudeness that caused Jorge to burn with anger.

"Why are these unprofessional idiots here?" he spoke to himself. "I am the security. Who authorized this?"

The sun was slowly climbing, and a gentle breeze was shifting. It was about seven in the morning, and the guests were coming to the windows and walking in clumps to see Mario's new toy.

"People everywhere," he mused to himself. "I need to end this—find Pena and Mario and end this!"

"*Jorge!*"

Jorge looked up. Mario the cousin was waving to him.

"Let us go inside and see this thing in action, eh?"

Jorge smiled. "No, no, sir, you go ahead."

He pulled his men close and whispered, with a smile on his face, "Frenchman, take Julio and Samuel with you. Go find out who authorized all these punks pulling security. Someone is stepping on my toes. Quietly get the men together and see what they are up to. When did they get here? How?"

Jorge watched his henchmen move off and then spoke loud enough for the fake Mario to hear him. "I am not feeling so good. Going to go sit and read for a bit."

"Ahhh, too much to drink last night?" The fake Mario shielded his eyes from the sun. The temperature was a mild eighty with a slight breeze. Mario seemed unconcerned, aloof. His bodyguards looked bored. They paid no attention.

Jorge smiled and looked at Mario's men. *Why are they showing such a presence? They are vulgar, not soldiers*, Jorge thought.

He was annoyed and a little bit suspicious. Mario had sometimes challenged him like this, questioning why he needed an elite guard, but this was over the top. He scanned the area and estimated nearly one hundred or more men, not his own.

Jorge smiled and nodded to Ivan and Tommy, who looked concerned.

"Excuse me, gentlemen." Jorge turned and left.

Andre Pena finished his walk on the beach. Now he sat at the far southern end of the small island. He had a decent amount of elevation, perhaps twenty feet, on his sand dunes. The beaches were much better on this section of the island. The north was too rocky with too many bugs and thorny bushes.

Early this morning he thought he had heard small boats near-by, circling the island. Andre sipped his coffee and looked at the beach house. The island had served as some sort of ancient trading post or perhaps military outpost in the colonial days of the Spanish. There were still remnants of old, crumbling walls as high as seven feet and worn-down battlements that at one time had protected something from the elements. The original beach house had been built in the 1940s and was added on to in the 1970s. Andre admired architecture and in a way regretted whenever something beautiful or with history had to be demolished. He had attended architecture school in the United States and worked for about a decade at his trade before he had fallen into demolition and then become what other people would define as a terrorist. Truth was, he had been trained by the CIA to help fight communist rebels.

Someone could hide pretty well on this island, he mused.

Lights were on and most of the guests were out, like tiny ants, swarming around the black submarine. The profile of the *Happy Mermaid* stood proudly above them all, making the other yachts look like toys.

"I could blow it all up now!" he said to the waves. He looked at the detonator in his hands.

The explosives were set as shape charges near the foundation and as incendiary in the attic. The explosion would at first rock the foundation and outer walls of the house. Anyone near a window would be shredded to bits. The weakening of the structure and holes where windows had been would allow a nice vacuum of oxygen when the fire started. The roof charges would detonate next, lighting the house up in a fiery furnace and bringing the whole thing down. Andre had always liked using charges from above. They were very effective when SWAT teams tried to land and assault from the roof.

"When you got something that works, you stick with it," he said to the sand and waves.

Andre settled down on his little hill and relaxed. He could see the plane and other boats at a dock to his right, a good half a mile down the beach. He strained to see if he could see the pretty girl who was fishing. The sun was too bright and he couldn't see anything.

Carla sat on the edge of the dock watching fish swim beneath the crystal-clear water. She wondered what they thought about, if anything at all. The large wing of the Albatross flying boat shielded her from the sun, and she began to feel sleepy.

"Hey, do you have any sodas?"

She put down her fishing pole and turned around to glance at the tiny brick guard shack where her friend had been sitting. She pouted and sighed. A five-foot cinder-block wall went from the block-shaped structure down to the water's edge, where it stopped by a rusty fence.

She looked around. There was a lonely wooden deck that zigzagged across the open sand back toward the house. Soon it would be too hot to walk on. The house was a good quarter mile away.

"Can you hear me?"

Carla felt her legs get numb. She had been dangling her bare feet off the dock and had been relaxing without a care in the world. She frowned at her black-and-red painted toenails. "You need a touch-up."

The wood seemed painful to the backs of her knees so she stood up and stamped her feet.

"You asleep?" she called out to the guard who had been assigned to watch this stretch of beach. He was a recent runaway from El Salvador, an artist with a shady past.

No answer.

Her father had told her to stay by the seaplane and when the time was right, to get on board and start it. He had texted her directions that made no sense. Now her feet began to feel like needles were in them as the sensation came back.

"When everything gets crazy, you will hear guns, explosions maybe, and lots of confusion. Shortly after that, I will arrive!" her father had texted her.

Carla walked quietly up the dock to the small house. She had removed her headphones and had the phone her father gave her secured in the waistband of her bikini bottoms. Something was not right.

Her father had made her nervous with his fear and constant repeating himself, as if she were stupid.

Carla made her way to the tiny guard shack and leaned against the doorframe. Her friend was holding a joint in one hand and a walkie-talkie in the other. His face was pale, as if the shock of some massive reality had just hit him between the shoulder blades. He muttered to himself and stared at the tile floor.

"Santiago, you OK? You're going to burn your fingers, hey!" She snapped her fingers.

"Carla." He shook his head and looked at her. His happy-go-lucky smile had gone. He was terrified.

Carla began to sweat and feel sick. "What's wrong?"

"Carla, sweetie, something bad, very bad, is about to happen. Men are coming down here."

"What are you talking about? You are freaking me out!"

"Hide."

"*What?*" Carla jumped at the panic in her own voice. She backed up.

"They…they are going to kill everyone on the island. They are going to…I can't repeat what they said will happen to girls. You have to hide. They are coming."

"What!"

"The plane. Go hide on it!"

Santiago looked around the guard shack, sucking madly on his joint. He saw some keys and lunged for them. His fingers shook as he put them in her hands. "They are coming here, right now! Go! Go! Hide on the plane. I have to wait. Carla, don't look at me like I am not speaking Spanish. *Go!*"

Carla felt sweat pouring down her face and neck. Her breasts heaved with panic, and she felt sick. She glanced at the plane and knew she had moments. She snatched the keys and ran.

CHAPTER 34

The Fan Hits the...

Evan watched Jorge leave with his men. He took a quick count of the four pickups with .50 calibers that had seemed to spread out from the beginning of the dock to where the sub was. This was a decent-sized area, but considering the effective range of a .50 caliber, it was overkill. Evan's biggest concern was that the intel they had gotten from the navy was so wrong. Four gun trucks were a big deal and could take some time to take out. The other concern was that Mario's army of thugs seemed very unruly. The numbers were vastly underestimated.

Evan smiled and listened to Tommy and Mario talk as they admired the submarine and talked about smuggling days. Tommy was dressed again like a Don Johnson stunt double. His black sunglasses covered the dark circles under his eyes. He wore an expensive Tommy Bahamas green silk shirt with a light-weight, white blazer and jeans. His alligator shoes looked new and clashed with his peach socks.

Evan watched guests from the house slowly spread out around the crushed-coral-and-concrete walkway and LZ. He looked at elderly men with young trophy wives with boob jobs that had probably been done in Miami. He gawked at the expensive clothes, waiters, and golf carts with breakfast dishes and coffee. The whole thing was an obscene spectacle financed by one country's insane obsession for pleasure and a quick escape from reality. *The irony*, Evan mused as he counted the armed guards and bikinis, *was that one country looked down its nose at the other. So pious, yet it relied on them to fuel their religion of self-satisfaction.*

Evan smirked and mumbled to himself, "Who's really getting the last laugh in this duel?"

"Ivan? Ivan!"

Evan snapped out of it and looked at Tommy. "Yes?"

"Can you take Mario on a tour? I have to make my way out back and talk to an old friend."

Evan nodded and looked at the seven armed guards who were with Mario. Evan stared for a second at Tommy.

Tommy frowned and shook his head slightly.

He realized that Tommy had no idea if this was Mario or not.

"Guess we're gonna do this the hard way," Evan said.

Evan looked at his guests and changed his demeanor to one of excitement.

"Come on down the ladder, sir; watch your step," Evan said and smiled, glancing back at the crowd. He estimated there were about seventy to one hundred armed men milling about in the crowd. *This is looking worse than I even thought.*

"Is there a bathroom in there?" a woman asked. She pressed up against Mario and held his arm.

"Watch your step and your head!" Evan said.

"Thanks, Ivan. You must understand my security is a bit over the top. I regret that we have never met, but I feel as though I know you," Mario said.

"Too kind, sir," Evan said respectfully.

Evan followed Mario down the ladder into the sub. Five of his bodyguards, the female, and three guests, who he assumed were politicians by their enlightened manner, also joined them.

"Where are the lights?" someone joked.

"Hey, someone is grabbing my ass! Mario!" The woman giggled as they came to the bottom of the ladder.

Mario paused in the narrow passage and turned around.

Evan felt claustrophobic and warm as he came face-to-face with Mario. He was more worried about the five armed men behind him. Any discharge of a weapon or worse, a hand grenade, could cause a fire or explosion that would kill them all.

"Is there a bar on this thing?" the girl joked.

Mario laughed. "It's morning time!"

The girl laughed. "It's five o'clock somewhere!"

Evan felt like choking her but smiled. "Watch your head, sweetheart. We may have to walk one at a time up here. It gets narrow and then opens up."

"Last time I went into such a dark place with a man, I ended up pregnant." The girl continued to laugh and talk.

"Ah, yes. Well, where to? I want to see the kitchen and the cargo hold. This thing is big, but it is all pipes and narrow passages," Mario said in amazement.

Evan nodded and encouraged Mario to move straight ahead. "Several tons of product can be moved in this thing. I suggest fastening it to the hull in Zodiac boats or launching it from the torpedo's tubes. You don't want to surface." Evan explained the same information again. *If only these idiots had read the stuff I gave them*, he thought. Evan followed Mario deeper into the sub.

The low light made things seem even more ominous, like a fun house on Halloween.

Mario was in the lead being steered by Evan, who was explaining the details of the sub. The girl was behind him, talking nonstop to the five bodyguards.

Evan knew what was lurking up ahead and just hoped he survived.

"You lead the way, Ivan. I just bumped my head!"

Evan smiled and moved to the head of the line. He thought about Tommy for a moment and hoped he made it to the plane and could get it started. Tommy had decided he could wait no longer to see his daughter and the plane.

"Right up here, men. Watch your step, and duck down. Mario, you first. I am right behind you...Doors on navy vessels are called hatches, and walls are called bulkheads." Evan helped Mario step through the next hatch ahead of him. Once he was sure he was through, he pulled the hatch shut, effectively locking Mario on the other side of the hatch.

The people on the other side locked it.

"This is when the proverbial shit hits the fan," Evan said matter-of-factly as he turned and smiled like a tour guide. No one had noticed the long flashlight-baton-looking thing that he had picked up by the hatch. The item was actually a combination stun gun flashlight.

"I have to get the lights on. It's too dark," Evan said exasperated.

"Hey, where did Mario go?" The girl stopped midsentence to ask the question and then kept right on talking. "One time when I was in Paris...There was a guy and a pool table—"

Evan pressed the baton up against her left breast and pushed a button. A quick blue arc shot through her tissue. She dropped like a rock.

The last security guard in line yelled with surprise and then dropped.

Juan, from Green Team Two, had moved up behind the guards with a silenced .22 pistol and started shooting them at point-blank.

Evan leapt forward over the stunned girl and brought his baton down hard on the forearm of the guard closest to him. He was trying to bring his Uzi up. Evan had his knife in his other hand and slashed it across the guard's neck less than a second after he delivered a massive undercut with his baton.

The next two guards dropped before they realized what happened, leaving the last one standing with his hands up.

"*No mas*. I give, please, please!" The man went to his knees, dropped his weapon, and began crying.

Juan put the pistol to the back of the man's head and frowned. He started to squeeze the trigger.

"*No*, wait." Evan stepped forward. "He can help us and get paid or die like a dog—no offense to dogs."

Juan shrugged, holstered his weapon, and zip-tied the man's hands behind him.

"You do that like you've done that before," Evan said with admiration.

"Used to be a cop. My whole force was corrupt, shot me twelve times and left me to die on the road," Juan said.

"Your new name is Lucky," Evan dubbed him.

"Been called worse, *amigo*." Juan laughed.

Evan pointed at the cowering politicians and the blubbering female, who was shaking and hyperventilating.

"At least she ain't talking." Evan scowled. He prodded the men to their feet with his baton. "Get up. You're lucky we are conserving ammo this week. Bad for the environment."

Roger watched El Coyote stack against the door with a team of five men. They would go topside and secure the trawler. Two of Mario's men were still on board, but not for long. The rest of the team gathered their supplies and made ready.

Two men opened the hatch quietly, and Roger watched as the team moved out. Roger looked at his watch.

El Coyote looked at Roger and said, "Let's go."

He stood up and moved out of the hold area with the rest of the operators. Once they were free, they would give the signal to the other two squads of Team One. Roger headed topside, being careful to step over a large puddle of blood that used to be Mario's guards.

"Set the snipers up. I have to get on board the *Happy Mermaid*. I can't take a shot from here with the AT-4. I need the bag of C-4! Gotta do this up close," Roger whispered.

"Fine. Save the AT-4s for the gun trucks," El Coyote said and then added, "We got a problem. Oscar radioed that there are four gun trucks in our LZ."

"What? I thought they only had two." Roger spoke quietly and was annoyed.

"There are still two on the other side of the island. They got six total!" El Coyote returned, listening to his headset. "No, they have more than we thought, and there are a huge group of civilians topside," El Coyote whispered. "I just took a peek."

Joaquin moved up to where Roger knelt and touched him on the shoulder. "Bravo Squad is up."

"Where's Luis?"

"Here, Charlie is up," Luis said.

"Aye, let's the four of us take a peek. Get your squads ready to get on that yacht," Roger said.

The three squad leaders took a quick peek from the fishing trawler at their surroundings.

The trawler's crew moved about their business, pretending that Roger and his men were invisible.

The LZ seemed alive with activity. Roger thought about a market or maybe a bazaar in some weird country. Well-dressed, well-poised men and women milled about, talking and sipping champagne or coffee. They looked at the sub and the surrounding boats as if they were at some sort of amusement park. Roger thought it was odd.

The thing that made Roger the most uneasy was that four F-150 pickups with .50-caliber machine guns were parked on the same side with the truck beds parallel to the beach house's walls. Roger was concerned. The weapons were pointed up at the sky, yet the gun operators were sitting close-by, the belts of .50-caliber rounds were loaded, and the trucks were idling. Mario's men looked either stoned, crazy, or like some type of medieval animals drooling over fresh meat.

"They could wipe out everyone in a matter of minutes," Roger muttered.

"*Sí*, and no one could make it to the house. Interlocking sectors of fire. How many soldiers you guess?" El Coyote asked, peeking from his concealed position.

"Lad, I'd say over a hundred at least!"

"Again, the navy was wrong!" El Coyote said.

Roger growled, "Or they lied."

Joaquin added, "Well, securing the LZ is going to take serious work."

El Coyote spoke urgently. "We need to get on with it, Roger. I will get guys to take a bead on the trucks. But the guests? They are toast when the shooting starts."

Roger shrugged and pointed at the *Happy Mermaid*, which towered above their fishing trawler. "We got to climb up on that thing. Unnoticed."

"Piece of cake." Joaquin laughed.

"Alpha goes first; it'll take us five minutes. We will cover Bravo and Charlie," El Coyote said, moving off.

Designated climbers had already been picked and were standing by. The men would use ropes with grappling hooks to get themselves up and then toss down several rope ladders. The actual climbing would be out of sight from prying eyes, thanks to the placement of the fishing trawler.

"We have to cripple that yacht, but I mainly want that mini-gun taken out," Roger told his leaders. They nodded.

El Coyote continued after some thought, "Well, if that sailboat from California had not taken our parking space, we could have parked in front of the boat as planned and *boom!*"

"Aye. Look, why don't we go with the other option we discussed?" Roger proposed.

El Coyote frowned again. "OK."

Roger said, "Let's get a move on, gents. Can't stand around all freakin' day."

Roger did a radio check with the whole Dark Cloud assault force and announced what he was doing.

Green Team Two

Oscar watched as his men grabbed the two men and one female as they neared the water. The second female was quicker than they expected and bolted. She had the build of a college athlete, which meant they would have to get her quickly.

Oscar lay prone among the flies and watched it go down. One of his men chased her until she got into the open field. She made it across the sand and began screaming. Oscar looked in the distance. Surely no one could hear or see her, but if she made it back, they were done.

Oscar's operative dropped down into the prone position and hid himself, taking aim. "Shit," he exclaimed.

The bullet tore through her, and she tumbled.

The four men and Tanya looked down at the unconscious body and then looked up and at each other.

"Well, Tanya?"

She shrugged. "I need light. Problem is they all look alike!" Tanya felt her heart race. She was not feeling so positive any longer.

Someone shone a flashlight in Mario's face. The team worked just as rehearsed. Mario had been hit with a stun gun and then injected with morphine. He groaned and mumbled.

The team stripped him naked, took dental x-rays with a small hand-held x-ray device, and checked his fingerprints on an electronic scanner.

"I think it's the Mario who I talked to, for whatever that means!" Tanya said, hopeful.

"Dental records don't match. Tattoos do, build does, and blood type. Fingerprints have been melted off with acid!" one of the team members said.

The team looked baffled.

"I say it's him," one of the team members stated with great confidence. Clearly he wanted this to end.

A loud scream could be heard on the other side of the door, and then silence.

"What do we do?" Tanya asked.

"It's him! We have to tell Roger and the rest," the team member with the portable x-ray machine, Eduardo, announced. He looked relieved.

"Wait!" Tanya knelt down and put her nose next to Mario's lips. She opened his mouth.

"We have to go, Tanya." Eduardo stepped past Tanya to bang on the hatch. This was the signal to open it.

"Hold on!" she screamed.

The three men stood and looked down at her as if she were nuts.

"What are you?" Eduardo asked, alarm rising in his voice.

"Not him. I know that Mario has a drink every morning. This guy's mouth smells like mouthwash. The more I look at him, *no!* I can tell this *is not* the man I spoke with!" She kicked his feet, and he stirred. "Platform shoes *and* watch on the wrong hand!"

"You may be wrong," Eduardo spoke rapidly.

The team members were beginning to sweat.

Tanya shook her head. "*Not him!*"

Fernando, who was a medic and member of the GAFE, spoke up quickly. "If it's not him, that means this whole mission could be a huge waste!"

"What's going on in there?"

Tanya heard Evan's voice on the other side of the hatch.

"One minute." Tanya began to pace and crossed her arms across her chest. She cursed and balled up her fists.

Eduardo shrugged and pulled out a syringe. He gave Mario a shot of Narcan and waited. The man came around and sat up.

"Are you the real Mario?" Eduardo asked.

"Who the hell are you?" The man looked terrified and tried to back across the floor.

"Mario?"

"Y-y…yes?"

"Not him!" Tanya had reached her snapping point. "Why won't you believe me?" She picked up an M-4 that had been propped against the bulkhead, aimed it at Mario's head, and pulled the trigger.

Mario's head exploded, and for a second they were all deaf.

CHAPTER 35

Dueling Lead

The first gunshots did little to alarm the guests. People screamed, but it could have been fireworks. Guests began looking around, and the occasional scream began to reproduce itself and multiply like a wave through the crowd.

Then the .50 calibers began.

Smoke, flesh, shell casings, and screams turned the scene into terror. Hysterically laughing teenagers and ex-cons began indiscriminately mowing down anyone who was not them. The guests were being herded toward the house, which was thick and walled like a fortress. Some of the thugs took it upon themselves to isolate some of the female victims and drag them into a secluded area behind a wall or vehicle.

The Scorpions first realized they were one of the targets when Mario's men turned the .50 calibers on them as they congregated in a large group in front of the *Happy Mermaid*.

Gerard had been sitting on a golf cart, smoking a cigarette and talking to a group of perhaps twenty of his comrades when the rounds began to fly.

Many of the Scorpions had already left the area in teams of ones and twos so they could take out sentries along the perimeter and scout out the movements of Mario's men. The arrival of the gun trucks had concerned Gerard, and he had called a quick meeting. Mario's thugs were all young, imitated the American gangsters they had seen in rap videos, and were usually stoned or amped up on meth. Many of them were ex-cons from L.A. and Texas and wanted nothing more than to prove themselves. Many of them, of course, had been through the weapons-training camps run by the Scorpions. They were not professional soldiers but psychopaths. They had something to prove. The triggermen possessed the innate insecurity of dysfunctional youth raised in a system that taught them that the world was all about them.

The guests, who, moments earlier, had been talking pleasantly and enjoying their morning coffee, were now running, screaming and panicked, toward the large beach house.

Gerard managed to leap off the golf cart and sprint onto the yacht as bullets literally ripped the golf cart and his men into shreds.

"No!" he yelled.

Gerard returned fire, but did not have the range to hit the men in the F-150s. He helped a few of his men to cover and then finally had to abandon them when he was overwhelmed by men running in his direction.

He had to find Jorge quickly, get some decent weapons, and then regroup his men. He knew that at least ten of his men were still on the yacht. Gerard was terrified that he had just been caught so off guard by such an insanely bold move. He had underestimated Mario's triggermen.

Within about five minutes, the dock began to clear, and the house began to fill. Bodies lay torn, twisted, and moaning along the dock.

Anyone unfortunate enough to not be killed outright was being treated to a particularly sick treatment.

Team Two, Five Minutes Earlier

Oscar and Pablo, the Alpha Squad leader, were at the partial shelter near the sub. Pablo sent a few guys forward to meet with Tanya's escort. They downloaded gear and carried no weapons. The point was to give the impression that they were part of the sub's maintenance crew. She would be placed in a Zodiac and moved to a different part of the island. Charlie Squad's sniper and spotter were back on the beach. His name was Kevin, and he was manning a Barrett .50-caliber sniper rifle. The Barrett was a large, cumbersome weapon, weighing thirty-plus pounds. It could take out vehicles or people at up to a mile.

Kevin confirmed that they had one gun truck marked as a target. A second gun truck was dangerously close to the sub and had been marked by Joaquin. Oscar glanced at his watch and listened to his squad leaders relay information. Details, counter-contingencies, and prayers were exchanged.

"Oscar, if I did not know better, I would say that these idiots are setting up to mow down all of the guests…along with Evan and his whole team," one of the team members said over the radio.

"Boss, Bravo Team has been spotted. They are moving toward their linkup with the *Mermaid*. I don't see any way to secure this LZ without a huge fight. We are outnumbered two to one and need more firepower."

"Airpower!" another member said excitedly over the radio.

The radio set made a sound and everyone listened.

"Oscar! This is Charlie Squad! We have about thirty men walking right up the beach toward our position. I think they know or suspect that something happened to the guests. If we hold and fight, your ass will be exposed. If we don't fight, we will all get flanked later. Please advise."

Oscar peeked behind a piece of concrete seawall and made out the outline of Evan and Bravo Squad. He spoke quickly to

Charlie Squad. "Charlie, when the signal from Team One goes down, you guys hold. Ambush the mob heading toward you. Eliminate them and then hightail it to our flank; sweep up. Your sniper assets have to take out these trucks!"

"What is going on? Why would these guys look like they wanna kill off their own people?" someone asked over the radio.

"I think we are caught in a civil war," Pablo replied.

"Roger's team is on the yacht. They are going to blow the minigun and then clear the *Happy Mermaid*. We have to clear this LZ so the birds can land!" said a voice over the radio. Oscar made a decision and turned to one of his men.

"Call Charlie Squad. Tell them to be ready!" Oscar said urgently.

Someone on his team relayed news to Oscar. He did not have time to see who it was.

"Oscar, we have Tanya. Tensions are rising. Get ready."

Thud! Thud! Thud! Thud! Thud!

All of the .50-caliber gun trucks began firing at once.

Oscar and his squad leaders took cover, exchanged confused looks, and then popped up and started sniping targets.

A white smoke trail, shot from the upper deck of the *Happy Mermaid*, hit the gun truck that was the closest to Bravo Team. The truck burst into a bright ball of orange-and-white light. Pieces of truck and glass went in all directions, ripping into pieces anyone who was too close. People with severe burns ran or rolled from the flames. Some just smoldered.

Oscar cursed as his men from Bravo Team were mowed down as they tried to bound and maneuver away from the superior force, which moved more like groups of frantic rats than organized troops.

Guests began running in all directions, and Mario's thugs began firing at anything that moved. They seemed to be enjoying themselves, as if they were in a game.

"Taking my shot," one of the snipers said over the radio.

Oscar could hear Charlie Squad's sniper whisper over the air.

A teenager was manning a .50 caliber and spraying into the crowd. He wore an iPod with earbuds and a Che Guevara T-shirt.

Thud! Thud! Thud!

Suddenly, the kid on the back of the truck was missing his torso. The two-hundred-yard shot was not difficult, but it also gave a sniper less room to evade and escape. The truck veered and hit a wall by the swimming pool as the driver was taken out.

Mario's thugs seemed to realize they were under attack now and began moving out toward the perimeter of the open area, which had become the kill zone. They dove for cover and fired wildly. Then they began to run and retreat. Bodies dropped, skidded, and twisted, and some crawled. The Dark Cloud shooters did their best to clear out bands of Mario's men near the guests. In one case, a woman was being dragged behind a wall by both her arms and one leg by three men who were frantic yet could not let go of their prize. Three coordinated head shots gave the woman the seconds she needed to flee and disappear. Smoke canisters with CS gas and red smoke began landing in the LZ, driving the remaining shooters and civilians to cover.

"We have to move now!" Oscar yelled.

Oscar and his team popped more smoke and began bonding and firing and maneuvering until they reached their objective near the sub. Superior training and fire discipline won out over the numbers and sheer chaos of Mario's fighters. Within thirty minutes, Alpha Squad had put Mario's warriors in full retreat. They had fired all five of their AT-4s, killing dozens of scrambling men, and had taken out all but one of the gun trucks. Charlie Squad's snipers had taken out anyone who had remotely looked as if they were giving orders. The remaining gun truck remained idling with no one in it. No one dared go near it.

CS gas began stinging eyes and making people cough and curse as the winds changed directions.

"Boss, we are getting low on ammo," someone yelled.

Oscar had linked up with the three surviving men from Bravo Squad and got a situation report from the men.

"Juan is dead." A situation report came over the net for all of Dark Cloud to hear. Things where deteriorating fast. Everyone listened. "Tanya is away on the Zodiac. All squads are at about fifty percent with ammo. AT-4's gone. Our heavy guns are gone. Half a dozen hand grenades. Mario's thugs have retreated behind the house's perimeter wall. Charlie Squad has taken five casualties and three wounded. Bravo Squad has lost all but three. Alpha Squad has lost one. They are moving our way. The enemy is at about sixty percent, which means they still outnumber us. They are afraid to show themselves."

"Kill all these bastards!" Oscar yelled out over the net. It was time for Dark Cloud to take the fight to the enemy, before there was no Dark Cloud.

Oscar listened to the sporadic small-arms fire and occasional explosions from a lobbed round from one of their M203s. He heard the occasional heavy thud of a .50 caliber. "Where's that coming from?" he yelled.

A report came in from one of their snipers who had a birds-eye view. "South of the island. Scorpions, we think, were decimated, but I suspect they are rallying. There are only two gun trucks left on the island, and the Scorpions have them!"

Oscar checked his magazines; he was down to one thirty-round magazine. He spoke out loud to anyone who could listen. The gunfire was deafening. The fog of war had begun.

"We still have not secured the LZ. We just killed half of our enemy, *but* when they mount a counterattack, we will be toast. Get the M203s up here. We have to start lobbing some explosives over that wall!"

A desperate voice came over the radio. "Team One is about to blow the minigun and breach the hull of the *Happy Mermaid*."

Boom! Boom!

The noise and percussion shook the very sand and concrete sea-wall that Oscar had been crouched behind. He popped up quickly with his rifle and scope. He looked quickly to see who would leave their covered position to peek at the explosion. Being a sniper, like being a hunter, required you to be a student of behavior.

Two of Mario's men suddenly stood up from behind their brick wall some hundred and fifty yards away. The men pointed and froze while they watched the front section of the yacht explode in a bright-orange fireball. They yelled and pointed with shock, arms moving.

Pop! Pop!

Both men collapsed immediately, a wisp of red briefly staining the air.

"Idiots," Oscar muttered. He finished speaking as if he had merely stopped to smash a fly. "OK, we have to drive those morons out from behind the walls, into the open," he said.

Everyone seemed to speak at once; no one could tell who was speaking. It did not matter, the pieces came together. Oscar listened to them all and got the big picture.

He shot thugs, listened, and gave orders all at the same time. Brass flew, bullets thudded, and people screamed. Oscar paused briefly to pull one of his teammates out of a hole he had stepped in.

"Choppers are inbound, ten minutes!"

"Civilians that are not dead are barricaded in the house."

"Something crazy is going on inside the house. Looks like they are segregating men from women."

"They must be preparing hostages."

"Charlie snipers just capped two men through the upstairs window. They are assaulting the women!"

Oscar cursed. "What is going on? It's like these guys are a bunch of Vikings raping and pillaging!"

"These are their own people!" Gustavo added as he capped two more of Mario's men, who had tried to run from an opening in the wall into the house. Their bodies landed in the swimming pool.

"Keep their heads down. Smoke them out!" Oscar yelled to his squad members.

Suddenly Oscar had an idea. "Where is Charlie Squad?"

"Coming up the beach now! They have lost one more," someone reported.

"OK, listen," Oscar began. "There is a minigun, a twenty-five-millimeter chain gun, on the back of the *Happy Mermaid*. I am going to get to it and rip that wall to shreds. Get online with everyone and start picking them off."

"Oscar! That's a forty-five-yard sprint," Pablo cautioned. "You will be ripped to shreds!"

"And?"

"Fine, we cover you." Pablo loaded another magazine and racked the chamber.

"We got problems." An operator named Julio moved down the column and spoke to Pablo. Julio was in charge of maintaining contact with the navy. "The navy just called, weather conditions. They are pushing back their arrival twenty minutes!"

"*What?* It's clear! Whatever. What about gunboats?" Pablo asked, his face visibly getting angry.

Julio shook his head and continued, "Against their SOP. They need to protect their landing craft!"

"The Scorpions are making a sweep from the north. They have about fifty guys. Two gun trucks. They know how to fight!" someone from the other end of the island, a spotter, said over the radio

One of the team members from Alpha Squad was looking at a tiny screen that gave a video feed from a tiny remote-controlled, hand-launched drone.

"Well, if you are going to do it. Do it now!" Pablo yelled to Oscar, who had moved several yards away to help someone who had tripped.

Oscar checked his weapon and looked at his men. "Throw some smoke. Shoot the suckers who try to get me."

Forty-Five Minutes Earlier

Evan heard the muffled shot and banged on the hatch. "Hey!" He stepped back and waited as the heavy door was unlocked and slowly opened.

Juan, or Lucky, as Evan called him, was in charge of Bravo Squad Team Two. He stood next to Evan and waited for the door to open. The dead bodies were being dragged from the passage, while the two prisoners were being taken to the galley. Someone had put duct tape over the female's mouth and zip-tied her hands in front of her. She still kept talking, upset from the burn mark on her flesh.

"Well?"

Evan and Lucky both had their answer as soon as the hatch swung completely open.

Tanya and the three men from Bravo Squad stood around the naked body of a Mario cousin.

"Not him," Tanya said flatly.

"OK." Evan motioned for the team to leave their equipment and follow him.

"Now what?" Tanya asked, annoyed and a little nervous.

Evan gave her a hug but not to patronize her. He just wanted to bring her energy down. She was amped up, most likely from exposure to so much violence in the last few days. Evan and most of the other operatives had been in enough combat of one form or another to know that you had to turn off the "spaz" in order to function smoothly; otherwise, you would wear out.

"Let's go to the galley, have some coffee, and I will call Roger," Lucky said.

Evan, Lucky, and all fifteen members of Bravo squad met in the galley. They readied their weapons, drank coffee or water, and rechecked gear.

Evan spoke quickly to Tanya while Lucky called Roger to report that it was not Mario.

"So you sure?" Evan asked.

"*Yes!* Yes I am sure! The man I spoke with on the yacht, he was Mario. Sure of it. That guy was close, real close…but not him. I…I remember the mannerisms of Jorge around Mario. Mario is a bigger-than-life kinda guy, a king. Holds himself like a cowboy king. Pearl-handled pistols and everything!" Tanya said and brought her hand down hard on the table and cursed as she almost spilled her coffee. "Oops, sorry—excited," she said.

"Bring it down, sweetheart." Evan laughed.

"Evan, come here a second!" Arturo said.

"Excuse me." Evan squeezed her hand, handed her a napkin, and then stood up.

Arturo stood over the captured and shaky security guard. The man was sipping coffee and talking a mile a minute to save his life.

"Hey, tell him what you told me!"

Arturo, who had been an interrogator for years, had the smooth, calm demeanor and quiet intelligence of someone who could size you up with a smile and get inside your head quickly.

"Have more coffee. You are doing great." Arturo was encouraging his prisoner.

The prisoner looked up at Evan, and began. "I…I took this job 'cause I just needed the money. Been in prison my whole adult life. Why…why did I get here? They said I would just have to protect Mario, go on the sub, but…but then there was more, much more. Look, I don't wanna kill anybody. I have seen too much, and where does it go? I saw a glimpse of hell, of eternity… my life."

Evan waved his hands to the man, trying to get him to speed up. "I get it. Look, this is your second chance. Things don't happen by accident. You were spared for a reason. I don't believe in luck, really. Just spit it out."

The prisoner nodded, accepted his coffee, and got to the point. "Mario's son is furious with Jorge. He hates Jorge, and he hates his arrogant Scorpions who strut around like they are supersoldiers. Everyone hates them, fears them! Well, this morning we were brought together by our leaders, and they say, 'Men, you have one job today—'" The guard stopped talking for a second.

Evan figured he was a bit of a drama queen but was being truthful.

"'Men, today your mission is to kill everyone who is not one of us! Start with the Scorpions, and when you are done with them, you can have the rich people. You can take whatever you can steal to include the women!'" He paused again. "I am with animals, I thought. Teenagers, boys who are cheering that they will kill people and preselecting which chicas they will drag off and violate…I don't want any of this! *All* of these men were recruited from prisons from Mexico and the United States. They were all brought here for one reason!"

Evan could not help but be shocked. He looked at Arturo and whistled. "How many of you are here?"

"Two hundred," the man said. "We snuck in at night. Jorge does not know we are here. We even smuggled in those extra machine-gun things."

"Oh, *boy!* Hey, Lucky! We are about to walk into a slaughter!"

"What?" Lucky asked. A shocked look moved across his face.

Evan walked over to the radio and held out his hand. There was no coverage inside the steel submarine, so they had to go low tech and use a radio that had an external antenna. Evan took the radio handset from Lucky and shook his head. He suddenly felt like he was in an old World War II movie, only they were fighting drug-crazed zombies with sombreros.

"Lucky, go see what you can on the external cameras. We gotta bolt in about twenty minutes!"

"Prisoners?" Lucky asked.

"They will be far safer here. *Do not* take the duct tape off that chick's mouth!" Evan said—the first serious thing he had said all week.

Lucky laughed and walked away.

Bravo Squad was making last-minute adjustments and preparations. They all had their own ritual. No one spoke.

"Roger?"

Evan heard static and frowned. Then he heard an angry grumble.

"Aye, Evan. They let you play with the radio?"

"Yes."

"What's up?" Roger asked.

Evan smiled. "OK, listen. We just got intel from a Mario triggerman that the purpose of those gun trucks and their whole freaking army is to kill the Scorpions. *And* everyone else. A jealousy love triangle. I...I don't get it, but that's it." Evan shook his head and felt confused, and then he finished. "Anyway, we are about to walk into a mini–Tiananmen Square. They also have orders to kill and loot, rape and pillage. Scorpions are the main course!" Evan listened to silence for a second.

"What? If this is true, it doesn't remotely make sense! Mario is celebrating his son's life and having his birthday. Turf war? Mario likes Jorge. I don't believe it."

"It makes perfect sense, Roger, if there is a coup!"

Roger sounded confused when said, "You lost me."

"Roger, the Scorpions are the target, and then rape, pillage, and burn. Mario is not behind this; his *other* son is!"

Tanya had been listening and walked over and stood next to Evan. She snapped her fingers and grabbed the handset from Evan.

"Roger! Hi, honey, this is me. I know Jorge has been planning something, but it's possible that Mario or Little Mario, as they call him, has been too. *None* of the brothers like Jorge. I think this is revenge. I don't think he has a clue of Jorge's bigger ambitions. This is a hunch."

"OK. This sucks. We have to move fast and end this. Only the navy can handle this!" Roger said.

"Use the chaos!" Evan blurted.

No one spoke for a moment.

Roger spoke before anyone else could. "OK, look, we stick to the plan. I am with Alpha and Bravo Teams right now on the yacht. We have taken out some guards. We are planting C-4 as we speak. Charlie Squad is waiting to cover your egress from the submarine. You got no cover, so ye better haul ass to the yacht!"

Roger paused.

"Where is Green Team Two Alpha and Charlie?" Evan asked.

"En route. Oscar says they had to take down some guests who got too close. Alpha is moving to you right now from the north. Got it?" Roger said.

"Called the navy yet?"

"Aye. You got Mario?"

"*No.* But tell the navy we do, in case they bail. Let's go on your signal like we planned, Roger. If the crap hits the fan, we all pile around the *Mermaid!*"

Evan spoke rapidly and toyed with his UMP.40 as it hung on his sling. He and the members of Dark Cloud now truly looked like a tactical team of some sort. Every man had a tactical vest crammed full of magazines, grenades, and personal weapons or blades of choice. Cargo pants, shorts, some even wore jeans. Almost everyone had on a pair of knee pads and shin guards.

The team members wore jackets of their own choosing, black or brown, and even a few different patterns of camouflage. No one could not mistake them for an army, but it would take careful observation to peg them as the same army.

Evan wore brown, tactical 5.11 cargo pants with a heavy web belt, on which hung a Leatherman tactical flashlight that could also serve as a concealable stun gun and his backup H&K handgun. He had shin pads on and kneepads around his ankles. His combat boots were fairly new, unfortunately. He wore a large bulletproof vest with a ceramic plate in the back. He cared less about standing out now than he did about surviving. His eye protection was on a strap that hung around his neck. And he wore a chewed-up olive-green baseball hat backward. Evan's second-most important accessory, besides his extra rounds, was his last can of Skoal in his cargo pocket.

Roger spoke quickly to Evan. His voice was tense. "You just get out of the sub. Charlie Squad Team One starts taking out gun trucks once you are clear. By then Team Two should be in position!"

CHAPTER 36

Son of a Drug Dealer

Jorge Valdez had left the sub ten minutes earlier. He had walked with his security detail back on board the *Happy Mermaid* and down below to where he had been told Mario was waiting for him. Gerard had elected to stay outside and on the docks with a group of Scorpions. They wanted to keep an eye on Mario's men and the guests without raising suspicion. Jorge had always had a little tension with Mario Jr. II and even more so with Mario's regular triggermen. Jorge viewed this as the same sort of rivalry that was common among regular infantry, who, deep down inside, wished they could be special forces but in reality could not make the cut. Jorge's men ran the training camps, the shooting ranges, and the kidnapping and surveillance classes that the regular triggermen attended. Jorge had seen waves of different types of killers over the years. The regular troops used to be respectful and look up to his more elite team. Years ago they used to strive to be like Scorpions or even join them, but now the new crop were just resentful punks. Many of them had spent time in prison in Mexico and in the States. They either had no education or very little. The new crop was just immature, sadistic, lazy, and all about pleasure and entitlement.

Jorge loathed them.

"Boss, can you share with me your barbecue secrets?" Marco walked next to Jorge. He loved to eat. Marco's, main job was to launder money through a chain of restaurants in Juárez and southern Arizona.

"Slow and low, my friend. The rub that I use, it is a family secret, but the key is always low heat over a day. Just like life, my friend, patience produces more results, huh?"

Marco laughed. "So true, boss. Just wanted to tell you, you are a great chef!"

"Thank you!"

Jorge and his five-man detail talked about the weather, food, and sports as they were led by a slim girl of about nineteen down into the bottom of the yacht.

"So where are the rest of the men, Marco?" Jorge asked. "I want everyone a little more alert."

"Almost everyone is at the garage or gym. I think Gerard told everyone to rally in the next hour. Dressed and ready to play."

Jorge smiled, but on the inside he was nervous. He was severely outnumbered by Mario's thugs, and this concerned him. They had lied about their numbers. Two boats showed up late last night, and each off-loaded about fifty more men and equipment.

Why do this in the cover of night? Jorge mused. He also knew that Mario was not behind it. Security was supposed to be Jorge's realm.

The six men were led into the *Happy Mermaid's* gymnasium at the bottom of the yacht. The area was not as large as the ship's hold, which could hold a few cars, Jet Skis, and a number of in-flatable boats. The gymnasium had a half-size basketball court, a glass-walled squash court, and a modest gym with some aerobics equipment. The free weights where his men regularly worked out were on the top deck.

Jorge smiled and thought about Tanya complaining to him about the gym filling up whenever she used it and the men staring too much.

"I will tell them to use the gym below," he had said.

"Jorge! How are you?"

Jorge paused and stared at Little Mario, who was perhaps the most fake person Jorge had ever known, and that included politicians. Little Mario had the nickname, from Jorge's men, of the White Mexican. He had a different mother than the other two sons.

"Your foot, what happened, my friend?" Jorge smiled on the outside only and extended his hand. Little Mario had a wimpy, soft handshake. He was not a small man, however. His shoulders were broad, and he liked steroids.

"Oh, polo accident in Buenos Aires. I was doing so good this year!"

"Unfortunate." Jorge looked at the plastic boot on his foot and the cane that he leaned heavily on. He was all alone and stood smiling at Jorge and his five killers.

"I have not been back to Mexico in a few months, and so much as changed!" Little Mario was the consummate playboy. He dabbled in marketing and making connections on the international scene for Mario's business. His best talent was being rich and spending daddy's money. Jorge did give him credit, however—he could charm and network, but without money he was an empty suit. Jorge regarded him as an amateur, a con man. Little Mario had solidified almost all of the European and Australian connections with Mario's product. He had villas in Spain and Italy and graced the organization with his presence a few times a year to brag about how lavish he had it.

Jorge frowned and folded his arms. "Your father, where is he?"

"He is still in bed. I have never seen him this depressed!"

Jorge nodded and felt a bit of pity for Mario. He understood the pain of a broken heart. In hindsight, he wished that he had not had to kill the other brother.

"He has lost a wonderful son, and, well, it is like losing a part of yourself. You see, Mario, the death of a child, it is an indescribable pain. Your father, he will mourn in his way."

"Well said, Jorge."

"So how have you been?" Jorge asked.

Jorge sized up the room and began to feel awkward. He had been lied to or given false information. He was told that Boss Mario wanted to speak with him. Jorge looked at his watch. He had to end this whole thing and soon. First, he wanted to have lunch.

Jorge pretended to listen to Little Mario Jr. for ten minutes as he bragged about his international exploits and travels. The girls, the important people, and the fun—yes, the fun.

"So, Mario, I have noticed a very large presence of security. Why is this necessary? You know that I have traditionally taken care of security."

"Oh, yes, yes. Well, I wanted more men here. I have some building projects, and, well, if they pose as security guards it makes us look more official. You know, some important people are here, and I—" Little Mario stopped speaking.

"Pardon, excuse me!" someone interrupted.

Jorge and Mario both paused. Jorge generally did not tolerate interruptions, but this was no ordinary day.

Jorge and his men turned around and froze.

A beautiful woman wearing a swimsuit leaned shyly against the door, half in the room. "I am sorry, honey, to interrupt, but I need some help moving some furniture. And with your foot—" She frowned and looked dejected for a moment. "I am interrupting, I can see that. No, no, sorry."

"One moment, miss. You are a very pleasant interruption." Jorge smiled and offered his hand.

The woman blushed for a moment and then walked into the basketball court. She carried her looks as a burden almost, as if she genuinely felt sorry for those who were normal.

"I have seen you on television, miss," Jorge said.

She blushed and flicked her black hair over her shoulder.

"And I have heard how charming you are, Mr. Valdez. You are even more so in person."

"You flatter an old man. Thank you."

Jorge and his men, who suddenly were no longer slouching or looking bored, stood up straight.

"I know you have important things to discuss. I just need two dressers moved."

She looked approvingly at the torsos of Mario's bodyguards. "Can I borrow muscle?"

Jorge shrugged and waved his men after the TV actress.

"Should we go sit while we wait for my father? Can I offer you some coffee?" Little Mario asked.

"Sure." Jorge followed Mario across the basketball court to a small oak desk that had drinks set out on a silver tray.

"So, Jorge, I have so many questions for you."

"OK." Jorge sat and poured a cup of coffee for himself.

Little Mario sat in his chair and put his cane across his knees. He began speaking. "As you know, my older half-brother, he handles, or handled, the procurement of items. Any big purchases. Boats, houses, submarines. I am more of a marketing guy. But I do have a degree in economics. My younger brother, he is the numbers guy: investments, banks stocks offshore, blah, blah."

"Yes, I know all this." Jorge sipped his coffee and let his right hand rest in his lap near his massive handgun.

"Well, I was coming back for the funeral, flying back from Venezuela. I go to withdraw money, and my account is closed. I talk to my younger brother. He tells me something crazy has happened. Can you imagine the number of bills a multibillion-dollar organization has to pay? Legitimate bills: rent, insurance, utilities on hundreds of properties, taxes! Not even touching personnel."

"Staggering, I am sure." Jorge inched his finger closer to his Smith & Wesson.

"Well, not as staggering as what my brother told me."

"Yes?" Jorge asked.

Little Mario continued. "Over the last several months, he has been having trouble with banks. At first he thought it was a fluke, you know, outsourcing jobs, stupid bank workers. But no! It has become more frequent."

Jorge sipped his coffee and looked concerned. "Yes?"

"Well, about the time that Mario my brother noticed this, he mentioned it to my other brother, Mario. God rest his soul."

Jorge and Mario both set their cups down to cross themselves.

"We have been defaulting on bills, loans. Cash shipments have not been making it to places. I tried to pay for an Italian police boat that we destroyed—you know, pay them back for damages. No money!"

"What?" Jorge put his left hand on the table.

"*Yes!* My brothers and I put our heads together last week and compared notes. It has been as if over the last few months, someone has been slowly draining our money, but worse than that, this person has been leaving just enough to pay our bills. When there is a default, I will look the next day, and the money is back"—Mario snapped his fingers—"and then gone again."

"Someone is skimming money?" Jorge looked puzzled. He did not need this additional headache.

"Funneling our money. *Then* this crazy submarine thing comes up." Mario started drumming his fingers on the table and looked up at the ceiling pleading with his eyes. "*Then!* My brother dies." He shook his head and looked at Jorge. "I…I—" Mario stopped as if he had a different train of thought.

"Then I heard about the new computers, that, oh…a girl named Tanya was installing? Tanya from Brazil. Tanya who has about ten different aliases, including Sophia Velazquez who formerly worked for the Brazilian Intelligence Agency! *Ha-ha!*"

Mario stood up and threw his head back in the air like a child who had just discovered someone had played a prank on him. "It all came together for me!"

Jorge felt pale and hot. He rested his hand on his weapon and felt his teeth begin to grind. Was this little shit trying to blame him?

"This is impossible!" Jorge whispered.

"*No*, it is not. *All* of—" Mario laughed as if he were in pain and slapped the desk. "*No*, you will love this part!"

"Speak, but speak carefully, son," Jorge said flatly.

"OK. Um, how do I put this?" Mario put one hand on his face and limped next to Jorge on his cane and then around the desk.

"Oh, oh, I will just say it: All of our freaking money is gone. The warehouses, everything, it is all gone, and you stole it to finance your overthrow of Mexico! Yes!" Mario Jr. II yelled at the top of his lungs. Then he got very quiet. "I know about the coup to consolidate all of the power."

Jorge heard a burst of machine-gun fire next door. "Shit!" Jorge kicked back from the table and drew his Smith & Wesson. He tried to get two hands on it.

Boom!

Jorge tumbled back over in his chair and began to scream as loud as he ever had. His fingers disappeared in a cloud of mist and smoke, and his handgun clanged on the floor.

Little Mario, who was younger and had the reflexes of an athlete, had touched his cane to Jorge's left hand. The cane was, in fact, not a cane but a hollow tube that held shotgun shells, triggered by a hidden squeeze.

"*Ahhh!*"

SILVER, LEAD, AND DEAD

"Scream, Jorge, scream! Your men are all dead! The guests, they are all gonna die! Your coup, it is over! You will live long enough to see your house of cards crumble! I know everything, you fuck!"

Mario started kicking Jorge as hard as he could with his plastic boot. Jorge did his best to stop the bleeding. He cursed and folded his hand, or what was left of it, under his body. Jorge's last thought before he passed out was that Mario did not have a broken foot.

Mario was in a frenzy. He flipped over the desk, threw the chair across the court, and jumped up and down. "Ahhhh!" he yelled.

His former-actress girlfriend walked into the room with two other girls and six men. She now wore a leather jacket over her one-piece bathing suit. She had blood splatter on her cheek, and on her it looked good.

"Darling, stop the yelling. It's not good for your inner peace!" She walked across the court and comforted her boyfriend as he stood over Jorge and sobbed.

"Sweetie, it's OK. I am here!"

Jocelyn handed her MP5 to one of the men who was with her and comforted Little Mario. She guided him from the room, soothing him like a child.

"Don't stand there!" she snapped at the men as she paused near the door. She had her arms around the much-taller man and dug her fingers through his hair. "Get that piece of crap. Bring him up to the observation room, Mario's father's room. He can watch the fireworks from there!" Jocelyn continued to speak and soothe her boyfriend. "I want him to see everyone die!"

Mario sobbed and said nothing.

"It's OK, baby. Yes, he will suffer, just like your father. He will pay!"

Jocelyn let her boyfriend lean on her and drape his arm over her shoulder and breast.

CHAPTER 37

Swiss Cheese and Hamburger

Evan, Juan, Tanya, and the remaining men of Bravo Squad moved quickly out of the submarine. The lone security guard stayed within reach of Evan. He had promised to get them through the crowd and alleviate suspicion in exchange for a large sum of cash and freedom.

Evan had agreed but on one condition: "You wear this explosive device. If you lie or turn on us, your head will explode."

The terrified guard agreed.

Juan had watched and kept a straight face as Evan attached what was actually chewing gum, a watch battery, wires, and duct tape between the man's shoulder blades.

Out of earshot Juan had laughed. "You are nuts, Evan. What if we do need to kill him?"

"Then shoot him, but right now he will only think about the explosive device." Evan smirked.

Evan and Juan made it to the pier first and were met by twenty-five men and teenagers with weapons at the ready. The crowd of civilians, which must have totaled about fifty, was milling about on the docks and the LZ in front of the house. Evan surveyed the near-football-field-size area that would serve as the LZ Mario.

How are we going to secure this thing? Evan mused. He did not want to kill a hundred-plus people, and how was he going to separate the civilians from the armed thugs? The situation was far worse than what he had imagined at the brief, but then again, nothing ever went according to plan. That was a fact you could depend on.

"Where is Mario?" a short, bald man with a pockmarked face asked Evan. He had tribal tattoos on his neck and face.

"He is getting a blow job. Told us to leave him alone. You see the girl is missing, huh?" Evan smiled and pointed back to the open hatch of the sub.

The short, bald thug seemed unconvinced and shifted his eyes among Evan's men.

They tried to appear relaxed yet were far from it. All eyes were on them, and surely questions began to move through the crowd as to why everyone was dressed in such a way and carrying weapons.

The security guard smoothed things over with his comrades, and Bravo Squad began to move toward the house.

The security guard repeated his lines just as he had been told. He seemed confident and able to deliver. "These men are Ivan's security detail and crew of the sub. Without them the sub does not work. They were promised food and a place to shower."

"Where are the rest of your friends?" another thug asked.

The guard shrugged. "Still inside. They are coming. Mario wanted them to wait."

"A shower? At the house? But they can't carry weapons around!" A tall man in his thirties who had an air about him of being in command of something had spoken. He stood right in front Evan and crossed his arms. He had a gold necklace around his neck.

Evan spoke with a warm smile as if making a case to be reasonable. "Why not? You guys have guns! And besides, this is supposed to be a party, a celebration. You guys got what, fifty cals and about a hundred guys milling around on the perimeter?" Evan shrugged and pointed. "Way I see it, we blend in. Only people unarmed are the guests."

"Sorry; we have rules, Ivan. I know you are supposed to have free rein, but your men?"

"Really?" Evan countered. He was taller than the thin commander and tried not to intimidate him. Evan politely moved into his space. "Mario himself said I could pack heat and keep my guys with me. None of my guys have their hands on their weapons; they are all slung. Your men though look like they are set to kill people!"

"Well, um—"

"Look, my guys are tired. You ever been in a sub for weeks? No beer, no good food, and no ladies?" Evan smiled and stuffed a one-hundred-dollar bill into his breast pocket.

The man smiled and showed gold teeth with a diamond stud. "They OK. They OK. Go have fun!"

Evan watched Juan creep his fingers to his trigger. Evan closed his eyes and reopened them.

Evan's earpiece cracked, and he heard El Coyote's voice. "I got you in sight. Watch that gun truck ten meters to your right. You need to move away from it. Blast radius. Be ready."

Evan's eyes got big. He knew what El Coyote had in mind. Evan looked at the gun truck and watched a kid looking at an iPod leaning on the .50 caliber. The whole crowd would die if these guys started shooting.

The crowd of civilians and thugs seemed to be intermixed. Evan estimated about one-hundred-plus people mingling around on the crushed coral and dock. The guards seemed to be staring at the guests and shadowing them, like wolves. The house was a

good fifty-yard run. He noted where all the cover and conceal-
ment was and then looked at the *Happy Mermaid*.

He made out the outline of a familiar face sitting on a golf
cart. "Oh, Gerard." He elbowed Juan and pointed.

"Nice." Juan smiled at a female who asked him his name and
then he turned to Evan and whispered, "Oscar says he is ready."

"Let's walk."

Evan gave Tanya a quick hug and kissed the top of her head.
"End of the line for you, cupcake. You are not even supposed to
be here."

"See you at the plane. Don't call me cupcake!" She smiled weak-
ly and then turned and walked with two men from Bravo Squad
down the length of the sub, and then between a seven-foot-tall co-
lonial-era wall and a stack of shipping boxes. She would get handed
off to Oscar and then be put on a Zodiac to zip around the island.

Evan listened to small talk, jokes, and dizzy houseguests. He
smiled, nodded, and moved slowly with his men. The twenty-five
men had moved toward the sub and were making their way into
the hatch.

Evan looked at Juan, who was looking at him. "Three, two,
one."

Juan smiled but was not happy. "You notice that three gun
trucks are aiming at the crowd and one at us?"

"Uh-huh."

Evan heard Roger's voice over his earpiece. "*Run, you wanker,
something is wrong!*"

One second, Juan, or Lucky, was standing next to him; the
next, his head and torso vanished in a spray of red. Evan felt the
remains of Lucky shower him, and bullets began to slam into the
people around him. Bravo Team raised their weapons.

Someone began laughing hysterically.

Three teenagers with guns began laughing, cheering, and
shooting.

One of the Bravo Squad operators hit a button, and the top portion of the submarine exploded, killing the twenty-five-man team that was trying to enter.

The four .50-caliber gun trucks began firing at once, sweeping through the crowd.

Bravo Squad began to disperse and take casualties.

Civilians tumbled, and people screamed, clawed, or trampled anyone who was in their way.

Evan brought his weapon up and squeezed a burst at a group who was pursuing Tanya and her escort.

Boom!

The gun truck nearest Evan went up in a fireball as an AT-4 hit it.

Evan tumbled backward and somersaulted into a group of bodies that lay still. His eye protection had broken, and he tasted blood. He was not sure whose it was but would sort that out later. He heard a ringing in his ears and stumbled to his feet.

Someone grabbed Evan as he turned to run. He flipped him over his shoulder and put a round in his face.

Thud! Thud! Thud!

Two gun trucks began shooting at targets on the beach.

"They are shooting at Green Team Two. They are cut off!" one of his men yelled.

Bravo Team's Team Two began diving for cover and assaulting the gun trucks and thugs, who were beginning to swarm like locusts.

Evan cursed and spoke into his headset. "Roger, start clearing the ship. Take out the guns! Bravo Team had to help Team Two. They are split up!"

"Lad! No! Get yur ass on the yacht."

Evan felt a round hit the Kevlar plate on his back, and he went down, rolled, and came up firing. He mowed down what looked like a twenty-year-old who was shooting at him.

Chunks of concrete, dust, screams, and blood began filling the air.

Evan found himself alone and too far from Bravo Team to help out, and then .50-caliber rounds began punching holes in the concrete and storage containers around him. Something exploded, and Evan moved out of the way.

Evan sprinted to the *Happy Mermaid*, yelling into his radio, "Roger, I am coming aboard. Bravo Squad is staying back to fight link up with Team Two!"

Andre Pena gripped his binoculars and cried out in shock and disbelief. *"What?"*

He had tried to call Jorge several times with no luck, and then he tried to call Gerard and other contacts. No one answered. Andre picked up the detonator and armed it.

"This is over. I knew I should not have come to this messed-up place!"

Andre watched as the area in front of the house was cleared by machine-gun fire. Less than half of the guests had made it into the house, where he was going to blow them up. Problem was, he had no idea why Mario's men had started shooting. Andre had second thoughts about blowing up the house. He had to escape. If Jorge was dead, what was the point of blowing up the house? The whole mission pivoted on Jorge blaming Mario for an atrocity and then living to be seen as the reasonable one or the savior.

Andre felt his heart race as he watched the scene before him.

The Scorpions had been ambushed, and then someone ambushed and began driving back Mario's army. The Scorpions had rallied, and he could see that they had the remaining two gun trucks.

"Two armies fighting Mario's guys? Huh? Then they fight?" Andre shook his head and considered three things: First, he looked at the seaplane, which was a mile run down the beach. Second, he looked at his detonator. Third, he raised the binoculars to his eyes and saw four, maybe five, specs on the horizon.

"Boats? The *navy?*"

Then the front of the *Happy Mermaid* blew up, and he made his decision. "Screw this. I am out of here!"

CHAPTER 38

Fish in a Barrel

Evan was done with explosions. He knew this one was coming, but it still hurt. He plugged his ears and gritted his teeth. The bow weapon system of the *Happy Mermaid* went up in a massive explosion that tilted the ship for a second and then caused it to dip down. The second explosion was a breaching charge that tore off a section of the hull and allowed Roger and Team One to spill into the yacht from the ocean side and away from the slaughter at LZ Mario.

"You gonna stand there looking at the beach, son, or you gonna join us?" Roger yelled to Evan.

Evan shook his head and focused his eyes on Roger. His ears were ringing, and he still tasted blood. "What squad?"

"Stay with me and Alpha Squad. We are going to the top deck—gonna look for Mario in his observation suite. Bravo secures the middle deck, keeps anyone from boarding. Charlie secures the lower deck!"

"And you want Team Two to keep fighting for the LZ?" Evan asked while wrapping his sling around his bicep.

"Aye, Napoleon, you got a better idea?"

"No," Evan admitted.

"Let's go!"

Evan packed a dip and then spoke while he followed Roger. "This better end soon. I got half a can left!"

Evan had trained in his early enlisted years with force reconnaissance before he became a marine corps pilot. He knew the value of being one with your team. And he had not been training with this squad.

Alpha Squad had trained together, breathed together, and bled together. Evan hung back near the rear and covered the flank. Roger, of course, was up front barking orders, like an ancient Scottish warlord.

The stairs to the top deck were guarded by three men, who, by now, knew they were coming. A hand grenade and brief firefight ended any delusions that they could hold off Dark Cloud. Doors were kicked in, rooms were marked as clear, and the advance was made. The noise outside was getting more and more muffled. Evan did his best just to keep up.

Evan counted six bodies as he stepped over them.

Evan heard the double thud of dueling .50 calibers right outside the ship. A round tore through the double hull and bulkhead and splattered Fernando in two. He had been standing several feet away from Evan. He was one of the most cautious men Evan had met on the team. He kept his gear immaculate and triple checked every angle before he spoke or moved. He was not a hesitant person, just thoughtful. Now he was dead.

"*Shit!*" Evan hit the deck.

"Scorpions are assaulting the yacht!"

Everyone heard the same message at the same time. The radio headsets came alive with chatter.

"*Move!*"

More holes began to appear throughout the walls as if they were walking through Swiss cheese.

Alpha Squad moved through a door at the end of the carpeted, smoke-filled hall and began moving quickly up a wide set of ornate wooden stairs. Half of Alpha Squad made it up the stairs to the final hallway that led to Mario's private observation deck and bunker.

That's when the ambush happened.

Oscar made it to the *Happy Mermaid* unseen until he began climbing on board via the tiny rope ladder that had been left behind. The bullets sounded like BBs pinging off the sides of the yacht as he climbed. Mario's men were taking potshots as he climbed onto the stern of the yacht. He leapt over the rail and felt a burn in his calf as he ducked and dragged himself behind a low bulkhead. The shooting stopped, and he heard a voice in his earpiece. It was one of his snipers.

"You OK? I got the bastards shooting at you. They are grouping it looks like near the south portion of the wall. Can you swivel that thing around enough to hit the two gun trucks that are putting holes in the yacht?"

Oscar cursed and wrapped a bandage around his calf.

The sound from the two .50 calibers was deafening. He knew Team One would not survive long under that much firepower. He also knew that the .50 calibers were laying down fire so that the Scorpions could maneuver and outflank. After all, they had all had the same training.

"Took one to the calf. Went clean through. Open up on those guys. Keep their heads down," Oscar reported back to his squad.

Bullets pinged sporadically around him as he lay underneath the twenty-five-millimeter chain gun. Oscar looked at the weapon. It appeared to be functional and loaded. He crawled and peeked underneath the railing of the yacht. He figured he could possibly hit one of the gun trucks. They were close, but the twenty-five-millimeter chain gun could only pivot so much.

"Contact! Contact!"

Evan heard Roger's voice as he sprinted down the hall to cover the last operator going up the steps. He fanned back to look at their rear and saw muzzle flashes.

"We missed some!" Evan yelled.

Three, maybe four, things happened at the same time, none of which could be controlled. Evan felt bullets thud into his body armor and the bulkhead near him as he backed through the door, protecting Roberto, who was moving up the stairs.

Suddenly, Roberto called out and screamed, "I am hit!"

That was the last thing he said. Evan thought about Roberto's six kids and three wives, two in the States and one in Mexico. A massive explosion from the deck above Evan's head rocked the yacht.

"Booby trap!" someone yelled over the net.

"Retreat!" Roger's voice could be heard and then stopped.

Evan heard static as Roger's voice cut out and went silent.

The rounds kept thudding around Evan, and he realized that there must be a secret compartment or hiding space where this group of men who were assaulting their six was shooting from.

Evan took out two shooters and ducked into the stairwell.

"Don't come back down the stairs!" Evan yelled.

It was too late. Eduardo and Alejandro leapt down the stairwell in their retreat and were shredded by rounds.

Evan found a hand grenade in his cargo pocket, pulled the pin, and prepared to toss it.

Pop! Pop! Pop! Pop!

"This is Bravo Squad. We are getting our ass kicked! Scorpions have breached! Reinforcements *now!*" The voice on the radio made Evan pause. *This is not good, we are surrounded.*

Evan peeked quickly around the six inches of steel that had been protecting him near the ladder. He was stuck. If he went upstairs, he was dead; if he stayed where he was, he was dead.

Evan tossed the hand grenade into a group of six men who were running toward him, more like barbarians assaulting a fortress than soldiers.

Boom!

Oscar had not fired a twenty-five-millimeter chain gun in years. It was, however, like sex: you never really forgot how to do it, and it was always over before you knew it and was way more messy than you remembered. Oscar annihilated the concrete wall protecting the house. He first started down by the swimming pool and walked the gun to the right, chewing up and vaporizing rock and pulverizing stone into fine dust. The rounds shredded and leveled the wall in moments and began to tear huge holes in the house. The dust and debris shot so high in the air that it was almost as if he were vaporizing his targets. The slow methodic *boom, boom, boom* of the chain gun drowned out the .50 calibers.

Oscar had no choice but to expose himself. He swiveled the chain gun around as far as it would go and caught the gun truck just as it was backing up to get a bead on him.

They both fired at the same time.

"Mine is bigger!"

Boom! Boom! Boom! Thud! Thud! Thud!

"Finish this thing! This th—"

Oscar's last words motivated Pablo, who was watching and listening to the whole ordeal from a semicovered position.

"Let's go!" Pablo stood up and sprinted with the buttstock of his M-4 squarely in his shoulder. He used his front-sight post to find targets and squeezed off rounds. Team Two, which now consisted of about twenty men who could run and five who had to just lay and shoot, bounded over their walls and covered the distance toward the Scorpion's force, which began to retreat down the gangplank and off the yacht.

The thud of Black Hawks began to get louder as they went from a distant rumble to an air-vibrating noise. The remaining gun truck swiveled its .50 caliber toward the sky.

Pablo felt rounds hit his vest and then he tripped, and he went down. The pain was not bad but he could not move immediately. He had twisted his ankle. He rolled and kept firing. Bullets where bouncing off the pavement near him.

The gun truck disappeared in a cloud of white dust, red fire, and black smoke.

The helicopter gunship continued to fire its weapons, which sounded like a giant buzz saw.

Brrrrrrrrr!

Gustavo and the rest of Team Two made it across the open LZ and fanned out just as a group of about twelve Scorpions made it back down the gangplank and tried to flee.

"Team One, this is Team Two. Choppers are here!" Pablo yelled into his head set.

Pablo shot several Scorpions as they made it off the gangplank. They stumbled or fell outright. Some returned fire. Pablo found cover behind a large steel shipping container. His men were ahead of him now.

The gunship stopped firing as the two forces met. The helicopter banked and made a wide circle to clean up the perimeter and provide security. Almost everyone was out of ammo at this point. Pablo watched Gustavo drag an injured teammate to safety behind a smoldering bulldozer. Two Scorpions converged on him. He was helpless. Pablo shot both of them.

"Thanks! Whoever that was."

Gustavo was relieved. He spoke into his headset not daring to look around for the shooter who had saved him.

"Welcome!" Pablo muttered.

Gustavo put his thumbs up, took care of the wounded teammate, and then got back in the fight.

The remaining Dark Cloud shooters where rallying together, guarding each other and moving forward.

Pablo limped as best he could and decided to use his last rounds to his advantage.

The machetes, batons, and knives came out as the two opposing forces began to lock in their final death match.

The navy began to fast rope onto the deck. Its soldiers headed toward the house. The Scorpions and Dark Cloud commandos began to circle and lock into what could only be described as a massive street fight.

CHAPTER 39

Hiding Places

C arla took off her headphones, pushed the blankets off her, and tried to control her breathing. She had tried texting her father fifteen minutes ago, and he had said to hide and stay hidden. Then there was nothing. She moved from the back of the plane as lightly and quietly as she could. She thought she had heard a few loud *booms* and now heard something very different. She thought she heard a boat's engine briefly, and then it cut off. Now, she heard *pops* off in the distance. She had been doing her best to make herself invisible in the back of the large moldy-smelling plane. She could not bear to sit still any longer.

"Dad, where are you?" She took a quick peek through a tiny window and froze.

"They are coming. This whole thing is falling apart!"

Carla could see the rear of the house about half a mile away up on a slight hill. It seemed to be busy with activity. She saw men with guns running and trying to get into the house. She also spotted what looked like guests being dragged into the house. Black smoke rose slowly from the docks on the other side of the house. She knew something had happened.

"A bomb?"

Carla saw a shadow move across the water and then on the lawn stretching up to the house. That's when she figured out what was going on.

"The military is attacking the island!"

She watched a helicopter with a gun of some sort circle and fire at something on the other side of the house. Carla looked at her texting device and frowned.

"Oh, my God; where are you?"

She heard loud, muffled noises like big weapons firing and saw pillars of smoke and dust rise up. Carla felt her heart begin to beat faster.

Carla held her breath when she spotted a figure on a motor scooter break away from the edge of the house, ride across the lawn, and then skid onto the gravel road leading to the pier.

"Man, Mario won't like someone on his lawn."

She watched the scooter get closer and then realized that it was her father. She moved quickly to a different window and spied the four men and, now, one smaller man, whom she recognized as a guy who had been sitting with Jorge this morning.

"Oh, no! Dad, answer your damn texts!" Carla looked at her texting device and then looked up at the front of the plane. She saw a sign that said "Signaling kit."

Tommy drove up to the four Scorpions who were guarding the docks. He recognized Andre Pena instantly. He shook his head and pointed with his thumb at four large UH46s that were circling over the island. Two Black Hawks came in low and disappeared in front of the house. Tommy could hear a massive firefight. Two gunships hovered and fired at something on the other side of the house.

"Hey! Navy is here. We gotta get this plane ready. Jorge is coming!" Tommy tried to sound in charge and pointed.

"How did you know to come here?" Andre asked.

"I am the pilot, idiot. Jorge told me to come here!" Tommy yelled. Tommy put his hands down and walked past the guards and Andre Pena. "I gotta turn that engine over."

"We haven't heard from Jorge."

"I was just with him. We gotta go!" Tommy lied. "He is coming."

Tommy looked out to sea past the plane and then scanned the docks and the rocky beaches to his right. The left was obscured by short block houses, a junkyard, and half of an ancient wall. He thought he heard the echo of a boat in the distance.

"Those helicopters are going to land, and when that happens, we are going to have to deal with hundreds of men!" Tommy yelled.

One of the Scorpions had had enough. He grabbed Tommy, punched him in the face, and dragged him into the guard shack.

"I am in charge here, you shit! We wait for Gerard. He just called. He's on his way. *He* is the pilot." The guard pushed Tommy into a chair and turned to face his comrades.

"He should be here by now."

"Dude, what is going on? The *Happy Mermaid* under assault?"

The guards continued to talk and try to sort things out. The helicopters circled again and lined up an approach. The Scorpions muttered.

Gerard had called them perhaps ten minutes earlier and mentioned that he was escaping. Everyone was lost. He was sure that Jorge was dead.

Andre Pena stared in amazement at the assault and destruction that was unfolding. He turned and looked at the airplane and then the guard shack. He shook his head. It was pointless to blow up the house at this point, and with the navy here, he would just seal his own execution.

No, escape is the only way now. He made up his mind and walked into the shack.

"We need him!" He pointed at Tommy.

Carla watched the thin, old guy follow the four big muscle guys into the concrete-block guard shack where her former friend's body still lay in a pool of blood. Her heart raced in her chest, her skin felt cold, and her mouth was dry. She tiptoed out of the plane and onto the floating dock that joined the seaplane to the elevated dock. She moved down the hot wooden dock and focused on the fifty feet or so she had to go. She ignored the helicopters, the smoke, the shooting, and the high-pitched whine of large speedboats.

She noticed wet footprints crossing her path as she neared the end of the dock and paused for a second. She lowered the flare gun and thought, *Wow they have not dried yet?*

Suddenly, muscular arms encircled her, and she felt her feet leave the ground. Small feminine hands snatched the flare gun from her. Carla tried to move against the man who picked her up.

"Quiet if you want to live," a gentle voice said.

Carla went limp as she was carried to the edge of a tin shed and gas pump. They put her down and made sure they were not seen. A thick wall halfway enclosed them and obscured them from the guard shack.

"Honey, listen, don't do anything rash. I am Tanya. This is Sergio and Victor. We know your dad. Don't speak. Shhh."

Carla nodded. She really had to pee.

"We have to fly out of here, but we need a few more passengers," Tanya whispered.

Carla nodded. "I have to pee."

Tanya looked from Sergio to Victor and shrugged.

"Go ahead. Climb down under the pier."

CHAPTER 40

Furious

Gerard had been on the bottom deck of the yacht when the force of the mercenaries, or whoever they were, attacked. He and nine men had snuck through a series of passages from the outside of the yacht and down a ladder into the bowels of the ship. His plan was to make it to a secret elevator that gave access to Mario's secret observation deck. He knew Jorge was alive and still up there. Jorge's watch had a powerful transmitter, camera, and microphone. Gerard's plan was to sneak up the elevator and kill the seven or so people who held Jorge hostage. Mario's observation suite was built to withstand a direct hit from large-caliber weapons and explosives, such as RPGs and breaching rounds. The glass surrounding his windows was ten inches thick.

Now everything was lost. The mercenaries had assaulted down and up at the same time.

The Scorpions' assault from outside had been repelled and countered by the navy and more troops. Gerard had barely escaped with his life. He had been shot several times in his vest and had taken shrapnel to his legs and arms. He was having trouble breathing and coughed up some blood. His team had been killed, and yet he lived.

Gerard had managed to kill several of the assaulters before dropping his handheld computer and fleeing.

Now he was on a Jet Ski that he had taken from the well deck of the yacht. He opened the throttle full and zipped around the island. He ignored the helicopters and dying gun battles. Smoke, sea spray, and sweat stung his eyes. He was furious. His vision was blurry still and began to clear.

Now they will no doubt figure out how to get into Mario's room.

He had been caught by surprise and in his haste had left the elevator door open. He knew who had Jorge and pieced together what he thought had happened. Somehow Mario, the White Mexican, had figured out their plans. He planned on killing everyone. Gerard was not quite sure how the Mexican navy became involved, but he suspected it had to do with Ivan or Tanya and the disappearance of Yuri.

"I was right all along!"

He cursed and ignored the pain in his legs. His only hope now was to make it to the plane and fly himself off the island. He had spoken to his men at the dock and assured them that he was coming to prepare the plane for their escape.

"Jorge is dead, I think," he had told them.

"Evan, what is going on up there?"

Evan listened to Joaquin's voice whisper into his ear. The whole yacht was mysteriously quiet now. Evan stayed at floor level and peered down the hall. He realized what must have happened. Roger and his squad were ambushed and taken out. He spotted large black panels in the walls, gun slits in a heavy iron door, and the dome of a camera. There was no way you could sneak in unnoticed. Mario's suite was basically an armored bunker.

"Mario had claymores built into his walls. He's got video and possibly a robot-controlled weapon of some sort," Evan whispered into his radio

"How many casualties?" Joaquin asked.

Evan peered down the hall, being careful to keep a low profile.

"Evan?"

"They walked into an ambush. Alpha Squad is dead. Hallway is littered with bodies. I see El Coyote next to Roger at the end of the hall. Looks like he tried to protect him from the blast," Evan said and then finished.

"It's time for the navy to handle this."

Evan shook his head and spat his dip onto the carpet. "Assaulting this door is suicide."

"Come back down, Evan. The Scorpions are starting to fall back. We have taken heavy casualties everywhere. Time to lick our wounds, regroup. Navy is touching down in five…Evan, you there?" A familiar voice joined the airwaves.

It was Roger. Evan closed his eyes and thanked God.

"Don't come in here. Door is armored like a bank vault."

"Can you move?" Evan asked.

"Yes. El Coyote's lying next to me. He's hurt. I have my hand on a grenade, but I dare not move. Playing dead is keeping us alive. I could drop a grenade through a slot in the door, reminds me of a mail slot. Would be the last thing I did though." Roger coughed and cursed.

Evan leaned against the wall at the bottom of the stairwell and watched Joaquin, David, and Adrian approach. They helped him to his feet. Adrian, who was a medic and obsessed with water intake, thrust a CamelBak valve into Evan's mouth.

"Roger, stay put!" Joaquin commanded into his microphone.

Evan nodded at them and said, "They were hiding in secret passages. We thought we cleared the rooms."

Evan gulped water and then spoke. "We have to rescue Roger before blowing that door."

No one spoke for a few moments. They stood still, drank water, and listened to the thump of helicopters.

Joaquin filled Evan in on what was transpiring outside.

Alpha Squad was dead, with the exception of Roger and a few others. Bravo Squad and Charlie were both down to about ten operators each. The tide was changing; the Scorpions were fleeing the ship and involved in hand-to-hand combat outside. The navy had its hands full securing the perimeter of the house and preparing the main assault.

"We got a lot of wounded. We have to get out of here!" Adrian said.

Evan thought about how he was going to get Roger.

Joaquin looked as if he had something on his mind and reached into his cargo pocket. "Evan, I think there is a way."

"Huh?"

"Trust me. Let's go!" Joaquin said then and pulled Evan along down the hall. Evan hurt in places that had not hurt in years. The men ran and limped as fast as they could.

CHAPTER 41

Not So Fast

Tanya peeked around the edge of the tin shed and counted the muscular backs of the four Scorpions and the thin outline of Andre Pena. The Scorpions were armed with a shotgun, AK-47s, and sidearms. Each man carried a machete, which seemed to be the fashion with Jorge's elite army. Tanya looked at her watch.

"We can't wait any longer. We gotta kill these guys. There is no need to escape in this plane, Tanya. The navy is here," Victor whispered.

Sergio pointed at a Black Hawk that was lifting away from the roof of the house. Its occupants had fast roped onto the roof and now were preparing to breach through the roof with explosives.

The gun battle for the rear exterior of the house was definitely going to the marines. Teams were preparing to enter the rear of the house. Troops were spread out, securing the grounds and flushing out resistance. There seemed to be a firefight in the woods.

"They will do it top down and then enter through the ground floor," Victor said.

Tanya looked at Sergio. She was exhausted and just wanted it all to end. "I got one question—" She never finished her sentence.

The roof of the house exploded and then caught fire. The helicopter backed away and spun as something hit its tail rotor.

It spun out of control.

Sergio took a step forward. A bullet thudded into the back of his head.

"Duck!" Victor yelled. He spun and raised his weapon but collapsed, meeting the same fate. Shot dead.

Tanya and Carla screamed at the same time and put their hands up. They backed into the tin shed and froze.

"Hello, Tanya!" The wet, bare-chested, sunburned, and bloody Frenchman limped down the dock. He was not smiling and held a short assault rifle with a scope out in front of him. He stumbled briefly but never took the weapon off of Tanya.

Tanya had no idea how he had made it behind them and onto the dock without making a noise. She had never seen so much fury in a man's eyes. She tried to process where he must have come from and saw that he was dripping wet. She backed up, covering the younger girl's body with her own. She braced herself for the bullets.

CHAPTER 42

Mexican Standoff

Gustavo cursed as the heavily tattooed Scorpion stabbed him in the side of the leg. Gustavo smashed him in the face with his buttstock. The Scorpion fell backward from Gustavo's blow. Gustavo dropped down to his knees and pushed the man onto his back. He dropped his empty weapon, drew his machete, and hacked down. There was a metallic thud and sparks as Gustavo separated the man's head from his neck.

Gustavo collapsed and grabbed his leg. He rolled over and accepted help from the navy's medics.

Every Scorpion was dead. The medics began clearing and triaging the wounded from the LZ. The entry teams were preparing to breach the house when the roof blew up.

Pablo accepted help getting to his feet and froze as he watched the explosion and the helicopter spin out of control. Fortunately, the pilot brought the bird down in the shallow water on the beach. The entry team on the roof was not so lucky.

"They must have wired the place to blow!" The medic helping Pablo said.

"You guys are running into a death trap!" Pablo told the medic.

The navy commandos backed off the LZ and took up a defensive perimeter as the house began to catch fire.

Pablo shook his head.

Guests and unarmed thugs began to stream out of the house with their hands up. The fight was over. It was now a rescue mission.

Evan put his next-to-last dip in his mouth and rode the one-person elevator to the top deck. He was sweating heavily and hoped the stream of adrenalin would keep him going. They figured that the elevator was used to bring up laundry or Mario from the bottom deck. The elevator stopped, and the door slid open. Evan turned on his red-lens flashlight, pushed open a small door, and stepped into a closet. He smelled expensive clothes and leather shoes. He clicked his UMP .40 onto "single shot" and slowly moved to the closet door.

"Roger?" Evan whispered.

"Aye?"

"Mail-delivery time."

Evan heard muffled voices and the sound of a radio in the main room. The closet in which he stood was a large walk-in that smelled of leather and cedar. He spied a couple of shirts that he liked.

The hand grenade dropped through the slot in the door, and Evan heard the screams.

"Grenade!"

"Blow the hallway up!"

"We can't!"

Three women screamed simultaneously, and the yells of several men could be heard.

Boom!

Evan felt the urge to yell something ridiculous and settled with, "Remember the Alamo, motherfuckers!" He burst into the room, preparing to shoot anyone who moved.

A man had either dove or been thrown onto the hand grenade. His body was torn in half and smoking like brisket.

Two men, wearing matching white T-shirts and camouflage pants, tried to pick themselves off the floor. They were bloody, stunned, and deaf. Evan popped them both in the head with a single round each.

Next he dropped to his knee and shot two clueless-looking men who stood on either side of the only remaining Mario. He ignored two young women who began to scream and cower in the corner of the cabin.

Mario dove from his hiding place behind the girls and took up a new hiding place behind Jorge Valdez, who was taped to a chair.

Evan felt someone grab him around the arms as he stepped from the closet. He realized it was a female by the hair in his face and the manicured nails that gouged at his eyes. She smelled great. Evan picked her up with one arm under her armpit and hip tossed her onto the wide bed that separated Evan from Mario and Jorge. She was light and landed soft.

Mario shot at him and missed.

The girl landed on a large, naked dead man, who Evan could only assume was the real Mario or Daddy Mario.

"*Stop! Stop!*" Mario screamed hysterically. He had almost shot his own girlfriend while trying to hit Evan.

"Stay there, sweetheart; don't move!"

"I am not lying on a stiff dead man!"

The beautiful woman he had hip tossed lay facedown with her head toward Evan and her feet facing Little Mario. Her torso was across the dead Mario's belly. It was a rather silly pose, and somewhat erotic in a sick sense.

Evan brought his weapon up to his cheek and got in a comfortable shooting position. He slowed down his breathing. His dip was going dry.

"I am in, Roger. You guys can blow the door."

"Aye, lad," Roger mumbled.

Evan never took his eyes off his target and spat onto the carpet. He could see video monitors through his peripheral vision. Dark Cloud operatives were clearing out the wounded and setting a breaching charge against the door.

"Gross!" exclaimed the girl on the bed.

"You a model or something?" Evan asked. His eyes and weapon did not move when he spoke.

"Yes. Look, can I get up?"

"Only if you wanna get shot."

"I am being poked by something hard. This is sick."

"I can shoot you."

"I fine here."

"Good girl. Looks like the late Mario is enjoying that!"

"You're sick," she exclaimed. "Who the hell are you people? Jorge, is this man yours?"

Little Mario tried to make himself smaller behind Jorge. He held a snub nose .357 to Jorge's head.

Evan took in the scene and calculated distances.

Jorge was pale and in a good deal of pain. He had a makeshift tourniquet around his wrist and a large bandage and ice pack duct-taped to it. His forearms were taped to the chair. His face was swollen. He regarded Evan with tired, defeated eyes, yet he was still in there. The arrogance, the fighting spirit.

"You go first," Evan said.

"You are not in a position!" Little Mario squealed. He sounded as if he might come unglued and either cry or start shooting.

The unstable ones were the worst. Evan regarded the gorgeous actress and figured she was what kept him calm.

"OK. Me first," Evan began. "Jorge, are you OK? I don't care about Mario. My real name is Evan by the way. Navy is here."

Jorge laughed more with pain than anything. He had figured most of it out by now. "Evan, tell this idiot that I did not steal his money!"

Evan smiled grimly. "Hey, idiot. Jorge did not steal your money. My boss did. The whole navy is right outside, so this thing is pointless."

"We negotiate," Mario said.

"Why?"

"'Cause I am rich!"

Evan tried not to laugh. "Not so much anymore!" Evan gently squeezed the trigger but did not let his round fly.

The girl began to cry. "Please, please no kill him. He is cornered; he needs a way out! I will do anything you want. Let us go, please!"

Jorge rallied and tried to sound reasonable.

"Evan, you killed all my men. You destroyed my chances at building a new Mexico! You owe me. My fight has never been with you. Kill Little Mario. He is a wuss. I *will* make you rich."

"No, no, don't kill my Mario!" The actress sobbed. "Kill Jorge! I will make you rich, Evan! This man is a liar!"

Mario pulled the hammer back on the handgun till it clicked.

Jorge remained calm, despite the fact that Mario was becoming hysterical. The actress was crying now. Jorge cleared his throat and spoke in a fatherly tone to Evan. "Evan, my friend, there is a million dollars in gold in Mario's safe. Kill this freak and set me free. I will owe you."

Jorge coughed and tilted his head to the side, waiting for an answer.

Evan saw movement on the monitors and knew his remaining teammates were clearing Roger out of the way and preparing to blow the door. Evan asked a very simple question: "Jorge, is the agency financing your political operation?"

Jorge got real quiet and for a second forgot about his hand. He looked Evan in the eye and whispered his words as if he was acknowledging a subtle truth that he wished he could deny. "Snake? Los Pepes?"

The model began to sniff and sob louder. Evan was not sure if she was acting or not, but she looked good doing it.

Little Mario yelled, "*Shoot* her. It was all her idea!"

The girl yelled louder; Little Mario shrieked. Evan was not amused and was beginning to get a headache again. He locked eyes with Jorge.

Jorge stared back, unblinking, and then he smiled.

That's when Evan knew the truth.

Jorge Valdez was working for the freaking CIA.

"I hate you, Mario. You would betray me after all the sex and crap I put up with from you?"

"You drove me to this, you crazy *bit*—"

"I am lying here on top of your stiff dead father. The man who used to grab my breasts in public while you did nothing! Now here you are again, afraid and doing nothing! *You* killed your father. Have some follow-through for once, you weak little coward!" she screamed with the high-pitched, shrill tone that only a woman could master.

Evan could not handle it anymore. He spat on the floor and shot Little Mario in the forehead.

The girl screamed.

The door blew off the hinges.

Jorge kept smiling.

Evan smiled back.

CHAPTER 43

What Goes Up

Tanya screamed as Gerard sliced a thin line across the top of her breasts with a razor blade. She fought hard against the duct tape that bound her ankles and wrists. The plastic bag over her face was beginning to suffocate her. She watched the world turn blue and then red.

"I am going to take you two somewhere far away and spend months working on the two of you, until there is nothing left!" Gerard said coldly.

He then pointed to Tommy with the razor blade and said, "I am going to make you two pay. The old man, he can watch!"

He left her on the floor of the idling airplane in between the seats next to Carla.

The massive flying boat was sixty feet long, which made it longer than the wooden pier. A tiny floating dock jutted off much lower than the main dock. The tail section of the Grumman Albatross flying boat towered over the end of the dock. The massive wingspan stretched out nearly one hundred feet. The noise of the twin propellers was deafening and drowned out all other noise from the chaos near the house.

Gerard stood up and wobbled a little unsteady. One of his men approached.

"*Boss!*"

"What!" Gerard said with a frustrated tone not unlike a child being interrupted from play.

"You won't believe this."

"At this point, you idiot, I will believe anything," Gerard shrieked.

He was beyond angry and doing his best to stay in control. The navy was taking the island. The fighting was all but dead from what he heard. It was only a matter of time before they came to this part of the island. He hoped to use his hostages as shields, and maybe they would not shoot him down.

"Try me," Gerard exclaimed. "*Well?*"

Gerard walked past his man and sat in the captain's seat. The nose of the plane faced out toward the open sea. Tanya strained to hear the muscle-bound thug who stood near her yelling to Gerard.

"Look! Jorge has escaped. He is down on the beach right now. He called me on the radio. Got away in a speedboat!" the Scorpion said loudly and waved his arms.

"*What!*"

"That is what I am trying to tell you! Pena and Raul and Paco, they are bringing him up from the beach. He is wounded badly!" the Scorpion exclaimed.

Tanya could not believe her ears. Her heart raced, and she said a quick prayer: "Either have Carla and me and Tommy die in a plane crash or, I don't know, just deliver me please!"

Carla was sobbing and shaking. Gerard had duct-taped a plastic bag over her head as well.

Tommy was tied to an empty seat, his white hair red with dripping blood.

Tanya was sure that he was dead. From her vantage point on the floor of the vibrating airplane, she could see his limp hand hanging into the aisle. Blood dripped off his fingers. He did not move.

Tanya tried to not breathe and conserve air. She knew that the four men and Andre Pena had untied the airplane and prepared it for takeoff. The twin propellers were whirring loudly, and the plane shuddered as Gerard hit the throttle. The door was open, and she could smell humidity, heat, and aviation fuel. Within moments the airplane would be airborne.

"Please let me die before that sadistic bastard touches me," she pleaded in her prayers.

Suddenly, Gerard leapt up and pointed at his bare-chested sidekick. The man had a tattoo on his back of a nude Mexican girl wearing a sombrero. He had scars that looked like puncture marks across his middle.

"*Go!* Go get him inside. Carry him if you have to, but we *have to go now!*" Gerard yelled.

"Will we make it?" the Scorpion demanded, uncertain.

"*Stop asking questions. Do it! Go!*" Gerard slapped his friend lightly.

Tanya watched the man grip his shotgun and leap from the plane's side door onto the floating dock.

Gerard went back to manning the controls.

"Please, God give me—"

That's when Tanya felt something touch her fingertips as she shoved her hands underneath the seats. Her hands were behind her, and she was slowly wiggling free of the duct tape. She brought her knees to her chest and used her core muscles to sit up. She was far enough behind Gerard that he did not notice.

Carla had stopped sobbing and was watching Tanya.

Tanya reached for the object. She about had her left hand free.

Gerard stood up suddenly and looked through the side door of the plane. He was smiling and clapped his hands.

Suddenly, he sprinted off the plane with a spring in his step.

"*Carla, sit up!*" Tanya grabbed the screwdriver. It was six inches long and rusty. "We have seconds!" Tanya ripped the bag off her own head and ripped at the duct tape around her ankles, stabbing it with the screwdriver.

Carla chewed like a mad hamster at the tape around her wrists until Tanya could free her. Carla pulled herself together and stood up, after almost tripping, and checked her father. "He is breathing!"

Tanya ran to the rear of the plane and looked at the emergency door. It was oval and large enough to push people or equipment through. She followed the printed directions on the door and pushed it open. She saw blue water and the end of the dock. She was sure that they could jump into the water, move underneath the pier, and then make it to the rocky beach and hide somewhere.

"*Tanya, look!*"

Tanya turned around, feeling a bit dizzy.

Carla was half dragging and half supporting her father, Tommy.

The three of them stared out of the tiny round windows from the tail section of the plane. They had an elevated perspective down the wooden pier, looking over smaller boats. They could see the hill and the concrete-block shacks where they believed that the men had gone.

"*Oh, shit!*" Carla screamed.

A Black Hawk helicopter seemed to come from nowhere. It hovered low while about half a dozen men wearing black and carrying weapons leapt off. Another helicopter was hovering near the beach slightly out of Tanya and Carla's view. Men were fast roping down and out of her sight.

"Look!"

Tommy began to moan, and Carla had to sit him down.

Carla and Tanya were so amazed by the assault that they failed to notice a figure running back to the plane.

"Gerard! Carla, find a weapon!"

Tanya was hysterical. She had to move.

The helicopters unloaded their teams while the door gunners sprayed a burst or two near the four fleeing Scorpions. Two paused to aim their weapons at the helicopters and were literally torn into pieces. The other two men dove to the ground and let themselves be attacked and secured by the commandos.

Gerard had managed to flee just in time. He realized that somehow Jorge had been used as bait to draw the Scorpions away from the plane. He did not bother to ask himself if Jorge had been tortured or went willingly. He had always been a master of the deal.

The Zodiac had landed on the beach driven by a man whom Gerard did not recognize. Jorge's appearance horrified him. His arm was in a sling, and he looked badly beaten. No sooner had he and his men begun helping him from the boat did the GAFE assault teams swoop in.

Gerard, Gerard, had no delusions of escape anymore.

"It's over, Gerard," were Jorge's only words.

Gerard Blaise, former French Foreign Legion member, pilot, outlaw, and commander of the most feared, brutal gang in Mexico ran for his life. "I am going to die fighting, but first I will kill that bitch!"

Gerard avoided the bullets and the men and made it through the sand onto the dock, running as fast as he could. He had his machete in his hand and cursed that he had left his handgun sitting on the pilot seat in the plane.

The sound of helicopters, the smell of exhaust, and short two-round bursts reminded Gerard that he used to be one of those guys. Now he was running down a dock with no shirt, wearing combat boots and cargo shorts. He would die by his own hand like a warrior, he hoped. "Only after I hack that computer girl to death!"

Gerard's rage against females burned deep inside and erupted in a white hot furry. He saw Tanya as the embodiment of every woman who had angered him. He loathed them and had only two uses for them.

He sprinted down the dock and leapt onto the floating pier. *Need my gun.*

He climbed into the cockpit and saw her.

The computer girl stood before him with her hands behind her back; she had managed to get free. The teenage girl in the bikini was holding a fire extinguisher. She tried to spray him but had not read the directions first. It would not fire.

"What's this? The wonder twins?" Gerard laughed.

He kicked the teenager in the abdomen. She buckled and went down like a sack of laundry. She began gasping for air. He looked Tanya straight in the eye and swung his blade with two hands right at her neck.

"*Die, bitch!*"

Suddenly, she was not there.

Tanya was not a physically strong girl, but she was, pound for pound, mighty for her size. She was quick and agile, and if she had anything, it was power and speed.

She dropped to her knees and thrust the screwdriver with all her might into Gerard's side between his ribs.

He yelled and then screamed. He suddenly could not breathe so well. He wrenched the screwdriver from her hand and his side, flung it, and started punching her in the face.

"Ahhh!" he yelled.

She felt his blood pour from the wound. His fists slammed into her jaw. She protected her face and collapsed in a defensive posture. He was losing strength and collapsed on top of her. He coughed up blood and tried to catch his breath. She had weakened him, but he could still kill her. She felt as though she was being crushed.

Tanya wrapped her legs around his middle and squeezed with all her might, and then she put her arms around his neck and tried to pull him close. He had less leverage to punch her, and she could bury her face into the side of his face. She sunk her teeth into his cheek.

Tanya was losing consciousness. Blood ran down the back of her throat. He was going to kill her. She began to lose strength as he fought to push her legs off him.

His pain intensified, and he tried to get a breath. He coughed and spat blood. He began to headbutt her and grip her elbows.

"He is too strong, Carla! *Help!*"

Tanya bit him again, as hard as she could, and visualized herself in one of those horror movies where people eat each other. She ripped a section out of his neck.

"*Aaahhhh! Ffff.*"

Gerard's fight went the other direction. He let go and tried to get away. He screamed and panicked. His lung was punctured and now part of his face was missing. He now sounded like a wounded pig instead of a sadistic killer. He tried to get away.

Tanya went on the offensive and tried to gouge out his eyes.

"*Carla! Help!*"

Tanya coughed blood and lost her grip on him.

Blood ran down the side of his face and his legs. "*I will not die from a woma—*"

Tanya realized he was looking for something. He stumbled to his feet and began looking around. She thought he might fall over on her.

That's when Carla shrieked, *"You looking for this, you sick freak!"*

Pop! Pop! Pop! Pop! Pop! Pop! Pop!

Carla kept shooting him until the gun was empty. Even after he collapsed in a bloody heap, she kept on pulling the trigger until the weapon stopped and the slide remained back. Smoke rose from the barrel.

"Wh-wh…where the hell did you get a gun?" Tanya's words sounded muffled through her swollen jaw. She moved to her knees and clutched her face. The pain was tremendous. She was drenched in Gerard's blood.

Carla dropped the gun and put her tiny hands on her narrow hips and then crossed her arms. She was in a state of shock, and within a few seconds, she began to realize she had saved their lives. Her pink earbuds hung around her neck. She squinted her eyes and pointed at the pilot seat, stamping her foot in a sassy posture.

"It was right there! The whole time! I just grabbed it!"

Tanya was dumbfounded and looked at the younger girl and tried to smile. Tanya sat in the pilot seat and shook her head. She was stunned and in shock. She regarded Gerard's bloody body as if she had just now noticed it.

Tanya felt like her jaw was going to come apart. "We killed him."

Carla seemed not to hear her and kept babbling. "It was right there, Tanya. The *whole* time, right there! If it would have been a snake…" Carla continued moving her hands wildly as she spoke.

Tanya shook her head and just held up her hand. "Shhhh, it's OK. You did good."

"I think soldiers are coming," Carla said flatly. "We look like crap."

CHAPTER 44

Finally Over

Four Hours Later

The most seriously wounded soldiers and Dark Cloud operatives were evacuated by air. Body bags were still being filled. The rest of the Dark Cloud team was shuttled onto a boat, given high fives by their counterparts in uniform, a few cases of ice-cold beer, food, and medical care. They were evacuated back to the mainland. The marines had secured the island and created a minicamp for Mario's soldiers and a separate processing area for the civilians. Law enforcement took charge of this group.

The main assault elements packed up and went home, leaving the marines and newly arrived regular troops to handle security. Law enforcement began the slow process of gathering human intelligence and confiscating computers and documents for evidence. The wounded prisoners were treated in place.

The fires had died down, the smoke had risen off and dissipated in the atmosphere, and now, once again, the island was semipeaceful. The beach house was ruined, and only the old stone colonial sections remained. Embers still smoldered.

Evan was aware now of how bad he smelled and how sore he felt. He glanced at his watch and frowned. The day was not over for him yet. He was thankful that he had no significant injuries other than bruised, banged-up knees and elbows, a sore back, pulled muscles, and a headache.

"You have five minutes. No weapons," the Admiral's XO said coldly and snapped his fingers. Evan was certain that he wanted all evidence of Dark Cloud to vanish.

"Sure, hold this. Be a minute."

Evan handed over his weapons.

Evan and a few naval officers stood outside a series of the concrete-block houses that had been turned into interrogation centers for the high-profile prisoners. The navy wanted to get to them now before they got back to the mainland, where they could start screaming in front of cameras and lawyer up. One high-profile prisoner had already threatened to sue and had met with an unfortunate accident. Cooperation was quite pleasant after that.

Evan put his hand on the doorknob and looked back at the XO. "My plane refueled?"

"Of course. The admiral wants to talk to you before you leave. Hopefully that will be soon!" The XO hinted with his eyes.

Evan nodded.

"Got it."

He stepped inside the concrete shack and faced a small, dejected man sitting at a table. The man's hands and feet were cuffed. He looked tired yet kept his composure.

"I have told them everything. You are?" Andre Pena looked at him and raised his eyebrows.

"Evan. Evan Hernandez."

"You are a soldier? One of the mercenaries?" Andre regarded him curiously.

"Yes. Yes and no."

"You here to kill me?"

Evan reached in his cargo pocket and pulled out his can of dip. It felt light. He packed his last little pinch and threw the can of Skoal on the table in front of Andre.

"I am not very good at these kinds of things." Evan brushed his hands across his face and took off his baseball hat. He flicked sweat off his head.

"Things?"

"I am the Snake. The man whose family you blew up. I killed your kids, revenge."

Andre Pena stared for a full minute. His eyes got red, and he visibly gulped. "That was a long time ago," he whispered. He stayed amazingly calm and looked at the table and then back at Evan. Tears welled in his eyes. "I…I sat in prison. You tormented me. I…I guess you are here to gloat. To kill me."

Andre seemed to drift off as if he were having a dialogue with himself. He stared through Evan and at the wall. "Lifetime ago. You killed them, but I guess you had your reason—you believed I killed your family."

Evan spat on the floor and hooked his thumbs into his belt loops. He felt uncomfortable but forced himself to stand firm. "I am not here to gloat. *Or* kill you. There has been enough of that today. You're evil, and so am I."

"What?" Andre looked at him with puzzlement and focused his eyes on Evan as if he had just now seen him.

"I need to change, Andre. I can't live like this. I mean, I can, don't get me wrong, but there are bigger things out there."

"What?"

Evan was not sure he could explain himself and took another stab at it. "I don't want the legacy of being evil. This is where it ends. You end up dead all the same."

"You are guilty?" Andre was perplexed.

"I am changed. I need to be free from my prison." Evan tapped his head and stared at the floor. He felt exposed and a bit insecure. "Only way I can have a clean break is to apologize."

"Changed? My kids are dead. You…um, what?"

"I am sorry for killing your kids."

Evan shook his head and tried to convey what he was thinking, but it was not working out. "No, Andre, I apologize. I forgive you for what you did. That frees me. Get it? Maybe you don't." Evan shook his head in frustration and cleared his throat. "They are dead, Andre."

Evan shook his head and turned to leave. He felt as if something had been lifted from his neck. He did not feel better but relieved. He felt as though he could see his misery with more clarity. The pain was not less—it was just not a barrier.

"Evan. Wait."

Evan paused near the door and turned around.

"You apologize, forgive?"

"Yes."

"I…I never killed your family. They were not in the car. A man, an American, framed you. It worked. You went nuts, worked for the enemy."

Evan stared at Andre. Now he felt worse. "What?"

"I learned years later that it was a CIA man who set you up. Your family was not there. He wanted the girl for himself. Simple. They are still alive, far as I know. In hiding maybe. Long time ago."

Evan stepped back and shook his head. "Nathan—it had… had to be Nathan."

"Now, you kill me?" It was more of a request than a question. Andre was not angry with Evan. He too wanted to be free from his ghosts.

Evan shook his head. "Already said no. I gotta go." Evan had his hand on the doorknob and opened it.

"I forgive, Evan if that sets you free. And I accept your apology."

"Ummm." Evan nodded and left.

CHAPTER 45

Landing Gear

Evan, Roger, Tanya, Tommy, and Carla stood on the pier near the large flying boat. Evan was still recovering from the shock of knowing his family had never really been killed. He could not process what to do next. Should he find them?

He was certain that Andre was telling the truth. He was also certain that he was not going to beat himself up over all of the wrong things he had done. He had murdered for no reason. Evan was not sure what he felt.

"You are not in a condition to fly," Roger said and handed Evan a beer; he refused.

Evan turned to the admiral and shook his hand. "Thanks for honoring our deal."

"Well, you made a convincing sales pitch, Mr. Hernandez. If we kill Jorge, he becomes a martyr. If we keep him in prison here, he becomes a cause célèbre; someone will try to rescue him. But in the States, he will be an example," the admiral said.

Evan smiled and sipped from a plastic water bottle. Evan finished the admiral's sentence.

"No, the DEA will lock him up tight, put him somewhere. No one will hear from him again."

The admiral squeezed Evan's arm and laughed. "And you collect a bounty."

"That too. This gives me some leverage with some issues I have with my former employer. Leave it at that!" Evan said.

"Right," the admiral agreed; he understood.

"And no side trips. Go home!" Roger growled.

"Will do. You can come with. Drop you off in Miami. Got a bar on board," Evan teased.

"Nooo. I am flying commercial. Going home! Mia is meeting me."

Evan smiled. His head was feeling better, but his back hurt worse.

"The bag of gold on Mario's yacht, it goes to the members of Dark Cloud, right?" Evan said and winked at the admiral.

He nodded. "That's several million. Yes, I never allowed it to be put on the property-seized manifest. You warriors are set for life!"

Tanya leaned against Evan. She was not very talkative since her face was swollen. She held an ice pack. Her eyes looked droopy from the Dilaudid. The medics had bandaged her and set her up with enough to keep her relatively pain free till they got to the States.

She nodded and pulled on Evan's hand.

"Let's go before I change my mind," she whispered.

"Well, this is it. Next time I come to Mexico, it's for fun!" Evan said.

"Let's toast Dark Cloud! To true warriors!" Roger raised his beer and toasted with everyone.

Evan drank his water and felt a stab of misery for the dead and guilt for being happy that he was not one of them.

"To the warriors!" Evan said.

Hugs, handshakes, pictures, and high fives were exchanged. Evan swallowed a couple of Motrin and helped Tanya get comfortable in the plane. She and Carla would no doubt fall asleep the moment they took off.

Tommy was feeling better; he had taken a quick rinse in the ocean and got some sutures and an IV. Mainly, he wanted to get in the air and get the hell out of Mexico.

The Grumman Albatross lifted off its blue runway and gained altitude in a slow, easy arc. Evan circled once around the tiny island and then set course out over the blue sea toward the States. He started to feel like a kid who was coming home from a late night, somewhere he should never have been. He looked at the satellite phone that he intended to use to call his older brother. His brother knew he was coming and had arranged for them to touch down at a naval air station in the Keys. Evan knew it would not be a friendly welcome. He knew his brother.

"He is gonna kill me," Evan muttered.

"Huh?" Tommy asked as he leaned back and let Evan do all the flying. He put his sunglasses low over his nose and looked for some CDs to play for the flight home. He had found a stash of CDs while rummaging through the plane.

"Can't fly without music. This thing has a good sound system. I was flying when you were an itch in your daddy's pocket," Tommy joked.

Evan nodded and looked at his altitude and wind speed. "Clear skies and perfect weather. Let's go home."

"That was my home we just left!" Tommy laughed.

Evan turned in his seat and glanced at his passengers. Jorge was snoring on a cot. Tanya and Carla were asleep in their seats. They were all in various contorted positions, enjoying a narcotic-induced slumber.

"Yeah, guess you won't be coming back here anytime soon. But I hear Italy is nice!" Evan said.

He resumed his attention on flying.

"And you, what's next?" Tommy asked.

Evan looked out at the sky and thought about Veronica and a grown-up daughter out there somewhere in the world, either in hiding or living happily free from him. Did they think he was dead? Who had protected them? What the hell had Andre meant by Nathan or someone had wanted her for himself?

"What's next for me?"

Evan shook his head and answered, "Sleep!"

Tommy laughed and then put some gum in his mouth. He was done with smoking.

"Did I tell you about the time I was flying medivac out of 'Nam?" he began.

"No, but I have a feeling I am about to hear it," Evan said, bored already.

"Well it was '68. We had to fly a VIP—a state department type—out of country. Seemed that the man had had an unfortunate accident with a hooker...A banana shoved up his—"

Evan held up his hand and tuned Tommy out. He watched the blue sky ahead of them. Tommy kept talking, and Evan kept wondering.

AUTHOR'S NOTE

They say truth is way stranger than fiction. They are right.

The actual facts regarding the drug war, human trafficking, and crime syndicates in Mexico are too vast to even list. Highlighted below are various headlines that may be of some interest. Visit Jamesgarmischbooks.com for news on up comping titles. Some proceeds from this book will go to the A21 Campaign, a nonprofit that helps fight human trafficking.

Mexico's Cartel-Fighting Vigilantes Get Closer to Texas Border (nbc.com)

Mexico Drug-Death Toll Double What Reported (latino. foxnews.com)

Americans Shot in Mexico Were CIA Operatives (nytimes. com)

Submarine Links Columbian Drug Traffickers with Russian Mafia (articles.latimes.com/2000/nov/10/news)

Mexican Cartel Accused of Killing Children to Harvest Organs (nydailynews.com)

Sexual Slavery in Mexico: A Pimp Tells His Story (theguardian.com)

US Legalization Hurts Mexican Drug Cartels (borderlandbeat.com)

Legalizing Pot Is Making Mexican Cartels Even More Dangerous (thefiscaltimes.com)

Stay tuned for upcoming books and news. Visit jamesgarmischbooks.com.

Made in the USA
Lexington, KY
09 July 2015